A TRIAL OF TWO WORLDS

J.E. LARSON

The Valdor Series

A Trial of Fate
A Trial of the Heart
A Trial of Two Worlds

Copyright © 2025 by J.E. Larson
Map Design by J.E. Larson
Copy Editing by Jen Boles
Proofreading by Eleanor Smith
Cover Design by cheriefox.com
Interior Design by J.E. Larson
All rights reserved.
No part of this book may be reproduced in any form or by any electronic or mechanical means, including information storage and retrieval systems, without written permission from the author, except for the use of brief quotations in book reviews.

All rights reserved.

Trigger/content warnings: Sexually explicit scenes, torture, language, violence, fighting, trauma rep.

ISBN 979-8-9900411-6-5

Dedication

To those brave enough to embrace our fears and transform them into the flames of inner strength.
Burn wild and free.

Pronunciation Guide:
Shifters
Skylar Cathal: Sky-ler | KA-hal
Neera Cathal: NEE- ruh
Rhea: REE- UH
Talon: (rhymes with gallon)
Shaw: SH-aw
Magnus: MAG- nuhs
Julia: JOO-Lee-uh
Alistar Warrick: AL-IS-ter | WOR-ik
Gilen Warrick: Gil (like a fish gill)- en | WOR-ik
Emery Cathal: EH-muh-ree | KA-hal

High Fae
Daxton Aegaeon: DAX- ton | ee(sounds like the letter a)-JEE-on
Castor Aegaeon: kast-er | ee(sounds like the letter a)-JEE-on
Idris Ekon: ID-riss | EE-kon
Adohan Ekon: ad-o- han | EE-kon
Minaeve: MIN-ayve
Seamus Duran: SHAY-mus | DUR-an
Anjani: ahn-JAH-nee
Gunnar: GUN-ner
Zola: ZOH-luh
Nyssa: NISS- uh

Humans
King Taran: TAHR-ən (like "car" and "run")
Istar: ISH-tar
Dawn: Daan

J.E. Larson

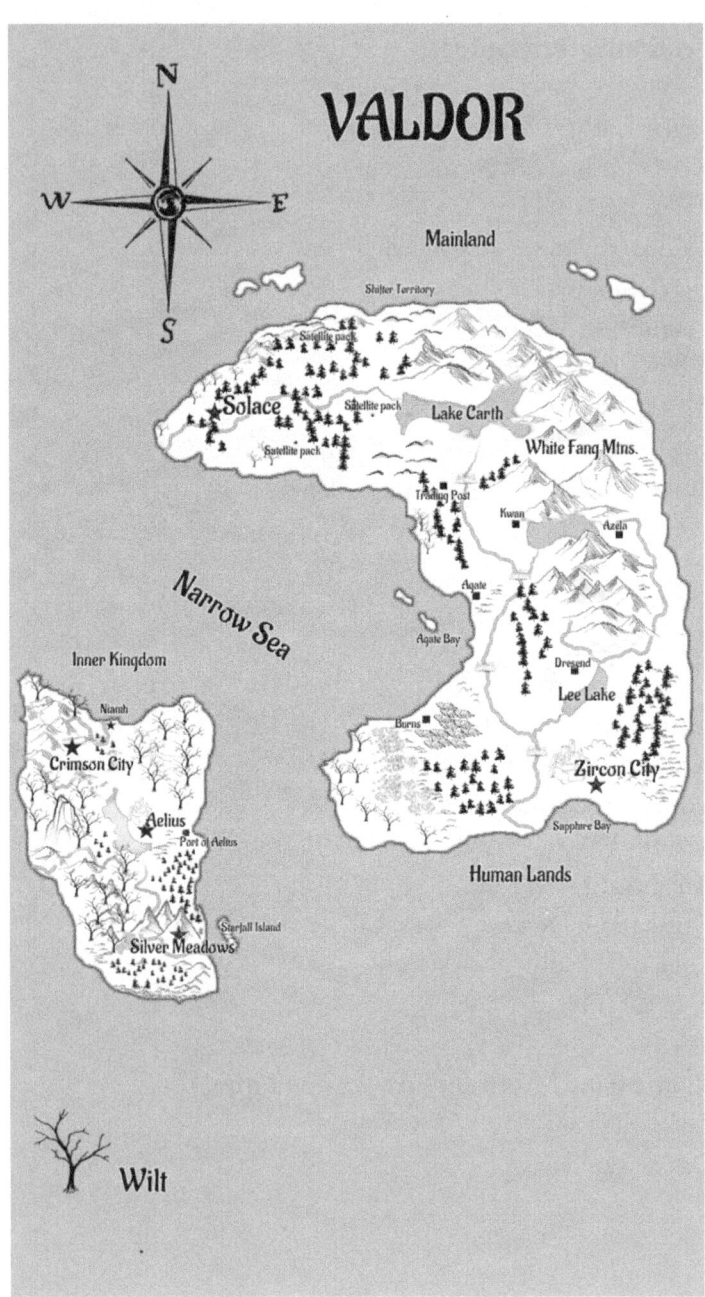

J.E. Larson

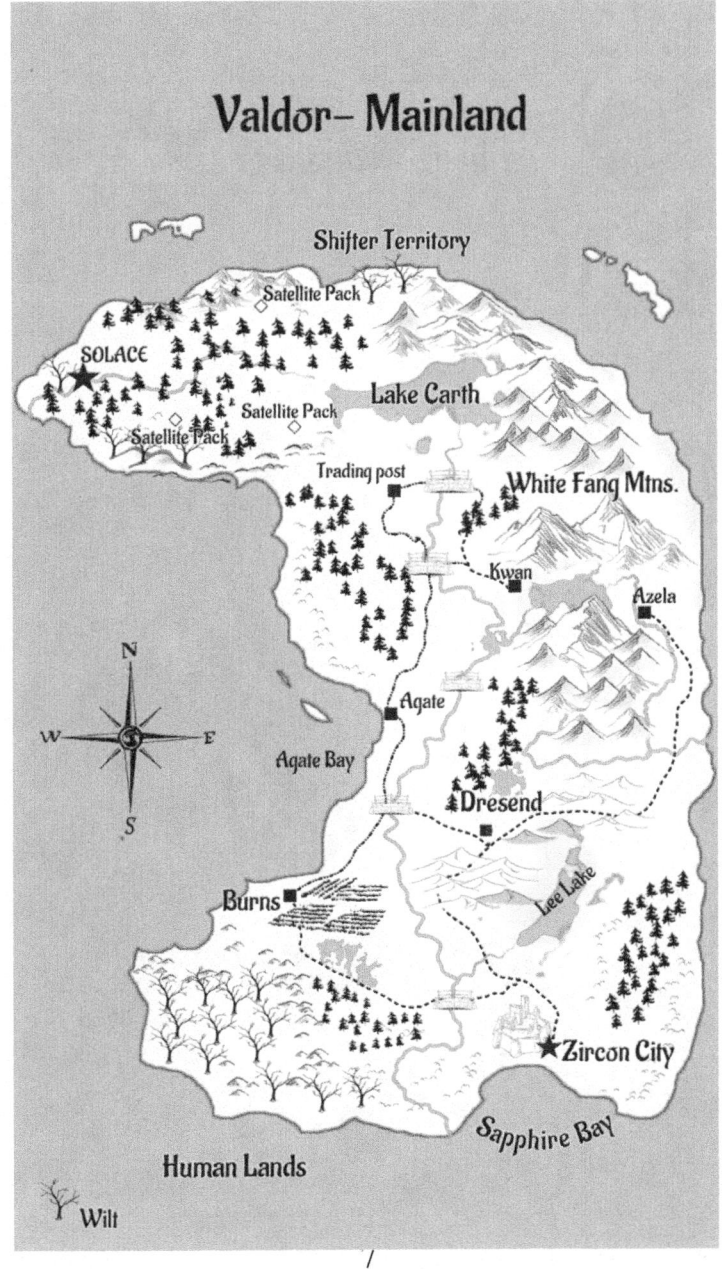

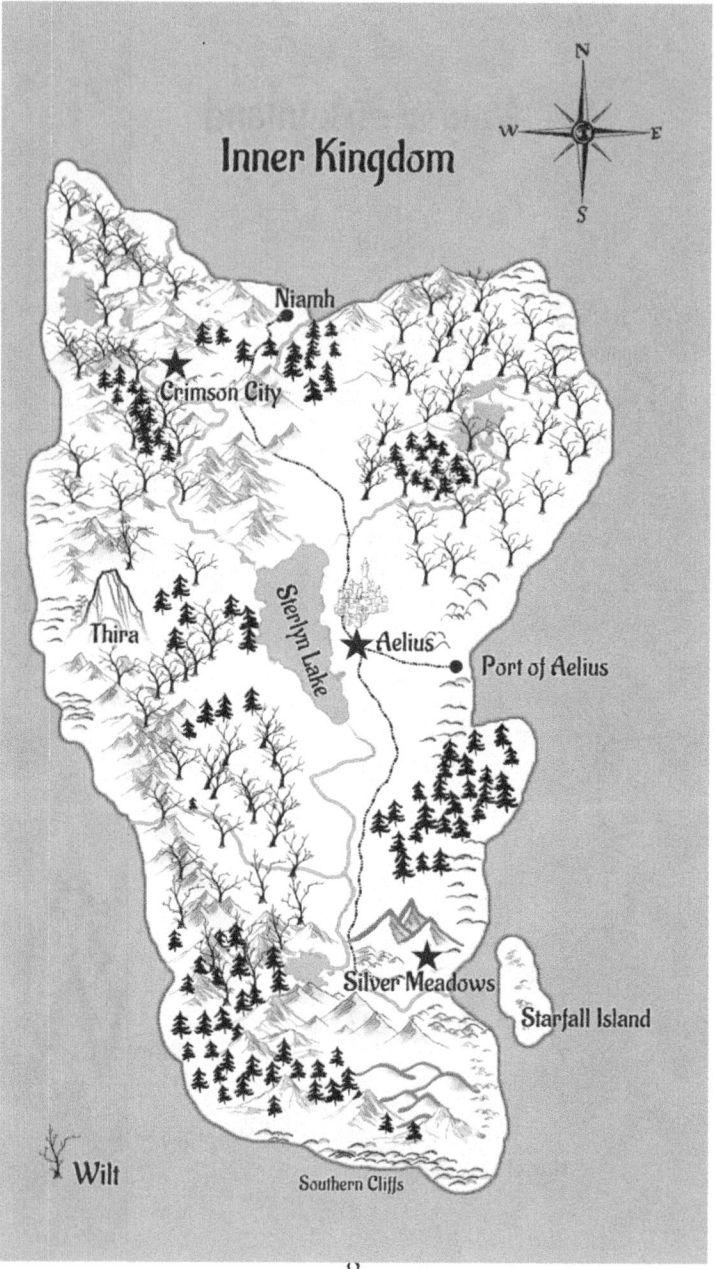

Recap as told by **Castor Aegaeon**

Well, well, well. Lucky for you, it's me, your favorite prince with a silver tongue. Yes, I talk fast, kiss better, and have a talent for *everything* in between.

Now, let's rewind to the glorious disaster that was the end of book two.

Hello, Crimson City. We arrive and meet with Adohan and Idris, along with a female fae, Nyssa, previously known as a fallen creature. Mute, yes, but so stunning it's hard to turn away. I'm still reeling at her existence. Healing her, however, nearly kills Skylar. So, yeah—good luck getting Daxton to approve *that* stunt again. Zola, our lovely shadow-jumping spymaster, is called to bring her into "safe-keeping" in Silver Meadows. Sensible, I'll admit, although I was not a fan of this.

We finally get some rest, and of course, that's when the prick, High Prince Seamus, decides to make his grand entrance. He starts screwing with Skylar's memories and tries to drag her off to Aelius like the absolute ass he is. Daxton steps in and goes all knight-in-brooding-armor to save her—yay. I was not invited to their private conversation later, so I can only imagine what happened behind Skylar's closed doors that night. But the next morning, they were both smiling...

Until our ruse is announced.

Trust me, I am annoyed by it almost as much as Skylar.

Aelius. Home of gloom, doom, and emotional constipation. Gods, this place is basically the wilted lands with better lighting. Then we have a "celebration," and an "offering of power..." *Offering*, my ass. And then Rhett unveils the trials scroll to Skylar... *alone*. I almost gutted the scroll keeper right then and there for that stunt. Seriously. And then, during the offering of the princes, I have to drag her out of the damn throne room before she tries to turn Minaeve into minced fae.

It would've been satisfying, but it also would've gotten us all killed.

At this point, I honestly can't believe Sky and Dax, the idiots, still haven't figured out their feelings for each other. I mean, we all *knew*, didn't we?

Reece and I carry Daxton back to his rooms. He is fucking heavy and out cold. Fortunately, he allowed Skylar to heal him a bit. And after? Let's just say when Daxton drops his voice and growls at me like *that*, I find better places to be.

The next morning, we're off to the first trial. Rhett, because the universe loves chaos, gifts Skylar the motherfucking *armor of Aegis*. Daxton was debating whether to trust him. Me? I was firmly team *fuck no*, this was somehow Minaeve's doing. I walk our fiery shifter to the trial entrance, and surprise, she wins. She tells me later it involved earthquakes, underground monsters, a bargain, a favor, and her soul getting ripped out. No big deal. Just your average Tuesday.

Of course, Minaeve, the venomous little cunt that she is, tries to paint Skylar as insane and dangerous. Classic move. We leave, but more trouble finds Skylar anyway. We run into the king of the water nymphs, Malek, who drops some juicy hints about Skylar's heritage. Then, we have a lovely reunion with Minaeve and Seamus and learn the second riddle for the trials before being sent off to Silver Meadows.

Idris gave me and her mate Adohan a gods-dammed heart attack as she almost went into labor on our journey. But thankfully, Skylar's healing powers save the day again. Once we cross into our own territory, I finally get to play a little card of my own and have Skylar swear a small oath to Silver Meadows. Nothing huge, just enough to give her access to our wards and magic. Look, we know the second trial is *somewhere* in our lands, and we all knew she'd do it for Daxton. So don't judge me for being clever.

We arrive home, thank fuck, and my brother shows her his little books and whatnot while I go and fetch—

Gunnar: *Me.* Yes, this is where I make my glorious entrance. You know, the moment things get interesting.

Castor: This is painful.

Gunnar: No, *this* is an amazing part of the story. This is where I come in, and *you* leave on your little side quest.

Castor: And I'm sad for the readers. I know they miss me.

Gunnar: *Fuck you*, Castor.

Castor: That's something I've never seriously considered, Gunnar.

Gunnar: I'm going to throw my axe, and we'll see if your premonitions can dodge *that*.

Castor: Gods. Enough. Can we *not* derail this gods-damn recap.

Gunnar: Fine, I'll be quiet... for now.

Castor: The gods have granted us a favor for once.
All right, Gunnar decides to have Skylar train for the Ice Gauntlet to prepare for slaying the unknown creature in the second trial, which is hiding somewhere in our lands. Daxton sends me away to find it, and I think it's because I don't agree with his decision to let Skylar train in the Gauntlet... but she's not my mate. So, I decide not to pick this fight.

(Shit, you don't know that yet, sorry. But I mean, come on... right?)

So, I leave. (*And yes, apologies to you for my absence.*) Anyway, Skylar's there, watching Daxton run the damn Gauntlet like it's a casual stroll through a garden... Show-off. Then, of course, the cadets give it a go, and that's when Reece—*Gods, Reece*—falls into the rocks. Skylar? She swoops in like a gods-damn hero and saves him. The whole Inner Kingdom's been practically worshipping her since she volunteered. And now? Well, it's *official*, Skylar's the People's Champion.

Then Daxton, ever the thinker, decides to take Sky and Gunnar on a training run through the mountains... with *heavy* fog. If *I* were there, I would've seen this coming. Skylar wouldn't have gotten hurt. But, hey, I wasn't, so she did.

And that's what sent Daxton off to hunt Anjani down, taking Zola with him. Oh, and guess what? That's when his *grand plan* kicks into motion. The storm begins, and trust me, it's one hell of a ride.

Now, while Skylar's recovering, I'm still out on my own little side quest, but don't worry, I'll be back soon enough. Daxton returns, looking all broody, with Zola and a new *handy* trinket that, spoiler alert, is going to lead us into war with Aelius. Adohan is pissed. *Great*. If I had been there, we could've handled it differently. But *nope*, fate is a fickle bitch.

So, Daxton storms off... *again*. Skylar follows him to his *secret meadow* with *fancy flowers* because, I guess, that's where all their feelings come out. He drops the "ask me" line.

Do you know what that means? Yes? Okay, great, moving on.

I finally return from my mission with the trial location, and of course, I swing by the archives, and I see... her. Nyssa. Still as silent and damn beautiful as ever. I take her to Skylar, where she shares the fun news: Skylar has to kill a basilisk. Yes, a basilisk. I'm sure that will be easy. Then my brother loses his mind, going full feral protective-mate mode. It's almost comical how much he loses his mind over it. So, of course, I stand off against him because... Well, more on that later.

Skylar and Daxton enter the second trial. They work together to kill the basilisk, which apparently talks to Skylar because of her shifter nature, and she is able to command it somehow before delivering the final strike. I mean, what the fuck? The creature's talking to her. Creepy much? They kill it and obtain the second key, but not before Daxton is injured. And... *this* is where everything begins to unravel.

Gods, here it comes.

Minaeve and Seamus attack Silver Meadows. Her lovely portals, powered by siphoning Daxton's magic, drop her warriors into the heart of my home. You can imagine how well that went.

Then Dax and Skylar show up.

Skylar tries to save Daxton after he throws her inside the wards, but Minaeve holds him hostage. The scroll reveals that Skylar must return to Solace to retrieve the final key, a dagger of some sort I vaguely remember seeing in the alpha's home. Needless to say, we are all pissed that Minaeve has Daxton. Furious actually. When Minaeve left with Seamus, it was like a piece of my soul was ripped out. Watching my brother being dragged back to the prisons beneath Aelius? Again? Gods, I can't even.

But here's the kicker: this is all part of Daxton's plan. His twisted, fucked-up plan. And despite how much it kills me, I'll help him see it through, whatever the cost.

There. That's the mess we're all in now.

Enjoy the read, my lovelies, especially to those lucky ***Fated Few***. Brace yourselves for the fallout.

Prologue

Stark Warrick
Fourth Shifter Champion (100 years prior)

As I descended the staircase to the labyrinth, I forced my shaking hands to quiet. My thoughts drifted as I absently rubbed my knuckles, trying to calm my trembling nerves, preparing myself for the unknown tasks that lay in wait for me.

Witnessing Queen Minaeve's power last night shook me to my core. I couldn't fathom how a ruler could be capable of such mistreatment of their subjects and still hold their throne. That the fae could stand to live like this.

But, then again, what choice did they have?

The wilt was growing, and the high queen's magic was fading. After arriving in Aelius nearly a month ago, waiting for all the high princes to heed her call, I witnessed the unspeakable depths of her wicked nature. Minaeve needed power, life's energy, to fuel her ability to combat the wilt—the price of safety resulting in the cost of life.

Last night, like a prized trophy, I was forced to watch from the side of Minaeve's golden throne as she siphoned not only magic but life forces from the three high princes of the Inner Kingdom.

I didn't bother familiarizing myself with all of their names. What was the point?

I was going to die today.

I'd even wager that the Gods themselves knew my fate was sealed. That all too soon, I would lay my eyes on the riverbanks of the crossing into the afterlife.

There was no hope of surviving these trials, let alone a labyrinth. In Solace, I was training to become a healer. My talents lay in nurturing and in the pursuit of knowledge. Yet somehow, I was selected for this task.

Was I simply chosen to fail? This question plagued my mind in a relentless cycle.

A piece of me still held onto the hope that there was a higher purpose to all this. Perhaps I was destined to be a stepping stone for the next shifter to be the last.

I prayed to the Mother and Father that my death would bring fortune to Valdor. That my life was worth more than a sacrifice to fuel a tyrant's reign.

The darkened stone hallway leading to the labyrinth's entrance was silent. The magical fae lights in the corners dimmed, depleting any source of comfort in the abyss beneath the keep of the palace above. The royals thankfully granted me a moment of solitude before I entered the trial of the mind.

Glancing toward my left, footsteps echoed along the gray cobblestones. Inhaling a jagged breath, I braced myself. As the glow of the fae lights unveiled the stranger's identity, my stomach leaped into my throat.

"What the fuck are you doing here?" I seethed in a hushed whisper, my hands shaking. "I told you—"

"You honestly expected me not to see you off before you enter the trial?" His deep laugh was laced with sarcasm and a dash of dark humor. "I'm hurt."

As he reached the final step, his piercing gaze seized the breath from my lungs. His presence jeopardized his very existence, but still, he was *here*.

I sighed, shaking my head. "You risk your life coming to see me like this."

"Ha," he scoffed. "You speak as if I have a life."

"You do." I frowned, my eyes never leaving his. "You *could*."

"Existing is not living," he said, stopping a length away and leaning his shoulder against the wall.

His handsome face held lines of secret sorrows, and I desperately wished I could do something, do *anything*, to make them disappear.

"It's more than I've got," I answered, leaning in.

"Don't," he rasped, retreating into the shadows along the corner.

"Why?" I asked, following his footsteps and closing the distance between us. "What hope is there for me to win this?"

"Your bloodline is—"

"I'm aware of my bloodline," I countered. "But *I* am not an alpha."

"How do you know? How are you so certain you won't succeed and win this trial?" His eyes snapped open as his shoulders heaved with the labored breaths that fought to contain his outrage. "This is a task for the mind, and yours is one of the brightest I have ever seen."

"Which is why I know," I tell him, anxiety winding up my throat and stilling my voice during our precious minutes remaining together. "I didn't ask for this. However... I'm grateful for fate bringing me here. That my journey in this life ends with—"

"This *journey* is not over yet!" he cut in, grasping my hands. "It's not over," he whispered, pressing his brow to mine.

Closing my eyes, I embraced him and inhaled his scent. The smell of him calmed my shaking nerves and settled my animal spiraling in my center. "I'll be waiting for you at the crossing."

"I've told you *not* to speak like that."

"Since the first day I arrived in Aelius," I said with a bright smile. "And every day since."

"Along with every night I've visited your room," he said as his lips brushed along the nape of my neck, causing me to moan. "I must admit those have been quite enjoyable." I chuckled, biting my lip. "I wasn't expecting to favor anything in this place, but fate had other ideas in mind."

Threading my fingers around the nape of his neck, I pulled his lips to mine. It was short but ever so sweet. His lips parted to taste me, and I lost myself in this blissful moment that would inevitably disappear. With a heaving breath, he broke our kiss, pulling back to gaze at me with those entrancing eyes I would never forget.

"This was worth it," I said, my heart thundering, threatening to break. "Meeting you was worth everything."

I couldn't make time stand still, but dear Gods, I wished I could. If I wielded the power to forbid time to continue, I would grant us eternity together.

Tilting his chin, I pressed my lips against his once more.

The sound of dungeon creatures broke our embrace as the darkened hallway behind me lurked with my impending doom. But to my surprise, my hands stopped shaking, my breathing slowed, and I was at peace.

"I love you." I whispered the words I'd known the day I arrived in the Inner Kingdom and saw him for the first time, lost in the depths of his stare that unlocked the secrets buried within my heart and mind.

The idea of love at first sight was a fleeting hope I never thought possible. That was, however, until I met *him*.

"Don't." He tensed, grip on my waist tightening, reluctant to succumb to the reality of what was to come. "You can't tell me this mere moments before you enter the trial."

"And why not?" I challenged him. "I have nothing holding me back."

In my youth, I knew I favored the company of males, thankful for having a brother to carry on our bloodline. Still, I never found someone worthy enough to say those three words to, until now.

"I love you," I said again, kissing him once more.

I memorized every fleeting second of his touch and the way his body pressed against mine. The way he smelled. The sensation of him in my arms, and most of all, the way he made me feel. With him, I was cherished and seen in a world of utter chaos.

"Love," he scoffed, pulling back. "Love is a foolish game in the lives of mortals and immortals alike."

I smiled, not needing to hear the words I knew he felt.

"Good thing you're smart enough to not only know the rules, but also how to break them." The very air around us seemed to tense as our moment together faded. "I must ask you something."

"Anything." His voice quivered despite his iron will.

"You must help whoever comes next. Whomever the queen chooses after me."

"Stark, I—"

"You must help the next shifter, *if* I fail." I paused, hearing him inhale a pained breath. "For the salvation of both our worlds, you must lend your aid, my love." I leaned back, my stare boring into his, preparing to confess what I've learned during my weeks captive in this palace. "There's a resistance forming amongst your people. There are whispers of overthrowing the queen and taking a stand against her. Together, you can help unite and free your realm."

"How do you know this?" he asked.

I tapped my ears and raised my brows with a taunting smirk. "I'm a shifter and, thankfully, constantly overlooked during my time here. Do you remember me telling you what I believe my animal would be if I could shift?" There was no guarantee, but if I ever got the chance, I knew in my heart that I would be an owl. "During my *stay* as an honored guest for nearly a month, I've been able to hear and see things missed by others. It's one of the reasons you fell for me so quickly. Remember?" I teased.

I felt him stiffen as I wrapped my arms around his neck. "What you suggest is a death sentence," he answered in a muffled voice.

"And living like *this* isn't?" I countered. "Constantly afraid of who the queen will destroy next based on a whim of desire or obsession over power. The high princes aren't the only ones she drains. I've seen others brought to her chambers."

He sucked in a pained breath. "I'm well aware of who she drains."

My heart shattered.

"My love." I sighed, tucking a strand of his hair behind his pointed ear. "You must fight back. You know and see too much to allow this to continue." I bent to gently kiss the unique patch of freckles in the shape of a crescent moon at the nape of his neck, hidden beneath his mesh of hair.

"I've stayed alive."

"But you've said it yourself, existing is not living." I paused as he looked up at me with tears in his eyes. "Fight. You must fight!"

"On one condition," he countered with an even tone. "*You*... must fight as well, Stark. Fight to make it out alive and return to me."

"It's a bargain."

I gave him a curt nod as I took one step back. Forcing myself to place distance between us, or else, I might never let him go. Despite my reservations, I knew this wasn't goodbye. Even if I died in the chasm below the palace, a piece of me would always remain with him.

I silently prayed the Gods would allow me to watch over him. To wait for him until our time together could finally begin. In this life or the next.

"I have to go," I said with a quivering voice, desperately reaching out to pull him toward me to kiss him, one last time. Savoring every ounce of him I could.

"I promise to fight, Stark," he said as I severed our kiss and forced myself to turn away. "For you. *Always*, for you."

"I know you will," I answered, my heart shattering as I marched toward my fate.

Chapter One

Skylar Cathal

Time was never an ally.

After healing the wounded and lending aid where I could, I retreated to the library in desperate need of solitude and rest.

The second I opened the doors leading to Daxton's personal collection, my rage morphed into a hollowed depth of sorrow that swallowed me whole. My footsteps heaved as I mustered my remaining threads of strength to scale the familiar steps I once cherished, seeking the chaise on the second floor, tucked away near the corner window.

The others tried to follow me, but Idris wisely stood in their path, telling them to give me a minute alone. The warning glare I caught from Castor before I disappeared served as a stark reminder of the true cost of these fleeting moments. His expression silently relayed what we dared not speak aloud.

Daxton was gone.

Imprisoned in a living state of his nightmares, held hostage under Queen Minaeve until I retrieved the third key and unlocked the location of the Heart of Valdor.

Daxton was a pawn in her scheme to ensure my return, but this was all part of his plan.

I collapsed onto the chaise, burying my face in the pillows, desperate to hide my falling tears. I knew I had to pull myself together, but for a moment, I allowed myself to feel the chasm of pain ripping through my chest.

I would *never* have enough time with Daxton.

"I will find you," I vowed to the cherished books adorning the library's collection, refusing to acknowledge an alternative fate.

A wave of stubborn determination settled in my chest as my animal sparked to life. I had to be strong. Crying about losing Daxton would not bring him back. I lifted my face from the pillow and closed my eyes, inhaling a deep breath of pine and mountain air, recognizing the scent of my mate that lingered in every corner of this palace, with the strongest essence of him emanating from this spot.

I recalled the nights we shared here. Before he confessed our bond, before I mustered the courage to tell him I loved him. He held me through my restless nights after the labyrinth, reassuring me with silent gestures of strength and comfort that I was safe and never alone.

"Skylar." Castor's voice crept through the outskirts of my thoughts. "Do you—"

"Tell me again," I said quickly. "Tell me the plan again. I... I... need you to tell me." I couldn't bear to look at him, keeping my eyes shut and clinging to the vivid memories of Daxton that grounded me like a lifeline.

Castor sighed, unhappy with my request. Even though he didn't admit it aloud, I knew his own guilt about allowing Daxton to be captured by Minaeve was eating him alive. "From the beginning, I assume?"

"Yes."

"You didn't listen carefully enough the first time?"

I grunted but otherwise disregarded his annoyance. I didn't have it in me to care, not now.

"Tell her again." Zola's brooding voice echoed from the shadows in the corner of the corridor near our hideaway.

"Oh joy, the shadow stalker is here. Why am I not surprised?" Castor muttered. "I thought Idris told *you* to stay out."

"I recall her telling you the same thing," Zola countered. "Idris is a respectable ruler and my closest friend. But I don't answer to Crimson City," Zola said before turning her gaze to me. "Daxton asked me to look after his mate, if and when he was *absent*."

My eyes darted to the shadows along the corner where Zola dwelled, finding only the faint outline of her face and arms.

"When did he ask this?" Castor asked.

"In Crimson City, after his mate healed Nyssa," Zola answered as she leaned against the bookcase, more of her torso coming into view. The shadows at her command recoiled farther. "She needs to hear it again, Castor. So, tell her. You're wasting valuable time. Don't get angry at the shifter for the delay when you're only adding to it yourself."

"Fine," Castor grunted, stuffing his hands into his pockets and scowling at the Spymaster. "It is a rare occasion when you make it difficult to argue with your logic. I'll make sure to put this to memory."

Zola bared her teeth and hissed. "Your insults were cute when you were no taller than my knee. But now, I'd be cautious, *Prince*."

Castor flashed Zola a cocky grin, folding his arms and leaning against a nearby chair. Even though Castor was now first in command of Silver Meadows with Daxton's absence, the orders of their high prince lived on. Zola was looking after me. I didn't know if it was comforting or unnerving to have her watching me so closely.

"Daxton knew, when he first felt your bond, that either he or you could be used as leverage in some way in the queen's favor," Castor said. "And if it came to a decision between you or him, he made it very clear that you would remain unharmed."

I nodded, understanding this part. "So, Dax created a contingency plan."

"Yes. He prepared himself for the possibility of this happening. When you were chosen as the champion and defeated the first trial, the reality of this outcome became more likely. We were given strict orders to allow this and not interfere with his capture if what he feared came to fruition."

"*Fucking Daxton*," I cursed under my breath.

"Minaeve's attack against Silver Meadows was predictable, but Daxton's actions added fuel to her already burning fires," Zola said.

"Which is why you were so furious at Daxton for taking Anjani's hand," I said.

"Exactly," Castor answered. "Daxton dismembered Anjani, knowing it would trigger Aelius's demand for revenge, making him the target and not you." Castor moved to sit in a cushion-backed chair near the chaise. "His imprisonment was even more likely, if not sealed at this point. So, we devised a plan to counter the queen's attack and, for once, take them by surprise. The only twist was that we didn't foresee Seamus's marriage to Minaeve."

"This is not a setback," Zola said. "It gives Daxton an opportunity to achieve the upper hand, for once."

"The bulk of Silver Meadows' armies," I spoke slowly, piecing it all together. "They aren't patrolling different areas of Daxton's realm, are they?"

"No, they're marching north in preparation for war," Castor answered, leaning forward with his forearms resting on his thighs.

It all made sense. Daxton was planning to overtake the queen, uniting with the allied forces of Crimson City. This was why Astro and Finn, Idris and Adohan's twin sons, didn't join them in Aelius or Silver Meadows. They were overseeing preparations of their own warriors. Ready to join Silver Meadows when the

Heart of Valdor healed the land to overthrow Aelius and the self-proclaimed queen, attacking from both sides.

"But why Daxton?" I asked again. "Why did he have to go?"

"You know he wouldn't let anyone else do this in his place," Castor said, bowing his head.

"Daxton understands the queen's desires more than most ever will," Zola answered. "He's the perfect distraction. The prize she has coveted since she came to power. And now, the mate of the champion. Holding him as her captive ensures your return with what she needs to seal her reign for eternity."

"And we need the scroll," Castor added. "When you have the alpha's dagger in your possession, we believe the final star will fill in. And then, when you return to the Inner Kingdom, the location of the Heart of Valdor should be unveiled once the final key comes into contact with the scroll."

"But how will Daxton steal this scroll if he's imprisoned?" I asked, recalling Seamus's warning to Minaeve, validating the presence of our mate bond, saving a piece of Daxton's soul. The taboo of the High Fae and mate bonds at least prevented her from forcing him into her bed.

"Minaeve and Seamus will want to celebrate." Castor glanced at his clenched hands, rage for his brother's imprisonment threatening to burst free. "And no celebration is worth the time and energy if you can't boast about your victory to those you deem beneath you.

They're in a position of power, Skylar. Their false sense of security will cause them to overlook small details. Once the idea of victory is achieved, their confidence will be their greatest downfall."

"Fuck!" I cursed, standing and bracing my head against my palm.

I was scared. Scared for Daxton, scared for his people, scared for all of us.

"This is all hanging in the balance based on your assumption that Minaeve is likely to brag? How is he supposed to escape?" I asked, clenching my fists so hard my knuckles turned white. My animal roared inside my head as my thoughts wandered to where my mate was being held captive. "I have no doubt the queen will siphon Daxton's magic over and over again, lock him in irons, and drug him to keep him under her control." Not to mention the beatings and other mindfucks that Seamus and Anjani likely had planned. "How will *he* be safe?"

"I'm the failsafe," Zola announced as shadows swirled around her frame with a life of their own. "The queen cannot detect my magic, and she can't siphon it away. A special adaptation thanks to my encounter with the wilt."

The tip of the dagger in her left hand picked at the dirt under her fingernails, such sharp, deadly weapons wielded like nothing more than mere toothpicks. A reminder that Zola had seen and endured trials in her immortal life that I didn't comprehend.

"I'll shadow-jump inside the palace and extract Daxton and the scroll when the time is right."

"And how will you know when the time is right?"

"I'll know," Zola said with absolute clarity. Almost looking bored at contemplating any further explanation.

"Zola will be able to visit Daxton in his cell," Castor said, sitting upright. "Waiting in the shadows just like she always does. As disturbing as her magic is at times, it comes in handy more often than not."

"I'll take that as a compliment." Zola chuckled, rolling her neck.

"Do you have an ally in the Aelius court?" I asked, hoping there was more to this plan.

Zola arched her brow with a toothless grin. "Of course I do. But their identity is unknown, even to me. They've requested to stay anonymous to ensure their position in the palace remains secure and their life unthreatened."

"With the vital information we've received this past century, Dax and I have agreed not to push our informant for their identity," Castor said.

"*Owl*... is their call sign," Zola said as she tapped her fingers along the blade of her dagger.

"Not my favorite, but it works." Castor scoffed. "Owl has helped us ferry groups of people out of Aelius and warned us of the queen's unexpected visits."

"You trust Owl?" My mate's life was not something I would put to chance.

"We do," Castor answered.

Chapter Two

Skylar Cathal

"Gunnar!" I called out, knowing he wasn't far, despite being told to keep away.

The steps of the spiral staircase in the corner creaked under his weight as he ascended to the second floor. Dressed and ready for battle.

"Daxton trusts you to lead the Silver Meadows Warriors in his place, Gunnar. So, I'm asking what you think of this plan."

"We are prepared for war," the general replied, his long brown, silver-streaked hair braided back against his half-shaven head.

Lightweight, black-scaled battle armor adorned with silver accents highlighted his muscular frame with three silver mountains etched on his shoulder. His dark brown eyes gleamed with the anticipation of battle and blood. Twin axes were strapped to his back.

"For too long, we've lived in fear... ruled by it," Gunnar announced with his shoulders back and chin held high. "When the wilt is eradicated, Silver Meadows will be ready to fight and break the chains of the self-proclaimed queen. And it's all tied to you, Skylar Cathal." Gunnar's grin widened as he bent his knee. "The feisty shifter who bested the labyrinth, earned her victory in the Ice Gauntlet, and slayed the serpent king himself. The true mate of my high prince. A warrior in her own right." He bowed his head. "I will raise my blades with your bow and proudly follow *you* and my high prince into battle."

I straightened as Gunnar raised his head, meeting my gaze. The pride in his expression was unmistakable, leaving me momentarily speechless. A steadfast belief that made my chest tighten and swell with emotion.

I swallowed a shuddering breath, bracing myself. "If I cannot convince the current alpha to give me the dagger, I'll have to declare a formal challenge."

"Good thing I trained you myself then." Gunnar grinned, rising to stand before me.

"Damn good thing," I said, giving him a firm nod before looping my arms around his neck to hug him tightly. Pulling back, I glanced at his left arm, the one I sliced with his blade to force him to let me leave the protection of the Summit wards. "Let me heal you."

"It'll heal on its own. It's not my first wound, nor will it be my last."

I gave him a stern look, and Gunnar sighed, reluctantly removing his armband. I immediately lifted my palm to his cut, allowing my magic to stitch the final pieces together.

"Thanks," Gunnar said with a sigh of relief.

"Did *none* of you listen to a *word* I said?" Idris's voice echoed through the library. "Adohan, put me down right now. I have some bones to break and heads to smack some sense into."

"I wouldn't dare unleash your temper right now, my love. Seeing as I'm the only one who can tame it," Adohan purred.

I could almost hear the prideful smirk he undoubtedly wore. Glancing over the railing, I watched as he carried his mate across the first floor of the library. Idris's muttering of select curses under her breath continued the entire way up to the second-floor landing.

"That's rich." Zola snickered under her breath. "You only think *you* can tame her, Crimson Prince. Be thankful for your mate bond."

"You two!" Idris shouted, glaring at the top of the stairs. "You are *so* lucky I'm about to have this baby. Or else I would throttle you and burn your insides myself." Her sharpened gaze turned toward Zola's hideaway. "And that includes you, Z! I know you're lurking in the shadows over there. I heard you." Flames danced around Idris's hands as her rage simmered.

Grinning, without showing her teeth, Zola unveiled her shadows, coming into full view.

"Thank you, Idris," I said, trying to calm her. "But I'm all right. I just needed a moment." Even though I knew we didn't have any to spare.

Idris motioned for Adohan to release her, and he reluctantly followed her request, never once taking his eyes off his very pregnant mate.

"None of them—" Idris paused, reaching for my hands. "None of them understand what it means to have your mate taken from you like that." She eyed the room, her gaze softening only when she turned back to meet mine. "Do you still feel your bond with him?" she asked. "I know it's unsealed, but can you still sense Daxton?"

I clutched my chest, closing my eyes and searching for the invisible tether. The pull that had always been a faint whisper guiding me toward my mate. "A little," I admitted in disappointment. "It's—"

"It's there," Idris encouraged, trying to comfort me in any way she could. "The bond is there, even if you haven't shifted. Your love is the bridge that connects you to him. Focus on that, and you'll *never* lose him."

Gods bless your fiery heart, Idris.

"I'll be taking Idris and Adohan back to Crimson City tonight," Zola announced. "Since Idris is close to birthing my godchild, and the twins were left in charge…"

"Finn and Astro are more than capable of assembling our forces and fortifying the city," Adohan boasted with a glower cast in the Shadow Jumper's direction.

Sensing her mate's emotions, Idris reached up to gently stroke his arm. "Our sons are young. But they've had us to teach them. They'll be ready, my love."

"It's imperative that we return home as soon as possible." Adohan paused as Castor suddenly shot up and stepped forward from his chair.

Nyssa, the fallen fae I healed in the wilt, glided up the staircase to join our group. Looking at Castor, I couldn't help but notice how tense and out of place he seemed to be. He was frozen like a statue, his attention isolated on only her.

"Nyssa." I spoke her name as her dark stare turned from Castor toward me.

Gunnar moved behind me, unsettled by her presence, preparing to defend me if necessary.

"I'm glad you're here," I said softly.

She nodded, gracefully lowering her petite frame to the floor, folding her fitted tan gown under her knees and bowing her head. She didn't speak. She hadn't spoken a word since I healed her as a fallen, and none of us questioned her for it.

Her raven hair cascaded over one shoulder, highlighting her beautiful, soft, pale skin with sharp, high cheekbones framing slanted eyes. When Nyssa looked at you, it was impossible to shake the feeling that she was more than she seemed, like her gaze carried the weight of untold stories and secrets waiting to unfold. Zola bore wisps of midnight stripes across her skin from the wilt, but Nyssa's scars were hidden from plain sight.

She gracefully raised her hands to begin signing, with Castor translating. "You must return to the mainland and retrieve the dagger of the Heart. The alpha's dagger."

"Yes," I answered.

"Are you afraid?"

I paused, this question catching me off guard. Of course I was afraid. I would be lying to myself if I said otherwise.

Nyssa tilted her head, searching for the words I had yet to speak, almost as if she was reading my mind. "I do not see fear for yourself. You're afraid for your friends and your family. But you are most of all afraid for your mate."

Gunnar took a step closer, with Zola moving to his side.

"Do you know?" Nyssa asked.

"Do I know what?"

"What the serpent king told you. Do you understand?"

"I—" To be honest, I hadn't had much time to think about it. "Do you?" I asked.

She nodded.

"What is she talking about, Skylar?" Idris chimed in, but my focus was only on the fallen fae kneeling before me.

A tingling sensation arose in my chest, my animal's presence rising to the surface.

"Your animal does," Nyssa signed, rising to place her palm on my heart.

I stilled, waiting to be taken under by her magic and shown a vision, but nothing happened. She withdrew her palm and folded it into itself, closing her eyes and breathing deeply.

"Look to her," Nyssa signed, with a kindness beaming brightly in her expression, paired with a soft smile. "Your animal will guide you in your time of need and bring you home."

Did her abilities allow her to sense my animal?

"Will you tell me what the serpent king meant?" I asked.

"No, only you can unveil the truth," she answered. "In time, you'll understand. This journey is meant to challenge you. Discovering the answers before you are ready will only steer you away from your path."

"Nyssa," Castor whispered, holding his hand to help her stand.

I watched them closely, her face softening at his kindness, accepting his offer and rising at his side, their hands united in a tender embrace.

I pulled my shoulders back and gazed out the nearby window. "I will travel to Solace alone," I said to the group.

Castor stiffened.

"I'm going alone," I repeated. "Daxton entered the second trial with me and almost died because of it. I'm willing to risk my life in these trials, but not yours."

"Skylar—"

"No," I said to Castor. I knew he was expecting to travel with me to Solace, but the Inner Kingdom couldn't spare him. Not now. "You each have a role to play in this rebellion. Each of you has a task to oversee while I'm gone."

"Daxton won't be pleased about this."

"I know," I said. "But this is something I must do on my own."

Zola fidgeted uneasily with the hilt of her dagger. "You're sure?" Zola dared to ask.

I shifted toward her, seeing a challenge spark in her midnight eyes. "Absolutely."

Zola sighed and clicked her tongue. "If this is your decision, I will respect it. You've earned my trust with all you've accomplished thus far. I will defer to your judgment on this matter," she answered, cocking her brow at Castor.

"If I fail…" The room went deathly silent as I looked down at the tattoo on my left arm. "If I die, another champion will come. Another will—"

"There will not be another champion," Adohan said slowly, his arm curling around his mate. The look in his eyes said more than his words ever could.

"Very well," I replied, clearing my throat. "Make sure you do your part, and I'll do mine."

Adohan gave me a curt nod, his flames dancing across his shoulders and through his hair. So many emotions were running wild it made it difficult to concentrate. There was fear, pain, dread, and selfishly, there was a hint of joy at returning to Solace.

If I succeeded in the final trial, I would have to ask the unthinkable, break traditions, and potentially shatter the world my people lived in.

Challenging the alpha was no small task.

Be ready. Be willing, the basilisk warned me. Was he referring to the birthright my father held? To my role as the next alpha of my pack?

"Call the *Opal*," Castor said.

Lifting my hand, I opened it to say, "Captain Fjorda of the *Opal*. I call upon your ship to ferry me across the seas and back. I call upon your aid in my final task of the trials."

Like magic, a loud horn blasted through the library's silence, echoing over Silver Meadows from the harbor to the east of the city.

"The *Opal*, it appears has answered your call," Gunnar said.

Chapter Three

Skylar Cathal

The city was frantic, and yet, I had never felt so calm.

Determination guided my footsteps as Castor escorted me through Silver Meadows and toward the harbor. The others would not be coming with us to say goodbye. It would be too difficult if they all came with me.

As we walked, I admired how resilient Silver Meadows was. The people were diligently repairing the damage caused by fires and the soldiers who had ravaged their homes. Even the children were lending a helping hand, caring for the wounded, or assisting the adults with various small tasks to rebuild their proud city.

Buckets of water were carried from the sea and the tranquil green river to cool the burning embers of the buildings that were left standing. The wounded were gathered near the archives tower for treatment, which thankfully was left untouched.

Not even Minaeve would threaten the guarded history of their people.

As Castor led me through the city, however, all eyes and busy hands paused to watch us pass through.

There were whispers back and forth, and I would be lying if I weren't afraid of what messages they might carry. Did the people blame me for all of this? For Daxton's imprisonment... For their home and families being destroyed?

As the harbor came into view, a familiar face stepped into our path.

"Stand aside," Castor said in a warning tone.

Despite a direct order from his prince, the male refused to move.

"We have something to say."

"You realize we're on a tight schedule, and more time wasted means—"

"I know," he cut in, hazel eyes highlighting contrasting whispers of silver that streaked his brown hair hanging just below his jawline. "We all know this, my prince." He paused, his gaze turning toward me. "I do not mean any disrespect, but I come here as the voice of your people. *She* needs to hear this."

I would always remember his face: the face of the High Fae cadet who helped carry Daxton into our rooms in Aelius. The male who fell from the Gauntlet and lived. Lived, because I was there in time to save him.

"Reece," I answered, placing a hand on Castor's shoulder, silently signaling to him that this was all right. We could spare this moment. "What do you have to say?"

"Be quick," Castor mumbled, the lines on his forehead creasing with unease.

Reece was not a Silver Meadows warrior, but it was evident that he still fought to protect his people, and I'd be damned if I didn't admire him for the strength of his heart. His fine clothing was torn, pieces of his shirt burned away from combating the flames, yet still, he carried a graceful, poised demeanor. One worthy of royalty himself.

Reece stepped closer, tilting his chin in my direction as his nostrils flared and his eyes widened. "It's true," he whispered.

"Careful," Castor said with a hard edge to his tone.

"It... It all makes perfect sense," he said, threading his fingers through his smoke residue hair. "You're the mate of our high prince."

"Yes," I answered, warmth spreading through my heart. "Daxton is my mate."

Reece dropped to his knee before me, bowing his head. "What I came to tell you rings true regardless of this fact." He paused, others around us stopping to watch with eyes and hearts full of wonder. "You have our gratitude, Skylar Cathal. We openly thank you for all you have done."

"Thank me?" I stammered. "Your city was burning, and..."

"Yes," Reece answered, raising his head. "Are you familiar with the concept of wildfires?"

"Well, yes," I answered, skeptical about where this was going.

"Nature has a way of cleansing the land and beginning anew. A delicate balance of life and death." His expression softened with kindness beaming from his smile. "But this cannot happen until the earth is burned and given a chance to start over. This is our chance. Silver Meadows is eternally loyal to our high prince. And..." Reece paused, rising to his feet. "We follow you, Champion. Our hope of rebirth and a new beginning."

Castor was no help. In his typical fashion, his mask of deception was firmly set in place.

And I... well, I didn't know what to say.

"I won't keep you any longer. Gods-speed, Champion." Reece smiled, gave me a final bow, and turned on his heels to leave.

The commotion of the city resumed its previous pace, confirming that Reece's confession was nothing of note because it was something they all believed to be true. A fact.

"Come, Skylar," Castor said, stepping to my side. "The *Opal* awaits."

I followed his guided touch, meandering through the final streets leading to the harbor. The wooden planks of the dock were steady against the crashing waves that swirled beneath the barrier. Reece's words on behalf of the citizens of Silver Meadows repeated over and over in my mind. I was honored by what he said, but the gravity of those words was not lost on me.

The fae would follow me, but would the Solace pack do the same?

Two worlds tied together by one fate.

"Welcome back," Fjorda announced as he lowered the walkway. He leaned over the edge of his beautiful ship, so cleverly named the *Opal*, after the elegant accents of white. "I knew you'd be calling sooner rather than later," he added with a smirk that no doubt had brought a fair share of females onto this very ship, and possibly a few water nymphs.

"Hello, Captain," I answered, stepping onto the walkway.

My boots creaked on the planks, my steps heavy, almost like stones were weighing them down.

"Are any companions coming with you this time?" Fjorda asked, his seafoam eyes churning with curiosity like the waves of the sea that held his heart.

His long brown hair swayed over his shoulder in tune with the wild ocean breeze. Reaching up a hand, he casually stroked his neatly trimmed beard, speckled with highlights of blond, patiently waiting for my reply.

Frozen in place, I paused at the final step on the plank. "No, not this time," I rasped.

"I imagine you have an idea of how to cross the veil?" Fjorda asked

"Of course." I scoffed. "I have a plan."

"Is it safe?"

"Is any of this safe?" I dared, knowing that nothing in Valdor was ever truly safe—not with the wilt or Minaeve in power.

His grin stretched, sharpened canines beaming brightly on display. "Nothing on the seas ever is."

"How fitting," I said.

"Indeed. It's part of the charm of my crew, and the fleet pledged to serve under my banner. The promise of the unknown. To live with the thrill of adventure."

"Well, prepare yourself for one hell of a ride."

"Gladly," Fjorda replied, crossing his arms and leaning against the railing. The smell of the salty sea air transported us from the commotion of the mainland. "Why do you think I gave you the mark?"

A piece of me wondered if his loyalty could be trusted or if the excitement of chaos was his driving purpose for lending his aid.

"And before you begin asking questions as to my intentions," he said, reading my unease, "the *Opal* will always answer the call from the High Prince of Silver Meadows. The prince who was promised, for I owe him a life debt, due countless times over, as does my ship and every member of my fleet, for the sacrifices he has made. The sea has our hearts, but he will always have our loyalty. Along with yours," he said with a half-grin.

"I'm honored."

Fjorda dipped his head and bit his bottom lip as his fingers tapped the hilt of the bejeweled sword at his hip. "Care to come aboard?"

Realizing I hadn't taken that final step, I took a deep breath and crossed the threshold.

"I see you come well-armed this time around, Champion," Fjorda added. "Is that the—"

"Yes," I answered, noticing his gaze fixated on my chest plate. "This is the armor of Aegis."

"I was commissioned to extract this armor from the depths of the Blue Hole. I know it well."

I made a silent note to inquire more about that comment later.

"And is that the bow of Arabella, Daxton's mother?"

I nodded, my fingers tracing over the silver-trimmed ebony weapon strapped to my back. I hoped my mate's mother would approve of me wielding it.

"I added a few others as well." I patted the hilt of a short sword, and daggers tucked along my outer thigh.

"Excellent," Fjorda said with a hint of mischief. "Females with more bark than their bite are not meant to rule."

Crew members moved around us, hurrying to prepare the ship for our voyage. Ropes were cast along the mast pillars, anchors raised from the sea floor, covered in seaweed with various small creatures clutching the metallic covering.

I gazed upward at the elegant white sails swaying in the wind. They waved with the circling gusts along the shoreline between Starfall Island and Silver Meadows. Riding the wildness of the currents that held the fate of countless seafarers.

"Skylar."

My spine stiffened in anticipation, knowing I couldn't refuse the call. I turned around to see Castor standing alone at the end of the dock. His head was held high with the regal air of his stature, in the steadying breaths he forced himself to take.

"Prove my brother right," Castor said on the wandering winds.

My heart surged, seeing the same look of determination and absolute faith I had seen in Daxton now reflected in Castor's stare. His silver and black fighting leathers shifted across his toned frame, his silver-white hair whipping across the hard lines of his face. Twin swords were strapped to his back, with three silver mountain peaks visible on his shoulder. He was ready to march north with Gunnar and the other Silver Meadows warriors.

Ready to fight and, if needed, die to free themselves.

"Return. And free us all," he said.

All I could do was nod and hold back my tears.

"Cast the sails," a sailor hollered as the white sheets filled above my head. The *Opal* drifted away from the shoreline.

My eyes never left Castor's. He stood at the edge of the docks, immovable against the fearsome weight threatening to tear us all down.

I recalled a portrait of the late rulers of Silver Meadows hanging in the grand hallway. While Daxton and Castor were the spitting image of their father, Castor had their mother's cunning dark eyes, inheriting this trait along with his unique gift to foresee death when it was near. I wondered what else he might see through the gifts of his mother's bloodline, and if they somehow allowed him to see the world in a different light compared to those around him.

Solace was my homeland, but this place had become a safe haven and a refuge for me. Silver Meadows was as much my home now as perhaps Solace was.

The ship drifted far enough to catch the current separating the island from the Inner Kingdom, and with a burst of speed, Castor and the rest of Silver Meadows faded in the distance.

Chapter Four

Skylar Cathal

I wandered along the outer railing of the ship, time passing in a fleeting memory, drifting in a blur like the beat of a hummingbird's wings.

The sun rose and fell over my head, once and then again, yet I still mindlessly paced. Restless and anxious, I continued my march across the ship. Not even the comfort of food or the aching need for sleep could break me from my trance.

I was adrift, losing myself within the lingering memories of Daxton, the fate of our worlds, and all that I had overcome. My mind wandered through the different scenarios I could face once I returned to Solace, searching for answers to questions I didn't know how to form. There was nothing I could do but wait.

And Gods above, I hate sitting and waiting.

The crew was a faint presence in my semi-conscious state of reality. Thankfully, they kept their distance, parting to grant me access to my weathered path, not daring to interfere. I was grateful for the space they granted me, for the solitude Fjorda and the crew seemed to understand I needed. In a tragic stroke of fate, they empathized with my pain, even though they didn't understand the gravity of the internal demons I was battling.

"I'm going to have to replace the decking if you keep this up," Fjorda said, standing against the wheel of the ship.

For the first time in days, I stopped pacing and turned to look at him, at anyone. The setting sun cast glowing orange and red rays of sunlight across his face, highlighting the blond speckles in his beard.

"The veil crossing is coming. You should—"

"I should what?" I stared at him with an emptiness in my gaze that forced him to pause.

Fjorda cleared his throat before shifting his stance against the wheel. "I know your pain, Champion," he said in a whisper. His wild eyes gleamed with a sense of understanding. "Nothing can be done to help alleviate the sorrow you're carrying in your heart."

Daxton. In the solitude of our voyage, my mind constantly circled back to him.

"The high prince is strong enough to survive this. He's already—"

"I know he is," I said in a pained voice. "I don't need a lecture about how strong my mate is. I know the odds he has faced. I know what he has struggled to fight against all these years."

"We all know," Fjorda replied. "The guilt you carry doesn't rest solely in your heart. It weighs on your very soul. In that, we are more alike than you might realize. Our pains share a common thread."

I scoffed and gazed upon the never-ending sea. "My soul feels—"

"Torn, like it's missing a piece you never realized was ever gone." Fjorda's words struck a chord. "The mate bond," he added, adjusting the wheel before stepping away and fronting me along the railing. "It's a gift, but also a curse."

"You speak from experience?"

"I do," he replied.

I was surprised to learn this about Fjorda. Carefully, I watched the sea captain, anxiously waiting to see if he would share more.

"My mate," Fjorda spoke slowly, as if the mere mention of her was like a knife to his gut. "She was as wild as the sea herself."

"What happened to her?"

"The wilt."

He didn't need to say any more.

"She became a—"

"Yes," he answered, hanging his head.

I knew from the grave look on his face that his mate was turned into a fallen, a nalusa falaya. A creature at the mercy of the wilt's poisonous magic that turned the infected host into something living, yet not alive.

"She's not gone, just... *lost*," Fjorda said. "I wander in this life waiting to find her again, living close to the wild sea that always reminds me of her."

I longed to offer the captain some form of comfort, but I held back. I didn't know if we would find her amongst the fallen, or if I was able to bring her back. Using my powers to heal Nyssa had almost killed me.

"You believe you'll see her again?" I asked.

"I believe I'll forever seek to find her, and whether it be in this life or the next, I'll be with her again. I've had time to make my peace with this." He tapped the center of his chest. "The bond brings you together, but your heart, your love, is the true bridge between your souls."

"You sound like Idris," I answered.

"Because she also knows from experience." The winds began to dance, swirling with the presence of wild magic nearing. "Are you ready to put your theory of crossing the veil to the test?"

"As ready as I'll ever be."

"Good," Fjorda replied, pushing from the railing and returning to his post at the helm. "In that case, as captain of this ship, I'm ordering you to rest and for you to head to your barracks."

"What?" I drawled, arching my brow.

"The dark circles under your eyes and the growling pit in your stomach over these past two days on the sea do not go unnoticed. You've been pacing relentlessly with no food, barely stopping to accept a ladle of water from my crew. Torturing yourself will not alleviate *his* pain."

"I'm not—"

"Correct. You're not anymore," Fjorda challenged. "It's enough. You'll need your strength in the trial to come. Withering away into nothing will not help our cause."

I glared at him, refusing to accept the roaring pains of my empty stomach and the aching muscles of my feet and legs. Two days. Had it really been two days of my mindless pacing and numbing awareness of everything around me?

"The winds indicate that our crossing is near," Fjorda said, adjusting the wheel. "We needed to sail the length of the Inner Kingdoms to the northern border. I don't dare enter the waters of the human lands."

"Why not the human lands?" I asked.

"Don't try to change the subject." Fjorda chuckled as a spray of seawater fell over us from a crashing wave. "Regardless of your station, here on my ship, you follow my command. You're ordered to return to your barracks and rest."

I placed my hands on my hips and glowered at him.

"Make that face all you want. It's not as intimidating as you think, with the roars of your hunger cutting through your silent threats."

I flinched as my stomach rumbled, clutching at my aching center and finally allowing myself to feel *something*.

"Go," Fjorda instructed. "There's food already waiting for you in the quarters you held during your initial stay aboard my ship."

I turned to walk away but paused. "What if I can't sleep? What if I am afraid to?" I confessed, biting my lip to try and keep steady.

"Was it not your dreams that led you to your mate in the first place? Where you found solace and comfort in your times of need?"

I pivoted, looking over my shoulder at the alluring sea captain. "It was."

"Then allow them to return and comfort you once again."

I nodded as he bowed his head toward me in farewell. I turned and began marching toward the rooms Dax, Castor, and I held during our initial stay on the *Opal*. Upon opening the door to my small, cozy room, my senses were filled with the amazing smell of fresh food waiting for me, just like Fjorda promised.

Without wasting another moment, I dove into the delicious plate delivered just before I arrived. The cooked fish and steamed rice soothed the relentless ache in the pit of my stomach. By the time my plate was devoured, night had fallen upon the sea, and my eyes could no longer keep themselves open. For two days, I had marched across the ship, locked inside my mind, tormenting myself.

Reluctantly, I lay my head on my pillow, giving in to my exhaustion and allowing my mind to drift into a dream.

Chapter Five

Skylar Cathal

I half expected to see the hanging valley beneath the Meja Mountain in my dream, but, to my surprise, that was not where I ended up.

A black slip dress allowed the breeze to dance along my knees, cooling me from the heat of the warm summer day. The rolling waves of the churning ocean currents splashed playfully against the olivine crystallized sand beneath my feet, bringing a serene smile to my face that lifted my darkened spirit.

I chuckled, glancing at the sand settling between my toes as the waves washed over my legs. I buried my feet farther in the layers of sparkling emerald grains with each cascading crescendo drifting over the shoreline. Leaning my head back, I inhaled the familiar scent of salty sea air, allowing this special place to surround me in a layer of tranquility that calmed the reckless animal spirit inside my chest.

This was my beach. A place of solace I could always count on to bring me peace.

"Spitfire?"

I froze.

A chill ran along my spine as hope dared to flutter in my heart.

"Spitfire," the voice rasped again. "Please, Gods, tell me it's really you."

I didn't dare breathe. The sound of his voice felt like a caress across my skin.

"Skylar?"

I turned so fast the world spun. My eyes widened in shock as I gawked at the sight of my mate standing across the way.

This was a dream, right? Or was this, on some level, perhaps real?

"Daxton?" I dared to whisper.

Gray eyes widened with the same look of shock I imagined mine held. He was barefoot, standing in the rolling waves, with his pants rolled up to his knees. The same black tunic with silver thread opened along his chest.

"Daxton!" I shouted.

He sprinted toward me. I lifted my buried feet from the sand and raced to meet him.

"Daxton!" I screamed once more, tears threatening to blur my vision.

"Skylar!" he yelled, a smile stretching across his face.

I soared into his open arms, spinning around in an all-consuming embrace that melted away every ounce of distress or dread, feeling his touch as if this were real. His grip was so tight it was difficult to breathe, but I didn't care. I wrapped my arms around my mate, burying my face in his neck.

Daxton was here.

Lowering me onto the sand, he released his hold on my waist, cupping my face and kissing me with a feverish need. His tongue swept through my open mouth, tasting me, reminding me what it was like to feel alive and whole. I threaded my fingers through his hair, pressing my body flush against his, needing to feel his touch on every inch of my skin. His hands moved to stroke my ribs as our kiss deepened, migrating over the curves of my hips as I moaned into his mouth.

Then, suddenly, Daxton stilled.

His entire body tensed like he was in pain. His eyes clutched shut, and he sucked in sharp breaths of air through his gritted teeth. The chasm in my chest widened as I helplessly watched him suffer.

"Dax?" I rasped, stroking his face with uneasiness etched in my voice. "What's wrong?"

"Nothing," he said, sucking in a pained breath through his teeth. "They... They're just moving me."

"Who's—"

His eyes snapped open to meet mine, and I understood. Gods above, I understood more than anyone what he meant. They were moving his body from wherever they deemed fit to torture him, back to his holding cell.

"I will kill them *all* for this. Every last one of them," I vowed. Their blood would be a welcome stain on my hands for harming my mate.

Daxton's body went taut again as the strength in his legs gave way. He crashed onto the sand, gripping the olivine crystals with his fists, groaning with agony at wounds I could not see. He was fighting to stay here, fighting to remain unconscious in this place with me.

I knelt next to him, placing my hands on his shoulders to call upon my magic, but nothing came.

"It's all right, Spitfire," Daxton said, inhaling a sharp breath. "But I don't have much time. I'll be awake soon." He moved to a sitting position on the beach, beckoning me to move into his lap so he could hold me.

I happily obliged, wrapping my arms around him and burying my head in his chest, trying to will his pain away. I listened to the thundering strength of his heart and his even breaths as the ocean waves gently rolled over our legs.

"You found me." There was a hint of a smile in his voice.

"Was there any doubt?" I answered.

He chuckled and drew me in closer, kissing the top of my head and inhaling deeply. "I believe you'll never stop surprising me."

"We were never meant to be mundane. You said so yourself," I said.

"I'm so wise."

"Oh Gods. Let's not stroke your already enlarged ego."

"Care to help it along?" He shifted, and despite himself, I could feel him hardening against me.

"Have you ever had these kinds of dreams about me before, Daxton Aegaeon?" I asked, giving him a playful smirk. "About touching me," I purred as I guided his hands between my thighs.

Arching my back, I moved against him. A deep moan escaped his lips as he moved to run his mouth along my neck.

"Can't say it would be a first," Daxton whispered against my fevered flesh. "I've dreamt about having you long before I had the privilege of doing so." His voice dropped into a more serious tone. "But I have to admit, it does not come close to the real thing."

I shuddered as his fingers brushed against my inner thighs, teasing me with a whisper of his touch. I pulled on the base of his neck, needing to kiss him, savoring every touch and feel of his lips as they brushed over mine.

"How did I find you, Dax?" I whispered between our kisses. "Here, of all places?"

"Why do you keep questioning magic and the limits of our bond?" Daxton answered with a hint of amusement. "You mentioned that you dreamed of the hanging valley in Silver Meadows."

"Yes," I breathed.

"In my darkest times, I dreamed of this beach. Over the past twenty years, or whenever I was at my lowest, I dreamt of this place, and it brought me comfort."

"My beach?" I questioned.

He gave me a half-smile that had me curling my toes. "Why do you think I wandered there during my first days in Solace? I had been dreaming about it for years. So, naturally, I had to see it with my own eyes, and then, I found a... book."

I grinned, remembering this all too well.

"And then," he continued.

"And then I showed up to retrieve it."

"And the reason for these dreams became crystal clear."

I threaded my fingers through his midnight silver-streaked hair, my eyes scanning over the face I treasured most in this world, memorizing every last detail I could.

"Skylar." Daxton sighed as he lowered his brow to mine. "I can't stay much longer."

"I know," I answered, not allowing my disappointment in his deception to taint these precious moments in our dream world. It could wait. For now, there was only us. "Will I see you again in our dreams? Here or in the hanging valley?"

"I'm not sure," Daxton answered.

I moved to straddle him in the sand, looking deep into his eyes that reflected his eternal devotion and immovable strength.

"Have you crossed the veil yet?"

"No, we're about to."

"I see." His lips pressed into a thin line, but he wouldn't dare confirm the dread pooling in my stomach.

I could see the answer written on his face. He doubted we could find each other in our dreams like this once I passed through the veil.

"I will find you," I whispered, kissing his cheek.

Daxton smiled as he tucked a strand of hair behind my ear, gazing at me with a depth of love and devotion you only read about in fairytales.

"We will always find each other," he answered as I kissed him.

Chapter Six

Skylar Cathal

I contemplated not waking up.

For a fraction of a second, I allowed myself to imagine staying there. But dreams are not reality. It was not in my nature to give up and surrender, no matter how tempting the latter might be.

The wooden panels above my head flickered with the rays of the morning sun through the window in the door. I turned on my side in the soft covers, adjusting my gaze to the light. I'd slept through the night for the first time in two days, and Gods above, I needed it.

"Ready yourselves for the crossing!" Fjorda's voice echoed, as rough as sea-salt winds.

Flinging the covers back, I quickly slipped into my boots. My dark gray pants paired with a white long-sleeve tunic were perfect for the sailing conditions. Before leaving, Gunnar almost convinced me that slaying the basilisk had earned me a second peak, but I couldn't accept it. To counter, I told him I'd consider it when I returned with the dagger, earning a true victory.

As I opened the door to my quarters, the morning sun's rays decorated the horizon in a magnanimous display. The glorious pink and yellow kisses of color were blessed by the Mother herself and danced across the distant lands of the Inner Kingdom.

We had to sail the length of the continent before reaching the northern pass, the departure site adding an extra day to our journey. And once we passed through, it would only be a few more days to Solace.

The distinct scent of the captain announced his presence before he spoke. "You ready?"

"As I'll ever be," I answered with a confident grin.

"Good. What do you have planned? I've tried crossing without Daxton a time or two—and it did not go well."

"Do I want to know what happened?"

"Let's just say this isn't the first ship under my command. Others have been claimed by the sea for attempting to pass through without magic to part the way." Fjorda crossed his arms and leaned against the paneled wall.

I reached into my pocket and wrapped my fingers around the solidified eye of the basilisk. The second key of the trials thrummed with power of its own in my grasp, almost begging to be released.

Here goes nothing.

"This should do it," I said, presenting the key to the captain.

Fjorda's eyes widened as he noted the eight-pointed star in the center, his gaze darting to the tattoo on my arm. "Let's hope so."

The ship's sails were fluttering in chaos, a clear sign that we were nearing our intended destination.

"Tie them down!" Fjorda hollered as he walked with me to the front of the ship, pointing to the sails. "Ready the oars. I believe we'll need the extra push through."

"You didn't have those out last time."

"No, but there's a different ambiance to the waters this time around." Fjorda stroked his blond-speckled beard, deep in thought, almost like he was listening to guidance from the waters themselves. "Trust me, we'll need them."

"The sea is alive today, Captain," a sailor said, his voice low and edged with unease. "The currents are restless. Churning, racing, spiraling in ways I've never felt before. This crossing isn't like the others. There's a tension in the air, a warning in my bones."

I hesitated, glancing at the darkened waters below. "What should we fear in the depths?"

The fae sailor's gaze flickered to me, his expression turning. "Some things, Champion," he said gravely, "are better left unknown."

My instincts told me not to push the matter further, and for once, I was inclined to listen.

"Your focus lies on getting us through. Mine is on keeping us alive on the journey across the seas," Fjorda said.

I nodded. "Very well, I'm trusting you."

"Likewise."

I stepped into position at the bow of the ship and braced myself, the salt wind tugging at my sleeves. A faint trickle of raw magic prickled across my skin before I connected with the dominant power of the veil. My animal stirred just beneath the surface, her essence sharpening, awakened by the veil's wild magic.

In my left hand, I held the eye of the basilisk, the power radiating from the small orb against my palm. Like a curtain drawn back by invisible hands, a route through the barrier appeared. The ship surged ahead with the synchronized power of the rowers, its rhythm steady and unyielding. At the forefront, the key glowed faintly, cutting through the unseen forces and carving a path forward.

Pricks of fire danced along my nerves as we moved through the veil. And just like before, it wasn't until we passed through the outer barrier that I finally saw the beauty of the magic hovering around me.

The crystalline colors danced around us, but unlike before, I didn't feel the intense waves of desire and lust running wild. There was a thrilling skip in my heart rate, but nothing compared to the first time I crossed.

"You're holding up better on this voyage, I see," Fjorda commented. "I'm glad to see your plan worked."

I turned to him, still holding the eye. "This crossing feels different."

The magic crackled along my skin, my senses sharp, alert, but the all-consuming heat I'd felt with

Daxton was absent. No breathless longing. No flood of adrenaline threatening to drown me.

"Each one is," he answered plainly. "Magic is as wild and unpredictable as the sea. And—" Fjorda paused as a half-grin slid along the corner of his mouth. "It is also known to heighten magic already present."

Our mate bond.

I silently cursed my shifter half for not being able to recognize the bond sooner.

"The veil's magic," I whispered. "It's strange how familiar it feels."

"Like waking up from a dream," Fjorda answered, leaning over the front and closing his eyes, allowing the sparkling crystalline colors to dance across his face. "But not remembering the details."

"Yes, that's exactly it," I said, arching my brow.

Fjorda kept his gaze toward the veil opening. "Not much longer now."

Suddenly, the air cleared around us as the crystallized layer disappeared, revealing a wide-open sea with nothing behind us. I retracted my arm, gently cradling the key in my palm as the orb began to crumble and vanish into specks of dust. The winding winds circled around me, almost as if they were alive, carrying the final remains of the fallen serpent king and whisking it away across the vast open waters to lands unknown, finally freeing him.

Perhaps now, the basilisk would find peace. I hoped that it would.

"Well, it seems that was a one-way key."

"The dagger," I said, twirling my hands in the wind, ensuring every last speck of the basilisk was freely floating away. "The dagger of the alpha can cut through anything, and since it is the third key to these trials, the magic of the blade will be able to part the way through and allow us to return."

"Clever." Fjorda clicked his tongue.

"Indeed. Now comes the more difficult task of obtaining it."

"Should be simple enough?"

I turned and glowered at Fjorda. "Sure, right." I scoffed.

"Isn't it, though?"

I raised a brow at him and laughed under my breath.

"What?" Fjorda replied, shrugging his shoulders. "You're trying to save Valdor. The wilt has likely spread to the mainland and through Solace by now. Surely, your alpha will relinquish the dagger?"

"It's more than that." I paused, dread pooling in my stomach. "It's the structure and hierarchy of our people. Our culture. To carry that weapon signifies more than just the title of alpha. It means you are sworn to protect the pack with your life, to guard it with your final breath in this world. To carry the dagger means you are bound to your people, and they to you."

I knew in my heart that the alpha, whoever it would be, would not release the dagger willingly. It wasn't in our nature.

"I will ask, but if the alpha denies my request, I'll have to issue a formal challenge and win."

"I see," Fjorda answered, stroking his chin. "Then you best prepare yourself and refrain from sulking around my ship like you've been the past few days. It would be embarrassing if you showed up starved, half-dead with exhaustion, and had to challenge the strongest shifter in your lands."

"True." *He had a valid point. I couldn't deny that.* "How long until we reach Solace?"

"Three days if the winds are in our favor," Fjorda said with a grin. "Now, aren't you glad I called for the oars?" He winked when his eyes found the mountain peak on my tunic. "I heard rumors through the harbor that you've been training in Silver Meadows."

"I have," I answered, my mind fondly thinking of Daxton and Gunnar. A half-smile dared to cross my face, even though I didn't believe I deserved to feel that spark of happiness.

"Then my advice..." Fjorda clasped a hand on my shoulder. "Win your challenge, Champion." And with that, the captain pushed off the railing and took his leave.

I smiled as he turned away, thanking him for lighting a fire under my ass.

I had work to do.

Chapter Seven

Daxton Aegaeon

On my first night in prison, Anjani laughed when she presented me with the iron collar. "Now, be a good *pet* like your mate, and try to behave."

Anjani Duran, Seamus's second in command, was a wicked and sadistic creature who was as lethal as she was alluring. The haunting Duran green eyes, the exact same shade Seamus held, were full of destruction and menace. The female prided herself on being able to extract anything from those in her *care*.

Blazing fury surged through me at the mention of my mate as a *pet*. The same name I knew Seamus had drawn from her memories to torment her in Crimson City. The same she heard in her nightmares when she woke up screaming in my arms.

I lunged forward, intending to break her neck with my bare hands, but a wall of shadow hurled me onto my back.

I thrashed against the grip of her dark magic, but Minaeve overpowered me. She appeared in the hallway, cloaked within Anjani's illusions, and laughed—sharp and cruel—at my feeble attempt to overtake her.

With my focus splintered, the queen seized the moment, siphoning a kernel of my power to weaken me further.

Minaeve's lips were poison.

Every time she forced the siphon, it felt like my life force was stolen from me. I could feel my magic churn inside my center, fighting against the pull. Fighting to remain in my veins, but alas, her shadows always found their way to my power and swept it away.

Ice trickled across my skin as she extracted my magic, followed by my essence in a flicker of silver light bound to my teleportation ability.

The intent of her siphons differed each time she forced it upon me, depending on which gifts she drew from, but this time, Gods above... This time, it felt as if my very soul was being devoured. My remaining threads of strength disintegrated.

The sheer look of glee on her face was monstrous, even beneath her glowing beauty. A surreal golden light enveloped her, casting an otherworldly sheen that seemed to breathe new life into her.

I had never seen such radiance from her before. It was mesmerizing, and deeply, *deeply* wrong.

That was the last thought I had before darkness claimed me once again.

When I awoke, my hands were bound above my head, and I was suspended off the ground with my toes barely touching the floor. My chest was bare, with my shirt discarded to the side.

Anjani stood across from me in the cave-like torture chamber. Through squinted eyes, the solitary fae light in the corner silhouetted her frame. I didn't dare open my eyes wider. The faint light was blinding after being confined in the dark for two days.

Anjani's cropped brown hair was braided to the side, her dark green leathers designed to conceal various torture weapons at the ready.

"Let the games begin," she sneered, reaching for a barbed whip.

I couldn't help the grin that spread across my face, followed by a low, maddening chuckle.

"Has your mind collapsed so soon, Aegaeon?" Anjani taunted.

"No," I answered with a dark laugh, my eyes snapping open to meet hers. "I just know you favor your right hand."

Anjani's jaw clenched as rage began boiling inside her. "Minaeve told me to have my way with you, to break your body and then your mind until there was nothing left but an empty vessel."

"Good luck." I met her stare, unafraid, challenging her to do her worst.

Without warning, she cracked the whip over my torso. The barbs ripped into my flesh, carving out gashes gushing with blood, turning the floor beneath me crimson. The warmth of my blood trickled down my front, my back, and my sides. There wasn't a single inch of me spared from her lashings.

Again and again, she struck.

Again and again, I met her stare.

I wanted to remind Anjani exactly who she held captive. I wanted her to report to her false king and queen about who lurked in their dungeons. I wanted them to remember what was born in these very cells.

Silver Shadow.

I received this name on the battlefields before my time locked within these walls. But it was here that the shadow was truly born. Surviving this place forced me to become something else. Something deadly that caused even Seamus to tremble with unease.

Eventually, Anjani grew tired, *or bored*, with no sign of breaking me.

"Guards," she called, placing her whip on the table near the far corner. "Until our next session, Aegaeon," she hissed, pulling a lever from the wall that dropped me to the floor like a stone. "Make sure the healing salve is applied. I prefer a blank canvas to resume my revenge." She snickered.

The chains rattled as they released me. My head collided violently with the ground as I finally gave in and lost consciousness once more.

At first, I thought Skylar was an illusion, a conjured desire manipulated into a new sense of torture.

In the past, Anjani hadn't been able to invade my dreams with her magic, but a drive for revenge was a powerful motivator.

The warm breeze lifted my sweat-slick hair from the base of my neck. The sunlight warmed my cold, broken skin as wisps of white clouds danced along the clear cerulean sky overhead. I reached up and tied my hair back, relishing in the serenity of this dream, this place that I'd dreamt of for the past twenty years.

I walked along the familiar breaking waves, praying for the waters to help wash away the lingering pains, when—there *she* was.

"Spitfire!" I called out, doubting, but praying it was truly her.

When she turned to look at me, my heart sang. The tether between us lit up and sang the beautiful melody only we could hear.

"Daxton!" she screamed. Her eyes pooled with tears.

It was her, Skylar.

My mate was a breathtakingly beautiful sight to behold. Even the Mother herself would be envious of her.

Luscious, thick golden-brown hair swept out behind her as Skylar began sprinting toward me. The black slip dress flared around her perfect curves, highlighting her strength and feminine grace that drove me wild. Her amber eyes blazed like living flames, drawing me in with their warmth and power.

"Skylar!" I roared as I crashed through the surf.

"Dax!"

When she leaped into my open arms, I could've died happy right then and there.

Holding her was a gift I would forever cherish. Her scent hit me, reminding me of burning cedar and open sky with a hint of pine from my homeland.

It was intoxicating.

This female was mine.

It didn't matter if our mate bond was sealed or not. Fuck that. Our love was strong enough to forge the threads of our unsealed bond.

I leaned in to kiss her, and it felt like I was flying.

I would never get enough of her. She was everything. I thanked the Gods above for granting me what time I had with her, even though I knew there would never be enough. I would never stop fighting to be back in her arms again, never.

All too soon, I was pulled from our shared dream, reluctantly rejoining the waking realm.

Still, that moment with her was enough to keep me going, strengthening me enough to push aside the haunting darkness and torment. The stunning details of her face, how she felt in my arms, and what her lips tasted like when I kissed her.

My spitfire. My heart and soul.

The masked High Fae guards hauled me down the darkened corridor that reeked of death itself. I was torn from my dream with Skylar, but I knew I carried her with me. Despite the distance separating us, we were never alone.

I will find you. We will always find each other.

"Pathetic," one of the guards seethed as they moved me.

"He won't last much longer if she keeps this up," the other guard replied. "Even with the healing salve for his wounds."

"Don't tell me Anjani's tired and already giving up?" I taunted in a rasped whisper.

"He's gone mad."

"Not yet." I laughed as my voice cracked. Every word was worth the pain.

The next day, in our second session, Anjani's lashings became personal. Not one ounce of remorse graced her expression. She enjoyed watching almost as much as partaking in my beatings.

I was drugged with the iron powder before being dragged out of my cell.

She and others under her command concentrated their efforts on inflicting deep wounds on my hands and feet. It was remarkable how blows to these areas almost hurt more than killing strikes. Anjani removed two of my fingernails from my right hand, while her cloaked footman broke the digits on my left. My feet were struck with the same barbed whip, making it impossible to walk even if I wanted to.

Fuck, this hurt.

Somehow, I managed to control my roars of pain, refusing to break. I retreated deep into the chasm of darkness inside myself, where no feelings existed, distancing myself from physical pain, and truly becoming Silver Shadow once more.

Chapter Eight

Skylar Cathal

The three days spent sailing to Solace were not wasted.

Winds were in our favor, almost like Valdor itself was helping us along the journey. No storm clouds threatened our passage, with only blue skies and warm winds to whisk us through the Narrow Sea.

And so, I trained from sunup to sundown. So exhausted that I couldn't keep my eyes open come nightfall, sinking into a dreamless sleep each time my head hit the pillow.

A part of me wished I could dream of Daxton again, but I also knew it was for the best. I needed to focus on the trial, and the temptation of drifting off with him was far too alluring.

I concentrated on working through the various movements Daxton and Gunnar had taught me during my time training in Silver Meadows. I knew I wouldn't be able to overpower the alpha with brute strength. I would have to use my head.

The question was, would the alpha be Alistar or Gilen?

Alistar had been our leader all my life. He was well-versed in combat and had access to his animal. But

Gilen was on his way to take his father's place. His power had likely grown since my departure, and if I were to wager who I thought held the position, it would be Gilen.

I hated the thought of challenging my childhood best friend. I hoped and prayed to the Gods that he would see reason and listen to me.

The scroll had deemed this task a trial of the soul, and I had to admit, before ever setting foot back on the mainland, I knew this would be the most difficult trial yet.

A long, high-pitched whistle sounded from a sailor high atop the crow's nest, signaling land was in sight.

We were here.

Solace.

I climbed the mast, wrapping a rope around my wrist and jumping onto the pristine white railing to lean over the starboard side of the ship. My heart leaped in my chest, seeing the shoreline I knew so well. The scent of the familiar forest, even at this distance, made my spirit soar.

Just as we rounded a cluster of sea rocks, revealing the cliffs plummeting into the waves, sheer dread replaced my joy.

"Dear... Gods," a nearby High Fae whispered and gasped in absolute horror.

No. I sucked in a sharp breath.

The cliffs between the green sand beach and the shoreline closest to Solace held threads of the wilt. Like ink spilled on parchment, it congregated near the sea and slowly spread across the land.

Black veins snaked along the shoreline, intruding into the forest that held trees resembling burnt skeletons. The once vibrant greenery now mimicked the territory overrun and controlled by the creatures of the dark magic in the Inner Kingdom. They were blackened with a lifeless sway from the sea breeze. Bare of any bark or leaves, even the pines farther inland were brown and wilted.

The decay of our world was no longer a threat but a reality. The wilt had finally made its way onto the mainland.

Valdor was in grave danger.

It was clear now, if I failed—if I didn't win the trials—everything would be lost. We would not survive another hundred years. The High Fae queen's magic might fend off the creatures and the progression of the decay in the Inner Kingdom, but the mainland would not be safe. We had no defenses against this. Nothing to combat the wilt that suffocated the land and everything in its path.

I swung back over the railing, sailors lining up along the side, gawking at the shoreline.

"I can't believe it," one of the High Fae females stammered. "How? How did this happen so quickly?"

That was the same question I had. It had only been three months, and when we left, the black veins of death did not yet cross into the mainland.

What made this progress so quickly? Did the human lands to the south hold these threads as well?

Fjorda appeared at my side. "You said the veil felt... different? That the magic at the crossing wasn't as strong?"

"Yes," I answered.

The others surrounding us nodded their heads as well.

"Gods above," Fjorda cursed.

I gasped. "Oh no!"

"What does this mean, Captain?" a beautiful blonde female asked, striding to his side.

I recognized her as Fjorda's first mate. The companion Castor had taken to his quarters on more than one occasion while we sailed to the Inner Kingdom.

"You want to tell them?" Fjorda inclined his head toward me, knowing I had reached the same awful conclusion he had.

"It means," I began, refusing to allow my voice to waver, determined to be strong, because, well, there was no other option at this point. "It means the veil is losing its power. It's weakening."

"How?" someone shouted from the crowd. The winds began to shift, bringing the *Opal* closer to the shoreline, revealing more evidence of the wilt's destruction.

"The veil has stood for five hundred years! How is it *now* failing?" another shouted.

I looked at Fjorda, and he gave me a curt nod, his eyes churning wild like the turquoise seas. He understood exactly why the veil was failing, why it was beginning to fall. There was one change, one definite difference.

"It's because of me," I said.

The High Fae on the ship stilled, their gazes all turning in my direction. Some looked confused, and others looked shocked, but there were a handful who realized the truth.

I inhaled a long breath, my animal sending a surge of courage through me. "The further I progress in the trials, the weaker the veil's magic becomes."

Whispers erupted amongst the crew.

I looked out onto the sands, sorrow threatening to shatter my beating heart at the state of my homeland, wishing I could have spared my people this deathly curse.

"They're linked. Gods be damned. Daxton was right," I said to myself.

Oh, Mother and Father, there would be no living with him after he heard of this. I shook my head as the chatter around me continued to build.

"The Silver Meadows high prince believed they were connected?" the first mate asked, overhearing me.

Her long braid fell over her shoulder in a cascade of blonde, almost white, silken locks. The slender sword at her back was paired with the daggers strapped to her thighs, sharpening her appearance and countering her feminine beauty with that of a lethal fighter.

"He did," I answered. "My mate had a theory that when I unlocked the Heart, the veil would fall, and our worlds would once again be open to one another."

"Your *mate*," she repeated, a half-smile appearing at the corner of her mouth. "That explains the scent change."

Others around her nodded in agreement.

"It makes sense," Fjorda said, silencing the muttering of his crew. "The veil appeared when the Heart was locked away. It's logical that they're linked."

"What do we do now?" a male sailor asked.

I glanced along the shoreline, recognizing my green sand beach before turning to Fjorda. "Do you have a rowboat you can spare?"

Chapter Nine

Daxton Aegaeon

"Gods a-fucking-bove!" I couldn't restrain the curse escaping my splintered lips as I forced myself to turn on the cobblestone floor of the dungeon.

If the constant darkness of the prison wasn't enough to break your spirits, then the stench of death paired with piss and shit certainly would. I doubted these cells were ever cleaned. Some of the dead were hauled away, but not all were fortunate enough to escape this place. Even in death, they lingered, with nothing but their skeletons as evidence of their time spent here.

Eventually, my eyes adjusted to the shadows. I was able to faintly detect the twists and turns of the catacomb's hallways meandering through the iron-caged holdings.

Sitting up, my hand traced the surface of the rock wall, locating a point where the iron bars of my cell fused with the rough stone. The iron wasn't only a physical barrier. It was a cruel trap for those of us with magic. Its presence stifled the flow of my powers, locking them away and gnawing at my sanity, amplifying the suffocating despair of this wretched prison.

There were undoubtedly hundreds of holdings here. I never traveled farther than my own section, so I didn't know for certain. But I *heard* them.

The cries of my kin echoing through the stone haunted my waking and sleeping mind. Dryads, nymphs, and High Fae were imprisoned here, doomed to suffer under a false queen's wrath, or worse, become a power source for siphoning magic.

I hated myself for not being able to come to their aid, but there was nothing I could do. The blackened pieces of my soul splintered, hearing their wails of agony.

"Fucking irons," I cursed, knowing the shackles were the least of my problems.

My limbs were in a constant state of agony. No, correction, Gods be damned, my entire body felt the effects of the enchanted metal shackling my hands, ankles, and neck. The iron collar was a new twist I hadn't had the pleasure of experiencing during my last visit to these dungeons. The chains interconnected at the front, making it nearly impossible for me to uncoil my body from a half-crouched position.

I managed to relieve myself in the corner bucket, gritting my teeth to fight back a groan as I slid next to the iron bars, searching for water to relieve my cracked throat.

Anjani would return soon, and I had no doubt Minaeve would accompany her. A week had passed since Silver Meadows. At least, that was what I overheard the masked guards mumbling after the second round of Anjani's torture.

A week.

Skylar, my brave spitfire, should be arriving in Solace soon.

I grunted, struggling to grasp the ladle outside the cell bars, resting in a leaking bucket of water. If I didn't drink from it soon, it would drain onto the floor.

My mangled fingers were swollen and twisted. Many of them were broken on my left hand, with two of my fingernails missing on the right. Still, I managed to grasp the ladle and gulp down the refreshing— *Shit.*

I coughed, spewing the water from my mouth. My shoulders heaved as I gasped for air, my entire body convulsing.

"Fuck!" I swore, tasting the familiar tang of iron in my mouth.

For a moment, I contemplated not drinking the soiled source, but I hadn't consumed a drop of water in nearly three days. I'd lasted five days without it before, but I dared not test that timeline again—not in here.

I glared at the bucket on the other side of the bars for what felt like hours. My throat splintered as I forced myself to swallow. My body's desperation overcame the need to feel and release my magic.

Reluctantly, I grasped the ladle and sipped the tainted water. The collar shackled around my throat rubbed my skin raw. The tension of the chain prevented me from shouting, swallowing, or even breathing without constraint. Every gulp I managed to take strained my throat. The iron particles infiltrated every inch of my body from the inside out.

After draining the contents of the bucket, I lay back against the stone, feeling defeated, but refusing to give up.

Chapter Ten

Skylar Cathal

"You don't have to go alone," Fjorda said for probably the tenth time since I shared my plan. "The *Opal* can easily dock—"

"No," I answered in a firm tone. "I will go ashore alone. I don't want to risk your crew's safety."

Fjorda crossed his arms with a firm scowl.

"Frown all you want. It's not going to make me change my mind," I said.

"Stubborn shifter," he seethed.

"One of our best traits," I replied with a playful wink, strapping my bow across my chest and shouldering my small bag of belongings. The letter from Daxton was tucked against the bindings on my chest, safe for the moment, even though I hadn't dared open and read it yet.

I decided to don my uniform from Silver Meadows: black fitted leathers with silver threaded trim, proudly displaying the single mountain peak on my shoulder. The armor of Aegis, however, I kept hidden safely in my bag, deciding not to reveal every tool in my arsenal if I could help it.

"Where will you wait?" I asked, approaching the railing.

"We'll remain close. Perhaps wander along the open seas to the northern tip of the mainland, but no farther should you need us in a hurry."

"And when I need you?"

"Your mark is still viable." Fjorda pointed to my palm. "The *Opal* will heed your call, just like before."

"Thank you," I answered as I swung myself over the railing, ready to scale the rope ladder to the small rowboat below.

"Was there doubt the magic would still work?" Fjorda challenged with a cocked brow.

"I thought it was just a one-time gift. Glad to know I can still use it."

"It will work as long as I grant you the mark," Fjorda said.

I thanked him once more before beginning my descent, settling onto the wooden bench and grasping the oars in each hand to carry me ashore.

"Hurry, Champion," Fjorda called out as I began my trek through the waters toward my homeland.

I gave him a nod in return as the sails of the ship opened and carried the magnificent white vessel away from the coastline.

I fell into a gentle rhythm with the strokes of my oars, little by little, carrying me to the green sand beach. The beach that Daxton had dreamt about, and I had called my sanctuary from the chaos of the world around me.

My own personal haven, just like the hanging valley in Silver Meadows was Daxton's.

With one final pull of my oars, I managed to catch a wave and glide easily onto the shoreline. My boat skidded into the sand with the sun hanging low against the western cliffs used by countless young ones to test their animal spirits.

The cooler winter temperatures were beginning to grip the land. The evening air held a crispness to it that differed from the long, warm months of summer. The snow would never settle in Solace itself, but the tops of the mountains to the north and east would hold white patches of snow on their peaks until spring and summer.

I steadied myself with my hands braced on either side as I stood and leaped out of the rowboat.

As soon as my feet hit the green sand, I felt alive. This beach always held a special place in my heart because, like me, it was different.

I bent to grasp a handful of the olivine grains and stood straight, taking a deep breath. Releasing my grip, I watched the grains trickle back to the earth. Each particle of sand fell like moments in time, causing me to reflect on the events that had happened since I last set foot in my homeland.

"I don't know if anyone is listening, or even if you can hear me," I said aloud to no one, to everyone. "I promise I will not give up. I may not win, but I swear I'll never give up."

The wilt hadn't destroyed this section of the shoreline yet, but soon, it would.

Glancing up, I noticed plumes of smoke rising from the direction of Solace. My heart jumped into my throat, and I took off at a run toward the cliffs, racing into unknown dangers that could be threatening my home and my family.

Chapter Eleven

Daxton Aegaeon

The chains binding my hands to the shackles at my ankles clinked against the floor, creating a brash echo across the chasm of despair that seemed to grow with each painstaking breath I forced myself to take.

Sleep would bring me little to no comfort. I could feel the iron from the water already beginning to take effect. Still, it was a welcome relief, despite the aftertaste and lingering effects on my magic.

Two pairs of footsteps echoed along the corridor. I recognized the rhythm of Anjani's gait, full of arrogance and false authority.

But the second surprised me.

"You've brought company with you today, Anjani?" I rasped, fighting back the pain in my hands and feet as I shifted onto my knees. "I didn't take you for the torturing soul, Rhett."

Peering through the bars leading down the hallway, I was stunned to see a torchlight, not a fae light, flickering along the cavern walls. The torch in Rhett's hand burned a deep blue, magically enchanted, but the Gods only knew what for.

Rhett appeared somewhat unamused at first, but then he glanced at Anjani. Together, they shared a spine-curling smirk, silently relishing in the joys of my pain and suffering.

"Oh, how the mighty have truly fallen, *High Prince of Silver Meadows*." Rhett snickered, exaggerating a well-practiced bow with a wide saccharine grin. His steel-blue eyes churned like the flames of the torch in his hand.

I knew we shouldn't have trusted him.

After he gifted Skylar the Aegis armor, I thought maybe, just maybe, we could recruit him for our efforts. But, no, he was just as twisted as his overseers. Even though Rhett was a distant relative of my mother's, it was clear where his loyalties truly lay.

"Are you going to behave?" Anjani asked as she leaned a slender arm against the bars. Her stump, where her hand once was, was wrapped and bound in a shiny metallic covering. She tapped it against the iron bars, displaying her impatience at my silence. "Well?"

My cold stare did not waver. "Fuck off."

"That's a *no*," Rhett said, sighing and leaning against the wall of dark stone. "I can't believe you managed to pull me out of bed for this—"

"You asked to come," Anjani spat, rolling her eyes. "I could've done this myself. I didn't need you here."

"I couldn't help it. I was curious about what you were doing with him," Rhett answered with an edge to his tone.

"Hence why I knocked on your door."

"I was pleasantly entertained with—"

"I'm aware," Anjani groaned and turned on Rhett, her eyes glowing with menace.

"You're always welcome to join. I wouldn't dream of turning away a beauty such as yourself, and I'm sure the others wouldn't mind."

I shook my head, barely able to stomach listening to them.

"My personal tastes are not as adventurous as yours, Rhett."

"You're missing out. To live unattached is *freeing*." Rhett narrowed his eyes, playfully cocking his brow and shamelessly flirting with Anjani.

Brave, if not slightly psychotic.

"This session was sanctioned by Queen Minaeve," Anjani said. "So, pay attention."

"I'm aware of what the queen wishes for me to document," Rhett answered in a low growl.

Rhett was not trained to wield a sword or a blade like Seamus or Anjani. His skillset resided in his vast web of knowledge. Only a fool would dare overlook it. The mind was a deadly weapon, and when utilized correctly, it could prove sharper and more lethal than any blade.

"Guards!" Anjani shouted up the corridor. "Restrain him in his cell."

"No special outing this time?" I snarled, never once dropping my stare.

"Not just yet," Anjani answered. "I want you to relive this over and over again. You will finally know what true suffering is, Aegaeon."

"Please," I huffed, "I've had the pleasure of your company for an entire week now. Trust me, I know what true suffering is."

"You *will* break," Anjani said.

The cloaked guards arrived just as Anjani glanced at the leaking wooden pail outside my cell.

"Good," she said with a vicious grin.

My eyes widened as my body began to convulse, roaring as a blinding pain shot through my center.

"I told you the iron would hide the taste," Rhett said as his smile began to widen. "It won't be long now before he falls asleep. We may not even need the guards to transport him. The portal will do the trick."

"No." I shifted forward, my forehead kissing the stone as my body began to betray me.

"Sleep, Prince," Rhett whispered as he knelt against the bars.

I collapsed onto my side, looking up at them through the iron.

"You will break," Anjani repeated, her eyes widening with a sickening delight.

Rhett's expression didn't waver. I watched as his cold eyes darkened, and the world around me faded to black.

Chapter Twelve

Daxton Aegaeon

Home, I was somehow *home* in... Silver Meadows.

I awoke to the familiar sensation of the plush chaise fabric beneath my palm. The smell of books paired with the wild mountain air through a cracked window settled my center, mending what was broken and torn apart in the dungeons beneath Aelius's keep. The sunlight, glorious, blazing sunlight, skittered along my lap as I sat up and gazed across my library.

It was quiet.

Warning bells sounded in my head, cautioning me of a looming doom hiding within the silence. I needed to investigate what was going on. I blinked, teleporting myself outside the palace, scanning over Silver Meadows below.

Tilting my chin upward, I detected the faint scent of smoke in the breeze. Spinning around, my breath stilled, witnessing the blazing scene unfolding before me.

The Summit was *burning*.

Screams echoed across the grounds, with countless fae frantically running, trying to stop the ravenous flames from burning them alive.

I reached for my ice magic to contain the destruction, but when I called, nothing came. My magic, my well of power, went silent. I could not call upon my father's gift to save my people.

How was I going to stop this?

"Dax!" Castor called from inside the flames.

"Daxton!" Gunnar's scream erupted next.

"No!" I lunged forward into the flames, disregarding the threat of the smoldering walls collapsing around me. "Cas! Gunnar!" I shouted, coughing as I pushed through the thick clouds of smoke.

I sprinted through the burning entryway. My arms brushed against the sweltering flames, but not even the pain of the burns could stop me from reaching them. I frantically ripped away the fabric along my arm, realizing this fire was magically conjured and hot enough to cause our stone walls to crumble. My skin bubbled and blistered, but I forced that matter aside.

"Cas!" I roared again. "Gunnar!"

This fire could not be doused by water or smothered by dirt. It burned until the source was extinguished, or the caster was killed or drained. I knew of only a handful of fae or mages capable of this type of magic, but they were nowhere in sight.

"Dax!" My brother's scream roared from the staircase.

Forgoing my own safety, I ran as fast as my feet could carry me toward the sound of his voice.

Smoke burned my lungs as my vision began to blur. The heat of the flames was hot enough to melt the surrounding stone. Skidding to a halt at the bottom of the broken stairs, my stomach dropped.

I tilted my head toward the glass skylight. The ceiling had shattered from the swell of gathering heat. The Summit was crumbling to pieces before my eyes.

"Daxton!"

At the top of the steps, I scarcely recognized the silhouette of Castor leaning on Gunnar's shoulder through the rising smoke. I sucked in a sharp breath as the fumes began to clear, revealing how badly their bodies were blistered and burned.

I watched in horror as my brother's eyes turned black.

Gunnar's head tilted to the side, sensing Castor's magic, and it only took a breath for him to understand.

"No! No, no, no!" I screamed as Gunnar's stare met mine.

He bravely gave me a nod, not a single ounce of fear in his eyes, as the ground beneath them collapsed and erupted in flames.

"Castor! Gunnar!" I screamed. "No!" I roared, crumbling to my knees, uncertain what to do or think.

"Your Highness!" a male exclaimed, grasping my smoldering flesh and forcing me to my feet. The pain from my burns brought me back. "You need to escape! We can't lose you, too!"

I blindly followed his lead, retreating to the main doors and jumping through the fires once more to the Summit entrance.

My heart shattered as the vision of Castor and Gunnar replayed inside my mind, a well of sorrow and regret drowning me on solid ground. The chasm of grief tore through me as a dark void settled in my center.

My brother and Gunnar were...

I couldn't breathe.

My brother was dead. Gunnar was dead.

"Witnessing this is far better than anything I could've hoped for."

Anjani...

I would eradicate her existence in this life and the next if it was the last thing I did.

Without warning, the sound of a blade slicing through flesh and bone rang out, followed by the muffled screams of death and a stream of crimson flowing toward my feet. Turning, I gasped in sheer horror at the sight of Adohan and Idris's headless corpses splayed across my own steps.

"The twins are already handled," Anjani said.

White-hot rage clouded my vision as I looked up to see none other than Anjani with a blood-soaked blade, with Rhett and Seamus standing on either side of her.

I lunged for them, summoning Valencia to my hand as I charged forward.

"Fool." Anjani laughed as she snapped her fingers.

My eyes sprang open, and I vomited across the cobblestones. My limbs convulsed uncontrollably as I struggled to remain upright.

I half-heartedly glanced at the burns along my arms. The pain of my wounds was the least of my concerns.

"Dreams can become reality when properly enticed within the confines of your mind," Anjani said in a low voice.

Rhett and Anjani were both inside the cell, but I couldn't muster the strength to attack. My chains were latched to bolts in the rock, and I was still shaken from the illusion, unable to right myself just yet.

Fucking hell, I watched them all die.

Everything about her illusion somehow seemed so real.

How?

"You record everything we needed?" Anjani asked Rhett. "The tonic seemed to help strengthen my magic."

I glanced sideways at the scroll keeper. My eyes burned with disgust and swirling rage.

"It was masterful," Rhett said with an all-knowing grin, jotting notes on parchment. "Losing your hand has not hindered the cunning nature of your magic, it seems."

Anjani scowled at Rhett, retrieving the torch that aided in the burns coating my arms. She walked to the door of the cell and held it open for her companion to pass through before locking it behind them.

"Oh, just wait," she purred in delight. "Wait until I add your pretty little mongrel of a mate to these illusions."

I growled at her, baring my teeth, unable to restrain my wrath.

"Protest all you want. You won't even know it's happening. This was a mere stop in our journey to break you from the inside out."

"You can... try," I rasped, forcing myself to sit upright.

"You do see the irony in this. Don't you?" Anjani asked with an inquisitive grin.

The silent, desolate stare of Silver Shadow was my only response.

"You didn't claim her."

Even Rhett tilted his head in curiosity at Anjani's words.

"What?" I rasped.

Anjani laughed wickedly as she tapped the base of her neck. "You didn't claim her according to shifter customs. And then *you* sent her straight into the arms of another male who would do *anything* to have her." Her piercing laughter mimicked the deafening screech of nails scratching against stone. "Into the hands of a powerful alpha who would love nothing more than to mark her as his chosen mate. Perhaps Gilen will believe this is fate finally turning in his favor. The Gods allowing her to return without a claiming mark."

"Skylar would never—"

"Never what?" Anjani challenged as she sucked her teeth. "She would never make a sacrifice to save those she loves? She would never trade herself to the alpha in exchange for the dagger in order to successfully complete the trials?"

My world stopped.

Anjani's wicked smile only grew, witnessing my reaction. "You didn't claim her!" she taunted, tapping her neck. "You didn't claim her! You didn't claim her!" She laughed again.

My stomach plummeted as despair wound its way through the cracks of my breaking heart. My chest ached. My center shredded apart as if my very soul was on the verge of fading into nothing.

"No," I rasped.

Rhett and Anjani exchanged smug glances before turning on their heels and leaving the prison cell, driving a fictional death blow straight through my bleeding heart.

Chapter Thirteen

Skylar Cathal

I was home, yet somehow, I wasn't.

Upon cresting the cliffs, I realized the smoke I'd seen from the green sand beach was carried from the eastern regions of our territory. The darker plumes in the distant hills were not an immediate threat to Solace, but still, the sight of them was unsettling.

My father, Emery, died fighting on those very fields. Countless battles had been fought between the dividing of shifter and human territories. With each new ruler of the human lands, a new divide and tentative peace treaty was struck, the binding law written in blood from lives lost fighting to protect our homes.

Humans were not born of Valdor, yet our history books and even the records of the High Fae lacked detailed accounts concerning their origins.

I remember attempting to read all I could about the humans' culture when I was young, naturally curious about the other half of my heritage. Our viable records stated that humans sailed across the vacant sea to the east, drawn to the magic of Valdor with the promise of peace, settling and creating a stronghold in the southern region of the mainland centuries ago.

Magic in humans appeared to be a rare stroke of genetic grace, while others inherited the ability passed down through a family bloodline. Some humans held the ability to manipulate and connect to the magic of our world, similar to shifters and fae, tapping into the raw magic and bending it to their will to create beautiful miracles like healing and, at times, dark weapons such as the hunters. Others could create weapons out of magical energy, and some were even rumored to have gifts of foresight.

But all too soon, a desire for power and control brought forth war and bloodshed between humans, shifters, and fae.

Kneeling, I placed my palm against the cold earth, grounding myself to the familiar presence of my homeland once again. A strong sense of unease swirled through my center, my instincts telling me something wasn't right.

Tugging the hood of my cloak over my head, I marched forward and entered the forest. My animal stirred with a potent surge of anxiety, putting all my senses on high alert.

The forest was quiet. Almost as if the wilderness embodied the bone-chilling stillness of death itself. Boisterous songbirds fell silent. The natural music of the land had become hushed.

The chilling feeling I had while in the hunters' keep crept along my spine, creating goosebumps at the nape of my neck.

Were hunters here?

No, not again. Not in *my* home.

I drew my knife and crouched in the nearby brush of ferns, carefully avoiding the patch of devil's club. My eyes meticulously scanned the bare willow and spruce trees. Utilizing my training from Daxton, I created a barrier to conceal my scent, cloaking myself in case anything nearby was trying to snuff me out of my hiding place.

Keeping my blade drawn, I waited and watched. But still, nothing seemed out of the ordinary.

Standing, I kept my knife at the ready, walking along the path I knew by heart. The route I had taken hundreds, if not thousands, of times before. The path that led me to my home. To Julia, to Neera, to Magnus.

I couldn't extinguish the spark of joy that flickered in my heart at the thought of seeing them again. Despite the despair and absolute horror of the trials thus far, reuniting with my family was a silver lining.

I felt my heart ache as I stilled.

Clenching my eyes shut, I reached to grip my chest. I could *feel* him. His pain morphed into my own through our bond. I shuddered, fighting the draw to succumb to the heartache of knowing he was being tortured. His presence was a mere flicker, disappearing in the next second, but still, it haunted me.

I will find you. We will always find each other.

Like magic, his words echoed in my mind, strengthening and comforting me like they always did.

And for once, I was not going to question how or why they appeared.

Dusk began to settle as I reached the thick patch of woods outside my family home. I could smell the scent of my cousin, Neera, first, followed by a trickle of Magnus and then, surprisingly, a strong presence of Shaw. Continuing forward, I also detected Rhea's scent faintly swirling into the mix.

Outside, the lanterns were not lit, and I couldn't smell anything brewing in the kitchens. *This is odd*. At this time of day, I would assume Julia would be brewing up a storm to feed Magnus and Neera. Even with me gone, Magnus alone could easily finish our entire family's helping of food if we allowed him to.

Tilting my chin up to investigate further, I detected the scent before hearing the commotion in the woods to the northern side of the clearing. If my animal had not pushed me to be on high alert, I might have missed it.

Exiting the condensed thicket of brush and trees across the way was a beautiful doe with dark brown fur, a golden hue decorating the ridge of her back. Calculating green eyes, the same Cathal green eyes that Neera and Magnus held, scanned the clearing. The doe tilted her head up to the sky and sniffed at the air before she released her magic with a green shimmer and shifted into her human form.

It was Neera.

Neera had shifted!

I moved to stand and call out to her, but the snap of a branch sounded behind me, followed by a low snarl that made every hair along my neck stand at attention. It wasn't the growl of a bear, a wolf, or even a mountain lion. This was something much bigger and much more terrifying.

I gripped the hilt of my dagger, preparing to defend myself. But before I could turn and make my move to attack, I had become the prey.

Ooof, I grunted as my back slammed into the ground.

A massive, black-furred paw pressed onto my chest, pinning me on my back. Sharp, deadly talons extended from beneath the layer of smooth midnight fur. The growl emanating from this animal was laced with a promise of death, and yet, I was not afraid.

I knew exactly who this was.

The hot breath of the beast brushed across my face as it pushed the hood of my cloak back with its nose. A massive panther, the size of a large horse, stood over me. Long, lethal ivory teeth bared and ready to rip out my throat, until... until his gaze finally met mine.

Shaw.

His bright hazel eyes were unmistakable, along with his scent I knew all too well. My dear friend, who, like me, held scars that dwelled deeper than the marks left on our skin. My friend, who faced his own fears to assist in my rescue and helped guide me through my recovery. The friend I could always count on, no matter what.

"Shaw," I said, releasing my shield and revealing my scent.

Slowly, his sharp claws retracted, and the pressure on my chest lessened. He blinked rapidly. Those predatory feline eyes scanned my face as he sniffed the air around me.

I remembered that my scent had altered, integrating with Daxton's, but surely he knew it was me? Right?

"Shaw, it's me!" I managed to sit up and unfasten my cloak. "It's me, Sky."

His lips pulled back, and his teeth flashed, the threatening growl of his animal radiating from his massive chest.

Shit, he wasn't entirely convinced.

I called upon my animal's help to bridge the connection with his panther. When I first saw Shaw after my capture, I was surprised by how they seemed to respond to each other's grief, comforting and strengthening each other with a unique bond.

My power began to build, filling my limbs with magic. I rose to stand, refusing to back down. "Shaw," I said slowly, my voice laced with a power I didn't completely understand. "It's me, Skylar."

The panther blinked, tilting his head to the side and looking me over once more. A soft purr replaced his menacing growl as he lowered his gaze and bowed his head in a sign of submission.

I released the tension in my shoulders with a soft sigh of relief. The panther and Shaw realized this was not some kind of trick or impersonation.

"Shift, Shaw," I commanded as I stepped closer.

The panther's eyes widened as it bent its head toward the earth, and in a flash, he shifted into his human form.

"What the—" Shaw didn't have a chance to finish.

I flung myself into his chest and wrapped my arms around him. He buried his head in my neck, squeezing me just as tightly. "What the hell was that? What the fuck are you doing here, Sky?" Shaw rasped in disbelief. "How—? How are you here?"

"That's a long story," I said, releasing my hold on Shaw so he could find some clothes, likely stashed in the nearby brush.

"Well, start talking then." Neera's sweet voice echoed behind me right before she jumped into my arms with tears streaming down her tanned, freckled cheeks.

I inhaled her sweet, flowery scent as I trembled from the weight of emotions rolling through me. I held onto my cousin with everything I had, cherishing the unconditional love we shared and thanking the Gods above for giving me this small piece of joy.

I pulled back to cup her sweet face, kissing her brow before pulling her back into my arms. "I missed you."

"Same." Neera's words were drowned by her tears. "More than you know, Skylar." She convulsed in my arms, her cries intensifying.

"Neera?" I questioned, looking down at her.

She kept her grip on my middle, pulling back to meet my gaze. The creased lines near the corners of her eyes twitched as she bit her lip to try to steady her quivering tears.

"Neera?" I asked again, my voice trailing off into a whisper. "What's happened?"

I glanced in Shaw's direction, hoping to see something, anything other than the excruciating heartache painted across my cousin's face.

"Come inside with us," Shaw said, his voice dropping, making my breath still. He walked toward us, his expression darkening. "There is a lot we need to tell you."

Chapter Fourteen

Skylar Cathal

"What?" I screamed, slamming my fists onto the counter.

My entire body began shaking, no longer in control, as my animal raged with sorrow inside my wounded heart. I clenched my jaw so tight I swear my teeth cracked as tears streamed down my face. My limbs trembled uncontrollably with anger, regret, and... unbelievable *grief*.

Julia, my aunt who raised me, who took me in and loved me as her own, was gone.

"Julia was leading a mission to patrol the southern borders of our land," Shaw said slowly. "It was routine. She knew those routes better than anyone."

"Except it wasn't routine," I snapped. "She's dead."

Shaw wisely took a step back, pressing his lips together as he swallowed, flinching at the booming magic laced within my harsh tone.

The tension in the kitchen was so thick you could cut it with a knife. The silence was deafening as my tears freely trickled onto the floor.

"Except," Neera said as she struggled to hold herself together, "Mother and others in her company were ambushed."

I lifted my head and gazed at my sweet cousin, knowing this loss hurt her just as much as it did me.

Shaw cleared his throat. "She and the others in her group were killed on sight by hunters accompanying King Taran's soldiers."

"Reckless," I seethed. "Tensions were already rising when I left. How could they—" Grief swallowed my words.

The southern region near Lake Carth was a known point of tension between our territories. It was never routine traveling through that stretch of land. Julia knew this...

"Julia," I sobbed, resting my head on the kitchen island. "No, no, no."

Shaw moved to try to comfort me, but I pushed him away. Turning from the table, I roared again, angrily running my hands through my hair before pounding my fist against the wall. The wood splintered beneath the force of my wrath. My breathing became rapid and uneven. Tears stung my eyes as my chest caved and my heart, my gods-damned heart, began breaking.

I glanced around the kitchen with all the cherished memories I held of her flashing inside my mind. My aunt showered those she loved with delicious meals, sprinkling her kindness and joy into every morsel. I absently traced my hand over the spoons and pots that looked untouched in the corner, stacked and cleaned but carrying a light layer of dust from the month since Julia's death.

Why... Why is she gone?

I turned to find Neera, and I could see my loss reflected ten times over in the creased lines and blackened bags under her tear-soaked eyes. Her head dropped as Shaw moved in behind her, gently cradling her hands as she turned to lean into his chest. Shaw stroked Neera's hair as her sobs soaked his shirt.

"Neera," I whispered as her eyes snapped to me. "I'm so *sorry*." It was all I could manage to say.

"War with the humans has begun," Shaw said.

Neera struggled to breathe, let alone articulate a response through her efforts to suppress her sobs.

"When you left, our alpha began gathering our defenses in preparation for an attack." Shaw paused.

"An attack?" I asked, my eyes widening as I returned to lean over the counter in the center of the kitchen.

"Yes," Neera sobbed.

"When? How long after I left did—"

"About three weeks after you left, Sky," Shaw said, his expression grim and cold. "The humans justified their attack, saying it was to protect themselves."

"Bullshit," I spat.

Neera managed to calm herself enough to lift her head, granting me the space to round the corner and quickly scoop her into my arms, needing to hold her as much as she needed me.

"How could the humans feel they were in danger? It's their hunters that are lurking on our lands and stealing shifters for..." My voice trailed off, watching Shaw's eyes flicker in understanding. "For their experiments."

"Things here have changed," Neera said, pulling back to look at me. "*We* became the threat."

"What changed?" I asked cautiously.

"Everyone in our pack felt it," Shaw said. "Two weeks after you left for the trials, there was a change in our power. Our magic evolved."

"Was it from the alpha?" I questioned, not yet brave enough to ask *who* the alpha was.

"Yes, well, not just the alpha," Neera answered, reaching back to grasp Shaw's hand.

My eyes took note of the casual familiarity laced between their intertwined fingers, and it took all my willpower to keep my mouth shut and just listen.

Neera inhaled deeply, preparing herself. "We *all* began to shift."

I raised my brows, glancing at Shaw, who gave me a firm nod to confirm Neera's account.

"And not just those of age, Sky."

"What?" I stammered, releasing my cousin, shocked by this news. "Do the elders have an explanation for this?"

"I wish they did," Neera said. "But for some reason, around two weeks after you left, we felt the call to shift. It was even on the night of a new moon."

I gasped, my eyes widening as my head began to spin, putting the pieces of all this together.

"Everyone who could sense their animal's presence was able to shift," Shaw explained. "The young ones who haven't sensed their animals yet haven't shifted, but even some as young as eleven can now change into their animal forms."

I rolled up the sleeves of my shirt, fidgeting with a strand of my hair as I paced back and forth along the familiar wooden floors of our kitchen. Out of the corner of my eye, I noticed Shaw glance at my tattoo.

"Did you—" He released Neera and stepped toward me to grasp my left forearm. His fingers traced over the two stars filled in on my skin. "You passed more than just one trial, didn't you?"

I blinked with a sigh, grateful for Shaw's clever mind. "Th-the veil," I stammered. "The trials, they are—"

"When?" Shaw asked. His breathing remained steady, despite his eyes being wild. His mind raced to discover answers.

"I passed the trial of the mind *two weeks* after I left. The labyrinth was a complete mind-fuck, which I'll tell you about later..." I paused, remembering Neera mentioning the new moon.

I remembered the faint outline of the new moon overhead when Daxton teleported us from the labyrinth, sensing a renewed wave of power and life rushing through me.

Shaw's gaze met mine, and I knew he had come to the same conclusion I had.

"The trials are not only linked to the Heart of Valdor, but also the veil and somehow *our* magic. Our ability to shift," I said.

"When did you complete the second trial?" Shaw asked.

"Last week." I tensed. "I killed the serpent king, a basilisk, just over a week ago."

Neera practically fainted at the news, and Shaw's gaping mouth was so wide it could catch a school of fish from the river.

"Again," I said, shifting on my feet. "I'll give you the details later."

"This all makes sense," Shaw said. "Last week, black veins appeared along the cliffs. The roots of the trees began to decay, along with the vegetation and wildlife closest to the Inner Kingdom."

"The veil is not merely a divide between our worlds. It's a cage to contain the wilt, possibly crafted with our magic along with the fae's." I slowly realized that the Heart of Valdor was locked away not only by the High Fae but somehow by shifters as well.

But why? What connection did our ancestors have to all this?

My mind was racing, searching through my memories for an answer, when suddenly, I recalled Malek, king of the water nymphs, and what he told me after my first trial victory.

We do not freely speak of the time before the wilt, young shifter—not yet, I'm afraid. Perhaps you truly are the one to free us all.

He knew something.

"Passing through the veil was different this time," I told Shaw and Neera.

"Different how?" Shaw asked, leaning in and eager to hear my response.

"It wasn't as powerful," I said. "Fjorda, the captain of the ship I traveled on, came to the same conclusion. He said it was due to the veil weakening."

"The further you progress in the trials," Shaw said, putting the pieces of this puzzle together, "the weaker the barrier becomes. The trials and the veil are linked, along with the magic of the shifters."

"But how? Why?" Neera asked.

I furrowed my brow, waiting a moment before answering. "We won't know for certain until I pass the final trial and unlock the Heart of Valdor."

"The final trial..." Neera trailed off. "It's of the soul, right?"

I nodded.

"Is this why you're here, Sky?" she asked. Her eyes were wide with worry. "What is it you have to do?"

"I've been tasked to retrieve an object."

"What object?" Shaw's voice deepened as he looped a protective arm over Neera's shoulder.

He knew.

Gods above, somehow, Shaw fucking knew.

"Also," an all-too-familiar voice boomed in behind me.

I spun around to see a petite yet feisty figure filling the doorway with a mesh of auburn hair flowing wildly around her striking azure eyes.

Rhea grinned and flashed me a wink. "Why the fuck do you smell like *that*?"

Chapter Fifteen

Skylar Cathal

"Rhea!" I screamed as we crashed into one another. "Rhea." Sobbing, I held her as tight as I could.

"Gods above, Sky," Rhea answered, her voice wavering as tears dampened my shoulder.

I pulled back, watching Rhea look at me with a forced smile. She was happy beyond words to see me, but I could see the broken pieces of her pain lingering in the cracks of her joy. I silently grasped her hands, giving her a knowing nod. War was brewing. The chaos of blood and lives lost was a heavy burden to carry.

"You've looked better," I said.

She rolled her eyes and managed a small laugh. "Not everyone gets to be ferried away to a magical land and doted on by towering High Fae princes." Rhea chuckled with a witty smirk. She leaned in and sniffed me. "That's Daxton's scent, right?"

"The Silver Meadows high prince," Talon answered, entering behind Rhea and pulling a shirt on over his head. "I knew it."

I glanced at Talon, his shaggy black hair and pale blue eyes shining like beacons against the oil lamps illuminating the space.

"Hey, Sky," he said, arms opening wide with a smile that made his crooked nose shift.

"Talon." I sighed as I eagerly fell into his embrace.

"Rhea won't admit it," he whispered in my ear. "But I told her, the night you almost killed him, that there was something there. Technically, I won that bet."

"All right, don't hog her attention," Rhea demanded, pulling me in for another hug as Talon greeted Shaw and Neera closed in around me.

"Glad to see you in one piece," Shaw said to his brother, clasping him on the shoulder.

"It was a close call this time around. Istar is sending in mages, along with King Taran's personal guard," Talon said, embracing Shaw.

I couldn't help but notice how Shaw tensed at Talon's news. With war at our doorstep, who knew which moments could be our last?

"Those bastard hunters don't go down easy, but we were lucky in this last fight. The Satellite pack to the south of Solace is thankfully safe, for now," Talon continued.

Istar was the lead mage of the human king, rumored to be as powerful as he was cunning. A deadly opponent known to hate our kind almost as much as the king.

"Have they told you about—" Rhea whispered as she squeezed me tighter.

I nodded in response, unable to say or do anything more than that, or risk falling apart in her arms.

"Julia will *never* be forgotten," Rhea said. "She lives through Neera and through you, Skylar. She lives through all of us who carry her memory and name."

I hugged her tighter, grateful for Rhea's kind words of comfort.

There would be time, I told myself.

Time to grieve Julia's passing properly and visit her final resting place to say goodbye. I wanted to tell her how much I loved her and thank her for everything, for the strength she instilled in me and the love she freely gave an orphaned child. I promised myself I would honor Julia's memory by never giving up. To hold my head high and keep fighting.

We're not just shifters; we're Cathals! I remember her telling me when I was just a child. *When we fall, what do we do?* It was her favorite lesson to teach me. *We get back up and try again.*

"All right," Rhea announced, clearing her throat. "Now spill."

"What do you want to know?"

"Everything. Starting with why you smell like the High Fae prince," she said with a wink, pulling me with her as she reached out for Talon.

"Daxton," I whispered. Everyone tensed, sensing my hesitation. "He's... He's my mate."

"Oh, Skylar." Neera sighed, clutching her hands at her heart.

"You can pay up later. I have some ideas on how we can settle this score." Talon snickered in Rhea's ear.

"So, it's more than just sex, then?" Rhea asked, shooing away Talon's taunting.

"Yes," I said, unable to keep the crimson flush from finding my cheeks.

"Well, I wouldn't blame you." Rhea sighed, ignoring her mate's *loud* eye roll. "You've been keeping yourself locked up for far too long, in my opinion."

"She was *waiting*," Neera said in my defense.

"Okay, fine. To each their own," Rhea said, waving Neera off. "Continue, Sky. How do you know he's your mate?"

"High Fae can sense a mate bond, but that doesn't matter, because honestly… I fell in love with him."

"That's not shocking news," Talon huffed.

Rhea playfully slapped Talon's chest. "We were surprised that Talon was able to pick up on the fact that Daxton was drawn to you, and you hadn't yet," Rhea muttered.

"Before the second trial, I told him I loved him," I said, "and he…" My voice trailed off, fondly remembering that night with perfect clarity. "He confessed that he'd known since the first time he met me in the meadow…That his soul had found its other half. That I was his mate, and he was hopelessly and eternally in love with me."

Neera sighed as her eyes softened.

"Which was so obvious that even my brother could see it," Shaw replied, giving me a half-smile.

"Both of you can go suck on a rock." Talon glowered at them, crossing his large arms over his chest.

"Am I going to be able to finish this story?" I asked.

"Not likely," Shaw answered for the group. "But you can try."

"Right." I chuckled. "You remember my dream? The one I had in the meadow?"

"Yes," Rhea and Neera answered, curiosity sparking in their expressions.

"That meadow is in Silver Meadows. And the orange and silver flower with an ebony stem?"

"That imaginary flower you obsessed over for years?" Rhea asked.

"Yes." I smiled. "It's real. Daxton created it."

"Gods above," Talon breathed. "That very well might be the new standard for *fated* mates."

"But you haven't shifted yet, right?" Neera asked.

"Our bond is unsealed, but it is there," I said, absently rubbing the scar on my wrist. My animal stirred to life in my chest, the thought of Daxton's love surrounding me like a shield of armor.

Rhea reached out and grasped my hand. "Like a spark, or the feeling of liquid fire stirring in your veins. You feel a pull toward him. Always aware of where he is and a sense of what he's feeling."

I nodded.

"*Love* is the bridge." Neera sighed.

"So, I have to ask, why is Daxton not here with you?" Shaw questioned.

I clenched my eyes, fighting back tears. "He was captured. And is being held as a bargaining tool for my return."

"Who the hell is powerful enough to capture Daxton?" Rhea asked, leaning to the side with her arms crossed.

"Queen Minaeve."

The room went silent.

"If I haven't said it before, I fuuucking *hate* her," Neera cursed.

We all raised our brows in surprise.

"Settle in and listen. I'm about to fill you in on everything," I said to my friends.

I recounted my time in the Inner Kingdom, backtracking to Crimson City, Aelius, Seamus, the scroll, and the trial of the mind. I even told them about how I healed Nyssa and the other fallen creatures in the wilt. And then I spoke of Silver Meadows. About Idris, Adohan, Zola, and Gunnar. I told them about the Ice Gauntlet, showing them the silver mountain peak on my black leathers. Then I told them about the trial of the body, the basilisk, and then the unfortunate plan that involved my mate being captured by the High Fae queen.

"Gods a-fucking-bove," Rhea cursed at my side.

"Right?" I said, glancing across the kitchen island at Shaw and Neera. My eyes darted between them, their familiarity and intimacy no longer something I could ignore. "Are you... Are you two..."

"Don't start," Talon warned with a palm raised.

"Please." Rhea sighed, squinting her eyes and pinching her brows.

"What?" I questioned.

Shaw reached for Neera's hand, giving her a soft smile. "No. We are not a mated pair, but—"

"But," Neera added, "perhaps a mate bond is not the *only* way to find happiness with another in this life."

"Oh," I replied with surprise—no, shock, actually.

Neera swore to us time and time again that she would only be sharing a claiming mark with her true mate. We *all* knew this.

I glared at Shaw, pinning him with my stare. He blinked at me, understanding my protective intent, and wisely shifted a half step from my cousin.

"Like we said." Talon chuckled with amusement. "Don't start."

"What does Magnus think about this?" I asked, turning my head and sniffing the air. "In fact, where is Magnus? Why is he not home? He should be here."

Knowing that Julia had passed less than a month ago, it was logical that Magnus would stay close to Neera, regardless of his role as beta.

"F-Father is—" Neera stammered as the room fell silent.

"Where is Magnus?" I asked again, looking at Talon and then Shaw.

"He's alive," Shaw answered. "But—"

I bit my lip, straightening my shoulders as my eyes blazed with the demand for an answer. The magic of my alpha command laced into my words. "Where is my uncle, Shaw?"

"He's lost. Lost to his animal form," Shaw answered, staggering back a step as my power filled the room.

I fought to catch my breath at Shaw's response.

When a shifter experienced a loss too great to carry, their animal spirit took control. They succumbed to their animal's power, and their human half faded into a distant memory. Some never came back, while others could return when the pain of their human soul was healed, or they were called back by something strong enough to guide them through a shift.

"What the hell was that power, Skylar?" Talon demanded, drawing me back as he instinctively moved closer to his mate.

"Oh, that." I shrugged as I scratched the back of my head. "It's new."

"Explain yourself," Talon snapped. His eyes flared as he tilted his head to the side to look me over. "That felt like a fucking alpha command, Sky."

Neera placed her hand on Shaw's shoulder, but he waved her off, insisting that he was all right.

"That makes a lot more sense now," Shaw said. "It's not the first time you've used it, is it?"

"No," I said in reply. I looked across the room, knowing they all felt the power of my alpha command. "All right, just to recap," I said, crossing my arms, "shifters and humans are on the brink of war, if not already in it."

They all nodded.

"My aunt is—" I didn't finish the thought. The sting of anguish cut me like a knife. I shook myself, biting my lip to keep the tears back. "Practically everyone can shift and... Magnus is lost in his bear form."

I looked at Neera as her eyes darkened, and I wished I could take away her pain, to bring back the light that used to shine so brightly in her eyes.

"And now, I have to complete the final trial. Who is..." I took a deep breath to prepare myself. "Who is the alpha?"

"Gilen," Rhea answered in a distasteful growl.

"Fantastic," I replied, glancing at Talon.

"What do you need to do for the final trial, Sky?" Neera asked.

"The alpha's dagger," I said.

"Shit," Talon swore.

Rhea's face paled as Neera clutched onto Shaw's arm with wide eyes.

"You plan to announce a challenge," Shaw said, not as a question but as a statement.

"Yes," I answered with confidence. "If it comes to that."

Shaw nodded. "I'll be there with you."

"So will we!" Rhea added with authority.

I looked at Rhea's mate, knowing I was asking Talon to do something practically unheard of.

"Call your alpha," I said. "As his beta, you can inform Gilen of what I intend to do."

Talon's expression dropped as his face hardened like stone. "I'm... I'm not the beta."

My eyes widened with shock. "What?"

Rhea scowled, a guttural growl sounding in the back of her throat in defense of her mate.

"I'm not Gilen's beta." Talon's crooked nose twitched to the side as he tried to mask his unease with the topic. "So, I'll have no problem standing on the sidelines as you challenge him."

I knew there was more to this story, but the looks Shaw and Rhea shot my way were a warning not to press the matter further.

The bond between a beta and an alpha had a will of its own.

"I'll ask Gilen to give me the dagger first and try the friendly approach," I said.

Everyone in the room just stared at me.

Shaw, the brave one, broke the silence of the group. "You'll have to—"

"I know," I interjected, understanding settling within my heart with what needed to be done. "I'll attempt to talk to him first. I have to try."

"Good fucking luck with that," Rhea mumbled. "My advice? Make sure your plan B is really plan A." She sighed deeply. "You'll have to challenge him, Sky. And you'll need to win."

Chapter Sixteen

Castor Aegaeon

Prayers are a final refuge for those clinging to the fragile threads of hope abiding within the depths of their darkened souls.

And I wasn't there yet.

The last time I prayed to the Gods was when my mother and father left this world, and then, my brother was deceived and taken prisoner, leaving me as the sole heir of Silver Meadows for the next century until he was released and allowed to return to us.

I was young and frightened, *so naive*.

Falling to my knees, I prayed to the Gods for help, and then they answered. Oh Gods, yes, they answered, granting me my "gift" to foresee death when it was near.

Even at the young age of eleven, I learned a valuable lesson that day. Physical strength could only take you so far. Your mind was the sharpest and most deadly tool you could carry. And I *never* allowed mine to dull.

Even now, I refused to pray to the Gods for their aid. I wasn't entirely devoid of hope, not yet.

I did, however, wish I could *forget*.

I wished I could forget about my brother in the prison of Aelius, *again*. Forget about his mate, a fearless half-shifter, whom I had also come to care for, fighting alone across the Narrow Sea. Forget that Seamus now called himself *High King*. Forget the smell of sweat, the ache of marching feet, and the constant, unnerving fear lurking in the shadows to the west. Forget the flashes of death that forever followed me. And most of all, forget—

"Prince Castor?" The flap of my canvas tent folded back, revealing a gorgeous female standing in the opening. "Is something wrong?" Her sweet voice purred as her hips seductively swayed from side to side as she entered, the opening of her robe revealing nothing but her naked flesh beneath.

I would be lying if I said I wasn't intrigued. She was exactly the type of distraction I needed. To become lost in the blissful ecstasy of finding my release with a female wrapped around me was an all-too-tempting escape.

I sat upright, my eyes shamelessly tracing over her seductive curves. Yet, despite the growing hunger to claim this female, my thoughts began to wander.

My cock hardened at the thought of *her* beneath me. Not the female standing naked in the opening... but *her*.

"Look, I don't intend to—" My words were cut short.

Clenching my fists, I felt the magic of my gift threatening to pull me under. My entire body tensed as every muscle of my frame tightened like a vice.

"Prince Castor?" the female at the opening questioned. "Are... Are you all right?"

I sealed my eyes, trying to decipher if this was a premonition of immediate death or simply another casualty of the decaying wilt that surrounded us on all sides.

Fuck. I hated being this close to the wilt.

Marching along the borders of the wilt twisted my magic, but there was no other choice. With Minaeve and Aelius to the east, this was the only route we could take and remain undetected. The false queen's reach was non-existent here, unable to fully penetrate the magic of the wilt, just like the rest of us.

I pushed myself upright on the cot, leaning over my thighs, grinding my teeth so tightly I was convinced they would shatter inside my mouth.

Breathe, I told myself. *Find the meaning... Look ahead, always look ahead.*

But before I could dive in, the vision disappeared, along with my arousal.

Fantastic.

"I'm no longer in the mood for company," I said in a half-truth.

"I see. Well, at least let me help you relax." The female's voice was heavy with need. "I'm certain I'll be able to change your mind about having company tonight."

Even in this darkened tent, I could see the hunger burning in her stare.

It would be so easy to fall into old habits and fuck the memories away. Closing my eyes, I tilted my head back and chuckled to myself. It used to be so simple. I could bury my cock inside a female and forget everything that pained me.

Gods knew, I needed it.

If I had half a mind remaining, I would succumb to my carnal needs and be done with this torment, finding my delicious release buried to the hilt, feeling her inner walls clenching around me as she moaned my name.

"Gods-fucking-dammit," I cursed, fisting my hair.

Her again. Always *her*.

It had been months since I'd had my fill. This female standing before me was not only willing but a beautiful opportunity I couldn't fucking bring myself to take.

"Prince?"

I turned to glance at the female, her russet eyes heavy with desire as she bit her bottom lip. Those perfect breasts made an appearance as she lowered the top of her robe, eager to have my undivided attention.

"It's—" I groaned in frustration. "Not tonight," I admitted in utter defeat. "I'll see myself out."

Abruptly, I stood, silencing her as I reached for my pants, pulling them up and fastening the belt along my hips. I didn't intend to be cruel, but sometimes, it was the kindest thing to do, especially in these instances.

She blinked rapidly, stumbling as she reached for the ends of her robe to cover herself. "What... What is it? Did I do—"

"You should get some rest. Take my tent for the night. I won't be using it," I said, my tone hardening. "We'll be marching again come dawn."

She shyly clutched at her robe, her brows narrowing in annoyance, and I couldn't blame her.

"Very well," she answered.

I turned to push the flap of the tent open when I heard her clear her throat.

"If there is something I did to upset my prince, I'm truly sorry."

Her tone made me pause. I wasn't a complete heartless monster. "My visions," I whispered without looking back.

It was a valid excuse, and partially true. Every good lie held fragments of the truth woven into the tapestry to make it all the more believable.

"I understand," she said as the sounds of the cot squeaked against her weight, signaling her acceptance of my offer.

Without looking back, I reached for my twin blades and threw my shirt over my shoulder as I stepped into the night.

Chapter Seventeen

Castor Aegaeon

One positive outcome of our escapade was a warmer climate during the evenings.

It was a pleasant change from the chill of the approaching winter months in Silver Meadows. The snow never stayed for long in our home, more of a dusting that blanketed the landscape for a handful of days and, if lucky, weeks. But it did reach freezing temperatures at night.

I stole a glance at the moon overhead, the watchful Father protecting us as his mate slumbered. My mind drifted to those I cared about who were miles and miles away, yet still under the same sky. A simple concept, knowing we were all connected regardless of the distance that separated us. We could all, in theory, be looking up at that exact same moment, reminding us that distance was merely a number that could never overcome kinship.

"Finished already?" Gunnar's taunting laughter pulled me from my trance. "That's fast, even for you."

Ignoring his snide remark, I meandered toward the fire, where he and a small handful of other warriors were gathered.

"Never began," I said to Gunnar as I stood across the flames from him.

Gunnar raised his brows in surprise. "You're off your game."

"If you play your cards right..." I gave him a half-cocked grin in amusement, knowing others were listening in. "*Someone* may be able to benefit from my absence."

A female and a male seated near the fire seemed intrigued, so I saw it as an opportunity to encourage them both to use my tent for the evening.

Anything to maintain the positive morale of the troops.

"The female in my tent, I believe, isn't particular about who pleases her tonight," I announced to the group, "or added company."

The male and female warriors sitting adjacent to Gunnar looked at each other.

The female's cheeks flushed a bit as she stood up and raised her brows at the male. "I'm not shy, and I like to share."

The male cleared his throat before eagerly jumping to his feet to follow her into my tent.

Good, at least someone will be easing some tension tonight.

"And I thought we were going to have a quiet evening during this watch," Gunnar teased, leaning back to continue carving a small figurine in his hands.

"What are you crafting tonight?" I asked.

"A snake," Gunnar answered, holding the carving upright, highlighting the unique pattern of scales imprinted across the back. "I thought of carving a basilisk, but I figured Skylar wouldn't appreciate it."

I huffed a laugh as I pulled my shirt over my head.

"Besides, the legs looked deformed. This is a much simpler design."

I eyed his work once more, admiring Gunnar's keen details in the fangs and the unique way the snake's body coiled.

Keeping himself busy so his mind would remain sharp. *Wise. I taught him that trick.*

"It's never an uneventful evening in a war camp," I said.

"And now we have a chorus of three at our backs instead of a duet." Gunnar chuckled. "How nice."

"I never want your watch to be dull," I added, strapping my swords across my back before scanning our surroundings. "Which is why I have graced you with my presence this evening."

Gunnar's scoff was all I needed to hear as I flashed a toothless grin and laced my hands behind my head.

We were on the southern end of Sterlyn Lake, veering toward the western side of the water's edge, only a short trek from the boundary of the wilt. Thick pine and birch trees somehow still stood their ground, with rolling hills and smaller mountains at our backs. I glanced toward the large boulders that once stood atop the mountains and wondered how they managed to make it here in one piece. Many were the size of a small house, while others were no bigger than a horse. Their varying sizes puzzled me, delightfully challenging my intellect as to how they were created.

This clearing was our rendezvous point, and we would remain here until Crimson City forces arrived from the north or word to advance came from my brother's command.

Through countless centuries of research, my best assumption was that the Heart of Valdor was in the center of the Inner Kingdom itself. But regardless of whether I was correct, this was a strong position to form an attack. Off to the east, along the shores of the lake, boats were tied off and secured in case the need to travel across the waters arose.

"All is fine," Gunnar said. "I checked the perimeter myself only thirty minutes ago."

"Good," I said.

"Anything from Skylar? Or Adohan?" Gunnar asked.

I reached into my pocket and retrieved the enchanted parchment, unfolding it and shaking my head. "Nothing," I mumbled. "Skylar has yet to open Daxton's letter and hasn't seen my message."

"What did you write her?" Gunnar said. "I've been meaning to ask."

I huffed a laugh, running my fingers through my hair. "How does fried roc taste?"

Gunnar doubled over laughing. "Well, that's one way to get her attention."

"I thought it was appropriate. And perhaps witty enough for her to reply back with some kind of snarky remark and—"

"So, we'd know that she was safe," Gunnar finished for me.

"Yes."

"You know she'll win the challenge against the alpha. I trained her myself."

"That's what I'm afraid of," I said.

Before Gunnar could move, a vision of death flashed across my mind, and I wisely shifted my weight to the right.

"Lucky bastard," Gunnar swore as his dagger embedded itself in the post of a nearby tent.

"Is it wise to insult your commanding officer like that? Or attempt to harm me?" I asked. "I thought better of you—"

"You knew better than to insult my teachings," Gunnar replied, standing to retrieve his weapon. "And I knew you'd get a premonition of your impending death and react in time to avoid it."

"Seems more like *luck* on your part."

"No," Gunnar boasted, "smarts." He grinned widely, tapping the tip of his dagger to his temple with a confident wink.

I shook my head and sighed.

Gunnar sat back with a disgruntled groan, sheathing his blade at his belt. An all-too-familiar smirk appeared on the side of his face as he reclined on the dirt near the roaring flames. "Has your hand not been enough for you these past few months, Cas? Has all that built-up tension made you *cranky*?"

"Careful," I warned, the tone of our conversation taking a drastic shift.

"Fair enough," Gunnar answered, knowing when our banter had reached a stopping point. And he knew that this topic was firmly off-limits.

I scanned the camp once more, looking for— Gods, I didn't even want to admit to myself what I was looking for.

"I'll take the next perimeter check," I told him, donning a black cloak hanging on the nearby rack.

"You'll want to end your patrol on the western rock faces," Gunnar said, resuming his carving. The flames gleaming off his half-shaved head highlighted the tattoos inked across his skull.

"Why?" I asked, skeptical.

"You'll see," he said, reaching for another log to begin carving through the night. "Just trust me on this one."

I sucked in a breath and gave him a curt nod as I pulled up the hood of my cloak and turned away from the fire.

Chapter Eighteen

Castor Aegaeon

The crisp night air was uniquely refreshing.

This close to the wilt, it was a blessing that life still found a way to flourish. The soft melody of the night birds and the scuffling of smaller nocturnal creatures meant all was well, for the moment. The magic of the land was still fighting to survive. I detected traces of it dancing along my skin like soft kisses a mother gives their newborn babe.

I didn't speak to anyone, only granting warriors a nod if any of them recognized me. I was consumed within the trenches of my own mind, thinking and plotting the next steps and then the ones after, tinkering with the different complexities of our strategy, and figuring out plan C, if plans A and B didn't work out. I was always calculating our subsequent efforts, always trying my best not to be surprised or caught off guard.

I reached a small outcrop of gray boulders that built a natural encampment overlooking the clearing below. I decided this would be an excellent vantage point and a separation from the commotion of the warriors. The natural rocky hill created a cascading staircase that I easily scaled. The boulders under my hands held streaks of sparkling minerals that stood out against the darker stones in the reflection of the moonlight.

Skylar would know the name of this.

A twinge of pain burrowed within my chest. I worried for her safety, along with my brother's.

When I reached the top, I searched for a restful dwelling to unwind in. A sound echoed from behind me. Against my best intentions not to be caught off guard, I froze in place, eyes wide with shock.

She was so still.

A stillness that I believed only the dead could truly achieve. Yet, she looked peaceful and, as always, exquisitely stunning.

I cleared my throat, half-wondering if she was asleep. "Nyssa," I announced as bravely as I could manage.

She didn't shift or even breathe.

"Nyssa." I didn't frame it as a question because I knew where she was, a part of me always knew—

A glimpse of fair skin atop a slender thigh drew my attention. The slit of her long ebony dress, which did little to curb my raging hunger, moved. I stilled as her leg straightened from its resting position and she sat up from the shadow cast by the large boulders and leaned into the moonlight.

Her narrowed almond-shaped eyes were so dark they were almost black, but she entranced me like none before. I knew that only in darkness could we see some of the treasures gifted to us in this life. Like the stars above, they shimmered with an ancient, all-knowing wisdom reflected in her gaze.

"Are you cold?" I asked, beginning to remove my cloak.

"No," she signed. "I'm fine, Prince Castor. You don't need to trouble yourself on my account." She exhaled a heavy breath, and I could see a hint of the chill clutching onto her exhalation despite her previous statement.

I disregarded her protest and continued to unfasten my cloak. Slowly, I walked to where she leaned against the rocks, securing it over her lap. "This isn't the most comfortable place for someone to sleep," I said. "But it might be the quietest," I added with a grin that had won me the beds of countless females in my past.

"I didn't want to worry anyone. I just wanted to find some peace," Nyssa signed.

I waited for her to ask me to leave, but to my surprise, she didn't. The fact that she didn't immediately try to decline my offering was promising.

"I can find another place to keep watch," I said, not wanting to leave, but still giving her the choice of privacy if that was what she desired.

Gods, I would give her anything if she only asked it of me. After what she was forced to endure and the courage it took to continue living, she deserved more than what I could give her.

"I don't mind your company if you're willing to give it. But *just* your company," she signed, with her brows raised in a warning.

"Many say that at first," I said with a flash of my smile, running a hand through my silver hair.

Nyssa tried to hold back her smirk as she signed, "Are all your female conquests so easily swayed with a simple bat of your long lashes and a sparkling smile?"

I couldn't tell if she was teasing me or insulting me, but regardless, I decided to play along. "Neither. It's the hair."

Nyssa chuckled and shook her head, motioning for me to rest next to her. I happily obliged, and she lifted my cloak so we could sit closer. With our backs against the rocks, we were able to gaze out across the moonlit camp and field below.

"There's more to you than just your handsome looks, Prince Castor," Nyssa signed. "The most beautiful pieces of you are concealed from the rest of the world, camouflaged with flamboyant charades and tricks."

I didn't dare meet her stare. My eyes were focused solely on her hands, not wanting to miss a single word she chose to tell me.

My heart was beating so fast that I swear Nyssa could feel the vibrations of its thundering rhythm. We were alone together, the first time since—

"You've been watching me, then?" I teased in a sing-song voice. "It's always the quiet ones you have to keep careful watch over."

Nyssa elbowed me, and I laughed.

"What do you see when you watch me, Nyssa?"

My question hung silently in the air between us for a long moment. Her hands remained still in her lap, forcing me to dare to look upon the face I had dreamed of each and every night since Skylar's healing magic saved her.

"Nyssa?"

Our eyes met, and my world stopped. My breathing became rapid as I recognized the desire I was feeling mirrored in her gaze. I shifted, daring to move closer, my lips only breaths away from hers.

Still, she didn't speak, and I didn't judge or blame her for this fact. Gods be damned, I spoke enough for ten people at times.

Nyssa silently raised her hands. Her fingertips grazed my chin before caressing the tips of my ears, causing my eyes to close and roll back. Her thumb traced along my bottom lip, and I could feel my cock throbbing against the restraint of my leathers.

Fuck, how could this female do this to me with only a whisper of her touch?

I felt Nyssa hesitate, and I opened my eyes to meet hers.

"Show me," I said.

Nyssa nodded, and in a flash, she pulled me into a vision.

Chapter Nineteen

Castor Aegaeon

A flicker of midnight entered my sight, and then... nothing.

The feeling of utter emptiness.

Not even sound existed here.

I wandered around in the abyss of shadows, the absence of hope, light, or anything worth living for. The only thing driving the breath in my chest was the instinct to survive. The primal feeling inside all of us that didn't allow us to give up, even if succumbing to death was the favorable option. I walked on feet that were not my own, wandering in a field of shadow.

Was this her life as a fallen?

This was not living. This was barely surviving.

Gods above. My heart broke for Nyssa. My very soul ached knowing she had to endure this.

Then suddenly, light began to filter in. Sound echoed and bounced off my ears amidst the deafening silence of my prison. I recognized the decay immediately. The territory of the wilt surrounded me, with black veins penetrating the roots of fallen and dead trees. The land was deprived of the life that once flourished here.

And then, I saw *me*.

I heard myself yell out for my brother as we attacked the harpies, as Skylar, Daxton, and I all huddled together with ice coating our skin.

A warmth or perhaps a sense of life sparked in my core. The glowing hands of Skylar reached for me, and I slowly began to feel the grip of death loosen its hold until, finally, I was free.

"What's your name?" I felt my head spin toward that voice that I knew was my own.

I felt a rush of emotion overtake Nyssa. Foreign to her for centuries, while she was in her fallen state. A warmth spread in my center as I stared upward. "You're safe."

As Nyssa, tranquility and an absolute feeling of safety encircled me. I knew that as long as I stayed by the silver-haired High Fae's side, I would be safe.

The vision faded, and I returned to my own body, with Nyssa sitting across from me.

She leaned back, bringing her hands up to sign. "I see your bravery, Castor. I see someone who conceals their pain with laughs and jokes, so others don't worry about what they are forced to endure each and every day. I see silent strength. Someone who is courageous and, above all, loyal to those they choose to love."

I stilled, unable to speak.

"You and I," she began, reaching out to touch my heart and then her own. "I know the burden you carry, for I have lived it."

"Death," I whispered, clenching my eyes shut. "I carry death with my every breath. And here near the wilt, it—"

I felt Nyssa's hand cup my cheek, forcing my eyes to open and meet hers.

"We're both able to see the beauty that only death can unveil," Nyssa signed.

My body began to tremble as I looked deep into her eyes, allowing myself to be swallowed and washed away by everything I witnessed through them.

"Nyssa," I whispered her name.

"The silence," she signed. "For me, it's the most difficult part of death when my life before was filled with such beauty."

I inclined my head, eager to hear more, learn anything more about her. "Tell me."

"I was eighteen when my gift first appeared. Far later than others, but there was no denying its presence."

"Your gift?" I asked.

Her half-smile was stunning, and one of the first I had truly seen from her. It made my heart soften.

"My voice." She traced her fingers along her throat.

My eyes were intently locked on every flex of her beautifully delicate hands.

"When I sing my wordless songs, the emotion from my music is felt by all those who hear it. I can invoke sorrow, joy, and, at times, inspire those who hear."

I blinked, in awe of the gift she was describing. "It is a gift of the mind to inspire emotion through your music. Were you born in Aelius?"

"Not Aelius, but I was traveling there when—" Her eyes grew distant as she looked away.

On instinct, I reached out to cup her face in my hand, turning her gaze back toward me. "You never need to hide when you are with me, Nyssa," I declared. "I will help carry your burdens. My strength is yours."

Could she sense it? Was she able to feel or understand the intent behind my declaration? Why I would gladly sacrifice my own sanity and well-being if it meant she would be safe?

She didn't move away from my touch or flinch as she had in the past. I swallowed my fears and pushed matters further.

I moved my brow to touch hers, feeling the caress of her smooth skin against mine. I breathed in her scent that sparked flames of desire in my soul. She was a survivor, healing in her own time. I had to respect that. I had to force myself not to give in to my throbbing need that was now painfully pushing against me.

Sensing that this might be the end of my limits, I took one final moment to memorize the feel of her, but as I moved to pull away, her hand threaded into the hair at the base of my neck.

I stilled. Seconds ticked by like years as she shifted her body closer to mine. I swallowed a heavy gulp, my breathing intensifying as my arousal throbbed with my racing heart.

"C–as-t-or." It was a faint whisper, almost inaudible even at this proximity, but I knew it came from Nyssa.

My name. She hadn't spoken since Skylar's healing, and her first word was *my name*.

I swiftly moved in, swallowing her whispers with my mouth on hers, devouring the forbidden fruit that had been looming over my head for too long. Nyssa's fingers curled into my hair as she pulled me closer. My mouth opened to taste her, and Gods above, she was delicious.

I reached a hand under the slit of her dress. But I sensed her hesitation, and I immediately pulled back.

"I'm sorry." I breathed heavily, apologizing for my boldness and giving in to my desires without thinking.

Gods, I wanted her. But I could never force anything she didn't wholeheartedly desire herself.

She unhooked her hand from behind my head. "Don't be," she signed. "It's just that—"

"It's me, Nyssa," I said. "You don't need to explain anything. I understand, and... I can be patient."

I had talked about this fact through countless nights with Zola. Like Nyssa, Zola had been infected by the wilt's magic, and lingering effects from the dark magic were likely still affecting her as they did Zola.

Time and understanding were what Zola had told me. And with the Gods as my witness, for *her*, I would gladly offer both.

Nyssa's shoulders relaxed, and a smirk worked its way to the corner of her mouth.

"What are you thinking?" I asked.

She lightly huffed. "I can't tell you."

"You also said you just wanted my company for the night, yet..." I trailed off, watching her bite the lip I had the pleasure of savoring only a moment before.

"*That* was not planned," she signed with a small grin hiding along the corner of her mouth.

"Sometimes, the best things in life aren't." I gazed at her expression, trying to decipher what she was feeling.

"That's surprising to hear from you."

"Sometimes, the beauty of the moment is enough," I said, repeating the words I remembered Daxton telling me after his first kiss with Skylar on the *Opal*.

I witnessed my brother fall more and more in love with his mate each and every second they spent together, despite the distance he tried and failed to keep between them. I smiled, knowing all too well how he was feeling.

"Do you think I will ever... heal? Will I ever be myself again, Castor?"

I paused, wanting to give her my full attention and honest words. "Yes," I told her, believing with every fiber of my soul that she would. "One day," I said into the crisp night air. "One day, something will inspire you enough to sing again, Nyssa. And that day will be one I carry with me for all eternity."

"Even in death?" she asked.

"Just your whispered word from before..." I paused, steadying myself. "...will be my beacon and strength, forever guiding me toward hope of a brighter tomorrow and a new beginning."

She stilled, her chest for a moment caught in suspension, and then she signed, "Your words were my light, Castor."

The world seemed to stop. The unspoken threads woven between us now glimmered when they were once unseen.

"Sleep, Nyssa," I said, opening my arm in an invitation for her to lean on my chest. "I'll keep you safe. Your nightmares will not dare invade your dreams while I'm with you."

To my elation, she granted me a half-smile and molded herself into my frame. The feel of her soft skin and slender curves under my palm ignited my desire. I used every ounce of strength I could because she was worth the wait.

She was worth *everything*.

"Sleep." I dared to kiss the crown of her midnight hair.

I felt her nuzzle further into my embrace, and I just about lost all my senses. I clutched her tightly, shifting so she could move closer, closing my eyes, and basking in the feel of her body atop mine.

Soon, Nyssa's rhythmic breaths indicated she had fallen asleep, and I cherished this tranquil moment tucked beneath the stars, knowing this memory would be one I would carry with me for the rest of my days, however long they lasted.

I gazed at the moon overhead as my thoughts traveled to all those under its same light. My heart ached for my brother and Skylar, knowing their sacrifices to save our world were immeasurable, hoping that everything we planned and worked for would be enough to save them.

To save us all.

Chapter Twenty

Skylar Cathal

Moonlight skittered across the worn cobblestone path, laced with patches of soil and weeds interwoven between the stones.

Stars twinkled overhead as wisps of clouds wandered within the cold winter winds. The frigid air filled my lungs. The comforting scent of the surrounding forest soothed my inner turmoil.

My footsteps felt heavy as I silently marched through the center of town, my animal on high alert. I didn't know if it was a combination of the grief I was forced to swallow from the loss of Julia, knowledge of Magnus's absence, or if it centered around my mate.

But regardless of my own sorrows, I had a trial to complete.

I turned north, away from the main streets, with my friends and cousin at my heels. The worn dirt path veering off to the side was familiar, but there was no denying that this time was different.

Winter was well underway, with a sting of cold lingering in the air that curled around my warm breath. Meanwhile, Solace remained uncharacteristically quiet.

News of Istar and King Taran's forces approaching meant there was little chance of a diplomatic solution on the horizon. And I knew Gilen would not back down from this threat. As a new alpha, he would see this as a way to prove himself, to solidify his claim by fighting to protect and defend our people, just like the alphas of our past. Like Alistar, like my father. I just hoped he and countless others wouldn't have to die in the process.

Shifters held an advantage over humans, but there was one problem with that advantage: humans outnumbered us. There were likely ten human soldiers for every shifter, and numbers often won a war.

As the alpha's manor came into view, I admired the sturdy structure framed by decorative gray and white stone. The weathered ivy vines snaking up from the bottom, with overgrown hedges encircling the complex, gave it a rustic beauty as if nature intertwined around the structure itself.

"You faced off against a mage on the last attack?" Shaw asked Talon.

"Yeah," Talon answered. "I never really understood what kind of magic they had until I had to fight one."

I couldn't help but slow my steps to listen in, noticing Neera and Rhea doing the same.

"They can somehow manipulate the energy and even the elements around them," Talon said, swirling his wrists and exaggerating by fidgeting his fingers.

"What happened with the mage you fought?" Shaw asked.

"Besides bleeding?" Talon smirked as his brother gave him a look. "All right, fine. Details... I know, I know. You want the details." Talon sighed. "The one I fought the other night made a shield of raw energy before trapping me on the ground. It felt like a cage."

I glanced at Rhea. Her eyes narrowed as she listened closely to her mate's story.

"Luckily," Talon continued, "my wolf's magic was amped up from the fight and wouldn't tolerate that shit. I was able to overpower his barrier and break through. He blasted me with a burst of magic that hit me like a hammer to the chest, but I was able to recover in time to snap his neck in my jaw."

"You didn't *eat* him, did you?" Neera's face went pale.

"No," Talon answered quickly. "But... can't lie and say I didn't taste him."

"I'm so glad my animal is a deer," Neera said, thankfully not vomiting along the path. "I think, after that story, I might become a vegetarian, though."

"That mage was fortunate I was busy dealing with a hunter," Rhea growled. "No one puts my mate in a cage and has the honor of a quick death."

Talon gave Rhea a half-smile and looped an arm around her shoulder. "You're as deadly as you are terrifying, my love."

Rhea turned and kissed his crooked nose. "No one but me is allowed to best you, Talon."

"When I let you," he countered.

Rhea raised a brow at her mate, bucking up her chin so she could meet his cocky grin. "Do you want to sleep outside for the rest of the week?"

"As long as you're with me, I'll happily sleep anywhere." Talon laughed, pulling Rhea closer, the only one who would ever dare to see her threat as playful mocking.

I sighed. Seeing them together tugged at my center, the longing for Daxton daring to pull me under in a wave of grief.

"Don't give in, Spitfire." I swear, I could hear Daxton's voice inside my head. *"Don't tell me you're doubting the magic of our bond... You know I'm right about this."*

I huffed a laugh, closing my eyes and picturing Daxton's amused grin. A true smile that exposed the hidden dimple on his cheek.

"You all right?" Shaw asked with Neera close at his side.

"As good as I can be," I answered, looking at him.

He nodded, not pressing the matter further, which I silently thanked him for.

"Where was Magnus last seen?" I hated asking, but I needed to know.

"When we buried Mother," Neera said with a shaking voice. "When we laid the stones on her grave, Father, he—"

We would both need time to grieve the loss of Julia, but right now, we had to be strong. And I needed Magnus.

We all needed him.

"Magnus shifted and disappeared into the forest and headed north," Talon said. His grip on Rhea tightened. "The loss of his mate—" Talon, for once, had trouble articulating his words. "It's..."

"You don't have to explain," I said quickly. "I get it."

Talon and Rhea both nodded as we continued marching onward.

"There have been sightings here and there. He hasn't left the pack lands, but we've been unable to reach him. We can't communicate with him even in our animal forms," Shaw added.

"I tried," Neera said, reaching for my hand, which I extended to try to comfort her.

"The reason he's still here," I said in a calm, steadying voice, "is because he still has you, Neera. He could never abandon you. I don't believe he's gone. He's just lost. We'll get him back."

"Promise?" Neera asked.

"Promise."

Her soft smile amongst her freckled cheeks held relief as she sighed. "Thank you, Sky."

"It's the truth. I wouldn't lie to you, and you know it."

"I know," Neera said as she hugged me, forcing our party to stop on the trail. "I'm just so glad you're back."

"For now," I answered, hugging her tightly and stroking her hair just like I remembered Julia doing countless times in our youth. "I'll have to leave again."

My cousin looked up at me, the jade in her eyes shining brightly with admiration and love. "I know you do. And you will win this final trial."

"You won't be alone in this, Sky," Shaw added, his voice collected and centered, just like him. "We know you will return to the Inner Kingdom with the alpha's dagger and unlock the Heart of Valdor."

"Besides," Rhea taunted, "I've been waiting years to help you convince—" Rhea's stopped as a loud call rang out overhead. A glimmer of gold and russet feathers soared through the clouds and away from Solace.

"Gods be damned!" I cursed. "Where's he going?" I turned to Talon and Shaw for an answer.

"Shit," Talon cursed. "He must be leaving on patrol."

"Well, stop him!" I demanded. "Shift and call out to him!"

"He's too far away, Skylar," Talon said, his lips pressed into a thin line. "Only his beta can call him at that distance."

"Then let's go find his beta."

Chapter Twenty-One

Skylar Cathal

I marched up the familiar steps of the alpha's manor. Shaw said he could smell the beta's scent from inside the compound. Raising my closed fist, I pounded on the doorframe.

"Xander!" I shouted at my ex-lover, my anger rising, cursing my luck. "Xander, it's me. Open the door. I need you to call the alpha back!"

A scuffle sounded along with hurried footsteps inside the manor. It was unusual for pack members to knock, as we were always welcome, but I had not sworn allegiance yet to our new alpha. In fact, I was preparing to do the opposite if he did not listen to reason.

The handle to the large double doors turned as Xander's tall, robust frame filled the entrance. "S-Skylar?" he stuttered, his eyes wide with shock and disbelief. "How? When did you—"

I held up my hand to silence him. "I'll explain later, but first, you must call Gilen and bring him back immediately."

I was done waiting.

Xander shook himself, his back straightening, embodying his role as second in our pack hierarchy. "The alpha will return tomorrow," he answered. "If you need a meeting with him, you'll have to wait until then."

"Bullshit!" I roared and stepped closer.

A low warning growl emanated from Xander's chest as his cocoa-colored eyes sharpened on me.

"Call him now," I demanded.

His threatening rumble didn't frighten me. After the basilisk and the labyrinth, I wondered if anything could.

"Gilen will return tomorrow." Xander didn't back down, his bear likely close to the surface as a light shimmer of green danced across his tanned skin. "Watch yourself, Skylar. You may be the champion, but—"

"But what?" I growled, refusing to back down.

"You don't hold a rank within our pack. You're only—"

"Careful how you choose to finish your words." Shaw cut in, stepping to my side, his magic flaring as he met Xander's stare. "As beta, it's your job to help protect our pack and ensure our alpha is guided and supported. I respect your position in this role. But if you dare speak of Skylar in that way again, you will feel my claws at your throat." Shaw's voice was as cold as death itself.

I watched Xander's brows narrow, his eyes fixated on my friend. "Brave of you to challenge me, Shaw. And here I thought you were the intelligent one of your little group."

Shaw's magic pulsed wildly from his center, followed by a deep, menacing growl at the back of his throat.

"Come on, Xander," Talon said, stepping to his brother's side to try and defuse the fight brewing at the alpha's doorstep. "You know Gilen will want to see her."

Xander's eyes didn't leave Shaw's as he spoke. "And your point?"

"Call him back," I said as Shaw's power continued to build.

"Shaw, back down," Talon whispered.

Shaw's growl only deepened as his magic flowed around him in response to Xander's challenge.

"Fat chance." Rhea sighed, leaning over the railing and picking at her nails, unimpressed at the scene playing out before us. "Are we really going to pretend you can take him, Xander?"

The beta's eyes dashed over to Rhea for a split second, his rage building. "That's enough."

"Really?" Rhea shrugged and rolled her shoulders. "Because we all know who our beta should've been. Who holds the most power aside from Gilen in this pack?"

Xander turned his attention to her. "You—"

"You can't do it," Rhea said, silencing him. "You can't reach Gilen when he's that far away, can you?"

I blinked, realizing what Rhea was insinuating.

"Can you?" Rhea challenged again. "You're not strong enough."

Xander's temper was on the verge of unleashing. "I—"

"Stop this!" I roared, putting myself between them, my power flowing through my words as a command.

They all stilled.

"Good. Thank you," I said, turning to Xander. "I don't want to fight. War is already here, and fighting amongst each other will only weaken us when we need to unite. I know this, and so do you."

Xander was difficult to read, but he remained silent, allowing me to continue.

"I need the alpha's dagger for the final trial, Xander." I helplessly watched as his expression fell on those final words.

"Sky." Xander sighed, his aggression softening. "What you're asking for is impossible."

"I know," I said, reaching for his hand, trying to find the rational male I once knew better than anyone. "I know the gravity of what I'm asking, but this is the final trial. I have to retrieve the dagger and return it to the Inner Kingdom."

"Whoever holds the dagger is the alpha, Sky. Gilen won't just hand it over to you."

"He might," I said, turning my lips in. "For me, Gilen might."

"Ha! You always did have an active imagination." Xander laughed, easing the tension.

I felt his magic simmer with Shaw following his lead. For the moment, there would be no blood spilled.

"But for you, he might," Xander said.

I knew this was a dangerous game to play.

Xander paused for a moment and leaned in closer to me, inhaling a deep breath. "Your scent... It's changed."

"Daxton Aegaeon," I said. "He is my mate."

Xander stepped back, glancing at the nape of my neck.

"But since I'm in the trials and can't shift, the bond is unsealed."

"He didn't mark you?" Xander asked slowly.

"No," I answered, my stomach churning as I silently cursed myself for that fact.

"Hmm," Xander hummed, stroking his chin. "Well, this may complicate things."

"When is my life ever uncomplicated?"

"Never," Rhea answered for me. "She does have a mate, Xander. Her scent and declaration alone are clear signs."

Xander was quiet, but I could tell his mind was racing. "Well, as always, if you wish to stay here, you're welcome to the rooms on the third floor. Dawn is fast approaching, and judging by the circles under Neera's eyes, I would assume that your group has been awake all night."

"Thank you, Xander," I said and entered the alpha's compound as he stepped aside.

Chapter Twenty-Two

Skylar Cathal

The five of us decided to share a room. None of them wanted to leave my side. I was thankful for their support and company. The last thing I wanted was to be alone right now.

We picked one of the largest rooms at the top of the staircase that overlooked the entrance to the manor, adjacent to Daxton and Castor's quarters when they were here.

Rhea and Talon slept together in a smaller bed tucked into the far corner, while Neera decided to sleep next to me, with Shaw on my other side. The three of us easily fit into one of the overly large wooden-framed beds. As we all settled in, Neera was the first to find sleep, her head tucked into my chest, holding onto me through the final hours of the night.

I glanced to my right, looking over the top of a slumbering Shaw, to see the branches of the spruce trees dancing in the breeze through the nearby window. Winter was well underway, with frost along the edges of the windowsill framing the outside world in a beautiful, iced silhouette.

"Can't sleep?"

I twitched, with Shaw's voice catching me off guard.

"Gods above," I hissed quietly. "I thought you were asleep."

He shrugged. "You thought wrong."

"Clearly."

"What's keeping you up?" Shaw whispered.

Neera stirred against me, but thankfully, she remained asleep.

"Too many things," I replied.

"Night terrors?"

"No, not really, not anymore…" I trailed off, realizing I hadn't had a dream about my capture since I'd arrived in Silver Meadows.

Gods, I missed him.

"That's good," Shaw said.

"Yours?" I dared to ask.

"They come and go, but none have ripped me from a good night's sleep for a few years now, thankfully." He stilled and turned onto his back to gaze at the wood panel ceiling. "Ask."

"Ask what?"

"Really?" Shaw murmured, casting me a brazen sideways glance. His black hair, so dark it seemed to shimmer blue in the light, tumbled effortlessly over his hazel eyes. "I know you better than that, Sky. Ask me about what happened on the steps with Xander."

"Fine." I sighed. "Why didn't you take the mantle? Why is Xander the beta and not you?"

I knew Xander's well of power deemed him strong enough to hold the position of beta within our pack, along with his strength and fighting abilities. But Shaw... Shaw's magic was undeniably *more*. Their scuffle on the steps and Rhea's comment about pretending only solidified my suspicion. I just didn't understand why.

"Not many know," Shaw whispered.

"Does Magnus?"

"Yes," Shaw said. "He was the first one I sought out when I shifted."

"And?"

"I asked him about what I should do. What role I needed to step into for the sake of our pack." Shaw went still, his face twisting as he dove deep within his thoughts. "I asked him if I should challenge Xander and become Gilen's beta."

"The beta," I whispered. "The bond between alpha and beta is different compared to the rest of the pack." I recalled Magnus describing the differences between his beta bonds with Alistar and my father, Emery. "Judging by the circumstances now, I assume you didn't challenge Xander?"

"In a way."

"Enlighten me."

He sighed. "It's hard to explain."

"You? Hard to explain?" I turned to look at him, "Now that's a first."

"It's hard to describe the feelings attached to it, Skylar," he whispered with a low growl laced in his words.

"For males, those tend to be difficult. I can agree with you on that."

"Gods." He sighed, palming his face, the scars along his forearms shimmering white against the splash of dawn trickling along the distant horizon. "Magnus asked me if I felt the pull."

"The pull?"

"Yes, the drive to become Gilen's beta. The call of the alpha to follow him. Like I said, it's hard to explain."

"Oh," I replied. "And I'm guessing you didn't?"

"No more than Rhea, Talon, or Neera," Shaw continued. "So, I decided to let it be. To continue in my current rank within the pack."

"But your magic is—"

"Is not meant to serve this alpha," Shaw cut in, sliding his gaze to me. "I'm not meant to serve as beta to Gilen."

It was my turn to be stunned into silence.

"That was all I could piece together anyways, because it wasn't long after that when Julia died..." Shaw trailed off. Losing Julia was devastating for all those who knew her. "It's been chaotic since then, and I stepped in to help however I could. And then Neera and I—"

"Do you love her?" I asked, my protective side emerging as I glared at the male.

Shaw flinched against my stare, feeling the power and meaning behind it. "Again, it's complicated."

"Because, Shaw, I love you like a brother, but if you hurt her... If you—"

"I know. Shh," he hushed, waving his hand. "Calm down, I know. We haven't done anything like that, Sky. Gods, I couldn't live with myself if I did. She just lost her mother."

"Good," I said with a sharp bite to my words.

"We were there for each other," Shaw said. "There's something that could be nurtured and eventually grow, but—"

"You're not a mated pair."

"No," he answered with a heavy sigh. "And we all know how Neera feels about finding her mate." Shaw shifted as he cleared his throat, his mind working to accurately articulate his emotions. "The blissful joy of a true mate bond is unlike anything else in this world. Witnessing Rhea and Talon's relationship unfold only helped solidify my desire to someday find my own mate." He chuckled with a grin, glancing at his brother on the far side of the room.

"I see," I answered, looking down at my sweet cousin sleeping on my chest. "Thank you," I breathed. "Thank you for being here when I couldn't, Shaw. For that, you will forever have my gratitude."

He gave me a soft smile and nodded. "We both need some sleep."

"It's almost daylight," I answered. "We should be waking up, not going to sleep."

"Then put a pillow over your eyes and pretend," Shaw said, rolling over. "Sky," he spoke my name, followed by a long silence. "You know that we're going to stand by you in this, right?"

I smiled. "Never a doubt."

"If he can't see the reason behind your request and he challenges you, I can fight in your place if—"

"Stop," I told him. "You don't need to do anything besides being my friend." Even though his back was turned toward me, I knew he was grinning. "No matter what, I'll complete the final trial."

"Never a doubt," Shaw answered. "Night."

"Almost morning," I replied, knowing sleep would likely not come for me.

"Please be quiet," Rhea grumbled across the room as she moved to curl against Talon's side. "If you two don't go to sleep, I'll put you to sleep with that gods-damned poppy tea."

"She'll do it," Talon grumbled, looping his arm over her middle.

"Fine," I answered, snuggling closer to Neera. I reluctantly closed my eyes, giving my body a chance to prepare for what the following day would bring.

Chapter Twenty-Three

Daxton Aegaeon

My chest ached like a blade through the center of my heart.

Throughout the long-shadowed hours locked away in my cell, I couldn't shake this feeling, this grief. I turned on my side in the darkened stone prison buried under Aelius's keep, unaware if it was the Mother or Father hovering in the sky.

"You've seen better days; I'll give you that."

I knew that voice.

"Are you still in there, Daxton?"

Zola.

I groaned against the aches and pains of my broken body.

"Ahh, there he is," Zola said with as much kindness as she could manage. "The stench indicated differently. Glad to see you're still alive. I was worried Castor would have to reign in your place."

"Going soft on me?" I whispered. My throat splintered as I forced the words from my cracked lips.

"Just checking in to see if we are at *that* place again."

Cloaked in shadows, I couldn't see her.

"I'm not," I said in a thundering voice, leaving nothing to question. "I won't allow myself to disappear like that again."

"Good," Zola said. "I won't break the vow I made to your mother to watch over you and Castor. Besides, I'm not the one who would be able to bring you back."

"Skylar—" As soon as I spoke her name aloud, I felt the fissure in my chest crack open.

Twenty years ago, I'd reached a breaking point. The constant pressure of Minaeve's hovering presence, the wilt, the death... everything. I was in a dark place. The thought of ending it all was an all-too-welcoming release.

Existing, that's all it was. I was living a life that wasn't truly worth living.

My people had become accustomed to living in a cage of fear for so long that it felt normal, even though it was far from it. I remembered what it was like before the wilt. I remembered peace and happiness and, most of all, hope.

But one night, twenty years ago, I forgot.

Zola recognized my withdrawal, lack of sleep, and extreme mood swings for months. Thankfully, that night, she refused to leave my side. She didn't breathe a word of what happened when she jumped into the shadows of my room. No one aside from her knew how close I had come to ending it all.

And as fate would have it, it was that very night when I finally closed my eyes that I dreamed of the green sand beach.

"Daxton?" Zola asked. I heard her footsteps echoing against the stone floor.

"I'm fine," I said. "My body is healing between sessions with a salve, and my mind remains unbroken. It's been days. Not years, Zola."

"My presence is not *all* about you today," she replied.

I glanced sideways and watched as her hand slid over the stone bricks near the bars of my cell. Her fingers wedged between a crack I hadn't noticed, pulling at the rock to reveal a secret alcove with a parchment tucked safely inside.

"Your informant?" I whispered. "You exchange your correspondence in *this* place?"

"Always have," Zola said, her face cloaked in shadow. "Wouldn't dare change the rendezvous point now. Besides, it helps me keep tabs on you."

Humph, I grunted. "How thoughtful."

Zola tucked the parchment into her fighting leathers and disappeared once more in shadow.

"There's no word from her yet."

"I didn't imagine there would be," I answered. "I never told her about this plan."

"Idiotic choice," Zola sneered.

"I couldn't tell her," I argued, still careful to keep my voice low. "If I had told her, she would've intervened."

"And I would've helped her do it, if she asked."

I leaned my head against the wall, chuckling softly to myself. "I know."

"None of us. And I mean *none* of us, Daxton, ever wanted to see you in here again."

"Good thing I have loyal subjects and friends who wouldn't dare disobey my commands."

"Stubborn—"

"I heard that," I said with a laugh that was worth the sting of pain from a cracked rib.

"I meant you to," Zola snapped.

"And here I thought you checking in on me meant you were going soft."

"Don't press your luck, High Prince."

A faint sound echoed from the underground hallway. I could hear Zola slide her hands to her weapons, but I remained where I was.

"It's just the rats," I told her. "After a while, you begin to recognize the difference. Besides, the guards are not due for a session with me today. They had their fill only a few hours ago."

"I know," she answered with a trace of unease that only those she kept in her inner circle would recognize. "I exchange communications when you are elsewhere," Zola said, trying to disguise the pain in her voice. "Our informant shares the whispers from the Aelius court. The people know you're here."

"And?"

"And, due to their oaths to Seamus, they are forced to follow him as their high king consort, but there are sections that are beginning to doubt the *queen*."

"Good." I groaned, absently rubbing my chest.

"What is it?" Zola asked as her eyes carefully scanned my movements.

"I—" I didn't know for certain what this was, but I did have a theory. "It's Skylar." Zola remained deathly still, anxiously waiting for me to continue. "Last night, I felt this aching pain fill my chest. Something is happening or has happened to her. She is drowning in grief, a deep sorrow that is threatening to swallow her whole."

"Is it regret?"

"No, I don't believe so. This stems from a deeper loss."

"Your bond," Zola muttered, shaking her head. "It's not yet sealed, and somehow, you're able to feel her emotions like this? Even through the veil?"

"How did I dream of her beach? And she of my meadow?" I asked with a half-smile. "I don't believe she's challenged Gilen yet."

"The trial of the soul will test her more than the others."

"She'll return," I said with absolute certainty.

"Like you," Zola said, raising her brows, "she's too stubborn to quit."

"Very true," I said with a light laugh. "I dreamed of her before she crossed the veil... Touched her. Held her one last time before she crossed."

Zola clicked her tongue. "I'm surprised she didn't punch you in the face for lying to her."

I shook my head with a forced laugh on a pained exhale. "That very well might still be coming."

"You told me in Crimson City that you were able to visit Skylar in her dreams when the hunters captured her."

"Yes."

Zola emerged from the shadows and knelt by my side. "It's logical that she comes to you while you're locked in this place. Sleep while you can, my high prince. You are both warring in your own battles, but you are *never* alone in your fight. Remember that."

I gazed at Zola, appreciating her more than words could say. She was a shadow jumper, my spymaster, and, most of all, a trusted friend. "I remember."

"I need to go," Zola said.

"I know."

"You remember what you must do?" Zola asked.

"Yes."

"You still believe they'll call for a celebration and bring you up to gloat about a victory?"

"Without a *shadow* of a doubt." I could practically hear Zola's eyes roll.

"Very well. Then I'll remain hidden in Aelius and await the cheers of victory. I'll jump us out of here when you're in possession of the scroll."

"Good," I said. "The final inscription won't be filled in until Skylar acquires the dagger and returns to the scroll, but the star begins to fill in the closer she is to achieving the task."

"The court will be in uproar when that final star is inked," Zola said. "I imagine the whole of Aelius will be drunk with glee when Rhett announces the final trial is complete."

"That's the plan," I said.

"I never said it was a *poor* one."

This time, footsteps echoed along the halls. Thankfully, not the marching tune of my torturers, but of the servants carrying a meal, if one could call it that.

Before I could warn Zola to leave, she was gone.

Good, I told myself, knowing she was never far and that she wanted to get me out of here almost as much as I did.

Chapter Twenty-Four

Skylar Cathal

I awoke to Neera loudly snoring in my ear.

It was hard to believe someone so temperate could snore louder than a bear, slumbering on without a care in the world.

I glanced to where Rhea and Talon were dozing, smiling at the fact that their limbs were locked in a tangled mess. Yet, they looked so peaceful, wrapped in each other's arms. Then, to my delight, I turned to notice Shaw was still fast asleep.

I managed to unravel myself from Neera's grasp and silently slip out of bed. The sunlight peeking through the shades indicated it was a few hours past midday.

In the northern regions of Valdor, during the winter months, we didn't have as much sunlight compared to the southern regions. Dinner would just begin brewing when the final rays of sunlight disappeared beyond the western horizon.

I managed to leave the room without disturbing anyone, creeping out of our quarters onto the third-floor landing. I meandered down the quiet hallway, ready to duck into a corner or spare room if anyone wandered my way. Most of the staff were busy preparing dinner or doing various chores outside the manor while it was still daylight. The manor would be quiet. A fact that I was going to use to my advantage.

Descending the staircase at the far end of the complex, I paused at the second-floor landing. The murals of our alphas adorned the tan-painted walls, decorated with various greenery near the base and along the frames themselves.

I glided my hand along the railing overlooking the open seating area below. A unique mixture of cedar and wildflowers that flourished in our lands thrived in this space. It was almost as if the trees and forest lived within the alpha's home—a haven for all shifters in our pack.

My eyes darted toward the portraits as I meandered down the hall, my feet silently guiding me through the history of our people. I held my breath as I stopped at the second-to-last portrait.

A pang of longing tugged at my heart as I gazed into his all-too-familiar green eyes.

There were endless questions I wished I could ask him. So many stories and memories I wanted to share. But most of all, I wished for the time I was never granted with him. With either of my parents.

My father, Emery, stood alone in a meadow surrounded by the thick, overgrown forest, holding the alpha's dagger in his left hand. Placing my hand along the canvas, I traced over the blade, and then, like magic, a tingling sensation fluttered across my skin where my fingers grazed the portrait.

"Father?"

A surge of strength and tranquility filled my heart as I gazed upon the male I knew I always carried with me. And, for the first time in my life, I had no questions. I didn't need to ask if my father believed in what I was doing, I knew I was on the right path.

I'm worthy to be his heir.

Gilen wasn't the only offspring of an alpha. He didn't hold the sole claim to the title.

"Can you and Mother do me a favor?" I whispered to the portrait. "Watch after Julia for us?" I chuckled despite myself. "She can be a handful sometimes." I paused, lowering my hand. "And I promise I'll make you all proud," I said with newfound strength. "I swear it."

A door behind me squeaked as it cracked open, likely from a gust of wind flowing through an open window pushing it ajar. I turned and boldly entered.

A room that I knew. One I had visited countless times before.

As I passed the threshold, the scent of salty sea air and the wild open sky filled my senses, transporting me through time to another life I thought I could have.

I glanced at the large windows across the way that allowed natural light in at every angle. A bed lay tucked in the corner, perfectly made and untouched for what looked like days or even weeks.

I smiled, knowing Gilen rarely slept in his bed. The ledge near the windowsill, with the supply of brushes, sketchpads, and canvas, was his favorite place to rest. He often fell asleep with a draft of his drawings on his chest or a paintbrush in his hand. I fondly remembered the quiet moments of our youth when he would sit with me, and we would talk about our dreams and desires for what fate had in store for us. I would read, and he would paint while we silently enjoyed each other's company.

Strange how our paths had turned and twisted from what we believed they would become.

Sunlight bending through the windows gave the room a serene, orange-tinted ambiance. I hugged myself, not daring to disturb the serenity of the space. A stack of canvases was arranged in the corner, with one draped in a brown cloth atop an easel. I tiptoed over and gently began pulling back the fabric, dying to see what he'd been working on.

I half-wondered if Gilen had begun painting his own portrait for the hallway with the other alphas. However, as I pulled back the fabric, I was proven incorrect.

My mouth fell open as my eyes widened in stunned silence.

This... This wasn't a portrait of Gilen.

It was a painting of *me*.

I didn't know how he managed to capture this moment with such utter perfection, but here it was.

The painting illustrated a stolen moment in time. Centered on me holding an open book on my chest, quietly reading alone on the green sand beach. I gulped loudly, turning around to investigate the other canvases in the corner. I carefully analyzed each one. My hands shook as I realized a handful were paintings of me. Some were half finished, with only portions of my face completed, and others had the background blurred, with me as the focus. However, one painting at the back of the stack took my breath away.

My hands trembled as I picked it up and strolled toward the bench under the window. This was the night of the full moon when I volunteered to be the shifter champion. The viewpoint was from above, and I realized this must have been Gilen's perspective from his animal form.

The meadow and surrounding trees were kissed by moonlight. Fine details in the tall blades of grass bending in the wind breathed life into the painting. The wildflowers were still in bloom from the late summer months, adding to the rich color scheme of the field.

Alone, I stood in the center. A look of pure determination was etched in every line of my face. With my hands clenched at my sides, I pulled my shoulders back. I was unafraid, unwavering in the presence of a terrifying destiny.

"Wow," I rasped.

A tug from my animal broke me from my trance and told me to look toward the door, alert to the presence of another powerful entity approaching.

I stood with my chin up and my shoulders back, summoning my magic and preparing for what would come next. The footsteps ascending the staircase just outside the room were hurried, taking two to three at a time, abruptly coming to a halt in the doorway.

Chapter Twenty-Five

Skylar Cathal

"Gilen."

Our stares met as broad shoulders filled the doorframe.

Gilen's eyes widened with disbelief as he took me in. His once clean-shaven face held a hint of stubble that made him appear older. The casualties of war had cut lines of worry and grief into his expression.

It was him, yet it wasn't. These months away had changed Gilen almost as much as they had changed me.

In disbelief, he whispered, "Skylar?"

"Hi, Gilen."

"You're back," he rasped, hope filling his expression as he entered. "And you've made yourself at home, I see." He raised his brows, glancing toward the uncovered painting on the stand and the canvas still clutched in my hands.

I opened my mouth to speak, but my words fell short, not knowing what to say.

"It's brave of you to enter the alpha's room without permission. The complex is open to the pack, but my room... Now that's bold."

"I'm surprised you didn't move to the alpha's wing. It's much larger."

Gilen stilled as he blinked, glancing toward his feet. "I couldn't do that to my father. Not after what happened."

I tilted my head, questioning his response. "But Alistar willingly submitted, right?"

"It's not that." Gilen swallowed heavily, pursing his lips as his grip tightened on the doorframe.

"What's wrong?" I asked, fighting the urge to reach out and comfort him.

"Julia wasn't the only mountain lion lost that day."

I gasped as my eyes watered. "Oh, my Gods. Gilen."

"They all fought bravely. Every casualty of this conflict is honored for their sacrifice, for protecting our people. My mother was no exception."

Gilen flicked his gaze to me, and I could see through his half-hearted attempt to hide his grief for his mother's passing. It was the same sorrow that stained my own heart at the knowledge of Julia's crossing into the afterlife.

"My parents did not have a mate bond, but they loved each other deeply. I can't force my father to leave the one space he shared with her. So, I remain here."

"I see," I answered, understanding Gilen's kind gesture.

"My father hasn't left his rooms since her burial. His grief, thankfully, didn't cause him to lose himself like Magnus, *but* it's changed him. I know a piece of him died with my mother that day."

"I'm so sorry, Gilen." I sent a silent prayer to the Gods to look after those we'd lost. "I shouldn't have barged into your room. I'm sorry about that, too."

"Sky," Gilen cut in, moving to close the door behind him. "You've been in here more times than I can count. It's fine."

"True. But that was then."

The door shut, and I could see Gilen's shoulders rise and fall as he inhaled a prolonged breath to try and steady himself.

"And now?" he asked as he turned. "Now what?"

"A lot has changed—"

"A lot hasn't," he interjected. "There are a lot of things that haven't changed since you've been gone."

The hairs on my neck stood at attention as Gilen's power began to pulse within the room, responding to his rising emotions.

"I just can't believe you're back," Gilen rasped, his voice heavy with emotion. A spark of hope rose to life from the depths of his obscured heartache. "Does this mean that you've won? Are the trials over?"

"No. There's one more I have to complete."

"The trial of—"

"The soul," I said.

Gilen stroked his chin and gazed out the window before turning to look at me his gaze softening. "Sit with me." He motioned to the bench along the windowsill. "And tell me what you need."

I was relieved to see remnants of my best friend living within the alpha standing before me, so I joined him. Gilen leaned against the wall on the opposite side with one knee bent beneath him, resting his forearms on his thighs.

It all felt so normal, just like when we were kids, or dare I say *friends*.

I took my place beside Gilen, crossing my legs as I prepared myself to tell him about the final trial.

"Start from the beginning," he said. "You really defeated the first two trials?"

I pulled up my sleeve, revealing the two ebony stars filled in on my skin. "I did."

His smile was soft. "Then, by all means, the floor is yours."

I told him everything about the labyrinth and the basilisk, including Daxton joining me in the second trial. "And now, I'm here for the final task."

"Why didn't Daxton come with you here?" Gilen asked with what appeared to be genuine interest.

"He—" I stumbled, biting my lip to prevent my feelings from spilling over. "He's with Queen Minaeve."

His brows furrowed. "Why would—"

"Gilen," I interjected, wanting to change the subject. "I need your help with the final trial."

He blinked as he leaned forward, his honey-colored eyes warming like the sun as his attention recentered on the reason I was here.

"How can I help?" Gilen's voice was easy and sincere.

I steadied myself, taking a deep breath before saying, "I need the alpha's dagger."

The softness in Gilen's expression hardened like the ice on the windowsill. "What?" he asked, sitting straight. "Skylar, do you realize what you're asking of me?"

"I do," I answered, reaching out to grasp his hand, pleading with him to listen. "Trust me, I understand."

Gilen shook his head, his eyes darting to where our hands met. "You're asking me to submit and grant you the role of alpha. Carrying that dagger is—"

"It's the crown of our people." The guilt threatened to silence my words, yet I couldn't allow it to hinder my actions. "I know what value it carries and what it means to our pack."

Gilen's fingers intertwined with mine. His familiar embrace, which brought me comfort in the past, now felt like needles against my skin.

"There's... I just..." Gilen stumbled. "What you're asking me to do, Sky, is—"

"I know." I clenched my eyes shut, fighting back a wave of unease as the tension thickened. Closing the distance between us, I could feel Gilen's chest rise and fall with heavy rasps. His racing heart matched my own.

"Gilen," I pleaded. "I need to take the dagger to the Inner Kingdom. It's the final key to unlocking the Heart of Valdor, so we can live without the threat of our world being consumed by darkness and death."

"And what happens then?" Gilen asked as he brought our hands to his chest. "What happens after the Heart of Valdor heals our world?"

I swallowed heavily.

"What then, Skylar?" he repeated, leaning toward me, his thumb gently caressing my cheek. "I know what I want, and I know what would grant you free rein to take the dagger."

I watched in stunned silence as his eyes slid to the nape of my neck that held no claiming mark from Daxton, and I swear my heart froze.

"The mate of the alpha could carry the dagger."

I moved backward, desperately needing to create space between us. "Gilen—"

"You're not claimed, Skylar."

My eyes widened in disbelief. "But we are not mates."

"Fate may have sent us on different paths at first, Sky. But I've seen the error of my ways, and I'm so sorry," Gilen said as he reached for me once more. "I can't take anything back, but I've learned from it. I understand how much I fucked up."

"Big time," I said.

"Big time," he repeated, nervously biting his lower lip. "But... you came back to me. Can't you see that this was all meant to happen?"

I stared at him, my chest heaving.

"Let me claim you, Skylar. Become my alpha female, and I'll give you the dagger."

"I-I..."

"I know you care for me, Sky." Gilen reached to cup my cheek. "We can be happy together. You will help me become the alpha our people need."

Could this be my fate?

Gilen leaned in, his eyes closing as his lips brushed against my brow. "You're mine, Skylar Cathal."

Giving myself to Gilen would ensure the success of the final trial, but in return, I would lose myself. Sacrificing my soul, knowing Gilen wasn't my true mate. That Daxton and I would—

No.

A rush of power fueled by my animal surged through me as Gilen's lips dared to touch mine. Dared to take what would *never* belong to him.

"No!" I roared, pushing him back.

He flinched. "No?"

"No," I repeated.

"Why?"

"I could *never* allow you to claim me."

"Even if it meant you would leave here tonight with the dagger in your hands and sail off to complete the final trial?"

My chest ached, understanding that I had no choice; I was going to hurt him.

"I see," Gilen muttered with discontent, his jaw clenching as he cocked his head to the side, trying to detect my scent. "Why can't I smell you?" he asked, his voice low and dangerous.

I hesitated.

"Why can't I smell your scent, Skylar?" he growled, rising to tower over me.

My animal fueled me with the power to meet his challenge. "Because I'm shielding it. I didn't want to draw unnecessary attention."

"Reveal it," he ordered, expecting me to follow his command.

I blinked as I looked at him. "Why?"

Gilen clutched his fists at his sides. "I don't know why I'm surprised at your defiance. It was a charming trait in our youth, but now... it's infuriating. This is not a game."

"You should've asked me nicely," I fired back at him. "This could've gone very differently."

Gilen was not my alpha.

"SSSkylar," Gilen snarled, frustration laced between each syllable of my name.

I refused to submit. "Gilen."

He slowly stalked to my right, cocking his head to the side, assessing me like I was a threat in his home instead of his childhood friend, recognizing the intent behind my stare.

"Where exactly is your High Fae protector?" he asked. "Did you lie to me? Are he and their queen hiding or simply waiting somewhere in the woods or on the ship that carried you back to the pack lands? Are you a threat?"

"Daxton is not here," I said, my voice steady despite my rage. "He's waiting for me to return."

"Daxton." Gilen rolled his neck, almost like his name made his skin crawl. "Pathetic."

"What did you say?" I narrowed my eyes as Gilen froze, feeling the pulse of my magic fill the room.

No one was allowed to insult my mate.

"He swears to protect you, yet in your final task, he's nowhere to be seen. Pathetic—"

Anger swelled in my chest, but instead of attacking him, I lifted my shield, allowing my scent to fill the room.

Castor would be proud.

Gilen staggered backward, bracing himself against the wall. "How?" he rasped with wide eyes.

"Daxton Aegaeon, High Prince of Silver Meadows, is my mate," I declared as I watched Gilen's hope of claiming me vanish.

"Your scent. You... You haven't shifted yet. How could this happen?"

"It doesn't matter right now, Gilen. Now, I'll ask you again." I sighed, softening my tone. "Will you give me the dagger?"

His lips pulled back in a snarl. "You dare ask this of me? You dare challenge my role in this pack? You?"

I met his snarl with my own.

"You," I roared, "are not the only heir of an alpha in this pack! You do not hold the sole claim to the title."

A flinch in his expression told me that Gilen had known the truth of this for longer than he cared to admit.

"You're not strong enough to defeat me," Gilen said. "You haven't mastered enough of your magic to shift, along with that mark on your arm that prevents you from doing so."

"I don't need to shift to overtake you in a formal challenge. I'm a Silver Meadows warrior," I announced. "Trained by Daxton Aegaeon and General Gunnar. I defeated the trial of the mind and the body, and I will complete this final task. I will not allow *you* to defeat me."

"Don't push this, Sky," Gilen growled.

The door behind him crashed open, with Shaw, Xander, and the others filling the frame.

Gilen's chest rose and fell with a mixture of rage and disbelief. "If you challenge me, I'll kill you. I won't have any other choice."

I know.

"I, Skylar Cathal, daughter of alpha Emery Cathal," I announced, my magic filling the space, "challenge Gilen Warrick as alpha of the Solace pack."

The world seemed to stop, everyone and everything becoming deathly silent.

I stared at Gilen, no longer scared of hiding my true power. "Do you accept?"

"Get out," Gilen snarled. "Leave my lands or pay with your life."

"Skylar has formally challenged your right as alpha," Shaw said, stepping into Gilen's room with Xander racing to front his approach.

Both males bared their teeth with green magic shimmering around them.

"It would be cowardice to deny this, Gilen. You would be forfeiting your right to be called our leader in the eyes of everyone in this pack," Shaw added.

Gilen cursed and turned on his heels to smash the canvases stacked in the corner. His rage took control, with his animal threatening to break through.

"Will you accept?" I repeated.

Gilen turned to me. My heart broke at the hurt and betrayal lurking behind his hardened stare.

"Let's end this," he answered. "Let this be the end of it all! I accept your challenge, Skylar Cathal. Tonight... Prepare yourself."

"Sky." Talon's voice cut through the tension as Gilen glared at him. "Come on, let's go."

Shaw continued to face off against Xander, with Rhea draping a protective arm around Neera in the hall.

"I should've known you four would be in on this," Gilen spat.

"Skylar is only doing this to protect us, Gilen," Rhea exclaimed. "The fact that you can't see past your own wounded pride is sad."

"Keep that tongue caged inside your mouth, Rhea," Gilen warned. "I'm still your alpha. I will punish those who dare speak against me and step out of line."

This time, Talon moved to confront Gilen. His teeth bared as his eyes hardened like sapphires. "Do not threaten my mate, Gilen. Alpha or not, I won't tolerate *anyone* speaking to her like that."

The two faced one another, the tension in the room thickening to an almost unbearable degree.

"Talon," Rhea said. "Don't. You're right. Let's go. It's not worth it."

Talon slid his eyes to me as I nodded, walking past Gilen and the face-off between Shaw and Xander. Neera reached out for me as I entered the hallway. I quickly met her embrace before returning my attention to those remaining in the room.

"I'm sorry it's come to this, Gilen," I said. "I truly am."

"Save your words for prayers to the Gods," Gilen said. "You'll need their strength in the fight if you truly believe you can overthrow me."

I glared at Gilen as Talon and then Shaw joined us in the hallway.

Xander remained at his alpha's side, his threatening growl echoing off the walls. "You're choosing this path. You're forcing Gilen's hand in this."

I held my head high and brought my shoulders back. "Or, I'm finally walking the path fate has destined me to find and embracing what and who I truly am."

I felt Shaw's approval first, his animal's presence flowing through a foreign bond in waves of quiet support, followed by the others standing at my side.

"We shall see." Gilen pushed open the window, leaped out, and shifted into his massive roc. Soaring high in the sky, his animal's voice rang clear, calling out to his people to bear witness to the challenge that would take place tonight.

To *my* challenge as alpha of the Solace pack.

Chapter Twenty-Six

Skylar Cathal

The final rays of sunlight kissed the canopies and scattered along the peaks of the distant mountains to the northern reaches of our territory. The air held a bite of cold that would chill you to the bone.

I marched to the center of the training grounds with countless pairs of eyes set on watching my every movement. The grass crinkled underneath my feet with the night's frost as the fog from my breath curled around my lips. My heart pounded inside my chest like the beating sounds of thunder in the sky.

"We're with you," Shaw said. "Don't forget that."

"I know," I answered, keeping my mind focused.

I knew I wouldn't enter this challenge alone. My animal stirred, preparing me for the fight ahead and fueling me with a serene sense of calm, telling me that this was the right choice.

"And what are we? Some sort of consolation prize or something?" Rhea asked, bumping Shaw's shoulder. "Don't forget who won a gold coin from you and Talon by betting on the right shifter from the start. I told you my girl would win." Rhea winked, giving me a confident smile I couldn't help but return.

"Where would I be without you, Rhea?" I teased.

"Yeah," Talon added in a flirtatious tone, his eyes focused solely on his mate. "I remember that day on the cliffs, and I still stand by what I said." We all looked at him, ready and waiting for his response. "I'd be *richer*."

Simultaneously, we all broke out into a half-hearted laugh.

Shaw shook his head, running his fingers through his tangled mesh of hair. "Nicely done, brother."

"I try." Talon grinned, flashing a smile that caused his crooked nose to twist.

"Skylar?" Neera's voice brought our laughter to a swift halt, her focus centered on me. "I-I'm not a fighter, a healer, or a high-standing member of this pack in power or strength. But I'm a Cathal." Neera's voice steadied as a warm hum of pride swelled within my chest. "Like you, I carry the honor of our family's name and heritage. And you—" She paused, her eyes glowing with a swell of magic. "You're my alpha, Skylar. I will forever follow you."

Despite the commotion of the gathering shifters, the world fell silent. I gazed at my cousin in awe. I cupped her sweet face between my palms and leaned my forehead against hers.

"You honor me, sister—blood of my blood. The strength of your heart is worth the might of a thousand swords," I said.

"Then take it. It's yours," Neera said as she placed her palm on my chest.

A rush of power emanated from her animal, reaching out to interact with my own. My soul blazed with the true magic of shifters. Of the strength woven within our pack that linked us to the land, our people, and our animals.

"Take what is rightfully yours, Sky," Neera told me. "We are with you."

Shaw came to my side next, placing a hand on my shoulder, his animal responding just as Neera's did. I noticed a green shimmer of his magic floating over his skin as it drifted toward me. A silent, foreign exchange passed between us, our animals recognizing one another as family. Rhea and Talon quickly followed suit, their animals calling out and linking with mine in the same manner.

"I've always known you were meant to do this," Rhea said with a smile. "Now prove it."

"I will."

The kinship I held with these four warmed my heart and mended the broken pieces of my soul. I would forever cherish their friendship and undying support.

"It's time," Shaw whispered to our group. "He's here."

I nodded as I adjusted the armor of Aegis, along with my bow, arrows, and blades strapped to my side.

After Gilen flew into the sky, calling out to our people to bear witness to the challenge, I raced home to gather my weapons. Without the ability to shift, I needed something to protect myself.

Shaw, being the diligent person he is, conversed with elders in the pack to confirm the rules and regulations of the challenge. Weapons would be allowed, and he warned me that Gilen could do the same if he chose. He could also fight me in his roc form.

The challenge was simple enough. A fight to the death or submission, without outside aid. The victor would hold the rightful claim to the role of the shifter defeated in combat.

Whoever won would become the alpha.

There hadn't been a formal challenge like this in our lifetimes, and never one from an unshifted pack member. Gilen and I were writing our own rules and breaking the norm.

I gave my family a nod as they stepped away, leaving me alone in the center of the clearing. I turned and watched as groups of shifters along the edge parted ways, giving their current alpha a wide berth as he made his way into the meadow.

The chill in the air turned frigid. The menacing glare from my opponent matched the dropping temperatures and the freezing ground we stood upon.

Gilen wore no armor, held no weapon aside from the alpha's dagger clutched in his hand.

I stilled when our stares locked. His gaze was sharp with anger, unflinching as he strode toward me. The lines etched in his face were rigid, remote, but beneath them, a deeper emotion surfaced... betrayal.

I steadied myself, shifting my feet in the grass. I knew this pain. I'd experienced this same heart-wrenching emotion the night before I left for the Inner Kingdom when he called me a half-breed.

I regretted the agony I was causing Gilen, but I didn't regret this challenge.

Gilen straightened to his full stature. His magic surged as he pulled back his shoulders to speak. "I'll ask you this one last time." He twirled the dagger in his hand. "You truly wish to challenge me?"

I squared my shoulders, fearless in his commanding presence. "I challenge you, Alpha of the Solace pack."

"So be it," Gilen growled, raising the dagger above his head. "I accept."

He threw the weapon toward the dirt, the blade embedding itself in the frozen ground beneath our feet.

Since Gilen didn't have weapons, I unstrapped my bow and quiver, but kept a blade strapped to my thigh. I placed them next to me in the grass, keeping them ready in case Gilen shifted into his animal form. He had an advantage over me with his physical strength, but thankfully, I had speed.

I crouched into a balanced fighting stance, and Gilen did the same.

For a moment, I closed my eyes and allowed myself to reach for my bond with Daxton, daring to search for his presence despite the distance that separated us.

And instantly, I felt it.

It was comforting and empowering. My animal sang inside my mind in response to his presence, knowing that no matter what, we would always find each other.

Xander cleared his throat and stepped between us, raising his arm to the sky before yelling, "Begin!"

Chapter Twenty-Seven

Skylar Cathal

In a flash, Gilen leaped to attack.

I dodged his initial strike, countering by blocking his punch with a swift sidestep and kicking his thigh as I spun in place.

My success in this fight was anchored to my ability to foresee my opponent's actions. If Gilen managed to capture me and take me to the ground, I would be dead. I needed to overpower him with my speed and technique.

This time, I pivoted on the balls of my feet, leaving an opening at my side that I knew Gilen would see. Keeping my balance, I adjusted my footing to transfer my counter into an attack. Just like Daxton taught me. My fist collided with Gilen's jaw. Not a powerful blow, but the first of many in this fight.

Gilen recovered, shaking his head while tasting the blood on his lip. His eyes transitioned into a haunting shade of gold that blazed with pure, unhinged rage.

"You've learned some new tricks," he sneered.

"My mate," I said, my voice ringing with power, "trained me himself. I won't dishonor him with anything less than victory."

The muscles along Gilen's shoulders flexed as his veins popped under his skin. "I'll be sure to send your regards to him... in the next century," he growled. "When the High Fae once again seek out a champion."

Hearing this, I charged at Gilen in a flash, knowing he could not match my speed. I withdrew a small blade and slashed along his bicep. Blood pooled along the wound as I ducked under his counter. Backing a few paces away, Gilen stilled, glancing at his wound and then at my blade dripping with his blood. It was already beginning to heal, but still, it sent a message.

I might not be able to shift, but I was far from defenseless.

"Cute." He snickered, reaching for the bottom of his shirt to pull it over his head. "This was beginning to become a nuisance anyway."

"The first blood belongs to me," I growled, sheathing my dagger.

"But not the last," Gilen roared as he rushed toward me.

We traded blow after blow, neither of us gaining the upper hand. An elbow caught my lip, splitting it in two as I spat the thick, hot, familiar iron-tasting blood onto the frozen ground.

I spun and answered with my own onslaught, gaining ground with swift knee strikes and kicks to his torso, bruising vital internal organs. Gilen's right hook found its mark on my eye, and I managed to roll backward with the momentum of his punch. I needed to put space between us to regain my senses and figure out my next move.

Despite my efforts, the fight turned in Gilen's favor.

A kick of his heel landed on the side of my knee, sending me stumbling onto the ground. Frantically, I gasped for breath through the pain, reaching for a dagger at my thigh to defend myself against his next attack. Gilen lunged toward me, but I was able to palm my blade just in time and slice my weapon across his chest, causing him to stagger back.

For the moment, I managed to escape death.

Groaning, I pushed myself onto my feet. My knee was unstable, but it could still hold *most* of my weight.

Dusk settled into the clearing, casting a silent shadow along the surrounding trees and vivacious forest. I glanced around at the pack members gathered near the tree line, witnessing our challenge.

"Giving up already?" Gilen taunted, circling me.

I noticed a slight limp in his gait as he stalked toward me, favoring his left side.

"Where's the fun in that?" I answered as my left eye began to swell.

"Enough, Skylar," Gilen said. "If you don't submit—"

"I will *never* submit," I growled, my power rising.

The gathered crowd of shifters hushed, carefully listening to our exchange.

"I'm the daughter of Emery Cathal, an alpha of this pack. The Cathal blood runs through *my* veins, along with the magic of my ancestors who were among the first chosen by the Gods themselves to become shifters."

Hushed whispers flooded the training field.

"I refuse to break. And I will *never* submit."

Gilen's eyes hardened. "Remember, it was you who pushed me to do this."

"Have at me, Gilen!" I roared, rising to my feet. "I'll take whatever you throw at me."

"I know," he answered. "You forget that not too long ago, I knew you better than anyone. I know that fire blazing inside you."

We both paced in a circular motion, never once taking our eyes off each other.

"I just didn't realize that I would be forced to extinguish your flames instead of tame them."

I growled at him. "That's the problem, Gilen. My fire was *never* meant to be caged!"

I dared a glance over to where Rhea and Shaw stood. Rhea gave me a cocky grin while Shaw nodded for me to keep fighting.

"Ha!" Gilen laughed, rolling his shoulders as a green shimmer danced across his skin. "Then, by all means, let's set you free."

The power emanating from Gilen was stronger than I remembered. In his short span as alpha, he'd fully grown into his magic, rising far above what his father,

Alistar, could ever muster. In less time than it took to blink, he shifted into his roc.

"Gods above." I gasped, swallowing heavily. "He's bigger than I remember."

Chapter Twenty-Eight

Skylar Cathal

The golden gaze of the massive roc blazed with fury.

Gilen moved so fast I narrowly dodged being snapped in two, leaping to the right and rolling into a balanced crouched position near the tree line. My knee buckled underneath me, but I gritted my teeth, ignoring the sting of pain, willing it to stay in one piece.

Shit, where did I leave my bow?

I spun, trying to locate my weapon, but Gilen lashed out before I had time to find it. His deadly, sharpened beak cracked inches above my neck as I avoided another assault. My pulse raced as my animal surged within me, feeling the depth of Gilen's power and fighting back against his will.

"*Submit!*" Gilen called out.

His command struck me like monstrous waves colliding against the sea cliffs. The force of it alone caused other shifters in the surrounding area to take a knee or drop their heads in a submissive stance.

He was trying to force me into submission, but it would never work.

Pivoting on the balls of my feet, I sprinted toward the safety of the forest at a hobbled run, heading toward a cluster of thick brush along the eastern area of the training field.

I dove headfirst into the mass of vegetation, towering trees providing a layer of protection from overhead, using one of Gilen's strengths to my advantage.

I heard his roc's song of frustration skitter across the ferns and brush that encased me. The thick cottonwoods prevented him from scooping me up with his talons. He was too large to fit between the trees. I scurried through the shrubbery, trying to steal a second from his hunt to locate my bow on the training field.

I was a gods-damned moron for thinking it was a good idea to take it off in the first place.

A low vibration began creeping along my senses. The melody of drums... No, correction, it was the pounding of massive wings resonating overhead.

I peered into the sky, searching for Gilen. The thundering of his wingbeats physically took me aback, each powerful flap of golden feathers causing the surrounding foliage to bend to his presence.

I swallowed heavily as I tried to remain calm. Imagining the three-foot talons sharpened to dangerous points did *not* help. More lethal than a sword or the dagger that I had strapped to my side.

The robust branches overhead created a protective barrier, but I knew it wouldn't be long until he found an opening. I had seconds, possibly minutes, to figure out a plan.

I needed to find my bow.

"Where the... Ah-ha!" I exclaimed, locating my prize in the clearing. "There you—"

My timeline was shorter than I thought.

Gilen utilized his speed from a free fall and the strength of his armored feathers to break through. The cracking sound of branches followed the body of a massive roc barreling through the treetops.

I was cornered.

Thankfully, two strong cottonwoods with a diameter wider than I was tall stood between us. Gilen reached his head through the barrier and screamed at me. His beak snapped at my heels as I began crawling through the brush.

"Gods," I cursed with a groan. "Not devil's club."

Not only were the stems covered in noxious, irritating spines, but the large palm leaves were as well. Still, I pushed on, crawling to the northern end of the field where my bow lay in wait next to the alpha dagger.

I could hear Gilen crashing through the trees behind me. He was deadly and graceful in the skies in his roc form, but here on land and in the thick brush, he was at a disadvantage.

Seeing the clearing come into view, I surged onward. My exposed skin was irritated from the thorns, but thankfully, my stubbornness didn't allow it to slow me down.

A rush of magic exploded behind me. Glancing over my shoulder, I could no longer see the golden feathers of the roc buried within the trees.

Shit, Gilen shifted back into his human form.

In a heightened state of urgency, I broke through the final layers of undergrowth and burst into the open field. I dove, somersaulting forward as I tried to regain my balance. Righting myself, I located my bow and quiver lying in the tall grass.

"Skylar!" Shaw's voice rang out in warning.

Gilen was right behind me, retaking his roc form once he cleared the forest. I pushed onto my feet, my boots digging into the dirt as I sprinted for my life.

How fast was Gilen able to shift?

I didn't have to ponder that question for long because, in my next step, I felt a wave of his magic build behind me as he shifted once again.

Gods above, he was powerful. If I weren't running for my life in a challenge for alpha, I would've paused to admire the speed at which he could transition between his two forms. Gilen's control over his magic was impressive, but then again, so was mine.

I was only three strides away from my silver bow, three lengths from a weapon I knew I could use to win this. Three steps away from—

A massive shadow blocked the moonlight, like something had reached up and extracted the luminous idol from the sky. The deep pounding of golden wings echoed across the field, ringing in my ears like claps of thunder from above, drowning out the rest of the world.

I was so close.

Bending to lean forward, I extended my hand to curl my fingers around the bow and quiver. Just as my hand slid into place, coiling around my salvation in this fight, something else also found its prize.

The wind was knocked out of me as Gilen's talons clutched me around my middle. The sharp talons encased me in a vice-like grip as he shot upward into the skies, with me in tow. The pressure of his hold dug into my chest, squeezing me tightly as the ground drifted away, my bow and quiver dangling in my outstretched hand.

As Gilen soared into the sky, I watched in horror as the arrows tumbled out of the quiver, skittering across the earth below.

"No!" I rasped as Gilen's talons attempted to penetrate my chest.

Gilen squawked in protest, hovering as his head tilted down to investigate. With one hand, I held a death grip on my bow as I reached for a dagger with my other.

The honey-colored stare of my childhood best friend was foreign to me. I could see in his eyes that he would not hesitate in this fight. He was ready and willing to kill me. Understanding this, I readied myself and struck true, my blade slicing deep within the golden stare I thought I knew so well.

Gilen roared in pain. The high-pitched howl shattered my eardrums, and I was... Oh Gods, I was falling.

"Ahhh!" I screamed, free-falling through the open sky.

Gods, I wished I had Daxton's teleporting magic. This was going to hurt.

Chapter Twenty-Nine

Skylar Cathal

In a panic, I dropped my weapons, desperate to try and slow my descent as I crashed through the canopy.

I reached out to grasp the branches, but I couldn't manage a firm enough hold to slow me down. A thick branch slammed into my chest, and I was able to grab hold to slow my descent. Still, I tumbled through the treetops, landing with a firm thud on the forest floor.

I lay on the ground for a moment, groaning as I assessed my injuries. Thankfully, the armor of Aegis saved my ass from dying, *again*. Rolling onto my back, I searched the skies for any sign of golden feathers.

None.

Thank the Gods, I might have bought myself a minute.

Sitting up, I found my bow and dagger lying near the trunk of a large tree off to the side. Favoring my uninjured knee, I crawled across the forest floor, and by the grace of the Gods, my bow appeared to be in pristine condition.

"Lucky break," I rasped. "Now to find an arrow."

I knew they likely tumbled into the clearing when Gilen first grabbed me, so I crept to the training field, my eyes searching the area when an ear-shattering scream echoed above.

Shit. I was out of time.

Ignoring the pain of my injuries, I forced myself to move. I was used to enduring pain. After the hunters' torture, these wounds were a motherfucking cakewalk.

Murmurs and gasps erupted on all sides as I entered the clearing, but my focus was set on reaching my arrows. My breathing quickened as I saw my prize embedded in the tall grass. One lone arrow stood upright in the clearing, and I knew this was my chance.

Dashing forward, I pumped my arms and legs harder than I thought possible. The pounding echo of wings became louder and louder with each step I forced myself to take. Gilen was closing in, ready for a final strike to end this challenge once and for all.

Except, so was I.

I readied my bow in my left hand. My grip was firm, yet relaxed, preparing to execute a blind-turn-around shot that I had perfected with Daxton and Gunnar.

The arrow's fletching traced over my fingers. The feathers caressed my palm as I grabbed the shaft and pulled it free from the dirt. Placing the arrow against the string of my bow, I inhaled a full breath, filling my lungs to the point of pain as I locked my left arm and pulled back on the bowstring with the other.

"I'm sorry, Gilen," I whispered as I turned, releasing my arrow on a calm, even breath.

I watched as the arrow soared through the air and embedded itself in the roc's shoulder. Gilen's screech of pain echoed loud enough for all of Solace to hear.

The arrow might not have penetrated his armored feathers if this had been an ordinary arrow. However, this was an iron-tipped arrow. The same weapon he gave me the night I shot and almost killed Daxton.

The roc screamed as it narrowly missed me overhead, tumbling and flailing into the grass field behind me. Gilen shifted into his human form, bloodied and wounded with an arrow protruding through his shoulder.

"Iron!" Gilen swore into the dirt. "You fucking shot me with an iron arrow!"

I swallowed heavily, sweat dripping from my brow.

Gilen was shaky but managed to push himself onto his feet. His body was battered and bruised, the iron weakening his magic as his muscles twitched.

"Your aim seems to have faltered during your time away," Gilen spat. "You missed."

"Did I?" I asked with a dark chuckle. "I *never* miss Gilen, you know that."

Naked and bloodied, he stood in the field, reaching up to break the shaft of the arrow and pull it free. His right eye was gone from when I struck him with my dagger, yet he still stared at me with unflinching determination and a will to fight.

There was no denying that Gilen was an alpha, but it wasn't enough to overpower me.

"Let's end this," Gilen roared as he sprinted toward me, picking up the alpha's dagger in the dirt as the distance between us disappeared with each charging footstep.

I remained utterly still as he raged in my direction, eye blazing, the dagger drawn and ready to strike me down where I stood.

My gaze rose to meet Gilen's as my magic surged to life, raging like wildfire, ready to consume everything in its path. I was ready to claim my father's mantle and unleash my true power.

"Stop, Gilen!" I roared, my magic exploding through each word of my command.

Instantly, he skidded to a halt. His one remaining eye flared with surprise at the force of my magic. His chest rose and fell in rapid beats, echoed by the gasps and whispers from those in attendance.

"Submit," I said in a low tone.

The well of power thrumming from my animal broke through the surface. The magic I had kept hidden for so long, never daring to reveal.

The power of an alpha.

Chapter Thirty

Skylar Cathal

"Submit!" I roared, stepping closer. My power blazed with the magnificence of a blinding sunrise. "You will submit to me, Gilen Warrick."

For a moment, I was afraid this wouldn't work, and I would have to kill Gilen to complete this task. But then... his gaze dropped. His shoulder slacked, and his animal's magic began to dissipate.

"Kneel," I commanded.

Gilen followed.

Gilen and every shifter surrounding us in the field.

I cautiously approached my childhood friend, waiting to see what would happen next. I swallowed heavily, not from fear but from the pang of sorrow that barreled through my heart. I took no pleasure in doing this to Gilen. I never wanted to hurt him like this.

"Gilen," I whispered.

He refused to look me in the eye, keeping his gaze cast down, drowning in a sea of shame.

"Gilen?" I said again.

"What does our *alpha* command of me?" he asked, throwing the dagger at my feet, his voice sounding broken. "Kill me and be done with it. Don't drag this out longer than it needs to."

My stomach dropped at the thought... I could kill Gilen. Any victor in a challenge would. Gods above, he would have killed me if the roles were reversed.

But I knew what was coming.

We were on the brink of another war with the humans. Battles and the promise of bloodshed were at our doorstep. I couldn't justify eradicating one of our strongest warriors simply out of spite or because of some bullshit politics.

Blame it on my human nature running interference, but I saw value in keeping Gilen alive. And as alpha, I could make my own rules.

Ignoring the dagger, I crossed the distance between us and called my healing magic as I gently placed my palm to his eye before seeking the wound in his shoulder. My power sought what was broken, mending what it could. I released my hand from his face and stepped back to give him space.

Gilen's fingers reached up to trace his injury. His brows shot upward in surprise as his chest heaved, a sea of questions swirling around him as he remained kneeling in the frozen grass, staring at me in awe.

My healing magic held limitations, but I was able to restore his vision. His eye, however, would forever hold a discoloration compared to the other. A lighter milky hue now clung to his iris.

"Why?" Gilen asked.

"I won't end the life of one of our strongest warriors when we're on the brink of war," I said, praying he would listen. "We need you, Gilen."

"I would've killed you, Skylar."

"Oh, trust me, I know. You sure as hell tried to." I winked, giving him a half-smile. "I'm looking toward the future of our pack, Gilen. We need strong warriors to defend our people and lands."

I was trying my best to appeal to his logic, hoping his pride would not force my hand yet again.

"Gilen!" Alistar's voice boomed as the crowds parted to allow the former alpha through.

"Father..." he rasped, biting his lip and looking down at the earth with a cloud of shame.

Alistar raced to Gilen's side, knelt beside him in the grass, threw a cloak around his shoulders, and wrapped his arms securely around his son.

Gilen gripped his father tightly. "I'm so sorry I failed you."

Alistar pulled back and sighed. "You didn't!" he exclaimed.

The two of them dropped their heads together, brows touching as their shoulders slackened, giving in to the weight of their reservations and accepting their pain.

"I'm so sorry I wasn't there to guide you when you needed me, son. But... I'm here now."

"I-I lost. Skylar is—" Gilen began.

"Skylar is finally accepting the mantle of her father," Alistar said in an even tone, holding his son.

"Emery was alpha before I stepped into the role. And I knew," Alistar said, looking at me. "I knew his heir would eventually rise to take his place."

I stepped backward, genuinely surprised by what I was hearing. "You knew." I didn't form it as a question.

Alistar nodded, the creased lines on his face deepening. "At first, I thought your rise in power meant you would become a mated partner with Gilen, but..." He paused, standing to meet my stare. "It has far exceeded what I had imagined. And there isn't a soul present here today who would deny your victory."

Alistar turned and gave his son a nod, a loving look full of pride despite his defeat, before returning to me.

"When I learned that you could ignore my commands at will, it was a clear sign of your true power. You were never meant to follow. You, Skylar, were meant to lead. As our alpha."

He knew.

"Yes, I knew." Alistar chuckled, watching my brows raise with surprise. "The strength of our pack lies within the alpha. To deny you this right would go against everything we stand for. Your strength becomes *our* strength and vice versa. This is why the shifter with the most power holds the title. It is a responsibility that only the alpha can carry."

I couldn't believe it. This whole time, Alistar knew I was able to ignore his commands. This realization shook me.

I had underestimated his depth of understanding and compassion as our alpha. He didn't see me as a threat. All these years... he saw me as the Solace pack's future alpha. A part of me wished he had told Gilen all this, but a part of me also understood why he hadn't.

Gasps echoed around me as Xander raced to Gilen's side. Gilen refused to look at him, but Xander remained where he was, silently giving his support. It was clear that the bond forged between them while Gilen was alpha still linked them to one another on a subconscious level.

Xander then turned to look at me. "Remember when I told you my animal was drawn to you? That your power exceeded the bullshit politics of our elders?"

"Yes," I answered, recalling our rendezvous before I was marked as the champion.

"It all makes sense. My bear was following an alpha. Even if she wasn't ready to reveal herself just yet," Xander said, looking at me.

"I remember feeling the same calling," Shaw announced, stepping to my side with the others not far behind. "In the meadow, when you didn't shift, my animal followed your lead."

I looked at Shaw, and something seemed to click. Like a turning of a lock, finally breaking free.

"We follow you," Shaw said with a curt nod.

"Told you," Rhea interjected with a smirk. "I told you that you were meant for more, Skylar. Why the fuck did you ever doubt me?"

Talon clicked his tongue and shook his head, wrapping an arm around his mate.

"What?" Rhea snapped.

"You have such a way with words, love," Talon answered.

"Skylar Cathal," Alistar said, standing to address the pack, "is our alpha!" He cheered, with everyone in attendance following his lead.

"Alpha," my pack whispered in a trickling pattern that echoed through the roots of the trees and the melody of the forest. "Alpha." The title rang more clearly. "Alpha!" The chant roared as the forest itself seemed to hum with magic.

On cue, the gathering clouds overhead cracked with thunder and a flash of lightning, draping over the sky as the rains began to fall. Hard, yet soft as it melted on my skin. The cold mixed with the falling waters, freezing the droplets as they fluttered to the ground, covering the earth in a pure blanket of fresh snow.

A new beginning.

Silently, I bent to take hold of the alpha's dagger. A strange silence engulfed me, with my focus solely locked on the third key in the trials of the Heart of Valdor.

The weapon hummed with a familiar magic that sang to my soul and my animal. As my fingers curled around the hilt, the cold kiss of the metal felt *perfect*. Like this weapon was crafted for me to wield.

I hoisted the dagger upward, stretching to the sky, yelling out a roar of victory to the Gods themselves.

My pack joined me, shifting into their animal forms, filling the night with roaring songs and calls. I closed my eyes. The snowflakes melted as they fell onto my cheeks, cleansing my soul and welcoming me into my new role. Magic trickled over my skin, and I felt threads of power reach out and connect me to each member of the Solace pack, linking them to me and me to them.

My power surging—growing.

I stilled with the dagger outstretched in my arm, realizing this trial of the soul was only a piece of my victory. I was meant to discover the truth about who I was. Who I was meant to be.

I lowered my arm, admiring the weapon my ancestors carried—that my father carried. I was honored that fate had brought me here. Honored that I was strong enough to hold this mantle.

"My people," I said for the first time as their leader, "with this dagger, I have completed the third trial, but now... I must leave."

"What?" a voice shouted.

"We're on the brink of war!" another declared.

"We need our alpha!"

"Settle down," I said inside their minds. *"I would never leave without leadership to guide you. But I must return to the Inner Kingdom. If I don't, then the wilt will ravage our home and destroy us all."*

I waited, trying to assess the reactions of my pack, wishing there was a better way to ease their fears.

This was why I didn't kill Gilen. Why I cherished Alistar and Xander's support. If I had to leave, then I knew I needed to supply our pack with the very best.

I turned to look at Shaw. "Up for a run?" I asked.

"A run?" Neera questioned at his side.

But Shaw… Oh, Shaw. He knew exactly what I was planning.

"You up for this?" Shaw asked.

"I don't have a choice," I said, readying myself.

"Where are you going?" Neera asked, stepping in my path. "You're hurt, Sky."

"I'll be fine," I said. "Besides, this new job as alpha comes with some perks. I'm now linked to everyone, and I think it's boosting my healing abilities." I lifted my leg, bending my knee that thankfully was already on the mend. "See?" I said with a grin. "The swelling on my eye has also stopped. It's almost like it never happened."

Neera pursed her lips, unconvinced by my attempt to reassure her.

"I'm going to find Magnus," I said.

Her eyes widened with a gasp. The light jade tint of her irises shimmered against a streak of tears she fought to keep at bay from her freckled face. "I'm coming."

"Good," I replied before turning to the pack. "I'm going to find Magnus. And I'm going to bring him back."

Chapter Thirty-One

Skylar Cathal

I knew exactly where to find my uncle.

Through the guiding moonlight, we sprinted along the vacant riverbank that meandered along the outskirts of Solace. The river, a lifeline for our people, fanned throughout our pack lands to nourish the lush forest and the myriad of wildlife that called this place home. It was a sight that always filled us with gratitude—a reminder of the constant flow of life. Of change.

Shaw shifted into his panther, running beside me with Rhea and Talon joining as wolves in the rear of our group. Neera, who remained on her two legs with me, followed my footsteps with graceful agility that transferred from her animal. I was thankful Neera didn't shift, giving me a two-legged companion on our journey to where Magnus and Julia first met—the waterfall.

There were many waterfalls in our territory, but this specific one held a special memory for our family. Every year on their anniversary, they returned to the place they met—with Neera and me in tow when we were younger.

Magnus was lost but not gone.

During our trek, the fresh layer of snow melted as it hit the ground, and I felt a strange tug at the back of my mind as the trees whipped past in a green blur. It was like a scratch on the back of my senses—something trying to gain my attention.

"The next turn, we should rest." A familiar voice sounded inside my head.

I skidded to a stop just before Neera collided against my backside, sending us tumbling onto the frozen ground.

"Ouch!" Neera groaned, rubbing her arm as she adjusted the bag of clothing slung across her shoulder. "What in the Gods' names was that for, Sky?"

"Hey, you're the one who landed on me," I grunted. "How do you think I feel?"

"I've seen who your mate is, Skylar," she grumbled. "Trust me, you're fine."

"That's... *bold* of you," I mumbled, narrowing my eyes at her.

Talon and Rhea avoided running into us as Shaw gripped the dirt with his massive claws and turned around on the trail.

"What made you stop, Sky?" Neera groaned, turning onto her side.

I didn't intentionally ignore my cousin's question, but my attention was elsewhere. My eyes were locked onto Shaw because... because—

Did I just hear him speak inside my mind?

"Shaw?" I asked aloud, pushing Neera off me and rising to my feet.

He tilted his feline head, stalking forward, his hazel eyes burning bright with a hint of mischief. His all-knowing demeanor translated perfectly into his animal. The midnight-black fur of his panther blended flawlessly with the surrounding night like a living shadow.

"It was you!" I exclaimed, my smile beaming. "I heard you... in here," I said, tapping my temple.

Shaw's tail twitched behind him as a low purr emanated from his chest. He stepped forward with his strong legs and bent his head toward my chest. His black velvet nose nuzzled me as I scratched his ear.

"What was...?" Neera trailed off. "Oh. You heard *him*?"

Barks and whines echoed from Talon and Rhea off to our left near the bank of the river. Their exhales of breath froze in a light fog around their muzzles. Shaw lifted his head and looked at them, his eyes narrowing, twitching his ears as his long tail flicked to the side.

"They're jealous," Shaw said

"What?" I asked. "Why?"

"Because you aren't answering them." Shaw's chuckle of amusement vibrated through our mental link.

I turned to Rhea and Talon. "I'm sorry. I'm not ignoring you. I just don't hear you."

Rhea growled, narrowing her eyes and baring her teeth. Not at me, but toward Shaw.

"Hey, Rhea. That's uncalled for. Knock it off," I said.

She immediately stifled her growl.

I stepped back, realizing that as her alpha, she would follow my commands. It was a strange dynamic that I would have to learn quickly and be careful not to abuse or overstep.

"You have a stronger connection with your pack when we're in our animal forms," Shaw told me. *"When I shifted, I could feel my connection with you strengthen. It was like you were standing on the other side of a door. So, I knocked."*

"You knocked?" I arched my brow and crossed my arms. "Really? That's the best analogy you can come up with?"

"It's the most basic," Shaw answered with a slight growl and flash of his teeth. *"Try describing what something smells like to someone without a nose and tell me how easy it is to explain."*

"I—" Dammit, he had a good point. I hadn't shifted yet. I wasn't familiar with this telepathic connection while in our animal form.

Shaw nudged my arm as he settled next to me on the frozen ground, the hint of a smirk stretching along his whiskers. His shoulder rested near my head.

"Like me, they've been knocking since we left Solace."

"They have?" I asked, tilting my head in Rhea and Talon's direction.

Shaw nodded.

"Try reaching out your mind to them," Neera suggested. "The alpha is linked to all of us. You should be able to communicate with anyone."

"Okay." I sighed, running a hand through my hair. My mouth twisted to the side.

"It'll help once we locate Father," Neera added. "You'll be able to reach out and speak to him."

I absently rubbed my neck, biting my lip and nodding in agreement. I knew I could reach Magnus and get him back, but I hadn't had time to figure out exactly *how* to do it. This very well might be the key.

"All right," I said. "Rhea, Talon, come over here, please."

The large midnight and golden-auburn wolves trotted from the riverbank to join us. Their gazes locked with mine as a wave of power settled in the distance between us, bridging a connection that was formed even before I had won the challenge against Gilen.

I decided to try to reach out to Rhea first. Her shade of blue was darker than her mate's gaze, giving her a mysterious edge that mimicked her wild, if at times unencumbered, personality.

Shaw said it was like being on the other side of the door. So, I listened, waiting to feel the pull against the back of my mind.

Closing my eyes, I searched for the faintest whisper of another's presence. The forest's melody and the river's steady trickle settled me into a trance. I felt the song of the wild calling me, and then... ever so faintly, I felt the same tug. The familiar pull of my attention drifted to this sensation, and the more I focused on the foreign feeling, the louder it became.

Imagining a doorway, I reached out and opened it.

"About fucking time!" Rhea's voice boomed inside my head.

"And Rhea has officially arrived." I laughed.

"Look," Rhea began, *"You're my best friend and my alpha, and I'll follow you to the ends of this world. But... I'll never shy away from speaking my mind or telling you the truth."*

The auburn wolf's tail wagged frantically with a spark of excitement. I took comfort in the honesty of Rhea's declaration.

"Now, listen for Talon," Rhea said. *"It should come easier the more you do it. It was like that for all of us when we shifted. But—"*

"But since Skylar is our alpha, she doesn't need to be in her animal form to do so," Shaw cut in.

Rhea growled and barked at him. *"I was getting to that! Gods above, Shaw. Other people have good ideas as well, you know."*

Shaw didn't say anything aloud, but I could tell his mind was formulating a witty remark he wisely chose to keep to himself for the time being.

Talon whined and nipped at Rhea's ear, trying to attract her attention. She growled but affectionately turned and nuzzled her mate.

"Okay," I said, raising my palms, stepping between Rhea and Shaw. "Talon, you're up."

I calmed my mind, searching for his, and thankfully, Rhea was right. It was much easier and faster to link my mind with his.

"Hey there, Sky! Glad I could finally join the party." Talon's voice joyfully echoed inside my mind.

"Me too," I answered with a smile. *"Didn't know it was so exclusive."*

"Did it work?" Neera asked.

"Yep," I answered. "Rhea was right. It's easier once you know what you're looking for. I was able to link with Talon almost instantly. I just—"

"Opened the door," Shaw said with a cocky flick of his tail.

"Yes..." I said, turning toward him. "Do I need to give you credit each and every time I successfully mind speak with a member of the pack?"

"No," he purred. *"You admitting it now will suffice. We'll always know whose clever idea it was for the analogy."*

"Seriously, Shaw."

"Know-it-all," Rhea teased, followed by a bark in her wolf form.

"Didn't I teach you not to brag so much growing up?" Talon added. *"Come on, brother, it's beneath you."*

"Fine," Shaw mumbled.

"Can you hear them, Neera?" I asked.

"No, not while I'm in my human form, thankfully. It's an ability only the alpha has," she answered, walking over to the river to cup a sip of water in her hand before bringing it to her lips. "But I can only imagine that Rhea is giving Shaw a hard time for... something. And then Talon is trying to stop them from bickering and eventually tackling each other."

I laughed to myself. "Keen observation."

"I try," she replied with a soft smile.

"A vital skillset, in my opinion," Shaw said, his eyes following Neera's every movement.

"I have a question," I stated aloud.

I heard the groans from Rhea first. *"Why am I not surprised?"*

"Did you hear Shaw's response just now? When you communicate in your animal forms, do others hear it? Or is it just a one-on-one conversation?" I asked.

"In my experience, it's a little bit of both, actually," Neera replied, wiping water droplets from her chin.

"We can either send a direct message," Talon said. *"Or broadcast it."*

"On the battlefield, it's a useful advantage when we need to adjust our attacks, to regroup or relay information," Shaw added.

"I see." I joined Neera and took a large gulp of icy water from the river, trying to wrap my head around this new branch of communication.

"How do you block others out?" I asked.

Shaw slid his eyes from Neera and glanced sideways at me, the corner of his lip turning upward in what I assumed to be a grin.

I placed a palm on my face and shook my head. "Gods. Let me guess, just close the door?"

A rumble from Shaw's panther mimicked the human equivalent of a laugh.

"If we hurry, we can reach the falls by morning, Sky," Talon said.

"Then let's keep moving," I announced as we gathered ourselves and continued following the riverbank.

Chapter Thirty-Two

Skylar Cathal

Sunlight peeked over the ridgeline of the surrounding mountains to the east.

The fresh layer of snow atop the daunting peaks reflected the rays of gold and yellow, mixed with a warming orange glow. I treasured watching the sunrise. I believed it was a gift from the Mother herself, granting us the blessing of a new day. A fresh breath of life with the sparking hope of what was to come.

As we neared the roaring sounds of the waterfall, I felt a surge of strength swell within me. My animal surged to the surface, her presence echoing through me with every step I took across the pristine blanket of snow.

"Slow," I commanded, reducing our speed to a walk.

I reached for the alpha's dagger belted at my hip, memorizing how the cold steel felt against the tips of my fingers. The chill from the crisp morning swirled around us, daring to freeze our breath from the labored journey.

"Up ahead," Shaw said to all of us as Rhea and Talon protectively leaped to either side of me and Neera. *"He's along the rocks, near the falls. I can smell him. His scent is strongest over there."*

I nodded, unafraid of what I needed to do next.

My shoulder brushed against Shaw as he scanned the rocks, searching for any other signs of danger.

"If you need me to step in—"

"I'll be fine, Shaw," I said, speaking only into his mind.

He turned his head to look at me, bright eyes shining against the shadow of his animal's fur as he sat down, flipping his tail side to side.

I reached out and grasped Neera's hand. "I'll bring him back."

"I know." Neera sighed, holding back her tears. "I just... We can't lose him, too, Sky."

"We won't," I answered with a firm tone. I clutched her hand once more before letting it go. "Guard Neera," I told Rhea and Talon, who nodded in understanding. *"If it comes to it, take her to safety, and leave me behind."*

Rhea released a small whine, followed by Talon's bark of understanding.

I approached the falls, the sound of the pounding waters drowning out the noise of my boots against the loosened rocks along the riverbed. The trees bent over the bank provided essential cover, allowing me time to scan the tranquil pool and large boulders near the base of the falls.

The cascading waters raced over the top of the ledge, almost fifty feet above, before crashing down with enough force to pound massive rocks into rubble. I fought to forget loving memories of this place, focusing solely on the task at hand... Rescuing my uncle.

"Where are you, Magnus?" I muttered to myself. *I know you're here somewhere.*

My heart skipped a beat when I felt a familiar brush of power toward the top of the falls.

The familiar knock of Shaw's presence brushed against my mind, but I pushed him away. I didn't need his help with this. If I acknowledged his presence, he would take it as a sign to jump in and interfere.

The large head of a ferocious grizzly bear looked down at me. The rich, solid, deep russet color of his coat was paired with the Cathal green eyes that I memorized as a small child. His sheer size alone confirmed that this was Magnus.

I held out my palms, trying to make myself seem smaller, projecting that I meant no harm. I had never encountered a shifter lost to their animal form. It was rare, an urban myth parents used as threats to ensure we fell in line and behaved, or else, when we grew up, our animals would take over and never let us go.

"Magnus," I bellowed over the roar of the crashing waters cascading over the falls.

The bear turned and looked at me momentarily before returning to foraging, oblivious to my call. A pain of grief shot through me as I questioned if we had lost him completely.

"Magnus!" I yelled, with a push of my magic, gaining his attention. "It's me, Skylar."

The bear's long claws clicked over the edge as he peered down the cliff face. I searched his eyes for any hint of my uncle still dwelling beneath. In one powerful movement, he launched from the rocks, bounding down the falls to land across from me.

Still, to this day, it amazed me how quick and agile Magnus was in his bear form. Standing on all fours, his shoulder was taller than my stature, and when he raised up onto his hind legs, he towered over everything in his path.

His magic pulsed, and I desperately reached to cling to it. The bear shook his head from side to side, clearly agitated as he clawed at the loose rubble, pushing against the link I was attempting to create through our minds.

"Don't fight it," I said across the waters separating us. "Magnus, come back to us. We need you."

The bear grunted and roared, his agitation rising as my proximity to him narrowed. Inside, my animal was cautious, urging me to be patient. I stalked to my uncle's side, biding my time. My animal was ready to send me a boost of magic to help forge a connection to the human residing within.

"Father," Neera's plea echoed from behind, but unfortunately, it only seemed to make matters worse.

The bear reared up on his hind legs and released a massive roar, baring his teeth and turning his gaze on the wolves and panther waiting behind me. He saw them now and knew I hadn't come alone.

Shit, this was not the plan.

"Take her away," I commanded Rhea and Talon. *"He's seeing this as a threat to his territory. Move Neera back now!"*

"Skylar—" Neera began.

"No, Neera," I said, taking my eyes off Magnus. "Go with Rhea and Talon."

"No, Skylar— Watch out!" Neera screamed as Magnus charged through the river, heading straight for me.

I pivoted and dove to my left, leaping over a boulder to avoid the swipe of his massive claws that would have easily shredded my flesh to pieces. In a flash, a large figure challenging Magnus's size and strength leaped from the cover of the trees and slammed into his frame, forcing him backward into the shallows along the river.

Shaw was leaner than Magnus, but my friend had his own set of lethal teeth and claws to combat his larger foe.

"Shaw!" Neera screamed as he stood between me and Magnus, baring his teeth and matching my uncle's roar with his own.

I reached out to Shaw's mind. *"Don't hurt him."*

"Are we sure there's any Magnus left in there, Sky?"

"I'm positive there is," I spat back.

"Really? 'Cause the Magnus I knew would never harm you or Neera. And he just tried to kill you."

"Tried," I corrected as I joined Shaw along the riverbank.

"Skylar," he warned.

"I've got this," I answered, patting his shoulder as I entered the river. *"Stay here,"* I commanded this time, using my alpha powers.

His ears twitched. I could tell he was not pleased, but he would obey. He had no choice but to follow my command as his alpha.

"Magnus," I said aloud, searching for the well of power I used to force Gilen to submit, when I forced the basilisk to bend to my will.

The bear's jade eyes locked with mine, and I swear I saw a flash of something sparking in them. A lifeline. A sign that there was more to this creature, that there was a human soul buried beneath the animal standing before me.

"Magnus," I boomed, power laced with my words. "Shift."

The bear staggered, trying to fight against my command. I boldly stepped closer to the creature, pushing a wave of power around him. "Shift," I commanded once more.

There was a green shimmer of magic hovering over the back of the bear's shoulder hump. It trickled along its forelegs and across the rest of its body. Magnus was fighting me, but it wouldn't last. I was the true alpha of the Solace pack, and I was going to bring my uncle back.

"Magnus. Shift!" I roared, putting everything I had into this command.

The bear moved onto the opposing riverbank, collapsing onto the ground. The animal roared, the ground shook, and the waters rippled out in waves with a burst of magic. Its stare locked with mine, and then, I felt it.

In a flash, the body of a man appeared across the riverbank.

"Release Neera," I told Talon and Rhea.

"Father!" Neera screamed as she raced past me through the river, unhooking a cloak from around her shoulders and draping it over Magnus.

Rhea and Talon joined Shaw behind me as I slowly crossed the shallow river. Wading through the water, my heart raced as fast as a hummingbird's wings, and my limbs felt like they were jolted with a bolt of lightning from the sky. The power humming through me was remarkable yet foreign. I would need to learn to control this magic, and with time, I knew I would.

But, like always, time never seemed to be on my side.

"Father?" Neera said between sobs. "It's us. Neera and Sky." Her gentle touch migrated in soft circles across Magnus's back as he sat up and clutched the cloak around him.

"Magnus," I said as I knelt before my uncle.

His eyes snapped open to meet my gaze. The forest-green tint was vivid and sparkling with a storm of emotions. I could feel the depths of his sorrow through his stare, and it stole the breath from my lungs. The agonizing pain of losing his mate threatened to swallow him whole, yet... another emotion began to take hold.

A swell of pride breathed life into his features as his stare softened at the corners, a sheen of wetness coating his eyes as he blinked. He granted me a hint of a smile as he tilted his head and lowered his gaze.

"Alpha," Magnus said before raising his head to meet me.

"You can still just call me Sky," I teased as a beaming smile crossed my face.

"Sky," Magnus whispered as he smiled.

Neera and I leaped into his embrace, his arms encircling and pulling us tightly to his chest. I could barely breathe, but I didn't care. Magnus was back. I'd brought my uncle back.

"My daughters," Magnus said softly, keeping his hold tight around us. "Thank you for never giving up on me. And thank you for saving me."

I pulled back, tilting my head to look upon the face of the male who raised me. "You would never give up on me." I sighed. "So, I would never give up on you. I love you, Magnus."

"I love you, Skylar." He closed his eyes and reached out to give me another hug. "And you, Neera," he said, kissing her brow. "I love you both so much."

Having Neera and Magnus reunited was magical, and yet, there was a tinge of loss from the missing piece of our family that I knew would never disappear. I only hoped it would be easier to swallow as time passed.

"All right, what else have I missed?" Magnus asked. "You're our alpha now?"

"It appears that way," I said, moving my hand to the dagger strapped at my hip. "Let's catch you up on the journey back home," I said as we rose to our feet. "Solace awaits."

Chapter Thirty-Three

Skylar Cathal

Magnus dressed in the spare clothes Neera brought for him, and Shaw shifted to join us, embracing my uncle and exchanging words of confidence before we started the journey home.

I retold my stories about the trials and the state of the Inner Kingdom. Rhea and Talon remained in their wolf forms, listening and adding in their own details while we informed my uncle about all that had happened. And then, when we stopped to rest and take a drink from the river, I told my uncle about Daxton.

"Are you officially mated and marked?" he asked, glancing at my neck.

"No." I blushed, only *slightly* embarrassed about discussing a claiming mark with my father figure. "We haven't marked each other yet. I wanted to wait until I shifted to claim him as well."

"I see." Magnus stepped closer and sniffed my head. "That's why my bear didn't recognize you at first. You smell *different*."

"That's the first thing I said," Rhea chimed in, paired with Talon's laughter.

"That makes sense," I said, giving Rhea and Talon a sideways glance.

Magnus stroked his beard as he sat back. "I'm surprised I didn't see it before."

"I did!" Talon boasted with a playful yelp in his wolf form. *"And I'm never going to let Rhea forget it."*

"You have one..." Rhea drawled. *"One accurate hunch in twenty—"*

I closed my connection with them, chuckling to myself at their banter.

"He truly is your mate... Daxton Aegaeon?" Magnus looked at me with a pang of sadness in his eyes, for Julia's passing.

"Yes. But regardless of the bond, I would still claim him. I fell in love with him before I recognized the bond linking us together. He's—"

"He's the other half to your whole," Magnus finished with a firm nod of understanding.

"Yes." I smiled, sitting cross-legged in the snow near the winding river. "I need to return to the Inner Kingdom to finish the trials and not only free Daxton, but his people as well."

"His people?" Magnus questioned.

"The queen?" Shaw asked.

I nodded.

"She is a tyrant, literally sucking the lives out of her people so she can remain in power. Daxton and his brother Castor have a plan to overtake her with the help of their allies in Crimson City once the Heart is free."

Magnus gave me a firm nod. "I see."

"War is surrounding us on all sides." Neera sighed. "When will all this fighting stop? I hate this. All of it."

I reached out and grasped her hand. "I understand your frustrations. And feel the loss just as much as you do. But, if we do nothing in the face of injustice, then what kind of creature does that make us?"

Neera started off across the river.

"Peace is won, my daughter," Magnus said. "Won after many are lost. Doing the right thing now allows others who follow to have a brighter future."

"Will we join forces with the High Fae, Sky?" Shaw asked, drawing our attention.

"I believe they will help us, yes."

Shaw nodded. "Good."

"Who will oversee the pack in your absence while you complete the final trial?" Magnus asked. "You'll need to select a sub-alpha."

"I already have," I replied, meeting his stare.

Magnus reached up to scratch his head. "Are you sure?"

"Are you questioning your alpha's decisions already?" I teased, cocking my head to the side. "By all means, keep doing it. I mean, I'm new at this, and I'll need your guidance. But I'm certain about placing you in charge while I'm gone. Our people need your experience to navigate the threat of the humans before I return with help."

"Then you... and our pack shall have it," Magnus answered with his ironclad loyalty to our people shining through to his core.

"Are you all right, Neera?" Shaw asked my cousin, kneeling at her side.

"I'll... I'll be all right," Neera answered as she smiled sweetly. "Thanks for asking."

"Are there any other mating bonds I need to be aware of?" Magnus asked, his eyes darting between Neera and Shaw.

"No," Neera quickly answered, putting distance between them.

Shaw shook his head in agreement. "No, no, there's not."

"Okay, what's going on?" I asked Rhea. *"I know you know something about this."*

I opened the connection to include Talon, hoping he might also have some insight.

"I know lots of things... Can you be more specific?"

"Rhea," I growled.

"Okay, fine. Don't need to go all alpha on me. I'll tell you what I know."

"This is fun," Talon teased as Rhea nipped at his tail.

"They're kind of on a pause."

"A pause?" I questioned. *"All right, Talon, your turn. Elaborate, please."*

"Gladly." Talon chuckled. *"When you were preparing to challenge Gilen, Shaw spoke privately with*

Neera. I don't know exactly what was said between them, but after that conversation, they've kept their distance."

"It's complicated," Rhea added, *"with the lack of a mate bond between them. They both care for each other, but we all know Neera's thoughts about this. And Shaw, well..."*

"He doesn't talk about it as much, but I know he secretly longs for a true mate bond," Talon said. *"He'd swim against the currents of the crossing itself if it meant he could find his mate."*

I sighed. "I see."

"See what?" Shaw asked as he moved to sit beside me. I couldn't help glancing over at Talon and Rhea, and Shaw, being the observant person he was, one hundred percent noticed. "Ah, well, good. That saves me time and an awkward conversation with you later."

I arched my brow. "Really? You think it does?"

"What's going on?" Magnus demanded in a deep, thundering tone.

"Nothing." My lips were sealed. "Shaw, Rhea, and Talon looked after Neera when you were gone, that's all."

Magnus's stare turned to Shaw as he sniffed the air between them before shifting back toward his daughter. "That seems to be accurate."

"Shaw and I are not together," Neera admitted. "We're friends. And he helped me when Mother passed, and you were lost."

Silence passed between our group as Magnus hugged his daughter tighter to him.

"Then you have my thanks, Shaw," Magnus said with a single nod.

I reached out to Shaw's mind. *"You know what you're doing?"*

"I try to."

"Why are you and Neera—"

"Skylar," Shaw interrupted. *"There's a reason we're not mates. We can't see it right now, but we both agreed to take a step back. With everything going on, this isn't the right time. Our pack is on the brink of war with the humans. You're our new alpha. The trials are still unfinished. We need to focus on other responsibilities for the time being. If it's meant to be, we'll find each other again."*

"I..." I stopped, understanding that Shaw and Neera agreed to place the duty to the pack before themselves. A selfless act that I needed to respect. *"That's very selfless of you and Neera."*

"If it were a mate bond, however, there would be no question," Shaw answered, giving me a half-grin.

"Well, at least this way, you don't have to have that awkward conversation with Magnus."

"Thank the Gods above." Shaw sighed.

Chapter Thirty-Four

Skylar Cathal

By midday, we had returned to Solace.

My pack welcomed us with open arms, gifting me words of gratitude and respect for bringing Magnus home.

"Thank you, Alpha," they said repeatedly, the title still new and startling.

I imagined it would take some time before I adjusted to the new role and the responsibility it carried.

I walked up the familiar steps to the alpha's estate, now *my* estate. Gods, this massive complex was now officially *my* home.

I outstretched my hand to the large double doors and, for the first time, entered the manor as the *alpha*. Shaw and the others rushed past me as we entered the large gathering area, making themselves comfortable in front of the ever-burning stone hearth.

The house was abuzz with an array of staff members scurrying this way and that.

I was greeted with, "Welcome home, Alpha," and "Can we get you anything, Alpha?"

I shook my head and thanked each of them for asking. But by the fourth greeting and inquiry about whether we needed anything, my stomach had begun to rumble.

"Actually, can we please have something to eat?" I asked one of the kitchen staff I recognized.

"Of course!" she said with a beaming grin. "Any requests?"

"Beef stew sounds delicious, if you have anything like that," I replied. "Something to warm us from the inside out."

"I'll get started right away."

"Oh, and—" I called out before she walked toward the kitchen. "Could you pack some sandwiches as well? I'd like to hold off on the fish and rice for as long as I can, but don't tell Fjorda or the crew that little secret."

Her bright brown eyes seemed to drop, realizing that I would only be staying for this meal and then have to depart for the Inner Kingdom. "So soon?"

"The sooner I leave, the sooner I will return." I winked.

She nodded and mirrored my grin.

"I'll take a whiskey, please," Magnus requested. "And a double wouldn't be the worst thing if you could manage it."

"Same," Rhea groaned as she dropped onto one of the large sectionals near the roaring fire.

"Right away," the kitchen worker said with a kind smile. "Anyone else want something stronger?"

The rest of us shook our heads.

"Their loss," Rhea mumbled.

"We made stew for lunch earlier today. Rewarming it won't be an issue. It shouldn't take long."

"Thank you," I said. "Oh, and I'm so sorry... I've forgotten your name."

"It's Wren," she said with a nod.

"Like the songbird."

"You got it," she answered with a wide grin as a dark curl fell in front of her tanned face. "Although I shift into a wolverine, so that didn't exactly match up." Wren laughed. "Both my parents shift into birds, so that's where they got the name."

I couldn't help chuckling with her. "What a unique story. I think that's amazing."

Wren smiled. "You're amazing, Alpha."

"I haven't done much to earn that level of praise, Wren."

"But you have," she replied, looking at me with a sense of awe and respect that humbled me.

"Your words honor me." I tilted my head to her as she bent forward, kneeling and bringing her fist to her chest before rising to her feet.

"As do you, Alpha." Wren's smile was infectious. "Whiskey is coming right up, Beta!"

"That's no longer my title," Magnus rumbled. "But I'll take the drink regardless."

"Oh." Wren blinked. "Sure thing, right away," she said as she made her way toward the kitchen.

Talon joined Rhea near the roaring hearth as I sank onto the soft, cushioned couch across from them.

Tilting my head back, I gazed upward at the large wooden beams that stretched across the exposed interior. The craftsmanship of this estate was beautiful. I had always admired the intricate framework of this room that reached the top of the second floor of the three-tiered mansion. Shaw stretched out on the nearby chaise adjacent to the large floor-to-ceiling A-frame window as Neera curled beside Magnus.

"So, Magnus," Talon casually said. "Not Beta?"

Magnus meticulously rubbed at his temples with his finger and thumb, releasing a small groan. "No."

Talon glanced at his mate, who shook her head. "Then who is, Sky?"

"I..." My words trailed off at the sound of thundering feet practically leaping down the stairs.

"Magnus!" To my surprise, Alistar barreled through the manor, anxiously rushing toward my uncle. "Magnus, my friend!" he exclaimed as they grasped each other's forearms, looping the other around their shoulders.

With firm thuds on each other's backs, they pulled away, both sporting smiles of exhaustion for the traumas they'd experienced these past months.

"I'm glad you've returned."

"Me too," Magnus answered as they embraced each other once more.

Next, the sound of a rolling cart entered the room, drawing our attention.

"Told you it wouldn't take long," Wren announced as she pushed the cart behind the backs of the couches and reached for two glasses to hand to Magnus and Rhea.

I jumped up, hurried over to Wren, and eagerly scooped up a bowl of stew. Rhea and Magnus received their drinks, which they eagerly finished before filling their bellies.

"It's going to take time, but it's good to be back," Magnus said, his eyes scanning the second-floor landing. "How's Gilen?"

"Gilen's doing the best he can," Alistar said with a crease in his brow as they joined us. "He's not here at the moment," he said, looking at me. "I suggested he fly to the eastern border to help with the patrol. Some space will do him good."

"A wise decision," Magnus answered.

I gave my uncle a nod as I finished my first helping of stew and looked at Wren's cart to see if there was more. To my delight, she was already ladling another helping just for me.

"It's different." Alistar paused, his gaze cautiously wandering toward me before returning to Magnus. "Skylar could've killed Gilen. But thankfully, our newest alpha has a compassionate heart and spared him."

"I've been told," Magnus answered, finishing his bowl. Leaning back, he scratched his beard, a clear sign that he was agitated or possibly worried. Magnus sighed as he set his bowl on the side table, his shoulders tense and his brow furrowed. "I can't remain silent on this, Sky. It worries me that you spared his life in the challenge."

"I stand by my decision," I replied coldly, my shoulders straightening at the tone of my uncle's words. "We'll need Gilen in the battles to come."

To my surprise, on our journey home, I learned that Magnus did not agree with my decision to spare Gilen's life and accept his submission.

"There's a reason why a challenge results in—" Magnus began.

"He submitted," I cut in, my tone firm with an authority that would not be questioned. "I felt Gilen link with me, along with every other pack member that night."

"He did," Alistar added, defending his son. "I witnessed it."

Magnus kept his gaze set firmly on me, bordering on a challenge. Right now, this was the last thing I needed. But this was also why I chose Magnus to oversee the pack in my absence. His loyalty to Solace and the people within it was ironclad. However, the responsibility of protecting our pack now rested on my shoulders.

Magnus dropped his stare, his thoughts swirling around him like the frigid winter winds.

"Gilen won't cause an uprising," Talon said. "He wouldn't do that to Skylar. Not after everything that's happened."

I internally sighed, thankful for Talon's attempt to keep the peace.

"Except," Shaw added, lounging in the chaise by the window, "that's exactly what Magnus is getting at."

I focused my attention on Shaw, who was staring off into the forest outside the window, seeing his concern mimic my uncle's.

"Are you worried?" I asked. "About Gilen trying to retake the pack in my absence?"

"He wouldn't do it while you are away," Shaw answered. "That's not what I'm worried about."

"Then what?"

"He's smart, but his pride is also wounded," Shaw began. "Thankfully, that'll take time to heal. Once he recovers, however..."

"I see," I said, absently reaching for the dagger strapped at my hip. My fingers traced the cold steel in light circles, sensing a comforting pull of magic from the blade.

"My son wouldn't do that," Alistar announced with confidence. "Skylar's power is undeniable as our alpha. It is the shifter way. Gilen would never break our customs or laws when it comes to that."

I silently agreed, knowing Gilen was the rule follower, always had been. But were Shaw's and Magnus's concerns valid? Could this be his breaking point?

"I'll watch over Gilen," Alistar said. "And ensure he doesn't step out of line."

"He's stronger than you," Shaw countered. "How will you tame him if he tries anything while Skylar is away?"

Good question.

"He's still *my* son. We are all each other has."

And there it was.

I nodded in understanding.

"I'll help," Rhea said, leaning forward so her forearms rested on her thighs. "I'll keep an eye on Gilen and make sure he doesn't start anything or get any fucked-up ideas in his head."

I glanced at Shaw and then at Magnus with a half-smirk. Rhea was the perfect solution to this potential issue.

"I almost feel sorry for Gilen now," I said, giving Rhea a wink. "I assume Talon will be with you?"

Talon nodded. Even though he was not chosen as Gilen's beta, it was evident that he still held their friendship in high regard. He would be able to help Gilen, while Rhea would ensure he didn't start something I would have to finish.

I reached out to Talon's mind, gently brushing against it. *"I'm trusting you with this. Keep the peace as best you can. But—"*

"If he begins threatening your position as alpha, I'll do what I must," Talon answered.

I gave him a firm nod, returning my attention to the others. "This is a good plan. Knowing that all of you are watching over Gilen while I'm gone helps put my mind at ease."

Alistar turned his lips inward, the look of disappointment flashing across his face.

"You have anything else you wish to say, Alistar?" I asked with an even tone. One I had heard him use countless times in my youth when addressing us from a place of authority.

"No, Alpha," he replied. "I understand your reasoning."

"This is not a reflection on you, Alistar," I said.

His eyes softened. "I understand, and I thank you for your reassurance. When will you leave?"

The question hung in the air as wordless seconds ticked by like hours, silently swirling around all of us like it had a life of its own.

"As soon as I can."

I didn't want to leave my pack, but I had to in order to protect them.

Glancing down, I opened my hand to see the opal tattoo on my palm. Bringing it to my lips, I whispered, "Captain Fjorda of the *Opal*. I call upon your ship to ferry me back across the open sea. I call upon your aid in my final task of the trials."

A loud horn blasted and echoed across the lands, the ship and its captain hearing my call.

Chapter Thirty-Five

Skylar Cathal

Before leaving to meet the ship, I gave Magnus instructions regarding our people.

"I want the other Satellite packs to relocate to Solace. We have to assess our strengths to properly defend ourselves. We're stronger together than we are apart, and right now, we must regroup."

I had a sinking feeling that when I unlocked the Heart of Valdor, the humans would launch a full-scale attack on our people.

"I agree," Magnus said. "Our numbers are nothing compared to that of the human population, but—"

"But we're growing in power and magic the further I progress through the trials. Becoming a legitimate threat in their eyes," I replied, recalling Minaeve and Gilen meeting while I was recovering from the hunters' capture. "I believe the mages can sense this and are advising King Taran to make a stand and attack."

"The human king is scared."

"As he should be," I replied with a spark of my power rising to the surface. "I want to do all I can to prevent a war from happening, but—"

"But we'll be ready if our hand is forced," Magnus finished.

"Exactly. I believe the High Fae will also come to our aid."

"Hard to deny the champion any favor after you save their homeland."

"Indeed," I said.

"I'll help keep watch on the human forces gathering south of the trading post," Neera added, joining us near the doorway of the alpha's estate. "In my doe form, I can easily sneak between the brush and watch without being seen."

"It's dangerous work patrolling the borders like that, Neera," Magnus warned.

"I know," Neera said. "But it's the least I can do to help. I am more than capable of doing this. I'm tired of sitting on the sidelines and not contributing."

I nodded in agreement, proud of my cousin's bravery. "I agree, Neera."

Saying my goodbyes once more to Neera and Magnus damn near broke me. My heart ached as I watched them leave the manor.

Refusing to allow my tears to fall, I steadied myself to read the letter Castor gave me before leaving Silver Meadows. Rhea and Talon joined me on the opposing side of the room, quietly waiting to see if they could help in any way.

I began unfolding the note from Daxton when another folded piece of paper tumbled free, humming with a strange sense of magic. I recognized it as the enchanted parchment Castor and Daxton used to communicate within the Inner Kingdom, along with Castor's elegant handwriting.

Skylar,
How does fried roc taste?
-Castor

I laughed aloud, showing Rhea and Talon the letter before the ink magically disappeared.

"So, you write a message, and it'll appear on the other half?" Talon asked. "It's that simple?"

"Yes," I replied. "Simple but brilliant."

"What're you going to write back?" Rhea asked as I located a writing utensil.

Castor,
The feathers get stuck in your teeth. I wouldn't recommend it. I'm coming back—be ready.
-Skylar

I lifted my pen and waited for the ink to dry.

"Nothing's happening..." Rhea's voice trailed off as the ink disappeared. "Wow! That's amazing! Let me try."

"Rhea," I scolded. "It's not a toy."

"Well, it's flashy like one, and it does cool tricks. Try to argue against that."

"Rhea..."

"Fine, fine. I'll behave."

"Good." I chuckled, shaking my head. "'Cause I'm leaving this with you."

"What, me?" she questioned, arching her brow. "Why?"

"I trust you," I said, carefully folding the parchment and placing it in her hands. "Castor has the other half of this. Any message you write on here will go to him, and then he will be able to relay it to me." I grasped her hands, holding them tight. I had missed her company more than words could express over these past few months. "You're the best one to keep this safe, and I know you'll be the first to warn me if something is amiss while I'm away."

"Bet your ass I will." She grinned, giving me a big hug, followed by Talon wrapping his long arms around us both and squeezing until it was hard to breathe.

Once again, I stood on the familiar olivine crystallized shores of the green sand beach. And, once again, I had to say goodbye.

The *Opal* docked just beyond the cliffs, waiting outside the outer rim of the ancient volcano's caldera.

Captain Fjorda himself rowed a small boat onto the shoreline to ferry me aboard. The one I took to shore likely drifted off. His beaming smile was contagious as he came ashore.

"It's about time," he said as he leaped out of the boat and scooped me into a giant spinning hug. "Don't you dare tell Silver Shadow I hugged you." He chuckled, setting me down on the sand.

"Can't promise that," I teased.

"Then I'll make sure to seize the day." He looked behind me at the gathering of shifters on the towering cliffs. "Alpha," he said with a bow as he moved back to the rowboat. "When you're ready."

"I'm ready," I said, following in his footsteps. He seemed surprised, but I had already said my goodbyes.

It was heartbreaking to say farewell to my friends and family again. But at least this time, they knew I was returning with the final key to the trials. That the wilt would be gone, and our world would soon be free. My mind drifted as Fjorda pushed the boat away from the beach.

It was difficult to explain, but I could feel the essence of my people floating with me along the gentle rolling waves. Regardless of where I ventured, I knew I would hold this connection to them, carrying them with me as their alpha.

Chapter Thirty-Six

Skylar Cathal

Fjorda pulled on the oars as we glided through the waves with barely a whisper of a breeze in the cove.

As the boat splashed into the swirling blues of the surrounding waters, I glanced at my tattoo with the alpha's dagger clutched in my right hand.

Magically, following the same pattern as the others, the third star began to fill in. The final trial of the Heart of Valdor was complete with my departure from my pack lands. With the dagger, the third key to the trials, in my possession.

"So that's it?" Fjorda asked as his lean muscles flexed to pull on the oars that propelled us through the surf. "That's the final key?"

"It is." I kept my eyes fixated on my tattoo.

"Now comes the hard part."

"The hard part?" I repeated, tilting my head to the side and looking across at the captain.

"Now you have to find the Heart and unlock it. Any idea where it could be?"

"Not exactly," I said, sheathing the dagger. "But I have a feeling I'll know soon enough."

As we ventured farther out into the alcove, I reached into my pocket and prepared myself to finally read my mate's letter.

Daxton's handwriting beamed in bold black lettering with my nickname written across the outer folds. I opened it and began to read:

Skylar,

As you read this, please know I hated keeping this secret from you. I will always do everything in my power to keep you safe, regardless of the outcome. My beautiful spitfire, whom I love with every beat of my heart and breath in my lungs. Again, I'm sorry for keeping this from you. I know you wouldn't hesitate to sacrifice yourself to keep me from returning here. However, this was the only way.

Remember—I will find you. We will always find each other.

Love, Daxton

"Daxton will be acquiring the Heart's location soon enough," I said. "It's all a part of his plan... and the reason he allowed himself to be captured and imprisoned."

Fjorda's brow creased before arching wide with understanding. "The scroll?"

I nodded. "With the final star filling in on my arm," I said, holding it out for him to see, "it's also filled in on the scroll."

"They'll know you're returning to the Inner Kingdom and celebrate your success—the queen believing that your victory ensures her own."

"Exactly."

"But you won't be going to Aelius." Fjorda grinned. "I might know some friends who can help sneak you ashore once we cross the veil."

"I was hoping you did."

"I'll rendezvous with our correspondents within Crimson City and send word to our allies once we set sail."

"Good. Thank you," I said.

"Thank you, Champion," Fjorda answered with a nod of his head as we approached the *Opal*.

A long rope ladder was draped over the side, and I reached up and began the climb to the top of the railing. I swung my leg over and landed on the deck, with Fjorda following close behind.

"We set sail for Niamh Bay!" Fjorda announced to his crew. "The champion has won the final trial. The Heart of Valdor is all but ours! Our world is on the brink of freedom!"

Cheers erupted amongst the crew of High Fae, followed by a booming horn blasting across the seas. The long white sails were released from their ties, and the wind filled the sheets, carrying the ship out to the open sea.

"Oh, by the way," Fjorda said, "it seems you're not the only shifter sailing with us on the journey this time around." He tilted his head toward the opposite side of the deck.

"I see," I said. "Thanks."

The captain gave me a nod as he turned to oversee his crew.

I smiled as I marched across the decking, leaning over the railing as we gazed across the disappearing landscape. The scars along his arms gleamed in the rays of the setting sun. His hazel eyes were set firmly on the shoreline as his black hair stirred in the winds. Turning to look at him, a familiar magic churned in the air, like a key turning in a lock, and something just clicked.

"Alpha." Shaw's deep voice boomed over the splash and spray from the churning waters below.

"Beta," I replied.

Chapter Thirty-Seven

Daxton Aegaeon

"Wake up!"

I didn't even bother flinching at the command. I was exhausted. Beaten down to a shell of my former self. Fuck, I just wanted to close my eyes and dream about anything other than this shit hole.

"Gods above... *Males*."

The scolding annoyance was almost enough to make me laugh, but those joyful feelings didn't exist here. I didn't dare allow those emotions to enter my mind, for I knew Anjani and Rhett would only use them against me.

"Please, Daxton!"

The plea caused me to turn over, followed by a faint recognition of who the voice belonged to.

"Good, you're still in there."

Barely.

"*Zola?*" I rasped. "What—"

"Daxton," Zola interjected. "She's coming!"

She?

My eyes snapped open at the mention of her, at the mere hope of what Zola was insinuating.

"You'd better be right," I groaned as the chains clinked against my efforts to rise from the cold stone floor.

"I value my position as spymaster in your realm," she sneered from the shadows. "Have you known me to ever be wrong in such matters?"

I sucked in a pained breath, cursing the iron chains that counteracted my healing abilities. "Not yet." I gritted my teeth as I moved to steady myself. "But this would be one hell of a way to tell me you've found another job title."

"Those chains will be gone soon," Zola encouraged. "Do you have enough magic stored away for the escape?"

I sat upright near the bars of my cell, clutching my eyes tightly. "As much as I could manage," I replied, struggling to brush my matted hair from my face, disgusted with myself at the state I was in.

"Let's hope it'll be enough," she whispered.

"It is," I snapped, baring my teeth toward the corner where I knew she lurked.

"There's the famed warrior under the layers of dirt and grime." Zola snickered. "I was wondering where he was hiding."

Bending my knees, I leaned forward, hanging my head and shutting my eyes once more so the world would stop spinning for one gods-damned moment.

"The last session was... *eventful*," I mumbled. "Never a dull moment in this place."

"How lucky for you."

The sound of keys echoed off the stone as the footsteps of four guards sounded down the corridor. Silently, I signed for Zola to disappear without rattling the chains, but she was already gone before I gave the command.

The guards began unlatching the locks on my door, not saying a word as to why they were coming to retrieve me.

"Hello," I said with a weak grin. "Are we having another go around already? Lucky me."

"On your feet, High Prince."

"Manners for once," I exclaimed in a sing-song voice I'd heard my brother use countless times. "I'm shocked you spoke to me, let alone addressed me by my title."

"Now," one of them barked with a swift kick to my feet that still held lashes from the previous meeting with Anjani. "You need to be washed."

"So Anjani can see where she marks my body beneath the grime of my holding cell? I don't think so. I'll pass," I replied.

"Either come with us or—"

"Or what?" I snarled, turning my eyes upward to look at each of them. The Silver Shadow, not Daxton Aegaeon, stared them down.

I noticed the two in the rear flinch, moving a half step backward before righting themselves. A wicked grin of amusement crossed my face, knowing I made them nervous. Knowing that even in this state, I could still kill them with my bare hands.

"Please," one of the guards asked.

Twice in one day? What the fuck was going on in this place?

"There's a gathering tonight to celebrate. The champion, she—"

The lead guard in the front turned to glare at the newest member, and even in the shadowed cell, I could tell he wasn't pleased. Yet he only confirmed what Zola had said moments ago.

Skylar was coming.

Chapter Thirty-Eight

Daxton Aegaeon

"The three of you should know the routine by now." I grinned, leaning back and laughing like a madman. "I don't make this easy."

I donned the Silver Shadow mask, daring them to approach, enticing them to try and force me to cooperate without one of them sporting a broken nose as a result. I glanced at the guard on the right, who had the privilege of this the last time I was forced from my cell.

"Which is why we brought *him*."

On cue, my arms began floating upward, and it took every ounce of my self-control not to push back against the magic encircling my limbs.

"Ahh, telekinesis. Clever." Next, my torso lifted off the ground, and my entire body was eventually suspended in mid-air.

"Bring him this way," the lead guard said to his companions as I was carried from my cell.

After every inch of me was scrubbed clean, I was escorted with blades drawn and held at my throat, then dressed in dark-colored fabric with rich gold thread, the opposite of my realm's colors, with far too many layers and finery for my liking.

"This way."

I obeyed, for now.

The evening sunset pierced my eyes with a bite of welcomed pain. I had not seen the light of day since my capture, and I embraced the stinging kiss of the light as it blurred my vision.

We halted as the guards readied themselves to lead me into the throne room. I turned toward the window and placed my forehead against the stained glass. Feeling the warmth of the setting sun through the painted window was foreign yet also calming.

I was free of the dungeons. I thanked the Mother and Father for giving me the strength to return and once again come out alive.

Yet, if I needed to remain in the dungeons for Skylar, I wouldn't hesitate to return. I would do *anything* to keep her safe. I would endure all this and more to protect her.

"Wait here," one of the guards said. "I will notify the queen of her newest guest's arrival."

"*Oddly generous*," I mumbled, my attention returning to the sunset along the western horizon. "We will always find each other," I whispered on a pained exhale of breath, believing in those words just as much now as the first day I said them to her. "See you soon, Spitfire."

"Bring him in."

"Wouldn't it be better if I didn't have these chains around my neck, wrist, and ankles?" I asked. "It would portray a stronger sense of unity for the High Fae gathered here today."

The lead guard contemplated my request, and it seemed like he was on the verge of bringing my suggestion to the queen when Rhett entered the doorway.

Fuck.

"Don't let his charming facade fool you," Rhett said, pushing the gold curtain aside as he entered the narrow hallway.

"Brave of you to be in such confined quarters with me," I snarled. "I thought you were wiser than that."

I hated this male. He and Anjani could drown in the crossing and be forever lost inside an eternal doom for all I cared.

"Bravery is such an elusive trait," Rhett said.

"I'm beginning to agree with my mate," I answered coldly.

"And what, pray tell, did the champion say? She's such a colorful specimen."

"You speak in twisted riddles."

"Obviously," Rhett countered. "While your strength lies in your brawn, mine lies within my cunning intellect. With the gift of my abilities from the Gods themselves, I have the honor to see many things that others don't. The knowledge locked inside my mind would even, dare I say, make the Silver Shadow pause with dread and fear."

"You're tiresome, And not worth the time or energy to try and decipher."

Rhett scowled but quickly recovered. "We shall see." His icy stare darted to the guards on either side of me. "She's ready for him," he said to the guard at my right.

"Oh, joy," I mumbled as I was led into the throne room.

The thick golden curtain was pulled aside with Rhett strutting out before me. "Bring him to the high queen," Rhett instructed.

"Move it," one of them barked at me. "Or will we have to force you?"

"I'll behave."

Compelling myself to stand straight, I held my head high, erasing any trace of pain from my expression and ignoring the bite of the iron shackled to my body. I would don the mask I'd perfected over centuries in her presence. Becoming Silver Shadow once more.

The clinking sounds of my shackles echoed across the large room, ricocheting from the crown moldings of the decorative ceiling along the columns and floor-to-ceiling windows overlooking Sterlyn Lake. The gold decor was flashy and far too much—a testament to the queen's desire to showcase anything and everything she could to display her rule.

I was led through the crowds of alternating shades of green. The High Fae in attendance did not even bat an eye at me as I entered, continuing with their conversations and generally ignoring my presence. After all, this wasn't a new scene for them to witness.

Under Seamus's rule, the Aelius court was the largest in the Inner Kingdom, but we all knew Minaeve was the true tyrant. When my realm allied with Crimson City, we became an even greater threat to Seamus and Minaeve. And judging by the looks from the sea of green dresses and tunics in the crowd, this fact was no longer a secret.

At the base of the steps, I was given a single command, "Kneel."

I refused.

Chapter Thirty-Nine

Daxton Aegaeon

I stared into the turquoise eyes of my personal damnation, standing before a ruler I had never wanted—a queen as cruel as she was beautiful.

She wore her power like a crown, veiling her tyranny beneath hollow promises of protection and prosperity. Yet, I refused to bow to the dictator who craved dominance, wielding fear and control in the name of safeguarding the very people she claimed to protect.

A maddening smile crossed my lips, knowing she would be forced to relinquish her claim once Skylar unlocked the Heart of Valdor.

The queen I despised with every fiber of my being and breath I fought to take met my stare. The memories of her carnal touch darkened pieces of my shattered soul.

Minaeve tilted her head to the side. Her crown of three glimmering gems shimmered in the fae lights as she relaxed on her single golden throne. Her raven hair cascaded down her shoulders, curling around her waist near the exposed front of her silky midnight gown.

"She said kneel!" a guard grunted, slamming their foot into the back of my knee.

I took the hit, my expression unchanged as I slammed into the marble floor. My stare remained forward, locked with the false queen sitting before me.

"Still defiant and ungrateful, I see."

Seamus.

I didn't have to glance in the direction of his vile voice to know who was speaking.

Hold your tongue, Daxton, I warned myself, clenching my jaw so tightly it practically shattered my teeth.

Puppet. False king. Weak.

That was all Seamus was.

I almost... almost felt sorry for the poor bastard. Like Minaeve, he desired power and control, ruling as the high prince of a realm longer than me or Adohan.

"Seamus, my king." Minaeve said his name without tearing her gaze from mine. "We're here to celebrate the success of the champion. Of Daxton's *mate*."

The crowd surrounding me now gasped, shocked at my presence. I blinked, and Anjani appeared in the corner, laughing to herself.

Gods above. I fucking hated her mind tricks.

"Mate?"

"Can this be true?"

"A shifter mated to a High Fae?"

"The bond is unsealed, yet true," Minaeve said as she stood with Seamus at her side. "Is it not?"

I attempted to rise to my feet, but the guard behind me held me down with his mind. If these fucking chains weren't on me, I could easily break through his hold and unleash hell upon this place.

"Are you ashamed of a bond to a shifter-human hybrid?" Seamus dared to ask.

"Skylar Cathal..." I said in a low tone that mimicked the icy kiss of death. Cold, lethal, and, above all, terrifying.

The crowds immediately hushed around me, hanging on the silence I commanded.

"...is my mate."

"But you didn't claim her," Anjani taunted.

I turned my gaze to Seamus's second, my eyes blazing with hatred. "She's mine," I growled. "I should've killed you when I had the chance."

Seamus smirked behind the safety of his queen's throne. "Your mistake."

"One I won't make again." I glared, doing everything in my power to keep the magic that I stored away quiet in my center.

"Enough," Minaeve commanded.

"You've had your fun, cousin," Seamus replied, glancing at Anjani as he stroked a hand along Minaeve's chest.

Minaeve grinned wickedly. "Now, it's time to celebrate. We've won."

My eyes widened by a fraction, turning to look at the queen once more. The smile caressing her scarlet-painted lips sent a chill along my spine and twisted my stomach into knots.

"Rhett, bring forth the scroll," Minaeve announced.

Like the loyal servant he was to the Aelius court, Rhett brought the scroll and unrolled it on the raised platform, displaying the enchanted parchment for all to view.

"As you can see, the third star is filled in," Rhett announced, "which means the champion has completed the trial of the soul and has obtained the third and final key to unlock the Heart of Valdor!"

Cheers erupted from the throne room. My presence and the declaration of Skylar as my mate disappeared from the forefront of their minds.

I smiled to myself as the commotion of the throne room spilled over to Minaeve and Seamus. They descended the steps and joined the boisterous crowd behind me, wisely giving me a wide berth. Even the guards at my side were distracted, their watch on me slipping.

The celebration was so loud I almost missed the familiar presence gliding toward me. His dress coat was a dark shade of green with a hint of silver thread along the collar.

Silver, not gold.

"Excuse me," a drunken male fae said to the guards as he looped his arm around one of them. He fumbled with the glass in his hand and threw it back, draining the contents. Once finished, he carelessly dropped it on the floor, and I watched as the golden chalice rolled near me along the bottom step.

"Gods. Get off me," a guard grunted.

"I'll be needing that, don't you agree?" The male euphorically slapped a guard on the chest as he pushed forward, his steps faltering as he attempted to reach his fallen cup. To any onlooker in attendance here tonight, he was staggering in a drunken haze.

Except, he wasn't.

The pine scent of my homeland was muffled, but still present. As the male bent to reach for his goblet, the guards turned away to scream their own cheers of delight, celebrating my mate's victory. Celebrating and overlooking the male in front of me.

The silver in his hair was dyed brown to disguise his allegiance—*clever*. His dark eyes snapped open as he looked me over, quickly sobering as they met my stare.

Reece.

His hands discreetly moved to sign, "Be ready, my high prince. You'll recognize the diversion when it's time." He paused and glanced at the guards, who were still distracted. "It'll be hard to miss."

I widened my eyes, trying not to draw any attention by scanning the room behind me.

Reece oversaw multiple types of trade in Silver Meadows, and recently, one item, in particular, was known to make a bang.

"Your job is to reach the scroll and head toward the shadows behind the throne. Zola will be waiting to shadow-jump you out of here," Reece signed.

I nodded, motioning to the chains. There was nothing I could do with these gods-damned chains still on me.

Reece tripped over his feet and laughed aloud. The guards turned their attention to him for a moment, shaking their heads before looking away, convinced he was nothing more than a foolish, drunken guest of the Aelius court.

"Here." Reece retrieved a small metal key from his jacket pocket and slid it along the floor.

Thank the Mother and Father.

Reece was able to pickpocket this off the lead guard when he stumbled past them onto the steps. I was more than grateful for his fast hands.

Still kneeling on the floor, I began working on the shackles along my ankles.

"Hurry," he signed as he stumbled on a step while attempting to rise to his feet. "It sss-eeee-mmms I need a refill!" Reece announced to the guards, who thankfully didn't turn and look at him, which meant they still had their attention away from me.

I quickly unshackled the cuffs along my feet, gently placing them on the ground without a sound. Next, I adjusted the iron encircling my neck. The skin beneath it stung as I moved the ring around my collar to find the lock. This one was more difficult to manage because I couldn't see the keyhole.

"Would you look at those females?" Reece joyfully said as he found his feet and looped an arm around the lead guard, keeping their attention on the crowds behind my back.

There. The lock turned, and I unlatched the iron around my neck. With my hair loose, I was able to conceal the area until finally, I worked on my wrists.

I sighed with relief as the iron chains and shackles finally dropped to the floor. I remained utterly still, silently waiting for the distraction Reece said I wouldn't miss.

"You know what thi-ssss party need-sss?" Reece asked.

"Less wine?" One of the guards snickered.

"Never!" Reece scoffed. "What'sss the matter wiitttth youuu two?"

Looking at their feet behind me, I could tell Reece had his arms around their shoulders and pulled them toward him. "Some pizzazz. Some excitement," he said in a hushed, sober tone that gained their attention. "Some *fireworks.*"

I grinned. *Here we go.*

Chapter Forty

Daxton Aegaeon

The room erupted in pandemonium.

Sparks of color and fire soared in every direction. Guests began screaming as the loud booms and explosions from the colorful displays meant to burst high in the sky erupted in the enclosed area. Panic set in as the blasts set fire to the draping curtains, blew holes through the walls, and shattered windows. I could smell the familiar scent of blood beginning to pool. Those injured by the blasts screamed in pain as the others trampled over them in fear for their own lives.

I sprang to my feet, forcing my aching body to push onward. Ignoring the shooting pains along my limbs, I raced toward the pedestal where the scroll lay untouched near the golden throne. I covered my skin in a thin layer of ice as I leaped over a fallen column, burning in decadent golden decor.

I glanced over my shoulder, thankfully not seeing Reece anywhere. I sighed in relief, hoping he had an escape route already planned and was able to find it without getting caught.

Skidding to a stop, I reached for the scroll and rolled it before quickly tucking it safely into my shirt.

Pivoting around the pedestal, I dashed toward the throne only a few lengths away. The center was covered in crumbling rubble and destruction.

Fireworks indeed. The entire structure was falling apart. It wouldn't be long before the ceiling came crashing down.

As I dashed toward the rendezvous point, my heart thundered inside my chest. I didn't see her. Zola wasn't waiting behind the... *Fuck*. There were no shadows cast around the throne. With the room illuminated by the explosions and fires, there were no shadows for her to hide in.

Where the hell was Zola?

"*Gahhh!*" I roared, feeling the force of the queen's magic, collapsing on my knees in front of the throne. I grasped my head in agony as she attacked my mind, attempting to split it in two and force it to explode like the fires swirling around us all. "No!" I screamed.

My eyes sprang open, finding her in the center of the chaos. Her hair was a tangled mess. Her crown was missing, with a large open wound along her black brow. If I could have managed to laugh at the state she was in, I would've.

"You!" she sneered as her magic flared with her finger pointed in my direction.

I simply smiled at her. "Me," I answered, unleashing the power I struggled to keep veiled during these weeks locked in Minaeve's dungeons. A blast of ice erupted from my hands, shards of deadly, sharpened points targeted straight for Minaeve's blackened heart.

"No!" Seamus screamed as he rushed to shield Minaeve, using his magic to create a barrier to protect them.

My shards slammed into his magic, knocking them backward into the rubble.

"Z!" I roared, frantically searching for my spymaster.

Where the fuck was she?

I collapsed onto my hands and knees, praying she was near and this wasn't all for nothing.

"Queen Minaeve!" Rhett hollered as he raced across the room.

Seamus and Minaeve slowly rose to their feet, ignoring Rhett's presence. Their eyes were solely locked on me. My heart began racing as Rhett bent to pick up Minaeve's fallen crown—his eyes turning stark white.

"Give that back to me!" Minaeve snatched the crown from his hands and placed it on her head.

Rhett remained still as the frantic screams and cries of the injured surrounded him, his vision slowly returning to an all-knowing deep-blue stare.

I watched him carefully. His emotions were quickly concealed, disguising any reaction to what he saw. But he wasn't fast enough to conceal it entirely.

"Of course," Rhett said, lowering his gaze and kneeling amongst the rubble. "I'm so sorry, my queen."

Another explosion boomed on the far side of the room, collapsing the main doors and trapping those of us who remained inside.

"Zola!" I roared once more.

My desperation rapidly grew as fear began to encircle me like a vice.

No, I told myself. *Fuck. No!* I would *not* fail. I refused to.

I needed to get the scroll to Skylar, ensuring that she didn't fall into Minaeve's hands and become a pawn in her quest for power. The primal need to protect my mate drove me past my exhaustion, urging me not to give up.

"Daxton!" Off to the side, cloaked in the shadows near the corner, I found Zola. Her eyes were wide with fear, her voice laced with panic.

Another explosion thundered in the throne room. The vibrations of the blast knocked everyone off their feet while vibrant colors danced over their heads. Sparks of energetic flames spiraled in different directions, causing everyone to take cover.

"Hurry, Daxton!" Zola called out. "I can't—"

"I know!" I yelled as I crawled toward the shadows.

Zola couldn't chance leaving her position. Her magic only remained undetectable as long as she stayed in the shadows.

With my power completely drained, I struggled to drag myself across the floor. Every muscle in my body screamed at me to stop. Begged me for a release.

My only solace was the hope of seeing Skylar again. When I would be able to hold her in my arms, and by the grace of the Gods, I would never let her go.

"Daxton!" Zola screamed. Her arm extended past her protective hideaway.

"Seize them!" Seamus commanded. "Before they escape!"

I forced my limbs to propel me forward. My roar of pain filled the room as I lunged for Zola's outstretched hand.

"Gotcha." Zola gasped as she helped pull me into the shadows.

Once my feet were tucked into the corner, Zola's magic encased us, transporting us outside the palace and away from the screams of terror and destruction.

The kiss of cold night air caressed my beaten body and felt like a gift from the Gods themselves. Before I could take a full breath, however, Zola jumped us into another shadow.

And again.

And again.

And... again.

Fifteen fucking jumps.

Each one twisted my stomach, making my body feel like it was being pulled through a hailstorm with gale-force winds. Zola's magic was a *gift* from the wilt.

Traveling within it held unpleasant side effects that I was unable to combat with my power drained. Each jump felt like an assault.

We finally came to a stop, and even in the dead of night, the waves of heat suffocated me. I fell to the floor, my eyes rolling to the back of my head as my vision began to blur.

"Hey!" Zola's voice was panicked. "Wake up!" she roared. "Adohan! Idris!"

I heard footsteps frantically speeding across the floor.

"Dax!" Adohan gasped. "Send for the healers! Quickly now!"

The world began to slip away. My limbs felt like slabs of stone as my breathing became labored. I'd drained my well of magic to the point of burning out, giving more than I was able to sustain. Only once had I felt this weak, so close to the crossing that I could feel the sprays of water from the river itself.

"Stay with us, Daxton." Idris's voice was soft and comforting. "Skylar is at the veil! We just received word from Fjorda. She's almost here... Hold on. You must hold on." Her plea was hopeful.

"Skylar," I rasped. "Tell her—"

"No," Adohan interjected, kneeling at my side. "Don't you dare say another fucking word. You tell her whatever you need to when you see her yourself."

I huffed a laugh, even though it pained me to do so. I tried to reach for the scroll tucked into my shirt, but despite my best efforts, I failed miserably.

Adohan noticed my feeble attempt and reached out to take the scroll. "You did good, my friend," he said.

"One more day, Dax," Idris encouraged as the sound of footsteps entered the room. The healers were already preparing some kind of concoction to try and heal me. "You just have to last one more day."

One day.

"Skylar will be here, Daxton," Zola said, quietly kneeling near my feet. "Keep fighting or else she'll kill you for giving up on her."

"*One day,*" I repeated.

I could manage that.

Chapter Forty-One

Skylar Cathal

"Are you sure about this, Sky?" Shaw leaned against the railing, his gaze narrowing as he looked across the vast ocean. "'Cause I'm not."

"I believe it's a reality we must face and can no longer ignore." I braced myself against the increased swaying of the ship as the crisscrossing winds near the veil pummeled the churning waves. "I don't see another option."

"They won't like it."

"Who exactly?" I asked as I steadied myself.

"The elders." Shaw pushed off the railing and sat across from me on the deck. His back rested against a barrel of wine we were tempted to drain after circling back to this conversation yet again. "Run me through your thought process once more."

"We're outnumbered," I said, internally sighing as I moved to sit upright. "If war is truly at our doorstep with the humans, they will slaughter us based on that fact alone. We're more powerful, but that won't last against the constant bombardment of never-ending troops."

"I understand that part," Shaw growled. "I've been in the thick of that very fight myself."

"I know," I answered with a narrowing glare at my beta.

"Keep going." Shaw took a deep breath, running through the different scenarios in his mind and thinking of every possible outcome.

"We need allies," I said.

"And the High Fae, who are at war within their own kingdoms... are the solution?"

I narrowed my eyes at Shaw in annoyance. "We help them, and they will help us in return."

"You must be certain about this, Skylar. Asking our people to abandon their homes is—"

"I know," I cut in, fidgeting with my hands. "An alliance with the High Fae is obtainable. I know Silver Meadows will welcome our pack, and I believe Crimson City will as well."

"But is the best solution to abandon our homeland?"

"The solution is to ferry our people to safety," I said. "There's no point staking claim to a land if the people inhabiting it are slaughtered trying to defend it." I slammed my fist into the deck as Shaw quieted, listening intently. "There are only a few thousand of us left. That's it, Shaw!" I exclaimed, rising to my feet to stand above him. "That's not enough to fend off the tens of thousands of soldiers King Taran has at his disposal, along with his hunters and mages."

"Go on," Shaw said.

"And not all of us are warriors. Not everyone will be able to fight on the front lines." Shaw nodded as I continued. "Shifters once called the Inner Kingdom home... It's time for our people to return. If war with the humans unfolds and they unleash a full-scale attack, we may have no other choice but to retreat or die."

"Some may choose to fight and die for Solace, Sky."

"I'm aware." I sighed. "That's what frightens me the most. The stubborn pride of our people will end up killing them faster than the wilt."

"Will you—"

"I'm prepared to enforce an alpha command if I must," I said with a firm stare.

Shaw nodded. "Good. It might just come to that."

"I hope it doesn't."

We were silent for a long while, with the evening sky blackening against the setting sun. We tirelessly worked through different strategies for defenses and attacks until I settled on this alternative plan.

"You won't have much pushback from me with this idea," Shaw said. "I agree with the logic of it."

"What?" I cocked my head at him. "Now you tell me? This whole time, I thought you were against this idea from the start."

"It's my job to make sure you're confident in your decisions for our pack, Sky." He gave me a half-smirk as he crossed his arms at his chest. "I've been on the front lines with Talon and Rhea, fighting against only a fraction of King Taran's forces, and you're right. We don't have the numbers to take on the humans alone."

"So, I'm not crazy."

"Now, don't get ahead of yourself." Shaw laughed. "I didn't say that."

I scowled at my beta. "Really?"

"Crazy can be a good thing." He winked. "Keeps everyone around you on their toes."

"I strive to entertain," I said with a melodramatic bow that made Shaw laugh.

"What performance did I miss?" Fjorda asked, joining us on the deck.

"Nothing," I answered. "Just some pack business."

"Very well," Fjorda answered. "I've come to inform you that I sent word to Crimson City about our impending arrival."

"Perfect," I said with a grin. "Also, you have impeccable timing… because you're just the male I wanted to see."

Fjorda paused and gave me a skeptical look. "Why am I now nervous?"

Shaw chuckled, stretching his arms and rising to his feet. "It's her crazy streak. Thankfully, it comes in handy more often than not."

"Anyways, I have a favor to ask, Fjorda," I said in a more serious tone.

He tilted his head, curiosity spiraling in his alluring emerald stare. "Now I'm intrigued."

"Good. 'Cause I'm hoping you're just as wild as the sea and possibly daring enough to pull this off."

Chapter Forty-Two

Skylar Cathal

"Your beta didn't exaggerate," Fjorda said, glancing between us. "But what you ask is not outside the realm of possibility."

"Can you secure other ships to sail with you? Enough to carry all my pack?"

"I have a fleet that docks on Starfall Island," Fjorda said, the corner of his mouth turning upward with a wink. "Did you really think I only oversaw the *Opal*?"

I was about to answer when he held up his hand.

"Don't bother." He sighed with a half-smile.

I chuckled. "So, you'll help us then?"

"I see this as a mutual benefit for your people and mine," Fjorda replied, extending his hand. "Heal the wilt, and you, Alpha of the Solace pack, will have the aid of my ships and the crews to ferry your people across the sea."

I grasped Fjorda's hand with a beaming grin. "Thank you."

"Thank *you*, Champion," Fjorda replied.

"But the veil?" Shaw asked. "Won't it prevent you from sailing through?"

"I believe it will fall after the Heart is unleashed and the wilt is destroyed," I answered.

"And then my ships will set sail."

"What if it doesn't?" Shaw asked.

"So negative," Fjorda teased. "Do you always have such a dark outlook?"

Shaw frowned. "I'm cautious. Unlike you," he said, glancing at me. "You're likely to act on the first thought that enters your head."

"Which is usually a good idea."

Shaw sighed. "Uh-huh."

"Can't deny it." I winked.

"Captain!" Fjorda's first mate called out from across the deck. "The veil. We're here."

"The ship awaits your key, Champion," Fjorda said, sweeping his arm to the side. "You part the way, and I'll steer us through."

I nodded and began making my way toward the front of the ship, with Shaw following close behind.

"You ready for this?" I asked, glancing over my shoulder at Shaw.

"As I'll ever be," he answered. "So, the dagger will cut through its magic?"

"That's the theory."

"*Theory?*"

"A well-tested and proven theory," I countered. "The second key opened the veil. Why wouldn't the third?"

"Didn't it dissolve? Or disappear?"

"Yes," I said, reaching the front of the ship.

"And don't you still need this alpha's dagger to unlock the Heart? What if it—"

"Shaw!" I said, cutting him off. "The alpha's dagger can cut through *anything*. And *I*... am wielding it. I have enough power to do this."

Shaw stopped and gave me a toothless grin. "As you say, *Alpha*."

I didn't miss the cunning gleam in his eye nor the smugness in his expression.

"Beta," I said with a firm nod.

Turning to the crisscrossing winds of the open sea and the twinkling ebony sky scattered with stars above our heads, I readied myself to pass through the magical barrier separating our worlds. It was just as I remembered. Unable to find the veil with my sight alone, I closed my eyes to search for it with my magic.

"This is..." I paused as I felt Shaw come to my side. "Strange."

"How so?"

"The veil is barely there."

"You said it was connected to the trials and the Heart, right?"

"Yes, but—"

"But," Shaw began, "doesn't it make sense that it's weaker?"

It did. However, the reality of this fact was more daunting than I had imagined. "I believe anyone with a thread of magic could pass through now. Which means the wilt—"

"The wilt will spread even faster," Shaw said.

I turned to him and nodded. The fear in my beta's eyes reflected my own. If I didn't reach the Heart in time, the wilt might very well destroy our home before we had a chance to fight for it. With the veil gone, the dark magic consuming Valdor would undoubtedly spread like wildfire.

"No turning back now," I said, steadying myself against the spiraling winds.

Holding out the dagger, I felt the blade pierce through the magic of the veil, creating an opening for Fjorda to sail his ship through.

"It's beautiful," Shaw whispered.

"It's nothing compared to the first time I crossed with Daxton." My heart ached at the mention of his name. "That's when I first kissed him."

"You... *kissed* him?" Shaw asked.

"Yeah, why?"

"Nothing. Just surprised it took that long."

"He was being a *gentleman*."

Shaw cocked his brow at me. "I don't need the details to deny *that* fact. Your scent gives that one away."

I stuck my tongue at him. "Prude."

Gods, I was beginning to remind myself of Castor. I smiled to myself at the thought of him and hoped he was all right. I hadn't received anything in return on the parchment attached to Daxton's letter before I left, which wasn't surprising, but it still caused me to worry.

Shaw huffed a laugh, his toothless grin spreading to the corner of his mouth. "Perhaps I'm just a little jealous."

"Really?" I rasped as we made the final push to pass through the veil.

"Really," Shaw replied in earnest. "You found your mate, Sky. That's not a guarantee for us in this life, and I'm happy for you."

I could see the longing he had to find his own mate one day, not missing the disappointment that he likely felt when Neera wasn't his.

"Don't count yourself out just yet. If I can find mine, then—"

"You're right." Shaw smacked the railing with a nod. "If *you* managed to find yours, mine must be just around the corner."

"Ha-ha-ha." I bumped his shoulder.

"You'll find your mate, Shaw."

"I know." He winked, forcing a smile.

Shaw turned his attention toward the shoreline, taking in the sight of the Inner Kingdom for the first time. His eyes widened as I sheathed the dagger at my hip, understanding the look of dread on his face all too well.

"Even the sand is black," Shaw whispered.

"It is," I answered. "Hard to see, isn't it?"

"That can't happen to Solace. That just can't—"

"It won't, Shaw." I reached out to calm his panther's anxiety spilling over into him. His eyes snapped to meet mine, and I drew a deep breath. *"It won't happen.*

I swear I will do everything in my power to prevent this. I'm ready. I'm willing." I said to my beta, my dear friend.

Refusing to allow my nerves take control I grounded myself in the knowledge that once the Heart was unleashed, everyone I loved would be safe. Our world would be free.

Shaw nodded. *"Only you can."*

"Fate has guided me to unite our two worlds and bring Valdor together again."

"I count myself lucky to be on this journey with you, Alpha."

I smiled at Shaw, thankful to have him with me, for his friendship and unflinching support.

"Let's go find Fjorda and figure out how we're getting onto the mainland," I said. "The *Opal* is too recognizable, and I fear the queen will have spies watching and waiting."

"She'll know you've completed the third trial, right?" Shaw asked.

"Yes," I said as we approached the ship's wheel. "And Daxton should have the scroll and be somewhere safe right now."

"Can you feel the bond or his magic now that we're inside the veil?"

I paused, "It's weak, almost like a whisper. Easy to overlook if I wasn't trying to search for it," I said, biting my lip. "And that fact alone terrifies me. Daxton was in the prison cells beneath Aelius... I know she drained his magic, tortured him—" I couldn't finish the thought, let alone the words.

Shaw placed a hand on my shoulder. "Easy."

"I know he's alive," I whispered, tears threatening to fall from my eyes.

"If he's your mate, I have no doubt."

"And then," I said, straightening my shoulders, "when I find him and make sure he's in one piece, I'm going to kill him for keeping this whole *plan* a secret from me."

"There she is." Shaw laughed. "Come on, let's find Captain Fjorda."

Chapter Forty-Three

Skylar Cathal

"On second thought, I'm not a fan of this plan," Shaw said in a shaky voice as he peered over the side of the ship.

"Why?" Fjorda asked with a raised brow. "Afraid of gettin' wet, kitty-cat?"

Shaw's deep growl rumbled the decking beneath our feet. "No."

"The water nymphs... You do realize they eat anyone they take under the waves? *I* was almost killed by them after the first trial."

"Ah, but who was it that vowed you would be unharmed?"

I paused, blinking against the shadows of the evening. "Their... their king."

"There is a water nymph king?" Shaw grumbled, palming his face with a weighted sigh. "Any other royalty I need to be aware of while I'm here?"

"King Malek," I answered, ignoring Shaw's complaining.

"Exactly!" Fjorda stepped to the railing and placed his fingers to his lips, releasing a long whistle that rose and fell in two swift breaths. "Prepare yourself for a trip under the waves."

My stomach turned as we waited. I recognized the familiar red-orange coloring of a scaled tail as the king of the water nymphs appeared along the surface.

"Champion," Malek greeted me with a knowing smile. "Glad to see I was right in sparing your life that day. You've done well for Valdor."

"You'll have one more to take with you!" Fjorda hollered over the railing.

Malek tilted his head to the side and glanced at Shaw. "Ahh, another shifter."

"This is Shaw. He's my beta," I answered. "It's good to see you, King Malek. And thank you for your aid."

"It is our pleasure. Hold on for a moment." The water nymph king nodded before he dove under the waves. When he reappeared, a beautiful raven-haired female with green scales and bright eyes swam at his side. "My queen, Iara, will escort your beta while I ferry you."

"Lovely as always to see you, Your Highness," Fjorda said, coming to my side, his eyes falling on the queen.

"Likewise, Fjorda," Iara answered, her angelic voice singing over the crashing waves under the enchanting moonlight. "May the seas be in your favor, and the winds watch over your ships."

"And may the grace of the sea be with you," Fjorda replied, bowing to the king and queen.

"You're familiar with them," I said.

"Yes, Champion," Fjorda replied. "Do you remember our conversation last week before setting sail through the veil? About—"

"I do," I quickly answered.

"She was..." Fjorda paused. "She *is* their daughter."

My eyes widened with surprise. "Their daughter was your mate?"

"*Is*," Fjorda corrected. "She is. Not even death itself can change that fact. My heart belongs to the sea from which she came, while my soul is anchored to hers. No matter where that soul is."

For a heartbeat, I witnessed the sea captain's sorrow emerge before swirling beneath the crashing waves of his caged grief.

"If my mate, Andrea, is no longer among the living, then she waits for me at the crossing."

"Waiting for you?"

"Yes," Fjorda said with a sad smile. "In our culture, fae believe when one mate passes on, they wait for their other half. They do not cross the great river to be with the Mother and Father until their mate can cross with them. A bond that stretches across eternity itself."

"That's..." I paused. "Beautiful."

"We must hurry," Malek cautioned from the churning seas below. "Word of your success in the trial of the soul has spread throughout the Inner Kingdom."

"Hold on," Shaw said, shaking his head. "How will we make it that far under the water?"

"Well," I began, "there's no time for the details of their magic, but they exhale into your mouth under the water, and you can breathe."

"And that's after we're already under the water?" Shaw didn't seem convinced.

"It's the only way to get you onto the mainland without raising suspicion," Fjorda said. "While you two go with the water nymphs, I'll sail to Starfall Island."

"The queen will believe we're still on board and returning to Daxton's territory," I added. "When in reality, you'll be gathering ships to sail to Solace." I fixed my bow across my back before securing the dagger strapped at my side.

"I know," Shaw groaned uneasily. "It's just that—"

"Come on," I said, grasping his arm as Fjorda moved the railing aside. "Don't overthink this. Just jump!"

I pulled Shaw with me as we leaped into the ocean, splashing next to Malek and Iara. Before we could resurface, Malek pulled me into his arms under the waves. His lips gently pressed over mine as he gifted me his magic, allowing me to breathe under the cerulean waters cast in the shadow of the clouds hovering in front of the beaming moon.

"It won't last long," Malek said as he turned to Iara, who finished gifting her magic to Shaw. "Let's go."

Tucked safely under their arms, the water nymphs gripped us tightly as the king and queen beat their magnificent tails, speeding off into the darkened abyss.

I could barely make out the surrounding ocean, the depths of which disappeared underneath us in an obscured trench of mystery. I grasped Malek's arm, not wishing to fall from his hold and be trapped in the open seas.

"I've got you," he whispered with a chuckle. "We need you to finish these trials. I wouldn't dare drop you into the abyss below."

"That's reassuring," I mumbled.

"It won't be much longer," Malek said.

The sea's sandy bottom began encroaching beneath us, and relief washed through me at the sight of it. We meandered along the tan sands. The powerful tails of the nymphs propelled us through the seas with ease, riding the natural flow of the waves that crashed along the shoreline.

Chapter Forty-Four

Skylar Cathal

Breaching the surface, I gasped, gulping a full breath of air. A second later, Shaw broke through the waves behind me, safely tucked under the queen's arm.

"I forget how difficult the transition from water to land is," Malek said. "You'll adjust in a few moments."

"You..." I rasped between coughs. "You don't say." My lungs burned as he released me onto the beach, water spewing between my heaving breaths.

King Malek's magic retreated from my system as I hurled water onto the rough sand, shaking as I steadied myself on my hands and knees. Shaw was not much better. Glancing behind me, I could sense a rise in his magic. His animal was close to the surface, ready to break through and force a shift in response to his distress.

"You all right?" I called out. "I don't know if your panther would have fared much better underwater." I spat the horrible taste of seawater from my mouth.

"*That was fucking horrible*," Shaw answered, violently coughing, followed by hacking noises as he tried to breathe.

"I hated every minute of that," he rasped. "Never again, Sky. *Never.*"

"Noted," I agreed. "But you've got to admit, it was effective."

"I see your next transport is already waiting," Malek said, motioning toward the large rock-faced cliffs trailing along the beach. "This is where we part ways."

I turned in the sand. "Thank you to you both," I said.

"Return our favor with your victory, Champion," Malek replied with a grin as a flash of orange and green splashed in the waves, disappearing beneath the night and the sea.

"What *now*?" Shaw groaned. "Please tell me it's a horse. Or at the very least something on land."

"Half-right," I grinned, recognizing the neigh and flaps of wings.

A dark-skinned rider dismounted a pegasus with a rusted auburn-colored coat. A bright, beaming smile stretched across his face, with his dreadlocked hair flowing behind him as he raced toward Shaw and me.

"Skylar!" Astro called out, reaching to help me onto my feet.

He pulled me into a strong hug, his fire magic warming me from the bite of cold night air and my soaked clothes.

"Good to see you, Astro," I said. "Finn didn't come with you?"

"Nah, he doesn't have the stealth or finesse with the pegasi like I do. Father sent him to oversee our troops marching south."

I raised my brows in surprise, and Astro nodded, a smirk creeping along the corner of his mouth.

"Didn't think we would be sitting idly by on the sidelines, did you?"

"No," I said with a determined grin. "Not one bit."

Astro's eyes darted beside me toward the drenched dark-haired shifter at my side.

"This is Shaw. He's my beta."

Astro turned to assess Shaw, offering him a hand to stand on his feet in the gentle waves. "Nice to meet you. What kind of animal do *you* turn into?"

"Strange question to ask someone you just met," Shaw replied, accepting Astro's hand.

"Just curious," Astro answered. "I've never met one of you who could actually shift."

I straightened. "You've only ever met me?"

"Right, so, naturally, I had to ask," Astro said. "Why wouldn't I want to know?"

Shaw seemed uncertain.

"So," I teased, speaking into Shaw's mind. *"Are you going to tell him or just shift and show him?"*

"There's no need to frighten the High Fae. I need to make a good impression if you're the only one of our kind he's met," Shaw said, making me chuckle.

"A panther," Shaw stated, closing our connection.

"A very large panther," I corrected. "His back stands just as high as your pegasus, if not taller."

"That's... oddly terrifying," Astro said with raised brows.

"You're younger than Daxton and Castor, aren't you?" Shaw asked, looking Astro over.

"Those old piles of bones. Ha—yeah. This is the first trial I've seen. High Fae stop aging once we turn twenty-five and our magic settles. Nice perk, am I right?"

"Thankfully, it doesn't diminish his ability to work with the pegasi." I glanced toward the magnificent beasts, and my stomach dropped. Astro was the only one here. "Where is Daxton?"

"I'm here to take you to him," Astro turned, his dark eyes churning with a hidden secret. "He's—"

"Tell me he's safe!" I exclaimed, frantically grasping Astro's shoulders.

"He is," he replied quickly. "He is, but... he's injured."

My heart skipped. The sand beneath me felt like it was falling away to nothing as I floated outside my body. I could barely swallow, let alone form a coherent thought.

My mate was hurt. Daxton was hurt.

Without hesitating, I ran to mount a pegasus. "Shaw, hurry up and get on the other pegasus. Astro, lead the way."

Shaw didn't argue, sensing my urgency.

Astro followed my lead as he leaped onto his red stallion's back. "I brought the three swiftest mounts in the herd."

"Good," I rasped. "We won't be stopping."

"I figured as much," Astro said, turning to Shaw. "Are you going to be able to keep up?"

"I don't believe I have much of a choice."

"That's the spirit." Astro grinned. "You'll catch on quickly with those feline reflexes, right?"

"He'll be fine," I said with a twinge of impatience. "Now, let's go." I kicked my pegasus, angling the reins to encourage him into the sky.

"I'm coming, Daxton," I shouted through the bond tethering me to him. *"I'll find you."*

Chapter Forty-Five

Skylar Cathal

The blistering heat from the sun beat across my back as I urged my mount through the open sky.

Astro thankfully slowed his pegasus to assist Shaw. I couldn't keep myself from barreling through the clouds at a reckless speed to reach him, to reunite with *Daxton*.

The high desert realm of Crimson City gleamed in the distance, its unique red sandstone buildings contrasting with the surrounding landscape. However, I ignored the sight of the city's beauty. I could feel the pulsating tug of our bond pulling me closer. The overwhelming sensation in my heart grew with each beat of my mount's wings as we soared past the rolling hills.

"Go!" Shaw screamed inside my mind. *"You need to go to your mate. Hurry. I'll be fine with Astro."*

"Thank you," I said, grateful for my friend's understanding.

Just as before, when Daxton was ensnared by the harpy and dragged into the wilt, I didn't need anyone to tell me where to find him. I could feel his magic.

My pegasus naturally flew toward the paddocks below Adohan and Idris's home, gracefully landing at a canter before extending its wings to help slow our momentum. Once its hooves touched the dirt, I leaped off its back and raced toward the raised plateau. My heart thundered inside my chest, along with my animal's power, urging me to push past the riding pains in my legs and race up the steps.

He's here.

This was not some cruel trick or a false hope. I could sense him. The faint tether linking our souls pulled taut through my center, instinctively guiding me—leading me to my mate. I leaped up the final steps, with my healing magic prickling beneath my skin, ready to heal whatever wounds Daxton had endured.

I would first heal him, kiss him, and then... Then, I would scold him for being a stubborn fucking idiot and placing himself in that kind of danger, for once again becoming the tortured hero and disregarding his own self-preservation.

"Daxton!" I screamed as I barreled through the open halls.

The airy atmosphere of this fortress carried my words across every inch of the estate. Anyone walking the corridors parted ways, giving me a clear path.

The scent of pine and cold mountain air encircled me, confirming where my instincts were guiding me. My animal erupted inside my center, urging my feet to move faster. I reached for the golden handle of a familiar large double door, recognizing the room we stayed in together the last time we were here.

As the door swung open, my eyes immediately drifted to the large white linen bed in the center of the tan-walled room, decorated with elegant red fabric highlighted by the heated sun. Tucked safely in the bedding was the sole owner of my heart, the only person who could ever claim me as their true mate. The soul I would sacrifice my life to save—without hesitation. The being I would always find.

"Daxton." I gasped as I flung my bow over my shoulder.

My body seemed to drift toward him, my feet barely touching the floor. He was unconscious, likely put into an induced sleep to help aid his healing.

"Dax," I sobbed, no longer able to hold back my tears as I melted next to his bedside. "I'm here," I said with a shaky breath as two healers wisely slipped out, giving us the room. "I'm not used to sitting at your bedside like this," I said with a half-hearted laugh. "This is horrible..."

Wet droplets dripped down my face as I beheld the sight of my mate. His face was bruised, with bandages covering gashes along the tops of his shoulders, likely littering his back with deep cuts to his skin. I reached out and gently cradled his broken hand in mine.

He'd been tortured.

A pound of flesh paid for his crimes against taking Anjani's hand in my defense.

"I'm here, Dax," I whispered again. "I've found *you*."

I gently cupped his cheek before tucking a strand of silver-ebony hair behind his pointed ear. He was beautiful, even in this state, even with his storm-gray eyes shut to the world.

"Daxton," I said, holding a captive breath as I pressed my brow to his. "I've won the trials, just like you said I would." I huffed a pitiful laugh, secretly hoping that admitting he was right would draw him out of his drugged sleep. "Come back to me."

I allowed my magic to flow into his body, healing wounds that went deeper than just marks on his flesh. The warming golden glow of my powers seeped into Daxton as the bruising on his face disappeared. I moved my hands across his skin, tracing over his shoulders, migrating across his chest before moving my hands toward his back.

Thankfully, my new rank as alpha granted me an increase in power, so I was not feeling the effects as much as I used to.

I closed my eyes and inhaled his sweet scent of open air and the cold—of everything that made my heart and my animal sing.

"Daxton," I used my alpha abilities to speak inside his mind, searching for my mate and desperately trying to bring him back to me. *"Daxton, I will find you..."*

Silence.

"I will find you," I repeated, sensing a faint whisper of something tugging at my words. *"Dax?"*

"We will always find each other."

Chapter Forty-Six

Skylar Cathal

My eyes snapped open, only to close once more as Daxton's lips came crashing into mine.

In a heartbeat, he wrapped me in his arms, his kiss consuming me with a ferocity that could shatter the world and everything within it. I moaned with pleasure as his tongue swept inside my mouth, swallowing my cry of passion, erasing every ounce of fear. I wrapped my arms around his neck as he shifted to sit upright, drawing me onto his lap, our bodies pressing even closer.

Gods above, it was hard to fathom that he was real. That this was not just a dream.

Moving my body flush against his, I sank into the seductive friction. Not daring to break away from his kiss.

Ice began trickling across my skin, sending sensual pulses of pleasure through my core, reminding me of the layers of clothing that divided us. I moved my hands to grasp the bottom of my shirt and eagerly discarded it onto the floor. Our lips parted for a fraction of a second, and somehow, even that felt too long to be apart. Daxton's mouth immediately returned to mine, catching my breath in the way only he could manage. His hands frantically reached for the bindings at my chest.

"Skylar," he rasped, barely breaking our kiss. "I knew you'd find your way back to me."

"Always." I threaded my fingers into his hair, tugging on the back of his head to devour his mouth once more.

Daxton happily followed my lead as he trailed a line of kisses from my mouth, along my ear, and down my neck. Until, finally, he cupped my breast in his rough, calloused hand, tearing away my bindings. Running his tongue across the hardened bud, he began teasing me with the promise of his sweet mouth soon to come.

My chest heaved as the built-up anticipation only made my need for him skyrocket to the surface. I pumped a wave of my magic to mix with his. Our powers intertwined and danced to a song only we could hear. The antagonizing pulsing between my thighs increased, driving me wild with need.

"This," Daxton rasped, his mouth devouring my nipple. "Is *mine*. You belong to me, Spitfire."

I tilted my head back, clutching onto him to keep from falling over as blissful pleasure rolled through me. He migrated toward my other breast, sucking before nipping at my pinked flesh with his teeth. His arms snaked around my middle, holding me tight as I rolled my hips across his hardened length, placing him exactly where I needed, nestled between my thighs.

"And you," I rasped, clenching my legs around his middle, "are mine."

Looking up, his eyes darkened with a burning hunger that mirrored my own. He slowly released my pebbled peak from his delicious mouth, and our breaths became rapid.

"Daxton," I growled, expelling a pulse of my power as my hand fastened tightly around my mate's throat.

I pushed him flat on the bed, my grip on him tightening as my power continued to flare around me.

"Listen carefully, my *mate*." I stared him down, magic woven in my words. "If you ever put yourself in that kind of danger again..." My thumb followed the line of his chin, forcing him to only look at me. "I can't lose you," I rasped. "Silver Meadows can't lose you. Valdor can't lose *you*, Daxton."

He met my stare, his chest steadily rising and falling, his pulse thundering beneath my hold on his throat.

"Daxton," I roared, my rage bubbling to the surface. "Promise me you won't put yourself in that kind of danger again without telling me."

He narrowed his eyes and gave me one firm nod in understanding.

"Good," I said as I released my hold. I bent forward, my lips brushing against his ear as my hardened nipples danced over his chest. "Now, fuck me."

"Yes, *Alpha*," Daxton growled in pleasure as he grabbed my hips and flipped me onto my back.

Without a stitch of clothing on him, Daxton towered over me, his eyes taking in every curve and inch of my body, making me feel like a masterpiece. "Any other commands you wish to give me before I take what is mine?"

Words escaped me as I eagerly reached for the tie on my leathers. The desire smoldering in his stare caused my breath to hitch.

"No," Daxton said, grasping my wrists, "allow me." His fingers laced into the waistline of my pants and undergarments, pulling them down to my boots as he stripped me bare. "Fancy blade," he added, carefully placing the alpha's dagger on the ground.

"Later," I whispered.

He nodded in response. On his knees, my mate relaxed backward onto his heels, his hard cock shooting upward as it pulsed between his thick thighs. His eyes slowly traced over me from head to toe as he began stroking himself.

"You're so fucking beautiful. Much better than my dreams."

"Are you trying to tease me?" I said, my eyes lowering to his cock.

"Possibly," he said. "Or savoring the moment with you spread before me, dripping wet at the sight of me towering over you."

"Dax, please," I begged. "I need you."

"Show me." His hooded eyes darkened with a seductive glee.

I moved my hand between my thighs as I began touching myself, showing Daxton exactly where I wanted him, where I needed him most.

My mate stilled.

Every muscle in his body tensed as his eyes locked onto the movement of my fingers migrating across my clit.

"You want my cock or my tongue first, my queen?"

"Your tongue first. Then your cock," I answered without hesitation.

"I love a female who knows exactly what she wants," Daxton rasped as he migrated his lips down my trembling body, guiding my thighs open so he could settle between them.

"*This*," he said in a deep, gravelly voice that made my heart race, "is also *mine*."

His tongue swirled in mind-blowing circles across my clit, followed by his mouth greedily coveting my apex as he began to devour me.

"I'm starving," he said between breaths, "and your pussy is the only thing that will satisfy my hunger, Spitfire."

"Oh Gods!" I moaned loudly, arching my back.

Reaching down, I threaded my fingers into Daxton's hair, rolling my hips and putting his talented mouth to use, no longer embarrassed to take every second of pleasure he was eager to give me.

"Don't hold back," Daxton purred.

"Then... don't— Don't stop," I rasped as my mate's deep chuckle vibrated along my thighs and across my clit.

His fingers graciously joined his mouth, and I almost blacked out from the euphoric rush of pleasure spiraling through my core. The additional touch sent me over the edge, my inner walls clenching as my back arched and I reached my climax.

"*Daxton*," I cried out, my body quivering.

Daxton rose up, brushing his fingers across his lips, savoring the taste of my release. "You're even sweeter than I remember."

"Better than a dream?" I teased.

"No comparison," he said, moving over me once more. "I know this is real."

"We're not done yet."

"Far from it," he said in a low growl as he kissed me.

Chapter Forty-Seven

Skylar Cathal

Without warning, I grasped Daxton's wrists and wrapped my legs around his waist. Sitting up, I launched myself forward, spinning him onto his back, straddling him.

"Now," I said with a dominating tone, "it's my turn."

I kept my grip firm, as my animal clawed at the confines of my self-control, desperate to claim my mate.

"Have your way with me, Spitfire. I'm yours to command. Yours to use. Yours for anything... for everything."

Excitement rushed through me, loving the control I had over this powerful male.

Bang, bang, bang.

A loud fist hammered against the door.

"Are you out of your gods-damned mind?" Shaw questioned.

"It's an emergency," a voice quivered with a sense of dread.

"They're—"

"Busy!" Daxton roared in response. "We're busy." His hold on me tightened as his gaze locked with mine, his voice dropping low as he whispered against the shell of my ear, "We're far from finished."

Even if I tried, I couldn't conceal the devilish grin on my lips.

"Daxton!"

My mate froze.

"Adohan?" Daxton mumbled, his expression changing from a hungry desire to one of question and unease. "What is it?"

"I need Skylar."

"Fucking horrible timing!" he growled.

"I wouldn't ask if it weren't dire... Trust me."

"What is it, Adohan?" I called out.

"It's Idris..."

I could feel the distress in his voice. My breath caught at the silent panic laced between his words.

"The baby is coming," Adohan said. "But Idris is bleeding... heavily. The healers say the babe is turned around. My mate is strong, but her stamina is wavering."

"The baby is likely breech," I whispered to Daxton as I dismounted his lap, and he searched for something to wear. I found my clothes and pulled up my pants before quickly fastening my boots. "Bottom instead of the head coming out first."

"Is that dangerous?" Daxton asked as he handed me my shirt, discarded along the bedside.

My binding was unsalvageable, but I didn't bother as I pulled my shirt over my head. "It can be, especially when accompanied by bleeding."

"She's scared." Adohan's plea tugged at my heartstrings. Hearing the voice of a father and a mate in fear for the mother and child. "She needs you, Skylar. They both need you."

"When did her labor start?" I asked as Daxton and I finished dressing.

"Late last night. Her water broke before the sun began to rise."

I stilled. That was well over ten hours. I looked at Daxton, who gave me a nod, understanding the gravity of the situation.

"I wouldn't have come if—" Adohan didn't have time to finish his thoughts as I opened the door to face him with Daxton standing beside me.

"Lead the way," I said.

Chapter Forty-Eight

Skylar Cathal

"Hurry!" Adohan's voice echoed with urgency as he led us through the inner passageways.

The tapestries adorning the red-colored walls shook as we sped past them. Even the ivy vines that adorned the open balconies seemed to part ways in response to the high prince's distress Adohan's feet thundered underneath the ground as he rounded a corner with the three of us close behind.

I could hear the screams of labor pains tearing through Idris, the echoes of her cries urging her mate to race faster, desperate to try and comfort her in any way he could. We hurried toward the estate's southern corner. Guards stood outside the room, with Astro anxiously pacing, hearing his mother's cries.

"Father," Astro said with a twinge of panic. "Is Mother..."

"It's normal, son," Adohan rasped as he reached for the handle. "You should've heard her screams when you and your brother were born into this world."

Gods, I felt my chest ache witnessing the sunken look on Astro's face. He knew his mother was in danger.

Childbirth, after all, was one of the most dangerous feats for females in this world.

"*Gods! Where is Adohan?*" Idris screamed as we entered through the large double doors.

"I believe that's my cue," Adohan said, his confident voice wavering, granting me a glimpse of the fear that lurked in his heart for his mate and unborn child.

"Fucking... God's above!" Idris roared. "Where have you been?"

"I went to find Skylar," Adohan said as he raced to his mate's side.

"I'll wait out here," Shaw said.

"Probably a good idea for now."

Shaw disappeared into the shadows, remaining with Astro, while Daxton and I entered and closed the doors behind us. The ornate bedroom was a frenzy with at least five different healers scattered with hushed whispers in the corner. I could smell the scent of Idris's blood as soon as we entered the hallways, but seeing it was another thing altogether.

Two healers bent over a wooden desk, scouring texts to find any resource that could help their lady of Crimson City, while others carefully monitored the baby's position and the mother's condition.

Zola was perched near Idris's head, gently wiping her friend's brow with a wet cloth. Her stare met mine, and I swear the shadows sprang to life in response to her silent pleas for me to help.

The room was in utter chaos.

"Everyone out!" I screamed.

An older-looking male, whom I inferred to be the elder healer, turned to look at me. "I beg your pardon, but—"

"Out!" I roared with a pulse of my power filling the space. There was simply too much going on, and the stress of everyone's panicked state was not helping the laboring mother. "This," I said, motioning around the room. "This chaos isn't helping Idris."

Thankfully, the healers followed my command and began filing out, muttering to themselves.

"And who exactly are you?" The lead healer glared as he flinched, trying his best to brush off my magic. "I brought both heirs into this world and intend to do the same with this one."

"Look, with all due respect—" I began.

"You give no respect," the lead healer said.

Daxton stepped to my side, causing him to stagger backward toward the door.

"I don't know what kind of powers you possess, shifter... but I will not leave Lady Idris."

"For Gods fucking sake!" Adohan's voice boomed as he stood at Idris's side, his eyes blazing to life with the flames at his command. "I don't care about your pride right now, Theo. What I care about is my mate and my child! Skylar is the only one who has the magic to help. Stay if you wish, but she's taking the lead." Flames erupted along Adohan's hands. "Move aside."

Theo's head bent forward, his dark tendrils of hair falling in front of his face as he followed the command of his ruler. "Yes, High Prince. As you wish."

I glanced sideways at Daxton, whose eyes were as hard as stone. His jaw was firmly set with displeasure at the healer's disrespect. A small part of me relished in his protective presence, but I quickly buried that glee and focused on my task.

"Look, I'm not as experienced as you are with bringing children into this world," I said softly. "And I'm also not afraid to admit when I need help."

Theo gazed at me with a raised brow, his expression uneasy.

"Will you help me deliver the baby and keep the mother safe?"

"That is my soul duty."

"Good," I said.

"Then both of you move it along and help!" Idris yelled as another contraction tore through her center. "The baby—" Idris could barely speak as she began to lose consciousness, her head falling to Adohan's chest.

"Skylar! Get over here and fucking help her," Zola cursed with fear.

"Idris!" Adohan roared in a blind panic. The heat of his flames spiraled around his touch, engulfing the space. "No, no, no! My love." He cradled her head in his trembling hands, his flames encircling his mate, desperately trying to fuel her with strength. "You must fight the pull. Do not give in. Stay with me. Idris— Idris!"

"Daxton, pull those curtains and let some fresh air in here."

Dax nodded as he combated Adohan's flames with his ice magic, following my lead as I moved toward Idris.

Idris's eyes thankfully fluttered open, finding Adohan.

"There you are, my love," he sobbed, releasing a caged breath.

Theo leaped into action, positioning himself at Idris's feet. "Do not fight the urge to push," he encouraged.

I rushed to the healer's side, my hands glowing with a golden hue in preparation to fix what was broken.

"The womb, I believe, is torn," he whispered to me.

Without hesitating, I moved my hands across Idris's belly. It felt like a stone under my palms as my magic began mending what it could.

"Gahhhhh!" Idris yelled as her contraction peaked once more.

Sensing the injury within the lining of her womb, I allowed my powers to flow into Idris, mending the torn tissue beneath the surface of her skin. Then, I searched for the baby.

"Is the baby...?" Idris rasped with a twinge of heart-wrenching fear in her voice. "Is the baby all right?"

Time slowed as the anxious parents waited for my reply, hanging on the silent seconds passing between us as

I assessed the baby's condition with my magic. It was faint, but the heartbeat was still there. I could feel the infant's distress from being wedged in the birthing canal. Idris needed to birth the child, or else I feared my magic wouldn't be enough to save them both.

"Idris," I began, "this is going to be—"

"*Difficult... Hard?*" Idris laughed with a shaking voice, trying to sit up. "Already there. What do you suggest?"

"Let's try an upright position," I said, looking to the healer, who gave me a firm nod, telling me he agreed with my suggestion.

"Gravity," Idris rasped with a side grin. "Worked last time."

I nodded. "Exactly."

"All right, let's get on with it then. I'm feeling the urge to push." Idris leaned forward with Adohan and Zola on either side, trying to help hold her up.

Theo silently moved into position below Idris as she rose to stand. Sweat pooled and dripped from her face as her brows pinched together, the lines on her forehead creased with hours of labor pains trying to bring her child into the world. Gritting her teeth, Idris groaned as she forced herself upright, bending her knees to try and widen her stance in preparation for the next contraction.

"Get ready," Idris said as a scream tore through her. Every muscle in her body clenched as she put all her energy into pushing the babe from her womb.

"Yes!" Theo said, his hands outstretched beneath Idris.

I stepped back, watching my friend convulse and shake with every last bit of strength she could muster. Daxton placed a hand on my back as he eagerly watched and waited alongside me.

"Yes, Lady Idris, one more push. The baby is right there!"

"Gahhhhh!" Idris roared as she took in one final breath and bore down.

Then, the most beautiful sound in all of Valdor silenced the room. The breathtakingly precious cry of an infant cradled in the healer's hands brought tears to my eyes.

Chapter Forty-Nine

Skylar Cathal

Idris collapsed into Adohan's arms as Zola gently cradled the baby.

The ebony stare of the feared spymaster, typically filled with hardened shadows, softened at the sight of her godchild.

A giant weight lifted in the room, the vice grip loosening from our chests as the baby's healthy cries continued to boom along the walls and into the halls.

Astro came bursting through the doors. "Mother?"

Zola smiled as she lay the baby on Idris's chest, with Adohan's arm draping over his mate and the newest addition to their family. "Looks like you're an older brother now, Astro. Finn alone can't claim the title any longer."

"I am?" Astro asked with a beaming grin.

"You have a sister now," Adohan said with a smile so wide and bright that even the mother's light couldn't outshine him.

Astro sprinted across the room and knelt at his mother's side. His hand trembled as he laid it atop the dark, curling locks of red and black. "She's got your nose, mother."

"Thank the Gods." Idris sighed.

In this one moment, joy flourished and sprang free from the grasp of dread and fear. The other woes plaguing our lives came to a swift halt as we basked in the miracle of this little girl's presence. A treasure more valuable than any trinket shining in the eyes of the proud, adoring parents.

Hearing the three of them laugh together as Idris brought the infant to her breast to feed sent butterflies spinning in my stomach. I smiled, relaxing my shoulders as Daxton's arm wrapped around my middle.

I immediately sank into his embrace, needing to feel his touch just as much as I knew he needed mine.

"You never cease to amaze me, Spitfire," Daxton said. "Crimson City will be forever grateful for what you accomplished here today."

I turned toward my mate, nuzzling into the nook of his neck as his arms wrapped securely around me. "Idris did most of the heavy lifting."

"Still." Daxton paused as he stroked my hair, sending tranquil waves of love and comfort through his gentle touch reserved just for me. "Without your aid, this realm would have been lost. If Adohan had lost Idris—"

"You don't need to say any more." I tilted to meet his gaze. "I understand."

I didn't dare allow my mind to venture down the path Daxton was suggesting. I couldn't allow myself to step into that pool of dread that could so easily swallow me whole without even a second thought.

"Skylar," Idris called out, stealing my attention. "You and Daxton need to meet her." Idris cradled the infant in her arms, moving her to her shoulder to try and coax a burp after her first feeding.

"I'm guessing it's Aunt Skylar now... Along with Uncle Dax," Astro said with a wink, his gaze returning to his newest sibling, whom he couldn't seem to get enough of.

"Fitting," Adohan agreed, his gaze never leaving his mate or daughter. "Seeing as you saved my family not only once but twice in the short time we've known you." Adohan finally tore his blazing stare from Idris and found mine. "Thank you will never be enough."

I swallowed, bowing my head to acknowledge his words, speechless by the depth of emotion beaming in Adohan's expression.

Daxton placed a hand on the small of my back, guiding me forward with him as we greeted the newest addition to the Ekon family together.

"Hello, little one," I whispered.

Her tiny, scrunched-up face with rounded cheeks was downright the most adorable thing I had ever seen. That, paired with the curled locks of auburn and ebony hair atop her head, was enough to make my heart burst with love.

"What are you going to name her?" I asked.

Idris looked at Adohan before answering. "Ember," Idris said with a wide smile. "Because she is our little light, our hope in this new world to come."

"Fine name," Daxton said, clasping Adohan on the shoulder. "I don't think any other would suffice."

"Would you like to hold her, Sky?" Idris asked me as she tucked the now-sleeping Ember into a soft blanket.

"Yes!" I answered, overjoyed to embrace the newest life in our world.

Idris handed me Ember, and right away, I became entranced in the sense of hope this tiny infant sparked. I realized that this, right here, was the reason. For every child born and those still to come, unlocking the Heart of Valdor and freeing our world would give Ember and countless others a new life. A life free of fear, free of the wilt, and if the Gods willed it, free of Minaeve's rule.

Ember cooed in my arms, making tiny noises and grunts as she nuzzled into my chest. I held her close, inhaling her scent and placing it in my memory so I could carry it with me.

To my dismay, however, she began crying. I tried to rock her back to sleep, but I wasn't experienced with caring for younglings.

"Give her to me," Dax said.

"Really?"

"Yes." Daxton chuckled softly. "I have a gift. Besides, you should eat something to replenish your strength after healing me and Idris. I can hear your stomach growling."

"A gift?" I repeated, placing Ember in his waiting hands.

One of the servants brought a tray of cold meats and cheeses, and I snagged a handful. I'd used a decent piece of my magic, but now that I was alpha, it was nothing a good meal couldn't fix. I sat down and devoured the first few bites, already feeling my reserves fill.

"He does," Idris scoffed. "I swear, when Finn was born, he wouldn't stop crying. I thought we would lose our minds until Uncle Daxton came to our rescue."

"We didn't let him leave for a solid month," Adohan added. "He has a special way with the young ones."

"Babies like me," Daxton whispered, followed by a soft *shhhh* to Ember. "Why is that so hard to believe?"

"You do own a mirror, right?" Astro asked. "Half the time your face says, 'Look at me wrong and I'll end you.'"

"Babies never look at me wrong." Daxton smiled as he gently touched Ember's nose with his finger before bouncing in place with her secured in his arms. Then, he began humming.

"Oh, *that* song." Astro grinned. "I still remember it."

"It was the only thing that silenced you and your brother's wailings when you had nightmares," Idris said, accepting a glass of water from Zola as we all tuned into Daxton's baritone melody.

Chapter Fifty

Skylar Cathal

I froze in place, recognizing the special music that drifted across time and space to shield me from my pain in the hunters' lair.

The same harmony that I swore I could hear whenever Daxton was near me. The same melody he sang to me on the green sand beach, he was singing to Ember.

"It's the song their mother sang to them," Zola said, coming to my side.

Startled, I blinked and turned to face her. "I've heard it."

"He's sung it to you?"

"Yes." I smiled softly as I continued to stare in awe at my mate with Ember gently cradled against his chest.

My heart caved as a deep longing began to fill in my middle. Seeing Daxton holding the baby made me realize how much I truly wanted to share this experience with him. For him to be singing this song to *our child* someday, for us to—

I bit my lip to keep myself together, trying my best to disguise my rising tears as joyful, instead of ones of secret sorrow.

"It's a beautiful moment," Zola said.

I nodded, wiping my cheek.

Daxton glanced up from Ember to find me, and I gave him a nod, indicating that I was fine, allowing the tears in my eyes to play the part.

My mate rocked the precious infant into a deep slumber, crossing the room to give her back to her parents. Watching how gentle he was with the baby astounded me, and for a moment everything seemed at peace, until—

Boom!

A loud banging echo broke our harmonious trance, putting Daxton and the others on high alert.

Boom!

It sounded again, followed by a powerful wave of magic that spiraled through the room, shoving us all back a step. Adohan bent over Idris and Ember with Astro on the other side of them, shielding the females from the blast of unknown magic.

Daxton wrapped his arms around me, helping me brace against the waves of magic that pulsed through the walls.

"Adohan!" Daxton shouted as he looked at Zola. "The wards!"

"I'm on it," Zola said as she leaped into the shadows and disappeared.

Finn and the majority of Crimson City's army were marching south to rendezvous with Castor and the Silver Meadow Warriors. This was not good.

On cue, Shaw came bursting through the doors, looking to me. *"What the fuck was that?"*

"I don't know," I said.

"Not something good, I imagine," Shaw answered.

"Judging by Daxton's response and Zola disappearing into the shadows, I'd say no."

"Wait, what?" Shaw paused in the doorway and shook his head. *"Did you say one of them disappeared into the shadows?"*

"Long story, but yes. Zola is—"

"Skylar," Daxton's voice boomed, interrupting my communication with Shaw. His lips were pressed into a thin line, his eyes strained with worry. "It's the wards guarding against the wilt. Do you remember me telling you about the borders around Crimson City, and—"

"Gods above." I gasped. "No."

Daxton nodded. "I'm afraid so. We've been preoccupied with Minaeve's retaliation that we overlooked the most menacing threat of all."

"Gather what forces you can," Adohan announced into the halls. "We will not allow those creatures to enter Crimson City. We will force them back into the cursed wilt!"

"Yes, Father. I'll gather the—"

"No, wait," Adohan said, turning to Astro. "I need you here protecting your mother and sister. If something happens, you must promise me you'll get them to safety. Protect our home for as long as you can, encourage those with no shelter to remain here, but if it comes to it, I need you to promise to keep them safe."

Astro's expression dropped, but instead of arguing, he gave his father a single nod.

"Good, my son." He leaned in and kissed his brow. "You're Ember's protector now, just as Finn is yours."

"Skylar," Dax whispered.

"Don't you dare," I began as I turned to face my mate.

"Spitfire—"

"Don't you fucking dare tell me to stay behind and not join you in this fight."

Daxton bit his lip, and I swear if the threat of the wilt was not at our backs, I would have blackened his eye for even allowing this thought to enter his mind.

"Dax!"

"I'm not telling you what to do, Skylar. I'm asking you to just—"

"I can hold my own, Daxton."

"Would you breathe and take a moment to listen to me?" Daxton shouted, shaking his head. "Gods above. I'm asking you to cover the interior before meeting us at the ward. With your healing gifts, you can tend to those who've been wounded while destroying any creatures already in the city."

"Oh."

"*Oh?*" Daxton repeated. "Nothing else, Spitfire?"

"For the moment, *no*."

"You never cease to surprise me," he said, leaning in to kiss me before I could muster a rebuttal. "I would never dream of keeping you out of the fight. My mate is strong enough to take on the trials and win. You can do anything."

"Good thing you're as wise as you are handsome."

"Fortunate indeed," he said, stealing another kiss.

"Where can I help fight?" Shaw asked.

"We've never fought alongside a shifter who could change into their animal form. This should be fun," Adohan said.

"Shaw is capable of holding his own on the front lines," I said.

"Very well." Daxton nodded, allowing me to give direction to my beta.

"Stay near the outer border with Daxton and Adohan," I said to Shaw. "You can work between me and them, filling in the gaps where needed."

"Easy enough," Shaw said, rolling his shoulders as his magic flickered and began to swirl around him.

Adohan came to my mate's side after kissing Idris and Ember's brow.

"I'll teleport us to the wards," Daxton said.

"All right. Astro, send word that those remaining who can fight should meet at the border, and those who cannot, gather here at our stronghold," Adohan instructed.

Then, in a flash of silver, Dax and Adohan were gone, leaving the rest of us to begin preparing for the attack.

Chapter Fifty-One

Skylar Cathal

"Astro," Idris called out, her eyes never leaving Ember as she spoke. "Take Shaw to the armory."

"Yes, Mother. Right away."

"And Astro," Idris added, "grab my knives and spear."

Astro froze in the arched doorway of tan and red sandstone, the intricate swirls of wind etched into the frame mirroring his bewildered expression.

"Mother?"

"You heard me. And do not argue. You know better."

Astro first looked at me and then Shaw, asking, "What are you comfortable wielding in battle? What weapons do you prefer?"

"*I* am the weapon," Shaw answered with a wide grin. "But my alpha will need hers. I'll go with you to fetch them."

I hadn't thought of bringing my bow or other blades. I only had time to bring the alpha's dagger with me.

"Good, hurry along then," Idris said.

He nodded to his mother and then led Shaw down the hall.

A female member of Idris's household cautiously strode over to her bedside, and Idris handed Ember to her.

"You know the passageway out of the city, correct?"

"Yes, Lady Idris."

"And you know what you must do if the city is breached. Where you must go to stay safe?"

"Yes," the maiden answered again.

"Good." Idris leaned forward and kissed the dark curls of her sleeping infant. "I love you, my Ember. Never forget to burn as bright as the sun."

And with that, the maiden tucked the baby to her chest and disappeared into a hidden corridor off to the side of the washroom.

"Idris—"

"Skylar." Idris pushed herself into an upright position, staring me down with fire blazing in her eyes.

"What do you plan on—"

"Do you really think I'm just going to sit here while my realm is attacked and swallowed by the wilt? That I'm not going to take up arms and fight to protect my people and my family?"

I curled my lips, fighting the knowing smile from spreading. "Even though you just—"

"You can heal me," Idris cut in. "Right?"

I blinked as I approached her bedside. "I mean, in theory."

"Well, let us put that theory to the test," Idris said as she raised her gown to reveal her midsection. "And be quick about it."

I allowed my magic to flow into Idris once more, and in the next minute, she was on her feet and dressing for battle.

"Do you need anything else?" Idris asked me as she fastened her tan and crimson armor into place. Her riding leathers were layered beneath her chest plate and gold armbands. Dark red fabric draped across her legs, paired with black boots that reached her knees.

"Shaw will bring my armor, and then I'll be ready to go," I answered.

Idris nodded, securing her chest plate before Astro and Shaw reentered the room. I eagerly accepted my bow and armor from Shaw as Astro greeted his mother, giving her a long spear with a sharp point resembling a blade.

Wisely, her son stepped back as Idris effortlessly spun the weapon in her hand and around her back before forcefully slamming the dull end into the ground. Idris made the movement appear effortless, as if she were born with the spear in her hands, as if it were an extension of her own being.

"Your magic seems to have healed her well enough," Shaw said.

"Appears so—"

"I didn't know you could do that."

"Me neither, but I'm glad I did. We're not entering an easy fight here, Shaw."

"I'm aware. Astro filled me in while we were gathering the weapons. Decapitate the dark-cloaked monsters called the fallen, don't let the hounds bite, and watch out for winged creatures from the sky. Did I hit all the high points?"

"Good thing you're a fast learner," I said, strapping the silver bow across my back, daggers along my thighs with the alpha's blade on my hip, and securing the armor of Aegis in place.

A loud horn echoed across the space, causing Idris and Astro to still.

"That's Father's call to arms," Astro said, his dark brows pinching together as his hand tightened around the sword strapped to his side. "The people will begin fortifying their homes or coming here in search of protection."

"Open the gates to let our people in," Idris called down the hall. "Help all that you can."

"Yes, Lady Idris," a High Fae called as he sprinted from the room, relaying Idris's command.

"Our turn." Idris marched toward the balcony, put her fingers to her mouth, and released three long whistles. "We'll fly into battle and eradicate the threat from above. Each of us can fly on one of the pegasi."

"I won't be needing one," Shaw said as he began removing his shirt, flexing his arms and rolling his thick shoulders corded with muscle. "I'll combat the hounds and any other creatures from the ground."

"What're you doing?" Astro asked as Shaw unfastened his boots and began untying his belt.

"I like these boots," Shaw said with a dark chuckle of humor in his chest. "I don't want to ruin them."

"He's preparing to shift, Astro," I said, averting my gaze. "His clothes would be destroyed if he kept them on while he shifted."

"Also, you'll want to open the other door," Shaw said with a dark gleam in his eyes, ready to give the Inner Kingdom a taste of the true power of our people.

I could feel my beta's animal's presence rising, his panther itching at the confines of his human skin, ready and eager to be unleashed into battle. A green shimmer of magic danced along the ridges and valleys of his muscles. The scars along his arms contrasted against his tanned skin, giving him a dangerous vibe that only scratched the surface of what he'd been strong enough to endure.

"If you don't," Shaw said with a deep growl in his voice, "I'll likely break it down, and I would hate for that to be the first impression you have of my kind."

"Break it down?" Idris asked as she moved to unlatch the second door to the balcony.

Shaw crouched, his panther roaring inside his chest, pulsing with power.

"Ready?" I asked my beta.

"On your command, Alpha."

"Give them hell."

With that command, Shaw released his magic, and in a flash that you would miss if you dared to blink, he shifted into his animal.

"Holy Gods!" Astro cursed as he staggered back a step, his eyes widening with awe and a sprinkle of fear. "He wasn't exaggerating about the door."

"I'd move aside," I said with a smirk.

Idris coughed to clear her throat, unable to keep her eyes off Shaw. "I-I'm..." she said, coming to my side. "If your people can transform into creatures like this, why aren't you controlling the mainland?"

"Numbers," I answered.

Idris nodded as Shaw stalked forward, lifting his massive head toward the air and sniffing.

"I'll cover you from below. The fighting is beginning."

"Be careful," I said.

My beta's large hazel eyes turned toward me, his whiskers twitching at the fluctuations in the different scents swirling in the air. His claws clicked on the hard stone beneath our feet as his power began building around his massive panther form. Shaw's long tail whipped to the right just before he sprang forward and swiftly leaped from the open balcony.

"Gods!" Astro stammered. "He's fast."

The neighs from the pegasi sounded from the sky, announcing their approach.

"Let's not allow him to have all the fun," I said as the three of us strode onto the balcony. I grinned, spotting Nisha in the sky. Her high-pitched neigh made my chest swell, and I knew she recognized me as well.

A crimson-colored stallion flew to Astro as a dark-colored mare glided to Idris. We all took our mounts, the wings of the pegasi flaring out and carrying us into the sky with the blazing sun beating down from above.

The Mother was shining down from her apex, the scorching heat from her rays blinding my eyes in our initial ascent into the blue skies above. I shielded my hand over my brow to scan the land below, hearing the panicked screams of the citizens rising through the clangs and growls from creatures in battle. The black tendrils of wilt migrated through the outer streets of the city.

"How are things going down there?" I asked Shaw.
"I'm hunting."

I could feel his mind focusing on a scent I knew all too well. The hounds of the wilt—the garmr were already running rampant through the streets of Crimson City.

"Remember, there's venom in their bite." My muscles tensed as I recalled their foul breath and stench from my first night in the Inner Kingdom. The four reddened eyes that made your skin crawl while fighting the urge to heave your guts out.

"Also, don't get lost or entangled in the mist."

From our vantage point in the sky, I could see patches of blackened mist entering the city and hear the frightened screams of citizens scrambling to run as far as they could. Anger rolled through my chest at the sight of this beautiful, vibrant realm on the verge of destruction.

"I've got it. You worry about the beasts in the sky. I'll handle things down here," Shaw said as he pulled his mind from mine.

Garmr, harpies, nalusa falaya, and who knew what other horrors borne of the wilt—only the Gods could fathom the dark magic that drained the life from the land.

Chapter Fifty-Two

Skylar Cathal

Nisha came to a sudden stop as the three of us hovered over the city.

My eyes darted to the western border, where strands of my bond with Daxton flickered within a bone-chilling shadow. The land stretching to the mountain range was as black as night, devoid of life, drained of the very magic our world was built upon.

Flames erupted along the border of tanned sand and blackened earth with warriors clad in crimson armor. There was a silver flash, and my heart skipped, knowing Daxton would put himself in the middle of the chaos and fight with everything he had to ensure the safety of his allied realm.

"Astro," Idris said in a firm tone, her eyes hardening as flames engulfed the tip of her spear. "Take the western side of the city and work your way toward your father's line. Skylar and I will circle the center before we—"

A mind-splitting screech forced us to cover our ears, our mounts neighing in protest. Then, my stomach dropped as a flock of harpies gathered within the skies of the wilted lands. A group so large it dared to block out the peaks of the far-off mountains along the horizon.

"Gods above." Idris gasped. "I've never seen them in numbers like this! There must be hundreds."

"Possibly thousands," I whispered as dread clenched the beats of my heart.

"We need more fighters in the sky, Mother!"

"Gather the herd and find riders," Idris said. "The harpies won't travel far from their masters. We need to keep the creatures and the wilt at bay while Adohan and Daxton reactivate the wards."

Astro followed his mother's command, pulling on his reins and guiding his pegasus toward the paddock.

I scanned the area beyond the wall, finding a single tower in the distance with crimson-clad warriors fighting to reach its base.

"If they're able to reach the tower, Dax and Adohan can reinforce the ward and repel the wilt," Idris said as she followed my gaze.

"Then let's make sure they do."

Idris and I guided our pegasi straight into the heart of the oncoming flock. The first wave of fifty or so harpies broke free from the circling mass, with the speed and grace of our steeds closing the distance. I kicked Nisha's side as I pulled an arrow from my quiver, knocking it against my bowstring. I'd fought against these creatures before, and unlike our first encounter, I was no longer afraid.

Adrenaline pumped through my veins, my animal's power surging through me as we flew forward. Crimson City disappeared beneath me in a blur, with my focus honed on the approaching flock of harpies. I could feel the threads of magic pass over my skin as we soared into the land claimed by the dark magic of the wilt. My animal roared inside me, the sensation of this power making her restless.

Nisha flapped her wings in a steady rhythm, allowing me to pull back on my bow, line up, and loose an arrow straight through the heart of my first target.

The brown-and-golden-feathered female screeched as the arrow struck her in the heart, sending her falling through the skies that she terrorized, dead before her body crashed into the scorched earth below. I relinquished control of my reins, giving Nisha her head, trusting her to keep us alive as we flew into the battle of the skies.

As soon as I released an arrow, I was grasping for another, ducking under swipes of elongated claws from outstretched hands and beats of colliding wings.

Draw, release.

Draw, release.

Draw, release.

I didn't dare break from this pattern. If I faltered for even a second, the surrounding harpies would overtake us.

With my string pulled back, I aimed for a creature swooping toward Idris's flaming spear. Anticipating its descent, I released the fletching, the tip of my arrow penetrating through the base of its neck as its scream sprayed blood across the open sky. Before Idris had a moment to thank me, we were once again on the defense.

"Astro should be here soon!" Idris roared through swipes of her weapon.

The fire-lit spear left devastation in its wake as Idris rode her pegasus through the mass of talons, wings, and clouds. Ending the life of any opponent who dared cross her path, the Lady of Crimson City proved her worth in battle, wearing the splattered blood of her enemies as a badge of honor.

The pegasi weaved through the sky as effortlessly as horses ran across the fields. Their instincts kept us alive as we continued to fight against the dreadful creatures of the sky. Relief rolled through me as the sight of a crimson-colored pegasus joined the fold of golden feathers. Astro and other riders rode into battle with us as another group from the main flock of harpies altered their circling course and attacked.

Nisha suddenly took a sharp roll to the right, causing me to drop an arrow and clutch onto her neck as she dove through the clouds. I dared a glance backward, seeing four harpies following us. One of them was noticeably different from the others.

Chapter Fifty-Three

Skylar Cathal

"It's an alan!" I cursed.

The male counterpart of the species was twice the size of the females, with black feathered wings and even deadlier talons at the tips of his feet and arms. "Hurry, Nisha!"

Sensing my urgency, Nisha folded her wings, sending us into a deadly dive straight toward the earth.

"Sky!"

Shaw's voice echoed across my mind, but I closed the door to his thoughts, needing to focus every ounce of my strength on clinging to Nisha's back and not splattering on the ground below.

The speed of our dive formed tears in my eyes as the winds whipped past us. I was helpless, putting all my faith into Nisha and praying she knew what to do. The female screeches faded as they broke off, but I could still feel the male lurking behind us, keeping pace with my mount's speed. I willed my eyes to open, fighting through the force of the swirling winds.

"Shit!" I cursed. "Nisha, fucking pull up!"

Before I could take another breath, Nisha's wings opened. My chest violently collided with the base of her neck as I fought against the force of gravity pulling us toward the earth. Nisha banked to the right, but she wasn't fast enough. The alan roared, his talons reaching for one of my pegasus's wings, slicing through the magnificent feathers, with blood staining his ebony claws.

"No, Nisha!" I screamed as my mount desperately tried to adjust our flight.

Struggling to remain upright, Nisha flapped her uninjured wing, fighting to extend the other to keep us from crashing into the dirt. She kicked and neighed in the air, but her efforts fell short. The pegasus's legs skittered across the blackened earth, buckling under the force of our landing and sending me tumbling over her body, crashing onto the ground. Somersaulting, I pulled my head in, protecting myself as best I could, relying on the armor of Aegis to help keep me alive.

As I came to a stop, I forced myself onto my hands and knees, shaky but thankfully alive, with my bow still clutched in my hand and my blades strapped to my thighs. Nisha was injured about twenty yards to my right. I rose onto my knees, strapping my bow across my back, unsheathing a short blade with the alpha's dagger in my other hand. Tilting my head upward, I scanned the midday skies above, searching for the male harpy.

Black wings blocked the rays overhead as the male dove toward me with vengeance in his menacing cry. Pivoting on my knees, I held out my weapon, ready to fight.

A roar sounded to my left as a giant panther leaped into the sky between me and the male harpy. Jaws open, teeth bared, and blood... So much blood.

Shaw latched onto the male's throat in mid-air. His teeth tore through the flesh of the creature with ease, the bones cracking as the neck severed in his mouth. The alan released a final cry before his decapitated body hit the ground.

The sky above us erupted in cries from the surrounding females. The ear-shattering scream sent a blinding pain through my skull. I fought to silence their magic, wrapping my own around me like a barrier. I reached for Shaw's mind, encouraging him to do the same.

"Link your mind with me," I told Shaw. *"Let me help guide your magic."*

Without hesitating, Shaw let me in, and he was able to follow my guidance to shield himself.

"Thanks for jumping in and saving the day," I said as I rose from the ground, thanking the Gods that our ears were no longer ringing.

"Being your beta is already proving to be a handful."

"Never boring."

Shaw released a shallow growl, sounding very similar to a curt laugh.

I glanced around, searching for Nisha, but she was nowhere to be found.

"The pegasus you were riding is fine. She trotted toward the outcrop near Crimson City lands. Her wing was injured, but she seems to be all right for now. She'll survive."

I nodded, trying to assess where we landed. Nisha must have flown toward Crimson City because the ground beneath our feet wasn't black and barren. It still held sagebrush and scattered desert flowers.

"We need to get back into this fight. The tower can't be far from here," I said as I bit my lip, searching for the pull of Daxton's magic. "That way," I said to Shaw, pointing west.

"Then let's go. Are you able to keep up?"

"Are you offering a ride?" I asked with a mischievous grin.

Shaw growled, baring his teeth. *"I'm not a fucking pony."*

Chapter Fifty-Four

Daxton Aegaeon

The wilt was death incarnate.

As soon as our feet touched the cursed ground, I could feel its magic threaten to tear us apart. I teleported Adohan and myself to the border, fighting our way through garmr and, by the grace of the Gods, only a handful of fallen creatures, for now.

Valencia sliced through the spinal cord of a garmr standing in our path, easily taking the life of the creature bred by darkness and birthed with the sole purpose of devouring any source of life it could find. Only a handful of hounds were able to pass us, but thankfully, Adohan's call to arms was answered faster than I anticipated.

"We must reach the ward, Adohan!" I shouted on the battlefield, forcing my friend to alter his focus and allow his warriors to handle the brunt of the attack.

The wilt's magic was unlike anything in this world, a dark curse that lurked in the shadows and in the blackened mist. No one ever emerged from the mists. If the toxic fog encased you, it was better to end your life with a blade than feel the life stripped from your bones and encase your very soul.

To this day, Zola was still the only one ever known to escape with her life.

"Hurry, Adohan!" I roared, my blade humming with the magic of my people, ready to eradicate any enemy who dared step in my path.

"Eager to take down another fallen, I see," Adohan rasped as he ran to my side. "Have you seen the flock circling overhead?"

I nodded, knowing exactly who was in the sky fighting against the threat looming from above. I sensed my mate the moment she joined the battle. "Idris with her?" I asked.

"Dammit. *Yes*," Adohan groaned. "I should've known better."

We ran in silence, our feet pounding into the ground as dust from the decaying land sprang from our footsteps. The magic of the wilt strengthened the farther we ran past the border.

It felt alive. How? I had no gods-damned idea, but I knew in my bones that it was watching us. Calculating when to strike. Searching for a weakness.

"There's the tower!" Adohan shouted.

From the shadows, Zola fought beside Crimson City warriors against harpies from the sky and garmr on the ground. Pushing my legs to move faster, I didn't dare teleport us to the tower, saving as much of my magic as I could to help strengthen Adohan's wards.

Using the rocky terrain to my advantage, I leaped onto a nearby boulder, raising Valencia overhead before my blade sliced through the middle of a hovering harpy. The creature wailed. The other High Fae turned their attention to our arrival, relief washing over their faces.

"The ward, Daxton, we need to climb!"

Fucking stairs, I internally groaned.

I told Adohan to build his relic on the ground level, but the bastard wanted to put it on a pedestal.

"We've got this under control," Zola roared. "But not if you don't get those wards up."

I sheathed Valencia across my back and darted toward the stone steps carved into the outer layer of the tower, combating my instinct to fight instead of run.

Climbing the steps, I searched down the bond for my mate. Relief and a swell of pride surged through my chest as I felt Skylar's presence. Her fiery spirit fueled me with a surge of power even from a distance.

Skylar was alive.

She was close, and she was heading this way.

Chapter Fifty-Five

Skylar Cathal

"You breathe a gods-damned word of this to Talon or Rhea, and I swear I will—"

"I know!" I said, gripping Shaw's coarse fur, urging him to run faster. "Hurry up, we're almost there."

Shaw's powerful legs thundered beneath him, carrying us across the wilted earth toward the tower where Daxton and Adohan were trying to fix the wards. Up ahead, I could see the mist encroaching on the tower. The remnants of dark magic were far too close, threatening to swallow the tower and everyone else with it. If Dax and Adohan didn't repair the ward, Crimson City would fall.

"Shift your weight!" Shaw shouted inside my head. *"And don't fall. It's embarrassing enough that I'm carrying you into battle like this."*

Shaw was right as usual, although I didn't dare admit it to his face. He was *not* a pony.

Riding on his back felt like tumbling down a cliffside while trying to remain balanced. He was remarkably fast and powerful, but riding along his shoulders and clinging to his neck for dear life was not the most enjoyable experience.

"You're the one that said I was too slow on my *two* legs."

"And I still stand by what I said."

Shaw took another sharp turn and leaped over a stack of boulders leading to the rolling hillside. The blackened earth and dried trees cracked under the force of his bounding paws as Shaw pushed forward.

"Warriors are fighting at the base, and I can see two figures climbing outside the structure up ahead."

"Dax and Adohan must be ascending to the relic at the top to reactivate the ward's magic—good. Let's help buy them some time."

"With pleasure."

Shaw surged forward, closing the distance, his roar causing even the garmr to flinch. He skidded to a stop, allowing me to slide from his back to join in the fight.

"Champion, here!" a dark-skinned warrior said as he tossed me a quiver of fresh arrows to draw from.

I was capable with a sword, but deadly with my bow. I nodded a quick thanks as I readied an arrow, searching for a new target. My silver bow felt weightless in my hands as I took a deep breath to steady my arm. The fletching of the feathers gently caressed my cheek before I released the string and sent my arrow flying.

Thud, one harpy down. Then two, and then three. Yet the massive horde looming against the horizon was still circling nearby, almost as if they were waiting for something.

Shaw released a deafening roar as he rounded on a pack of four garmr, attempting to guard the base of the stairs Daxton and Adohan were climbing.

"Shaw?" I reached out to my friend and listened for his answer. *"Shaw!"* I screamed.

"I'm fine."

"Why am I having a hard time believing you?" I grabbed the quiver, attached it to my side, and ran for the stairs outside the sandstone tower. *"Give me a way through, then. I'll have a vantage point from the steps to cover you."*

Shaw swiped at the garmr, forcing them to step back and create a small opening for me to leap onto the steps. From there, I could keep the wall to my back and help cover the others from above. I drew on my bow, arrow after arrow soaring across the battlefield. Crimson entrails stained the scorched earth. My nose wrinkled at the aroma from the High Fae and wilted creatures alike.

There was so much death… And *why*?

Why were these creatures here? Why did the ward fall? Why was all this happening now?

A chill crept up my spine as I turned to see black mist gathering fifty yards from the tower's base. As the seconds turned into minutes during the fighting, the enemy silently grew right in front of our eyes. I cursed myself for being foolish enough not to recognize this sooner. The fear-gripping feeling of death loomed around us as the mists began to encircle the tower.

Fuck, this was a trap.

And we were caught in the dead center.

"Daxton!" I called with my mind.

Reaching along the fragments of our bond, I searched for him. Desperately trying to relay the pangs of dread that kept words from escaping my lips. The whisper of his presence in response sent my heart soaring, hope fueling me from within as my animal began to sing in response to him.

I wasn't afraid to die.

But I was terrified of the others dying before their time was done. Before we could eradicate the wilt and set Valdor free.

Daxton's exhaustion carried through our bond as if it were my own. His magic was wavering, and I knew they needed my help. Strapping my bow across my back, I flew up the steps, taking two at a time, desperate to reach the top.

"Dax!" I yelled as my eyes met his from across a pedestal.

Adohan gave me a firm nod as his brows narrowed in concentration, his hands shaking atop the stone relic.

"You made it," Daxton said with a broken voice, shoulders trembling.

"Right on time, it seems," I answered, running to his side, placing a hand on each of their forearms.

"This ward shouldn't have been this weak," Adohan said as he and Daxton wrapped their hands around a small stone carved into the shape of a flame. "Minaeve should've—"

"Minaeve should've done a lot of things," I growled, allowing my magic to gather in my center. "Including dropping dead. But that hasn't happened just yet, so she can just fuck off. We can handle this ourselves."

"I second that," Daxton rasped.

"Agreed," Adohan said, bearing down and preparing himself for one last effort.

I didn't know the limits of this ward, but I knew it required the majority of their magic, which the queen herself most recently siphoned away. Just add it to the gods-damned list of reasons why killing her wouldn't be revenge enough.

Concentrating, I willed my power to flow through my touch, healing Adohan and Daxton's depleted reserves and attempting to fill them with my own. My status as alpha granted me a stronger burst of power I didn't have access to before, *thank the Gods*. I could feel Shaw's presence knocking at my mental door, but I pushed it aside, focusing on giving Dax and Adohan all I could.

The seconds ticked slowly: five, seven, ten, fifteen... It only took fifteen seconds for my knees to buckle, and I collapsed to the floor.

"That's enough, Skylar," Daxton roared. "Adohan, now!"

I cursed my inability to keep my feet underneath me, hating that I couldn't give them more. Daxton and Adohan bared their teeth and clenched every muscle in their bodies as they made one final push with their magic.

The blue hue of the stone flame sprang to life, the magic thundering like a wave crashing against the sands.

"Skylar." Daxton knelt beside me, cupping my face and inspecting me for other injuries.

"I'm good, Dax."

"That's yet to be determined," he answered. "But for now, I'd agree."

"Did it work?"

"Yes," Adohan said, panting as he backed toward the steps, gazing into the skies above. "It's working! The flock of harpies is returning toward the mountains, and the garmr also appear to be retreating."

"What about the mist?" I dared to ask, silence filling the space, followed by a prickling grasp of dread pooling in my gut. "Adohan?"

"*No.*" The Crimson City prince's voice was barely audible. He swallowed a heavy breath as he staggered back from the open ledge. The whites of his eyes were wide with fear as he tilted his gaze upward to where Idris and Astro were soaring overhead. "Daxton, they're here. There's, there's—"

"I sense them." Daxton's grip tightened on my arm as he moved me to his side. "Gods."

The cold whisper of death brushed against me, fear becoming a physical entity that wrapped around my spine, squeezing it like a vice. The stench of sulfur mingled with a chilling emptiness could only come from one thing.

Nalusa falaya—the fallen.

And judging by Daxton and Adohan's grim expressions, there were far too many for us to fight.

Pushing past the fatigue in my legs, I forced myself to stand at Daxton's side, my jaw dropping to the floor at what my eyes beheld. Within the mist, dark-cloaked figures began to appear out of the tendrils of air. One after another materialized out of nowhere, creating a line of hundreds, if not thousands, of fallen standing shoulder to shoulder with the moving ebony mists at their backs.

The wilt was finally showing its true hand. The weapon that had been growing since the curse first fell upon Valdor. An army of the undead triggered by my victories in the trials and a sense that their hold on Valdor would soon come to an end.

"Daxton." I coughed to try and clear my throat. "Have you ever seen this many gathered before?"

"No," he answered. "I've never witnessed this many fallen creatures together like this."

For once, words from my mate did little to comfort me.

"But," Adohan said nervously, "it does make sense. The wilt has been growing for five centuries. Taking High Fae and other creatures under its control. This... This must be the result."

I knew my magic could heal the fallen of the wilt, but I couldn't even begin making a dent in the numbers standing before us.

"The wards will keep them back," Adohan said with confidence. "We just need to get to safety behind Crimson City's walls."

"Get ready to run, Spitfire," Daxton told me. "I can teleport us once we're closer, but right now at this distance, I—"

"I know," I breathed. "We'll make it."

"Shaw," I said, reaching out for my beta. *"We need to retreat. Get yourself, and anyone else you can, back inside Crimson City walls."*

"Already on it," he said.

I felt Daxton tense beside me as he pushed forward to the opening. His eyes widened with fear as he screamed, "Zola!"

My eyes darted to the Shadow Jumper as she alone began marching toward the hundreds of fallen creatures materializing in the blackened mists.

Chapter Fifty-Six

Skylar Cathal

"Zola!" Daxton roared her name with desperation, his shoulders heaving as his gaze fixed on his spymaster's trail.

She paused and turned her head. "Go," she signed as she began charging forward once more.

"What is she doing?" Adohan demanded.

"She's—" I could barely form the words. "She's trying to give us time to escape."

The three of us raced down the stone steps, leaping from the final level as we looked out onto the wilted land between us and the fallen.

"We can't leave her," I told Daxton, knowing he felt the same.

"I'm not planning on it." My mate's jaw clenched as Valencia appeared in his hand. "You're going, though."

"Fat chance!"

"Skylar!" Daxton yelled as he turned toward me. "For me. Keep your promise. Turn and run."

Bastard.

"Daxton, I can't—"

"You must!" His eyes darted to Adohan, who came to my side.

"Don't fucking touch me," I snarled.

"Skylar," Adohan began, but stopped when the rasped voice from a nalusa falaya silenced us all.

"*You—*" One of the hooded figures stepped forward, its long, bony hand extending from its cloak, pointed directly at Zola. "*You're the one who escaped. You're the one our shadows seek. The powers you wield are not for you to keep.*" It glided forward with three others behind it.

"They can't cross the ward line, right?" I asked.

Their lack of response gave me no comfort. Zola was in grave danger.

"The ward begins at the city gates," Adohan said, stepping closer to my side.

"I've heard your whispers for nearly five hundred years," Zola said in a deathly calm voice. "The time has come to put your words to the test."

In a flash, shadows encircled Zola as a handful of fallen creatures surrounded her, beginning their assault.

"No!" Daxton roared, but Adohan jumped to restrain my mate from following.

Zola's cries of pain tore through my center. They were killing her, using her gifts against her. The magic that flowed through her veins was now used as a tool for her destruction and torment. Summoning my courage, I darted around the two High Fae males and ran straight for Zola.

"Skylar!" my mate roared from behind me.

Zola's screams muffled his cries.

Was it my brightest idea in the world? No, most definitely not. But I couldn't just stand there as I watched my friend being torn to pieces.

Then, out of the corner of my eye, Shaw leaped ahead of me. His teeth were bared, claws outstretched, the look of death reflected in his eyes. I had never seen my friend hold this much hatred, this much rage. I slowed as I watched him lunge into the circle of nalusa falaya.

Shaw began shredding the creature with its hands on Zola's throat. The circle of fallen creatures erupted in panic as Shaw stood protectively over Zola, shielding her body with his own, blood dripping from teeth and claws from his victory—a nalusa falaya slain.

"Z!" Idris's voice bellowed from above as she and Astro swooped down from the sky astride their pegasi.

"Idris!" Adohan screamed in a panic as he and Daxton reached me. "Get back here now!"

Idris, a female after my own heart, ignored the command and flew with her blazing spear into the fight. I grinned, regaining my footing as I joined, with the males following.

"With me," Daxton growled. "Stay right beside me. Guard my back, and I'll guard yours. We fight together, Spitfire, or Gods help me, I'll drain my reserves and teleport you to the wall myself."

"Understood," I rasped as I drew my alpha's dagger, a twinge of guilt eating at me for trying to run off without him by my side. I knew I would be angry at him if the roles were reversed. "This will do the trick if Valencia doesn't."

Daxton nodded as Adohan sprinted with unparalleled speed, the urge to protect his mate driving him past his physical limitations.

In the circle of fallen creatures, Idris and Astro managed to corner one of them and break to the right. Shaw stood protectively over Zola's limp body as three remaining fallen creatures circled him like sharks in the water.

"What the hell are you doing?" I yelled at my beta as Daxton and I charged into the doom ring. *"Shaw!"*

Silence.

"Answer me!" I roared with the power of my alpha command.

"I had no choice."

If the threat to our lives wasn't knocking at my door, I could have pried more out of him, but for now, that would have to do.

Charging ahead, Valencia sliced through the air, colliding with a blackened blade drawn by the fallen who spoke to Zola from the mists. A shield of ice sprang from the ground to block the escape for Shaw to attack while I fronted the other with my short sword drawn and dagger at the ready.

"Champion," a fallen creature rasped as a dark blade appeared from its hand. "Not all of us want to be saved."

"I didn't know I was offering," I grunted as I swung my sword, blocking a strike to my right and left, trying to inch close enough to decapitate the creature.

"Fuck, Skylar!"

My attention snapped toward Shaw just as his teeth sank into the creature's flesh. His claws tore at the sickly gray skin along its neck, and a severed head rolled along the dirt. It would have been a moment of relief, but the bleeding wound on Shaw's shoulder wasn't closing or healing. It should've been healing.

"I-it bit me, Sky. I-I can't..."

"Shaw!" I screamed in a panic, feeling his tether to me beginning to fade.

The fallen I was facing took advantage of the distraction, lashing out at my side and making me dive into a roll and expose my backside. An ice dagger flew through the air, colliding with the shoulder of the fallen, granting me the time to quickly roll to my left just as the blade came crashing down where I once was. The creature roared in frustration.

I kicked out against the flat side of the blade to disarm it and drew on my animal's rising power. Without hesitating, I flung myself onto the fallen's injured shoulder, and with my alpha blade drawn, I sliced through its neck. Black blood spewed outward in a fan as the headless body collapsed to the ground.

My hands began trembling as I clenched the head of the creature in my grasp, unable to look away at the life

I was forced to take. At the face of the beast that I could have saved.

"Skylar!" Daxton came to my side, his hand gliding over mine, urging me to let go. "It's done. You can't carry the burden of their death. They were dead long before your blade made this cut."

He knew. Gods be damned, he knew that guilt of taking the life of this nalusa falaya had struck a chord in my center, holding me frozen in place.

"But I—"

"Unlock the Heart," my mate said. "Unlock the Heart, and perhaps not all those who were taken will be lost."

I released the head, letting it fall to my feet as I stepped back and shook myself to try and regain my senses.

"Skylar!" Idris's cry broke me from my trance.

"Shaw!" I yelled in a panic as I rushed to my beta's side. "Shift," I commanded, needing to assess the damage masked under his blanket of midnight fur.

"How bad?" Shaw's voice was barely a whisper as he lay motionless on the earth in his human form.

"You've been through worse," I lied.

"That's a relief."

Even though I was drained, I needed to do this. I couldn't sit here, watch my beta become a nalusa falaya, and do nothing. The black threads of poison were already coursing through his veins. There wasn't enough time to move him inside the wards. I had to heal him here, or else he—

"Here," Daxton said, placing a hand on my shoulder, "take what you need. Heal him, Skylar."

Placing my hands on Shaw, I gave a nod of thanks to my mate, feeling his magic flowing throughout our bond and somehow fueling my wells of power. My palms glowed in a golden hue, erasing the remnants of the fallen's bite and eradicating the poison.

I gasped, collapsing backward into Daxton's arms. Despite his help, I was exhausted. "Gods above," I cursed. "Don't do that again, Shaw."

"I'll do my best," Shaw said in an unsteady voice. His wound was healed, but he was still a bit shaky.

Daxton cradled me in his arms, and for once, I didn't fight against him doing so. "We need to get out of here."

"Zola?" I asked.

"She's alive but unconscious. We've got her," Idris answered as she released a long whistle into the sky to call riders down to us.

"Let me take her," Shaw said, rising to his feet. "I'm strong enough to ride."

"Put a cloak on your lap, and then maybe I'll let you," Idris snapped.

"You are riding with me, Idris." There was no room for argument in Adohan's tone.

"The only reason why I'm even thinking of letting my best friend go with you is because you did just jump into a death circle and save her life," Idris said.

"Shaw will look after her," I mumbled, my head falling into Daxton's chest.

I didn't know how I knew this, but something told me that the safest place for Zola right now was with Shaw.

Idris glanced at me and flipped her eyes back at Shaw with a skeptical glare as Adohan jumped behind her in the saddle. Two riderless pegasi swooped down on the earth, their neighs alerting us to the ever-approaching mist that held more nalusa falaya ready to attack if we didn't retreat soon.

With a wave of Adohan's hand, loose pants appeared across Shaw's bottom half. "Stop arguing about this. We need to get to safety. *Our* fight is far from over tonight, my mate," Adohan growled as he took hold of the reins.

"I swear on my life she'll be safe," Shaw said with absolute clarity.

I tried to sit up to find my beta, but my vision swirled, unable to focus. I had depleted my magic reserves, and I was on the brink of a shifter's sleep taking me under.

"It's time to go, Spitfire," Daxton said as he mounted one of the pegasus with me in his arms. "Idris, hand Zola over to Shaw. We need to get out of here now."

Idris released her friend into Shaw's outstretched arms as he dashed toward the waiting pegasus.

"Let's get out of here!" Astro yelled as he ignited a wall of fire between us and the approaching mists. "I'll be faster riding alone. The rest of you go. I'll follow."

Adohan gave his son a nod, and then the rest of us flew toward the safety of Crimson City.

Chapter Fifty-Seven

Skylar Cathal

As Daxton and I walked down the hallway from the healers' quarters, I couldn't help leaning into him as he draped an arm around my waist.

Once we safely landed inside Crimson City walls, Daxton refused to release me from his hold and promptly carried me into the healers' quarters. Thankfully, the healers agreed that I was suitable and simply needed rest and sustenance to recover. They gave us a delicious broth-like remedy to help replenish our stamina and magic.

I immediately started asking questions about what was in it. They kindly obliged my ramblings, not giving all their secrets away, but they did tell me they utilized the red healing waters in their recipe that gave Crimson City its name.

Staying true to her mysterious nature, Zola miraculously awoke once we landed, seemingly unharmed.

Thank the Gods above.

Zola promptly jumped off the back of the pegasus, marched to her room, and slammed the door shut behind her. Not even Idris was permitted entrance to speak with her, which surprised all of us.

Shaw remained close by my side. He gladly accepted the red-broth remedy from the healers but remained distant and oddly quiet.

"Sky, mind if I venture into the city and have some space from everyone?" Shaw asked. "I-I need to clear my head."

"Yes, of course. Anything you need."

"Thanks."

"You sure you want to be alone?" I asked.

"Yes, unless you need me for anything else?"

"No, go ahead, Shaw, we'll see you soon." I granted him leave, knowing I was safe with Daxton.

The encounter with the fallen had shaken him, and instead of prying, I decided to give him space.

"I'm not letting you out of my sight," Daxton said with a piercing gaze.

My mate wasn't entirely convinced I was out of the woods just yet and watched over me like a newborn babe, but I didn't mind. For once, I relished in his attentiveness. I needed Daxton to be near me. I craved his presence, to touch him, see him, and at the very least, simply hear his voice.

Gods, there would never be enough time with him.

After a few more hours rest and a hearty meal, the night was well upon us. Dax and I walked toward the center of Idris and Adohan's home. I could still hear the echoes of Adohan's rage while we were in the healers' quarters. He was furious at Idris for charging mindlessly into battle. But then, in the end, his roars of madness turned to ones of passion, and we all knew the argument was settled for now.

Turning down the familiar corridor, the gathering area came into view with the Ekon family in the center. Fae lights illuminated the space with the gleaming moon and twinkling stars overhead. A fire peacefully roared in the center of a raised iron pit, warming the area despite the cooler night air, painting our surroundings with crimson and gold hues. Idris and Adohan were seated on one side of the cushioned seats with Ember cradled safely in her mother's arms. Astro stood behind them, affectionately gazing at his sister with love only a sibling could give.

"Where's Shaw?" I asked, glancing around the space. "Is he not back yet?"

"I'm here," Shaw announced, stepping into view along the opposite wall.

I gave him a curt nod as Zola silently appeared in the shadows behind me and Daxton. I jumped, swallowing my gasp of surprise as I turned, realizing she held the magical scroll linked to the Heart of Valdor clutched in her hands.

"Pardon my delay," Zola announced as her eyes flickered over my shoulder to pause on Shaw.

I watched Zola carefully, noticing how her throat bobbed with unease and her breath stilled in her chest when her line of sight met my beta's.

Shaw uncomfortably cleared his throat and pushed off the wall to cross the distance to reach my side.

His gaze narrowed on the scroll, and if I didn't know him better, I would assume that was the intent of his stare.

"So, this is the scroll that Daxton sacrificed himself to retrieve?" Shaw asked, his eyes trailing up to meet Zola's. "It'll reveal the location of the Heart?"

"It should," I answered, watching Zola and Shaw's interactions with keen interest.

"Yes," Zola said, shaking her head as she unrolled the parchment. "You have the dagger, I assume?"

"I appreciate the confidence, Zola," I answered, moving from Daxton's embrace to retrieve the alpha's dagger attached to my side. "Here it is."

Carefully, I raised the dagger to the unfolded scroll. Like the other two keys, I could feel the same powerful hum emanating from the weapon's hilt in my hand. I took a deep breath and gently dragged the blade's tip over the final star. Immediately, writing appeared across the page, and I readied myself to read it aloud.

"'The champion shall know the way. Follow your heart. You must be ready—must be willing.'"

As I finished reading the final words aloud, a vision overtook me.

Flashes of wilt swallowed my sight. A winding path through the dense collections of dead and dying foliage appeared through the lifting fog. A large body of water expanded behind me with a small clearing of rolling hills and scattered boulders. Then I was rushed forward along the path and thrust toward the base of a towering mountain—no, a volcano. Lava was spewing along the edges as an entrance along the base appeared. In a flash, I was pushed forward once again, and then, there it was.

A stone the size of my palm lay guarded by a shimmering veil of magic. Red and vibrant like the molten rock surrounding the cavern, the Heart of Valdor waited for me to unlock its power.

Be willing.

The final words from the scroll echoed inside my mind as I hurtled back into my body.

Daxton's arms cradled me, his face pinched in concern, brows creased. "Skylar?" he asked with unease.

"I'm all right. It was a vision," I said, shaking my head and pushing to stand.

"What did you see?" Daxton asked as he swallowed heavily.

"I saw the Heart of Valdor. Where it's hidden and how to find it."

"Where is it, Sky?" Shaw asked.

"It's inside the wilt."

"Of course it is," Idris scoffed as she stood to bounce her baby back to sleep. "Why wouldn't it be someplace safe and easy to find?"

"The active volcano," I said, looking toward Daxton.

"Thira," Dax answered, "at the heart of the wilt itself."

I nodded. "Yes, there's a tunnel at the volcano's base that leads to the Heart. It's also protected by a veil of magic." I looked at the dagger clutched in my hand. "And the final key, the blade that can magically cut through anything, will grant me access to the stone."

"So, we're traveling inside the territory of the wilt then," Shaw stated. "Good. I'd like to have another run at—"

"I believe there's a safe way through," I said. "In my vision, the mist parted, and a pathway appeared. But I don't know where the pathway begins. I don't believe the creatures of the wilt will be able to attack us if we stay on the path."

"What else do you remember about the clearing?" Adohan asked.

"Any details will help," Idris added.

"I remember grassy rolling hills with large boulders and a body of water behind me."

"I believe I know where this path begins," Zola said. "I've spent more time than any other living soul venturing across that desolate piece of our land, and luckily, Gunnar and Castor are already there waiting for us."

"Of course," Daxton said in agreement. "It seems our luck has changed, Spitfire. And fate is finally smiling on us."

"Let's hope."

Chapter Fifty-Eight

Daxton Aegaeon

My mate had been quiet—*too quiet*.

It was decided that Adohan, Idris, and Astro would remain in Crimson City, as Finn and his legion of warriors had likely reached Castor and Gunnar. The rest of us would venture toward the clearing where my armies lay in wait, and the pathway toward Thira would be unveiled.

Adohan argued against not going, but in the end, I couldn't allow him to come. Not with their realm under the threat of another attack and their newest addition needing them now more than ever. I was thankful he didn't protest much further than he did. When the morning rays peeked over the horizon, Zola, Shaw, Skylar, and I would depart to meet the others.

And maybe, just maybe, by this time tomorrow, we would be free of the wilt.

However, something felt off. Amongst the discussions and various strategies that Shaw suggested, which Zola grudgingly agreed with, my spitfire was uncharacteristically quiet.

Shaw and Zola seemed at odds with each other, fighting a silent battle that I honestly didn't have the time or energy to begin to decipher.

Skylar seemed to be drifting, silently floating amongst the chatter surrounding her. She was content to hide amongst the chaos, but she could never hide with me.

"Are you hungry?" I asked Skylar as we departed the gathering area.

I selfishly longed to whisk her away and keep her all to myself. So many aspects of our lives were drowning in disarray, yet all I wanted to do was steal the next few hours alone with her.

"It's late," Skylar said, shrugging her shoulders. "I don't want to bother anyone."

"I'm sure the staff would be happy to—"

"I'm not hungry," she snapped, stopping me in my tracks.

I glanced over my shoulder, half expecting to see Shaw nearby, but to my surprise, he wasn't. I was unfamiliar with the inner workings of the beta and alpha bond, but I knew he wasn't a threat. And thankfully, Shaw seemed to understand this and made himself scarce when Skylar and I needed to be alone.

"What's wrong?" I asked

"I don't have an appetite."

"Since when?" I challenged, not buying for one second that she was all right.

Something was troubling her. Through our bond, I could sense her emotions rising and falling with waves of fear and uncertainty.

"It's nothing, Dax." Skylar sighed as she meandered to the railing and gazed upon the slumbering city below a blanket of moonlight and stars.

"Bullshit," I cursed as I leaned my shoulder against hers, reaching out to brush her hair and tucking a strand behind her curved ear.

She was hiding something. I knew my mate. Whether she intended to or not, the pain swirling in her heart worked its way through my center. Her sorrow became my own.

"Tell me what's wrong. You've been quiet since you read the scroll."

"Leave it alone, Dax," she said, refusing to meet my stare. "I don't want to do this right now. I'm trying to keep myself together. I just—"

"You know I won't stop until you tell me."

"Gahh," she groaned, knowing I wouldn't let up. "Fine."

Skylar turned to face me, and I could see the shimmer of grief threatening to break through her brave facade. I reached to cup her cheek, desperate to catch her falling tears and make them disappear.

"Skylar," I said softly as she nuzzled her cheek into my hand, a stray tear dampening my palm. "What is it?" I asked, pulling her close to my chest.

The feel of Skylar in my arms centered my world in a way that still managed to take my breath away. She was my anchor to this life, the tether of sanity that kept my heart beating, my lungs breathing, and my soul from crumbling to pieces.

Whatever was ailing her, whoever hurt her, would feel the wrath of Valencia as I tore through the fabric of their world—because she was mine.

"It happened in Solace."

I stopped breathing at the mention of her time parted from me. My mind jumped to thoughts of Gilen. Anjani's sick and twisted visions of them together after she taunted me about not claiming her flashed in my mind's eye all over again.

"What happened?" My voice rumbled with a caged fury as my blood began to boil. If that fucking male did anything to my mate, I would end his life without a second of remorse. "Did Gilen—"

"No," Skylar said, pushing back to meet my stare. "No, it wasn't Gilen. It—" My mate's voice trailed off as grief swallowed her words. "It's Julia. She's gone. She died in battle against the humans."

"Gone?" My chest ached as I felt my mate's heart shatter from the grief of losing her surrogate mother.

"I'm sorry, love," I whispered, wrapping my arms tightly around Skylar as she openly sobbed into my shirt. I stroked her hair softly, laying a gentle kiss against her brow. "I'm so sorry."

I knew the pain of losing a parent, of someone who loved you unconditionally with all they had. These emotions were not something she could bury within herself and ignore. The blow inevitably softened over time, but you would never forget.

"Shhh," I hushed, trying to calm her sobs. "Let's go to our room."

In my mind, I pictured where I wanted to go, and in a silver flash, there we were.

Cradling Skylar on our bed, I leaned against the headboard, content with holding her until she no longer had the energy or need to cry, lending her my strength in any way I could.

The night was well underway before she was able to calm herself. The cool breeze drifted through the open window, lifting the crimson curtain to allow the moonlight to flood the space.

"Skylar, look," I said, gently encouraging her to lift her head to gaze upon the idol symbolizing our protective Father hanging in the night sky.

"It's beautiful," she whispered, her sobs thankfully halting.

"The Father and the Mother watch over the living and those who have passed. When one slumbers in this realm, the other guards over those at the great crossing. Speak to him," I said. "Ask him to send a prayer to Julia. I know she'll be listening."

"Do you think it'll help?" Skylar asked me with tear-soaked eyes, nearly breaking my heart.

"It helped me," I said. "When my parents died, I prayed each morning and night for years. Telling them about anything and everything. I don't know if they heard me, but regardless, it aided in lifting the weight of the loss."

Skylar summoned her well of courage as she squared her shoulders and gazed upon the face of the moon peering through the window, allowing herself a moment to grieve. It pained me to witness the weight of the Meja Mountain carried on her shoulders. Her chest heaved, and her soaked eyes looked weathered with worry.

I sent my own prayer to the ever-watchful Father, asking him to help me shoulder what Skylar could not. And when the time came that she could no longer carry the weight of the world alone, I would be strong enough to help her.

To the Mother, I prayed for her guidance. To lead me to do what was right and to shine a light on the path that would lead us to a long, beautiful life together.

I watched as Skylar bent her head, mouthing a silent prayer to the Gods. Her shoulders slowly dropped as the tension in them subsided. When she finished, I watched as my mate bucked up her chin, the fire I loved rekindling and burning bright within her. She turned to me, and my soul felt whole. I reached out to grasp her hand as she folded against me.

"At least..." Skylar whispered. "At least I know I'll see her again."

"You will, but not for a very long time, Spitfire," I answered as the gripping fear of losing her damn near stilled my beating heart.

I reached out my hand and guided her to our bed. As she curled into my chest, I held her close, willing sleep to come swiftly, to wash away the weight of the day and bring the promise of a brighter dawn.

Chapter Fifty-Nine

Skylar Cathal

Sleep didn't come for me.

I needed to savor each moment with him in my arms. I wanted to remember everything with Daxton. Every second, every minute, every breath and kiss shared in his presence. He was a treasured gift, the person I cherished most in this world.

Daxton stirred and looked down at me through a haze of exhaustion. "Why are you not asleep?"

"Why aren't you?" I asked in return, arching a brow. "Daxton," I said in a low tone, pushing up to straddle his waist.

"Skylar?" he answered, lifting his hands behind his head and smiling at me with an all-too-knowing smirk. "If we both can't sleep, then—"

In one swift movement, I leaned forward and silenced his words with an all-consuming kiss. The taste of his lips against mine dragged me into a well of desire that I didn't want to ever break away from. He reached up to thread his fingers through my hair. Our breaths became rapid with each thundering pulse of our racing hearts.

The threads of our bond shone so bright that I could have sworn it was sealed—that our love was enough.

"Dax," I moaned into his mouth as he ground his length between my thighs. "Daxton!" I roared this time, forcefully pushing on his chest and pinning him flat on the bed. Desire and a rush of power from my animal flooded me, driving my arousal wild and pushing me for control. "Remove our clothes."

I watched as the curve on my mate's sinister grin stretched across his lips. His eyes narrowed as his canines gleamed against his dark beard. With a wave of his hand, nothing separated us.

"Good," I growled.

Rising, I grasped the base of his shaft with my free hand and guided it to where I needed him most. In one swift movement, I sat down, his girth stretching and filling me in all the right ways.

"Fuck," he moaned, his eyes rolling back.

I squeezed my legs around his waist, keeping him exactly where I wanted. "I'm going to have my fill of you tonight, Daxton, and then some."

Bucking my hips, I rode my mate hard, reveling in the intoxicating friction between our thriving bodies. Taking every solid inch of him, I rode the waves of pleasure erupting from my core. Daxton's hands gripped my hips, fingers leaving crescent marks on my skin as he matched my pace. Our bodies moved as one in an entanglement of lust and need.

I leaned forward, and my mate consumed my mouth with his, sucking on my bottom lip. Ice trickled along my nipples, causing me to release a sharp gasp as his tongue slid inside my mouth.

And Gods above, his tongue.

Our kisses grew hot and heavy as Daxton thrust his hips upward, slamming himself to the hilt. He held me in place as he slammed into me again, and again, and again, fucking me within an inch of sanity, teetering on the edge of blissful release.

"Turn around," Daxton rasped. "Sit on my lap with your legs spread and your back to me."

I obliged his request, eager to follow his lead.

"Place your hands here," Daxton said, guiding them into position on the bed, his teeth scraping against the base of my neck as he leaned forward.

My entire body trembled in response to his touch, feeling his cock pulse against my backside. The tip sliding between the seam of my ass.

"Good," he purred. "Now, spread those stunning legs let me fuck you from behind." Daxton's fingers reached around to press on my clit. "I'm going to make you come so hard you forget your gods-damned name."

My chest heaved as a thrumming pulsed between my thighs.

"You're unbelievably stunning spread out for me like this—so eager to be fucked by your *mate*," he growled in a deep guttural voice.

I tilted my head back as he continued to stroke my clit, using my arousal to slide his delicious cock across my center, teasing me until I was trembling—until I was whimpering for him.

"Dax—"

"Manners... Spitfire."

"Please, Daxton."

"Good girl," he growled. "Now, tilt your hips."

I obeyed, and Daxton rewarded me by pressing the tip of his cock inside me before burying himself to hilt with one firm thrust. With a loud moan my head fell back, my entire body quivering with pleasure.

"Now, ride me, Spitfire."

Straddling him in reverse, I moved against him, my hips swirling in rhythm with his thrusts, feeling Daxton fill every inch of me.

He released a sensual groan as I rolled my hips, riding his cock and taking exactly what I needed. Without warning, he sat up and leaned forward to grasp my breast, his other thumb continuing to circle my clit.

"I can't wait to mark you here with my bite," Dax growled as his teeth nipped at the base of my neck.

"Along with my own on you," I rasped, leaning back to find his lips.

I eased myself down his length until he was once again fully seated inside me, loving the feeling of him stretching and filling every part of me in this position. Daxton's moan echoed against the walls as he rolled my nipple between his knuckles, ice kissing the base of my neck.

"Dax!" I moaned, finding my release.

"Skylar!" Daxton roared as his hips bucked one final time.

Rolling to our sides, I reveled in the bond I had with my mate. Turning my head, I kissed him, savoring the feel of his lips that I knew I would never have enough of.

"Keep kissing me like this, Spitfire," Daxton said with a dark chuckle, "and we'll never find rest tonight."

"Who needs sleep?" I answered with a humorless laugh, allowing the quiet night to seep into the space around us. "Daxton..."

I could feel him tense against me, sensing the unease through our bond. "Skylar?"

No. Not now, not yet. I can't—

I shuddered as I took in a long breath, clutching onto my mate with every ounce of strength I had in me.

"Turn toward me," Daxton said.

Curling into his chest, I buried my face in the nook of his neck. I inhaled deeply, the fresh aroma of pine and mountain air helped settle my rush of anxiety.

"Skylar?" Daxton asked, his beard brushing my brow as he kissed my forehead. "Are you frightened?"

"No," I answered quickly.

"I can tell when you're lying."

"I'm not afraid for myself," I dared to admit aloud.

"Who are you afraid for?"

I swallowed heavily, the truth dangling at the tip of my tongue.

"Who?" he asked again.

"My pack." He needed to know. "I asked Fjorda to sail to Solace once the veil is gone. I'm afraid the humans will launch an all-out attack against shifters, and many of my people will die. We are strong, but the number of soldiers in Taran's army is—"

"I promise we will help protect your pack, Skylar."

"You will?"

Daxton gave me a firm nod. "I swear on the Mother and Father above that Silver Meadows will aid your pack in any way we can. *I* swear to protect them, just as I would you."

I unfolded my arm to cup Daxton's cheek, giving him a soft smile and a loving kiss. "Thank you. It puts me at ease knowing we'll have your support."

"Anything for you, Skylar," Daxton said, looking deep into my eyes and searching for the words I was not saying. Gods above, he somehow knew there was more lingering below the surface. "Anything else on your mind?"

"There's always something," I answered, earning a half-smirk from him in reply, exposing the dimple on his right cheek. "But nothing I wish to talk about tonight." I leaned in and kissed him.

All my fears momentarily disappeared as his tongue danced inside my mouth. His hands caressed my curves in a possessive hold as a moan escaped his lips. The head of his cock brushed against my lower stomach, already hardening.

"I need you, Daxton," I said, my voice quivering.

I needed him to whisk me away and make me forget, stealing a moment dedicated to only us.

"Please."

"As you command, my alpha queen."

Chapter Sixty

Skylar Cathal

The morning arrived all too soon.

I bit my swollen lip, trying to remain focused on our task at hand as the memories of what Daxton and I shared last night flashed inside my mind. My cheeks flushed crimson as I glanced his way, admiring the sight of him from across the room.

Our combined scent filled the space, embodying a raging bonfire atop an icy snowcapped mountain.

Daxton and I dressed, donning our armor and preparing for whatever challenges the wilt or the final trek to the Heart of Valdor held. I was just about to clasp the final straps of the armor of Aegis over my fighting leathers when Daxton stopped me.

"Wait," he said, raising his hand to my shoulder, "you've earned this."

His magic caressed my single mountain peak, granting me a second and then... a third.

"Dax," I stammered, "I haven't won a victory yet. I haven't brought honor to—"

"You have, Skylar Cathal," Daxton said in a voice that would not be challenged. "You've won all three trials, and you honor Silver Meadows by wearing these peaks on your shoulder as you unlock the Heart of Valdor."

I glanced at his hand as he lifted his palm to reveal the three silver mountain peaks. A deep sense of gratitude flowed through me, with pride beaming in Daxton's eyes that forced me to swallow any words of protest I dared to speak.

"I'll make you proud, Dax," I declared.

"You already have, my mate," he answered as he bent to kiss me. "In more ways than you know."

"I'm deeply honored by this," I said, tracing my fingers over the silver thread, knowing how much it meant to him and his people to carry this mark.

"Are you ready?" he asked, those three words carrying the weight of our entire world with them.

Gazing into Daxton's eyes, I gave him a firm nod. I was ready. My animal hummed in my center, sending a warmth through my middle and throughout my limbs that granted me comfort. Reminding me that we were in this together.

I fastened the remaining armor pieces before strapping my bow across my chest with the alpha's dagger secured along my back. "Let's go."

"Wait, please. Don't leave," Shaw said in angst as Daxton and I approached the paddock. "We need to talk. You can't just disappear and ignore this."

Hearing the urgency and pleading sound of Shaw's voice made me uneasy, and I rushed ahead to investigate.

"Watch me," Zola said with crossed arms as she turned and stepped into the shadows cast along the wall of the paddock.

"Zola," Daxton hollered, reaching my side.

His eyes dashed between her and Shaw. His brows pinched with the same confused expression mirrored in mine.

"Daxton," Zola said with a low growl, her eyes cast down and away. "I'm jumping ahead to camp. Is there any objection to my early departure?" Her gaze snapped open to meet my mate's, refusing to glance in Shaw's direction or acknowledge his presence.

She might have asked permission, but even I knew it was only a courtesy.

"You may go," Daxton said, giving her a nod. "Inform Gunnar and Castor we'll be arriving just after midday."

"Zola," Shaw pleaded, yet she still refused to turn toward him. Shaw's jaw tightened as his fists clenched, shaking with frustration. "I should go with you."

"I've handled myself just fine for well over six hundred years, shifter. I don't need you to tag along. You'll only slow me down."

Before Shaw could begin his protest, Zola faded into the shadows and jumped away.

"Gods a-fucking-bove," Shaw cursed, glaring up at the rays of the rising sun peeking out beyond the mountains. He turned and kicked a post, dislodging it from the ground as it splintered and shattered under the force of his frustrations. The pegasi were startled, neighing and bucking with unease, scattering toward the far side of their holding.

Shifters. I sighed, patting Daxton's arm as I approached the paddock.

"Hey, Shaw," I said, cautiously stepping closer.

I didn't dare reach out my mind to invade or link with his. I'd only seen him frustrated like this a handful of times, and I knew better than to push him once he reached this limit of his self-control. But it didn't stop me from asking, "What's going on?"

Shaw's shoulders began to shake, his frustration transforming into rage. I could sense his animal's presence, buried just beneath the surface, ready and eager to shift and release his pent-up irritations from his human form.

"It's... It's not the right time," Shaw said through gritted teeth.

Bullshit. I was not buying that for one second.

"Like hell it isn't," I said, confronting him.

Daxton shifted uneasily, his eyes locking onto my beta, ready to step in at a moment's notice if Shaw's temper got the better of him.

"If it's bothering you enough to shatter that post, then it matters enough to talk about it."

"I don't—"

"I know you don't like to talk about your feelings, but it's me. You can tell me. At the very least, you can show me."

The bond linking us as alpha and beta was new, but the magic connecting me to Shaw and to each pack member in Solace was old and very powerful.

"Show you?" Shaw asked.

"Yes, let me in. Let me help you. Your magic and your animal are spiraling."

I could feel the threads of Shaw's consciousness brushing against my mind, opening the doorway into his thoughts and emotions that were driving his animal into a frenzy.

Immediately, I felt his rage and frustration, and surprisingly, a deep sense of longing and sorrow swirling around a centralized thought. I focused on the eye of the storm whipping through his consciousness and gasped when the image of none other than Zola appeared before my eyes.

"Wait? What does this mean, Shaw?" I asked, needing to hear him say it.

"It means I no longer have any questions," Shaw said, his gaze wandering to where we last saw Zola.

I cocked my head to the side, trying to grasp the gravity of what Shaw was implying. "All right, elaborate a little more, please." I needed to be sure. I needed to hear him say it aloud.

"Skylar," Daxton said, stepping forward, Shaw's attention turning to meet his gaze. "Skylar," Daxton repeated as he gave Shaw a nod and sighed, placing a hand on Shaw's shoulder in silent support.

"Oh Gods," I groaned, firmly slapping my palm to my face. "Are you certain?" I asked, peeking through my fingers.

"Like I said, it's not the time or place to discuss this," Shaw answered. "But yes."

I gazed at my friend, understanding what was happening. His animal's roars of confusion and driving instinct to follow and protect her all made sense. The emotions spiraling inside Shaw's mind was, ironically, rational. Controlled even.

Shaw and Zola.

Gods above. Shaw felt the call of the mate bond.

It was why he leaped into danger and selflessly protected her against the fallen, and why there was awkward tension between them last night.

But why was she running away?

"It's the wilt's magic," Daxton said. "Zola has never been the same since—"

"So I've learned," Shaw answered, taking a deep breath to try and steady himself. "We discussed this last night, and again this morning. But still, she's reluctant to explore this matter further."

Without asking, I leaped forward and encircled my arms around my friend, holding him close and giving him every ounce of comfort and protection I could muster. At the end of the day, I was his alpha, driven by instinct to protect my pack.

Daxton released a low rumble in his throat next to me as a warning, but I waved him off.

Clearly, Shaw was not a threat.

Shaw's arms tightened around me in response. "I've fought for every gods-damned thing in my life, Sky. Why would my mate be any different?"

Mate.

I pulled back, reaching up to tousle his hair with a playful touch, just as I had when we were young. The glimmer of hope in his eyes returned, mirrored by the faint smile tugging at the corner of his mouth.

"Like always, you're right."

Shaw huffed a laugh. "Can I get that in writing?"

I gave him a beaming smile, and thankfully, he returned the gesture. "There will be time to figure this all out, Shaw. I promise you'll have that time with Zola."

"I'll hold you to it."

Daxton stepped to my side and draped an arm over my shoulder, pulling me close to his chest. Shaw looked up at him and wisely took a step back, giving my mate a shallow nod in understanding.

Gah, males.

Chapter Sixty-One

Skylar Cathal

"Wait up!" Idris bellowed. "Did you think you could sneak away that easily?"

"Idris." I sighed as she dropped a bag onto the ground before looping her arms around me and Daxton. "Wouldn't dream of it." I gasped under the intensity of her hold. "How is Ember?"

"She's here," Adohan said with a beaming smile. "My daughter wished to bid you luck as well." Adohan approached us with Ember cradled in his arms.

I smiled brightly, seeing the precious babe happily cooing with her eyes directed at the male holding her.

"Besides, Shaw," the Crimson City high prince said, turning his attention to my beta, "my mate has a special gift for you."

"What is it?" Shaw's brows arched at an angle as his eyes narrowed in the morning sun's rays.

"This," Idris announced, turning toward her dropped bag and extracting what looked to be a set of clothing. "Here, put these on."

"What is it exactly?" Shaw asked with hesitation.

"Think of it as a base layer." Idris beamed. "I got the idea when Skylar first mentioned how you shifters shred through your clothing when you change into your animal forms."

"And what is it supposed to do?" Shaw asked, lifting what looked to be a fitted dark shirt and pants.

"I did mention that our tailors have a magical touch," Idris said with a wide smile. "Now, hurry along and put that on. We don't have time for you to dawdle."

Shaw shook his head but obliged Idris's request.

"I gave you this idea?" I asked her. "How? When?"

"You'll see. Just be patient and wait, Skylar. I want to see if it works."

"Alright..."

Shaw groaned from around the corner, making me chuckle.

"What now?" he asked.

"Shift!" Idris said.

On cue, I sensed Shaw change into his animal, and from around the corner, a large panther stalked into our view. I felt my own animal spirit awaken, sensing Shaw's. The pegasi shifted restlessly at his presence, their ears twitching and hooves striking the ground as instinctive neighs and nervous bucks betrayed their unease with a predator so near their paddock.

"Now," Idris said with a cunning smirk, "shift back."

"Do we really have time for this?" Shaw asked me.

"You already started this by agreeing to try it on. I'd humor her for now."

"Fine," Shaw grumbled.

I watched his long tail twitch to the side as he rolled his shoulders. A green shimmer spread across his midnight coat, releasing his magic to transform into his human form.

"Look, I don't—" Shaw stopped as his hands ran over the clothing still intact on his body. The stitched leather seams followed the natural lines of his muscular frame, with faint outlines of what appeared to be scales that resembled a dragon's or snake's skin. "What the...?"

"Yes!" Idris screeched with joy, marching forward with a blade drawn in her hand. "And look," she said, slicing her weapon across his chest. "It's strong enough to withstand a blade, too!"

"Gods!" Shaw stammered as he jumped back, inspecting his chest for any sign of injury.

"Some weapons will cut through. But at least in battle, when you shift back and forth, you'll now have a layer of protection instead of running around butt-ass naked amongst swords and spears aimed to remove what qualifies you as a male."

"Uh, thanks," Shaw answered with a hint of sarcasm.

"Idris, this is amazing," I said, moving forward with Daxton to inspect the material. "How does it feel, Shaw?"

"Lightweight, flexible, and surprisingly breathable despite the dark coloring. I can easily wear this under my other clothes," he said as he redressed, keeping the base layer on.

"Can you make more, Idris?" I asked. "Enough for my entire pack?"

"Already on it," Idris answered. "You said close to a couple thousand, correct?"

"Yes," I replied.

"Good, that's what I assumed." Idris looked at me. "And yours will be ready when you return with the Heart. Promise."

I smiled and hugged her tight. "Thank you, Idris."

"Thank you, Skylar."

I didn't dare say any more. I simply released my hold on my friend with a kind smile and meandered over to kiss baby Ember's brow. I absently squeezed Adohan's forearm, thanking him for all he had done and would continue to do once the Heart of Valdor was released.

"Spitfire." Daxton's voice immediately drew my attention. He was already astride a powerful ebony-colored pegasus, with the reins held at the ready. "You're flying with me."

Wait, what?

I narrowed my eyes at him. "And why is this? I'm perfectly capable of flying on my own."

"Please, Skylar," Daxton said, his eyes softening as I approached his side.

I felt a deep sense of longing through the threads of our bond. He was asking to protect me because he yearned to have me close at his side. And to be honest, I wasn't one to push against that—not now.

"A bit overprotective, are we?" I teased.

"I do not safeguard my mate because she is weak or unable to defend herself," Daxton said, extending his hand. "I protect her because she's too important to lose."

"All right." I sighed as I accepted his hand and climbed into the saddle in front of him.

"Thank you," Daxton whispered against my ear with a soft kiss.

"Only for you," I whispered.

His arms encircled me in a fortitude of unwavering strength. My animal sang at our proximity, his grip on my waist tightening as I leaned into him.

"I'll take it," Daxton purred as his hands slid across my inner thigh to regain control of the reins. His touch lingered, and I tilted my head to see the corner of his mouth turning up.

"I have a question," Shaw said as he found his seat on a tan-colored mare. "Why are we not teleporting directly to the clearing like Zola?"

"My teleporting magic radiates a specific signature," Daxton answered. "I've learned over the years that Minaeve can detect where I leave from but not where I'm going. I don't want to take the chance of her sensing our departure from here and endangering Crimson City."

"She can detect it?" Shaw asked.

"She's siphoned Daxton's magic for centuries," I said with a cringe. "I wouldn't put it past her to recognize the power she's acquired and desires above all else." I tightened my hand along Daxton's arm. "But never again."

Daxton brushed his lips along my cheek in a silent thanks. "Once we're airborne and over the western edge of the wilt, we can link, and I'll teleport us the remainder of the way. Even her powers of detection have limits. The wilt interferes with magical signatures."

"Sound plan," Shaw said. "Thankfully, we won't have to be flying for long."

"Nervous about flying again, Shaw?" I asked as Daxton readied our mount.

"No." Shaw scowled.

"Good," Daxton said. "Let's go."

Chapter Sixty-Two

Skylar Cathal

Flying above the clouds brought tranquil ease to my mind, my animal rolling within me at the open sky above us, with the looming threat out of reach below.

The entanglement of the sun's rays painted magnificent pinks and dashes of yellow and orange across the horizon. Nature orchestrated a masterpiece that artists could never accurately articulate with their canvases and brushes.

"You enjoy flying, don't you?" Daxton asked.

"It appears so."

"I can feel your power surging through your center, your magic interloping with mine. Do you have any assumptions about what your animal will be?"

"A stubborn one, most likely." I laughed.

"I'm looking forward to meeting your animal form, Spitfire."

I squeezed his hand. "Me too."

"Whichever creature you shift into, I know it'll be a magnificent sight to behold."

I felt my animal surge in my center, her power drifting around me in a comforting embrace, linking our spirits until we blended into one. I had never felt this deep a connection with her before, and I assumed it was because we were ready to shift—ready, yet unable until the mark of the trials was no longer inked on my skin.

"Shaw," Daxton called out. "Take this." Daxton tossed the end of a long rope through the open sky to Shaw. "Don't let go."

Shaw nodded in understanding, and in a silver flash, Daxton teleported us through the Inner Kingdom. The pegasi bolted as their hooves touched down on soft grass, their wings beating as they adjusted to the change of scenery. I glanced around the clearing and realized this was exactly where we needed to be.

The rolling hills, with large rocky boulders along the tops, were identical to my vision. Then, when I looked behind me, I recognized the deep, tranquil blue waters of Sterlyn Lake. Thick pine and birch trees stood their ground where the barrier of the wilt halted, with hills and smaller mountains at our backs and a war camp stretching out before us. I glanced ahead at the wilted landscape to the west and then, farther off in the distance, the looming volcano, Thira.

This is it. We've made it.

"Daxton! Skylar!" Castor's voice thundered across the distance separating us as we dismounted.

"Cas." My mate's warm smile at seeing his brother lifted my spirits.

Castor ran to Daxton as they openly embraced one another. "That was one hell of a plan, Dax. But next time, let's not willingly sacrifice ourselves to the enemy, all right?"

"Fair point." Daxton chuckled as he released his brother.

Castor then turned his attention to me and quickly scooped me into his arms. "I'm so fucking grateful my brother was right about you," Castor said.

"Me too," I agreed with a soft smile, wrapping my arms around his neck.

"Sky! Dax!" Gunnar was next to join us and promptly hauled me into his chest, spinning me around on the grass before gently setting me back down on my feet. "Glad you made it, little shifter. I have to admit I've missed you."

Gunnar turned to Daxton with a bright, beaming smile, bowing his head. "My high prince. Your army is ready."

Daxton placed a hand on his general's shoulder before embracing his friend. "Has Finn arrived yet?" Daxton asked, pulling back as his eyes scanned the camp.

"No, he hasn't," Gunnar answered, "but we expect him to arrive soon. Zola has already informed us what happened in Crimson City, and she is patrolling the camp as we speak, gracing us all with her sparkling mood today… which is more pleasant than usual."

I glanced over my shoulder at Shaw and noted his interest when Zola's whereabouts were mentioned.

"Make sure there's room for Finn when he arrives and that our warriors are ready. We're leaving for Thira immediately."

"Thira?" Gunnar asked, looking over his shoulder toward the towering volcano in the distant territory of the wilt.

"The Heart of Valdor is inside a volcano?" Castor asked, arching his brow as he glanced sideways toward me.

I nodded. "It is."

My eyes locked onto the towering figure that held the key to our freedom. To Valdor's freedom.

"Let's get moving then," Shaw said, joining the group.

"Brought along a friend, I see," Gunnar said as he tilted his head toward Shaw, looking him over. "Brawny one, aren't you?"

Shaw scowled, seeming unimpressed, and remained silent through Gunnar's speculations.

"Shaw is my beta," I said, "and he's coming with us to Thira."

"As am I," Castor added.

"Brother, I—"

"Don't," Castor said, raising his palm toward Daxton. "You need me with you."

With the brothers beginning to argue, their attention elsewhere for the moment, I reached out to Shaw's mind. *"Find Zola before we leave."*

"We don't have time for—"

"Yes, we do," I said in a firm tone. *"Now go. We'll see you at the border of the wilt near the western side of the clearing. Promise I won't leave without you."*

"You'd better not," Shaw growled as he slipped away from the group to find Zola.

I didn't know if they would solve anything in these brief moments, but I knew he needed to see her. The least I could do was give him this moment.

"Dax," I said, turning to my mate. "Don't fight Castor on this. Let him come with us."

Daxton furrowed his brow at my request, grey eyes swirling, searching for an answer.

"I knew she was clever," Castor snickered.

Daxton ignored him, his ever-watchful gaze never leaving mine. "You're sure about this, Spitfire?"

"Yes," I said, "trust me on this one."

Castor sighed. "And here I thought you were finally granting me a compliment, or at the very least appreciating my unique skillsets and what they can bring to this final dalliance of the trials."

"Don't push it, Castor." I sighed as I shook my head. "I believe we'll need him, Dax. I know you don't want to put anyone else in harm's way, but—"

"I know." Daxton's shoulders heaved as he sighed heavily. "I see your point."

"You see hers and not mine?" Castor clicked his tongue and rubbed his fingers across his brow. "Honestly, we are on the brink of war. Safe is a rapidly fleeting state of being."

"True," Daxton agreed. "Is everything else in order for you to leave with us, Cas?"

"It is," Castor replied, his voice holding a twinge of annoyance.

"You're sure?"

"Yes," Castor said firmly, reaching back to stroke the pommels of his twin blades strapped across his back. "I don't carry these around just for show, you know."

"Gunnar," Daxton commanded, "ready the warriors, break down the main camp, and make sure to station the healers' quarters near the base of the rolling hills. I have a feeling we'll soon be at war."

"Yes, High Prince," Gunnar said with a shallow bow. "Anything else?"

"Honor the three peaks on your chest," Daxton said with a half-grin, placing his hand on his general's shoulder. "Accomplish this, and freedom will finally be within our grasp."

Gunnar stood tall, his features hardening, preparing for battle. "I'll see it done."

"I know you will," Daxton said, giving Gunnar a firm nod before turning back to me. "I can't risk teleporting us from camp, but once we are a safe distance inside the wilt, then I believe I can jump all of us to the base of the volcano."

"All right, well," I said with a gleam in my eye, "let's not keep the Heart of Valdor waiting."

Chapter Sixty-Three

Castor Aegaeon

As we marched through the camp, warriors paused, their actions a testament to the reverence they held not just for my brother but also for his mate, our *champion*.

Of course, there were a handful of nods my way. I couldn't blame them. The pair ahead was undoubtedly at the lead of this endeavor. However, I knew it was impossible to overlook the stunning brilliance that followed in their wake—*me*.

Skylar walked beside Daxton, where she would reside in power and governing station within Silver Meadows once we were no longer under Minaeve's control.

I don't believe Dax had shared this idea with her yet, but I knew he intended to declare her as his equal regarding our realm's ruling seat of power, breaking the mold and setting a new tone for the bright future ahead. Because of her, he dared to dream of a life beyond this day or the next. Dared to dream of a better tomorrow for all of us, and she was the key.

The fact that Skylar was the alpha of her pack sprinkled the idea with complexity, but it only added to the unique nature of their mate bond. Once the bond was sealed, Daxton and Skylar would become a united force to rival the Mother and Father above. If I could predict the future beyond emanating threats of death, I would say that the Solace pack would soon reside inside Silver Meadows, with a potential war brewing with humans and Aelius alike.

The Gods truly had wicked minds when weaving fate's design.

Glancing ahead, I couldn't seem to pry my gaze from Skylar. Her shoulders were pushed back, her head held high—the power of an alpha queen radiating from every facet of her being. Despite her age, she had a sharp mind that I had helped mold, of course, but most of all, she was brave.

That bravery shone like a badge of honor, highlighted by the three mountain peaks on her shoulder. The newest addition was not missed by the watchful eyes of our gathered warriors, and thankfully, it appeared that they agreed with Daxton's decision to award them to his mate.

A commanding aura glowed within Skylar. That blazing fire my brother fell in love with was beaming bright and true. Even with the midday sun shining in a cloudless sky overhead, she was the shining ray of light we were all drawn to.

The end of the camp rested along the base of a small hill that dipped into the landscape before the borderline of the wilt. Reaching the top of the hill, I noted Zola at the border, listening as Shaw spoke to her in a hushed whisper.

I didn't envy the male.

When Zola shadow-jumped into the center of our camp this morning, she called out for Nyssa, who was enjoying a peaceful moment with me on the outskirts of the boulder field after we finished our breakfast. I was furious about the intrusion, but when she met Nyssa's stare, a silent understanding passed between them that I didn't dare intrude.

Well, almost.

They didn't venture far from where Nyssa and I were sitting. I leaned back and focused my fae hearing on Zola's questions, picking out keywords related to the topic: *mate bond*, *Shaw*, *fallen attack*, and the *wilt*.

I forced myself to pull away. Nyssa would have answers for Zola, but I wasn't privy to Nyssa's responses—not yet, not until she shared them with me herself.

I empathized with any male foolish enough to try and seek more than a single night with Zola. She'd looked after me when Daxton couldn't, raising me as her ward after Minaeve took control of our land. Her shadows and daggers guarded a heart hardened over centuries. Only a handful were ever granted access to witness her less prickly side. I'd never known her to take a long-term lover, let alone desire a mate bond.

The wilt had changed her. It marked her in a way that darkened her soul, which was difficult to understand

and relate to. Yet—then again—I knew of the violent history Shaw was forced to endure as a youngling from Skylar's brief account.

Hmm, perhaps the mate bond held validity. But, at the very least, I empathized with the shifter.

On cue, I felt the familiar tug at my center that I could not deny or turn from if I tried. And trust me, I did try. With every fiber of my being, I tried to ignore this primal call, but in the end, I could not.

All right, gods-dammit, I didn't want to.

I glanced over my shoulder, scanning the clusters of boulders to our left, where a High Fae female patiently waited amongst the debris. I gazed ahead at my brother as his eyes locked on Nyssa before turning to me. Daxton's expression softened as he wrapped his arm around Skylar, silently granting me his approval to answer the call he knew all too well.

"Wait a second," Daxton whispered to Skylar.

The first part of her reply was inaudible, yet the final words were as clear as day. "You've got to be kidding me."

And now she also knew.

"I assure you, it is not a joking matter." My brother chuckled softly, pulling his mate to his side as the sun above their heads highlighted them in a natural spotlight.

Daxton intertwined their fingers as he held Skylar. The world around them disappeared for the moment. My brother's touch, so often steeped in menace and violence, softened in her presence. Skylar was the one who pulled him back from the abyss that had turned him into a shell of his former self.

Their palpable devotion to each other, regardless of a sealed mate bond, was clear. It was... Well, beautiful would still be an inadequate way to describe it. With a tenderness I thought he reserved solely for books or his beloved plants, Daxton tilted her chin upward and kissed her.

"But—" Skylar stammered.

Daxton's toothless grin was his only response.

I gave Skylar a playful wink before turning on my heels and marching toward the one soul who silenced the call of death and destruction, bringing me peace I never thought I would find.

Chapter Sixty-Four

Castor Aegaeon

"Nyssa." I spoke the name that would forever linger on my lips, dwelling in the confines of my scheming mind and eternally branded into my dreams.

Her dark oval eyes snapped open, stopping me in place. "Did you eavesdrop on my conversation with Zola?" she signed.

Shit.

"No," I answered, in a half-truth.

She narrowed her eyes at me and tilted her head. Gods above, she held a gorgeous, calculating intellect that dared to match her beauty.

"Not all of it," I admitted.

"I appreciate your honesty," she signed, her expression softening. "I knew you could hear her questions. I was unsure if you knew my answers."

"I stepped away," I admitted with a touch of unease in my voice, something I was far from accustomed to feeling in another's presence. "With you..." I said, daring to step closer, hoping she would catch my falling heart. "I will always be honest with you."

"Thank you," she signed, mercifully not moving away. "So, you're going to Thira?"

"Yes," I said, unable to meet her gaze.

That was until Nyssa reached out and cupped my cheek in her delicate palm, directing my attention to her stunning face that I'd dreamt about more times than I'd care to admit.

She licked her lips, and I felt myself leaning in, desperately wanting to taste them again. We'd spent time together since the night we shared our first kiss, not far from where we now stood, but it remained platonic.

Despite the dangers and the fabric of our world on the tip of a sword dangling in the balance of everything, I still wanted her. I still craved her like a fine wine, waiting for any signal to act on the desire pooling like magma underneath my skin.

Nyssa stepped closer, and I felt my breath halt. Her eyes locked on mine in a sea of endless emotions that were far too deep to express with words alone.

Did she—

A spark ignited within my chest, a secret hope kindling to life that I kept buried deep within the depths of my darkened soul.

"Nyssa?"

I was honest with her question. I hadn't stayed to listen to her response or try to watch her sign her answers with Zola. I'd never been on this side of things. Feeling uneasy and nervous around those I desired was far from my norm. Fidgeting and shifting my feet, the unfamiliar waves of tension rolled over me as Nyssa's arms circled around my neck.

On instinct, I wrapped my arms around her waist, my hands tracing over her delicate curves that sent my heart racing.

Gods, it'd been far too long since I'd had a proper lay, since I'd been able to feel the glorious sensation of my cock sliding between a woman's thighs. I bit my lip as I clenched my eyes. My cock pulsed, begging to be unleashed and allowed to satisfy the one female who consumed my every waking thought and dream.

"Did you want something?" I whispered, because Gods above, I sure as fuck did.

Nyssa's brows rose as she smiled softly, rising onto her tiptoes before she pulled at the base of my neck and kissed me.

My hands ravaged her, pulling her close as her tongue wound inside my mouth. I moaned in response, our kiss deepening as I lifted her off her feet.

My, my... *mate*.

Our tongues danced as she threaded her fingers in my hair. I pressed her back against the divide in the rocks, her legs eagerly spreading to wrap around my waist. I ground my length between her willing thighs that were spread so beautifully for me to take, so eager for me to devour and worship.

This was *my* female.

Mine to take. Mine to claim.

The roaring drive to have her was deafening. The wilt would never touch her again. No fucking thing in this world would ever have her, aside from me.

Cupping my face, Nyssa pulled back.

"Wait," she signed.

I stilled, willingly obedient only to her.

Her eyes scanned my face as her fingers traced over the contours that defined my nose, cheeks, chin, and eyes, lingering finally on my lips. I playfully nipped and kissed her delicate fingertips, adoring her taste. I swallowed heavily, trembling under the restraint to keep myself from kissing her. My right hand silently slid up her thigh, cupping her ass and gripping it tightly as I rolled my hips and thrust my hardened cock against her sex.

My female moaned in delight as her eyes fluttered, chest heaving in response to my touch.

Fuck, yes.

I desperately wanted to take her right here, right now. I wanted to claim her mouth, her pussy, and then fuck her gorgeous ass that was clutched in my eager hands.

Nyssa bit her lip, fighting against the longing I knew she felt between us. This was no longer just a one-sided attraction. She motioned for me to release her back to the ground. I followed her command. However, my grip on her perfect ass did not move.

And, to my delight, I didn't believe she minded it one bit.

"Come back," Nyssa signed. "Come back to me, Castor."

I raised my left arm against the stone above her head, leaning forward and shifting my weight to the side. I released my hold, trailing my fingertips along the seam of her dress. I watched her reaction to my touch as I traced over the body I desperately needed to bury myself within. When I reached her breasts, I circled a hardened nipple as she inhaled a sharp breath. Her body instinctively leaned against me, silently asking me for more.

"Oh, Nyssa," I purred, dropping my lips to the shell of her ear. "Was this your way of incentivizing me to come out of this suicide mission alive?"

I felt her nod as her arms encircled my middle. I cradled the back of her head as she buried her face in my chest, molding her flawless body against mine. I felt her hands unlatch as she placed two fingers against my thundering heart. She tapped it three times before removing it and resting on her own.

I mimicked her motion, tapping her heart three times before returning it to my chest.

"Castor!" Daxton called out. "It's time."

I pressed my brow to Nyssa, inhaling a sharp breath and holding it captive before daring to release it, willing time itself to stop. "I swear on the Mother and Father, I will return to you, Nyssa. Death would only delay my arrival, never stop it."

I leaned in and kissed her. The overwhelming pull to remain with my mate countered my sense of duty to help my brother and Skylar. If it meant staying here with Nyssa, I was teetering on throwing it all away, casting my middle fingers up at the world, and laughing as we disappeared.

"Castor!"

"Fuck," I cursed as I pulled back in a snarl.

Nyssa gave me a half-smile and a nod, encouraging me to fulfill my duty toward my brother. Understanding that if I turned away from him, I would never truly be able to live with myself.

"I'll be waiting," Nyssa signed with a devilish smile.

I returned one of my own, biting my bottom lip as my eyes trailed over the gorgeous figure and even more breathtaking soul I was forever bound to. When my eyes met hers, I felt a connection begin to fall into place, and I knew—I knew I would carry Nyssa with me no matter where my path wandered in this life or the next.

I silently tapped my heart once more, and she smiled with a nod, doing the same. Pushing off the rock face, I forced myself to turn away, rejoining my brother and the shifters for the final trek of the trials to free our world.

Chapter Sixty-Five

Castor Aegaeon

"You ready?" Daxton asked me.

"Let's make this journey a quick one, shall we?"

My brother nodded as we joined Skylar and Shaw, who were waiting at the bottom of the hill at the border of the wilt. Zola was no longer within the vicinity, and I could only imagine that Skylar was interrogating her beta for more information.

"For now," Shaw said as we approached. "We'll have to wait and see what becomes of it."

"I'm—" Skylar's expression dropped, almost as if she could feel Shaw's emotions as her own. "I'm sorry, Shaw."

"It's not a rejection, Sky," Shaw answered. "And with everything that's happening, I would be concerned if she didn't react this way. It took almost four months for you to accept your feelings and even imagine that a mate bond with Daxton was possible."

"True," Skylar said, looking at my brother, a spark igniting in her amber eyes in a special way reserved only for him. Turning her gaze, she asked, "So you're all right, Shaw?"

Crossing his arms, Shaw looked over the camp. "I have something to fight for beyond today. Something that I know will be worth the wait."

Hmm, perhaps Shaw was a perfect match for Zola after all. He would need that blessed patience to understand her.

"All right, I don't see a pathway. Is there a magic incantation we need to say to make it appear?" I said in a mocking tone, waving my fingers at the wilt.

"Seriously, Castor?" Skylar clicked her tongue, making me chuckle.

I always enjoyed ruffling her feathers.

Our champion strode forward, reaching to unsheathe the alpha's dagger from her back. The blade was humming with magic, similar to her armor and Daxton's sword. It seemed plain, yet power lay embedded within the ancient steel. Magic was utilized to forge this weapon and give it a purpose beyond our comprehension.

Skylar raised the blade to her palm and sliced her hand. Daxton tensed, being the overbearing male he was despite his mate's independence, as Skylar kneeled on the wilted earth and placed her bleeding palm on the ground. Once her blood trickled onto the dying earth, the blood of the shifter champion, a pathway appeared.

Not just a clearing, a gods-damned pathway with thriving, living, no longer decaying land.

Gasps erupted behind us as a trail of green grass and living trees appeared, leading directly to the volcano's base on the far side of the wilted territory.

No longer was the soil black on this magical trail. It was alive with bursts of white flowers embedded in the moss and leaves of long-forgotten trees blooming in the sunlight. It was as if the forest was never dead, just sleeping. Waiting for someone to simply come and awaken it from a forced slumber, or perhaps more accurately, a nightmare.

"Come on," Skylar said, stepping onto the path as more flowers and fresh patches of grass sprang to life in her presence. She turned and cocked her hip to the side, impatiently waiting for us to join her. "Are you surprised? I told you a pathway would appear."

I muttered to myself, "Not this type of path."

Her blood healed the land. I had expected some trees to part, granting us an opening, but I did not expect the fucking forest to awaken back to life.

Daxton was the first to join Skylar, with Shaw close behind. I skeptically took my time, seeing if any trickery was lying about in disguise.

"Do you want me to shift to keep a better lookout, Skylar?" Shaw asked.

"That may draw too much attention for now," she answered. "Besides, you'd take up most of the space on the trail."

"Let's not waste any more time. Move out," Daxton's voice commanded, following Skylar's lead with Shaw in tow.

I felt a calming presence flood my center, and I forced myself not to turn and find the source of my tranquility. If I did, I wouldn't be able to follow the others. Knowing Nyssa was here and had braved returning to the wilt after what she endured for centuries inspired me to confront my lingering fears. So, I sprinted off after the others without looking back.

The plan was simple. We were to follow this pathway until we were too tired or far enough in the wilted area for Daxton to use his magic to teleport us the remaining distance.

No words were spoken as the four of us pounded our feet against the greenery, surrounded by the looming decay outside our route. As the hours passed and our trek farther into the wilt progressed, my magic swirled inside me with unease. The flashes of visions threatened to overtake me and pull me under.

I never fared well inside the wilt. Dark magic pressed against my senses as if someone held my head between their hands and slowly began compressing my skull.

Over time, I mastered my ability to control the minor flashes of looming death and the continuous unease that came with it. When Skylar and I charged in to save Daxton, the pull of my visions was constant. It still drained my concentration to keep them at bay.

The smell of decay in this land was putrid despite the thriving greenery beneath our feet. I dared to run closer to the edge of the pathway to test the confines of the barrier separating us from the dark magic. As I suspected, the pull intensified, and I jumped back to the center behind the others. Thankfully, my head cleared, and I could focus on keeping my visions at bay.

"You all right?" Shaw asked me as he slowed his strides to match my own.

"Is it that obvious?" I whispered so Daxton and Skylar would not hear me from up ahead.

"I'm observant," Shaw stated plainly, his breathing steady despite our thunderous pace.

"It's the wilt," I said as we continued to run. "My gifts allow me to foresee imminent death, and in this place, it tends to happen more often than not."

Shaw nodded in understanding, his mind calculating as he narrowed his eyes and scanned our surroundings as we continued.

"It won't be easy," I said, "with her." Shaw didn't break his stride. "The wilt—"

"I'm aware," Shaw answered. "I may be young, but I have seen and lived through my fair share of horrors in this life. I understand what many will thankfully never experience."

I stared at the male at my side, surprised by his reply.

"Death does not scare me. I've fought through that seed of darkness that attempted to engulf my soul. I was molded into a survivor and became a fighter. My mate—" He paused as we bounded over a fallen tree. "My mate has lived through this and more."

"She has," I said as our feet landed on the grass, returning to our run.

"Zola has taken on the dark magic of the wilt and morphed it into a weapon to use for good despite its cruel nature."

"You see Zola's marks and abilities as a strength."

Shaw nodded. "I don't know her as you do, but my soul, my animal... Zola seems to be the answer to all my questions."

"You're an old soul," I said with a humorless laugh.

"Not the first time I've heard that. Come on, we'd better keep up with Sky and Dax."

Glancing ahead, I could see Skylar gliding across skewed boulders with Daxton only steps behind her, their focus fixated on what looked to be a clearing five miles or so down the trail. Sweat coated our brows as our breathing became labored from the exertion, but the look of determination never left our champion's face.

"Stop here," Daxton announced, turning toward me and Shaw.

My breath heaved as I reached for my canteen. I relished in the clean, rejuvenating water that coated my cracked throat. My legs were taxed from the hours racing through the wilt, but I was still ready for more. I offered the canteen to the shifter male at my side, who accepted the offer and finished the remaining contents as he leaned against the trunk of a barren tree just off the green pathway.

My attention drifted to Skylar, who stood with her back toward us, her eyes locked on the looming volcano in the distance. The setting sun kissed her face as it dared to dip below the horizon.

"From here?" Skylar asked Daxton. "Is this far enough?"

"Yes," Daxton answered.

Thank the Gods above.

Chapter Sixty-Six

Skylar Cathal

Thira.

"This way," I announced as the four of us rematerialized.

The setting sun behind the volcano painted the sky in glorious crimson with kisses of pink and orange. The magnificent spectacle that birthed the Inner Kingdom towered over us as the ground beneath our feet trembled.

As if the dark magic of the wilt sensed our arrival, a veil of fog trickled in from all sides, blinding our approach toward the entrance.

The smell of sulfur coated my nose, the uncomfortable stench twisting my senses and growing stronger the closer we marched toward the base. I tilted my head skyward, scanning the mixture of heavy clouds covering a vast blanket of twinkling stars and searching for any threat from an attack above.

Nothing. As if the night had swept through the area and quieted the land. It was unnerving that we hadn't encountered any creatures of the wilt.

Be ready, I told myself as my feet glided across the jagged rocks and fallen boulders encased by the blinding mists. *Be willing.*

The others followed my lead in deafening silence, blanketed by the baritone rumbles of the active volcano. The tension in our group mimicked the thickening fog surrounding the base, making it impossible to see farther than a body length ahead. But I wasn't following the route to the Heart of Valdor with my eyes. I was following the pulsing magic that trickled across my champion mark, pulling me toward the stone that would heal our world.

"Stay close," I called out as I came to a stop. "Don't get lost in this fog."

Daxton paused beside me, Shaw only a few paces behind, with Castor lingering farther back. I halted our party to make sure he was still with us.

"Don't stop on my account." Castor chuckled as he rejoined our group.

I could feel Daxton's stare over my shoulder as he glared at his brother.

"I'm just admiring this delightful scenery," Castor said in a false sincerity.

"I'm not planning on losing anyone here today," I said.

"I'm touched." Castor winked as he placed a hand on his chest with a cocky grin.

I shook my head, trying to hide a half-hearted smile at his remark. Gods, I needed Castor here, even though I wish I didn't.

"How are you navigating through this mist, Sky?" Shaw asked, his eyes scanning our surroundings. His animal helped him analyze every sight, sound, smell, and change he detected.

I took a moment to admire Shaw and how much he'd grown in these past months, becoming the brave and powerful leader that I was honored to call my beta. Shaw was a worthy male who deserved happiness and to find peace within himself after fighting for so long.

"The Heart is calling to me," I said. "I'm following the pull of its magic through my mark."

"It's calling to a worthy champion," Daxton whispered, placing a protective hand on my shoulder.

I turned and grinned at Dax, his unconditional love shining through his softened stare. He never doubted this fate. Never once did he falter in his belief that I would be here as the champion of the trials.

My mate was strong—so gods-damned strong. Valdor would need that strength in the fight to come.

"*Dax,*" I stammered as my limbs began to shake.

Daxton's arms looped around me as I swallowed a heavy breath. I buried my face in his neck as I breathed him in deeply, putting his scent to memory, marking his essence as my beacon of light and hope.

"I know," he whispered against my brow with a gentle kiss. "Everything's coming together, Skylar. It's natural to feel overwhelmed when we're finally here. Lean on me. We're in this together."

Without saying a word, I clung to his sturdy frame, focusing on slowing my breathing to match his steady heartbeat.

"I've got you, Spitfire," Daxton said.

"It's this way," I announced as I reluctantly stepped out of Daxton's arms.

Before letting me go, Daxton brought my wrist to his lips, kissing the scar he left on the night we first met, giving me one final push of encouragement to continue.

Finding him, loving him, was a blessed gift I would forever cherish.

I led us to the tunnel entrance, with my animal's magic rising within me to answer a call that sang to our souls. I could sense Shaw's magic rising with my own the closer we were to the Heart of Valdor.

The entrance to the rocky tunnel was narrow at first, but thankfully, it widened as we stepped through. Daxton and Castor conjured fae lights to hover above our heads, illuminating the winding pathway carved from what appeared to be *magic*. Steps materialized before us, smooth and unencumbered, starkly different from the uneven ground here and outside the tunnel.

"Finally, an *easy* path," Castor said with amusement.

"Thank the Gods above."

"It's too simple," Shaw said with unease. "I don't trust it."

"Oh, because reaching this luxurious destination was a leisurely stroll through the palace gardens?" Castor said with a sideways glance.

"I'm not saying that—" Shaw grumbled.

The two of them bickered back and forth while I stared ahead at the inclined steps. My heart raced despite my feet remaining still.

"Skylar," Daxton whispered as he stepped beside me.

I kept my stare forward, refusing to meet his gaze. "Let's keep moving."

The smooth volcanic rocks along the walls seemed to hum in my presence. My animal's magic rose within my center, pulsating in unexpected waves to match the magic embedded in this ancient dwelling.

The cavern trail wound over small pockets of bubbling magma, bending and twisting in on itself as we ventured farther into the center, closer to where the Heart lay in wait. We meandered for hours in the tunnel, carefully traversing the passage, not knowing when or where we would reach the end.

Shaw paused on a turn, causing me to glance over my shoulder to see what halted his trek. A hint of green magic shimmered along his back, paired with a wave of unease. He shook himself to try and remain calm. His panther fought against his will, the magic of this place calling for him to shift.

"Let's stop for a second," I announced to the group.

"Are you all right?" I asked Shaw.

"It's hard to explain," he answered with a growl. *"I don't know how much longer I can keep myself from shifting."*

"I understand," I answered. *"It can't be much farther. Try your best to remain in your human form."*

"Do you feel the urge to shift, Sky?"

"I do," I said. *"But with the champion's mark, I can't."*

"Right," Shaw grunted as he rolled his shoulders, focusing on regaining control. *"Let's hurry up and get the fuck out of here."*

"Couldn't agree more."

"Is he going to shift?" Castor asked. "Do we need to brace ourselves for an overcrowded tunnel?"

"He'll be fine," I answered.

Shaw gave me a firm nod in agreement.

Daxton came to my side. "I can feel your magic growing the farther we travel along the pathway, Skylar."

His scent of cold mountain air granted me a moment of clarity and ease.

"I believe it's due to our proximity to the Heart of Valdor," I said. "Shaw's magic is responding in a similar way. It's putting his panther on edge."

I paused and recalled what the basilisk told me before he died. *When your kind first sealed it away.*

"It's our shifter magic."

"So, we're close then." Castor clapped his hands, readying himself. "That's great news. I was beginning to wonder if this passageway led to the dungeons below Aelius. We've been walking for hours with no end in sight."

Daxton scowled and shook his head, turning his attention back toward me. "Are you all right?"

"Never better," I replied quickly, forcing a smile.

Daxton narrowed his eyes, unconvinced by my answer.

"Are you ready for what happens after we reach the end?" I asked, trying to divert his attention. "When the wilt is gone and—"

"War," Daxton answered, with a sober look haunting his expression. "War is a sacrifice I'm all too familiar with, but... we can't turn away when there's something worth fighting for."

"Agreed," I said. "You're the prince who was promised to unite your people and lead Valdor toward freedom, Dax." I gazed at my mate, sensing Shaw and Castor intently listening nearby. "*Never* forget that."

Daxton tilted his head, looking me over, searching for the hidden meanings laced between my words.

"Let's keep going," I said to our group as I forced my feet to continue marching forward.

The closer we ventured toward the Heart, the stronger I felt, almost like the Heart was fueling the blaze of my magic burning in my soul. Our trek continued well into the late hours of the night, but it wouldn't be much farther. Perhaps one more turn and then—

"Hey, wait a second," Shaw called out. "Did anyone else notice these markings?"

I froze in place. I'd seen them. I just wish they hadn't.

Daxton stopped, turning toward Shaw with a fae light glowing overhead. My eyes glided toward Shaw's hand as he traced over the carvings on the blackened stone wall.

"What is it?" Castor asked, stepping closer to examine the carving.

"It... It appears to be a—"

"It's the Heart of Valdor," I whispered.

"How do you know this, Spitfire?" Daxton asked.

"I-I just know," I answered without meeting his gaze.

Shaw raised his hand to study the markings. "I think our ancestors carved these," he whispered.

"Likely the shifter who sealed the Heart of Valdor away," I said.

The depiction showed a male holding a stone in the center of his chest, with radiating lines encircling him and spanning through the edges of the carving. A protective circle encased him, with what appeared to be his animal's spirit or magic flowing toward the stone. A stream of vertical light soared skyward from the center of his chest, cresting in a circular barrier surrounding him and the Heart of Valdor.

"What does this mean?" Shaw asked.

Daxton remained silent, carefully examining the rippling lines from the stone clutched in the male's hands. "Do you feel it, Cas?" Daxton asked, turning toward his brother.

Castor raised his brows in surprise. "Thought it was just me."

"Feel what?" I asked.

"Your power is more responsive as shifters," Daxton said, "but I can also feel mine stirring. I feel *stronger* somehow."

"The Heart of Valdor is affecting all of us," I said, finally understanding what power this object truly held. "We're all linked to it."

Castor joined the others and traced his fingers over the markings resembling waves surrounding the stone. "It amplifies the holder's magic," he stated, coming to the same conclusion I did, "but how?" He paused on the wisps of white emitting from the shifter male that drifted into the stone. "What does this mean regarding..." Castor's voice trailed off as his eyes turned black.

Without warning, I turned on my heels and began sprinting toward the end of the tunnel.

Chapter Sixty-Seven

Skylar Cathal

"Skylar!" Daxton called out, racing to catch me. "Skylar, wait!"

"Sky!" Shaw's voice echoed in a panic.

I knew he'd figured it out. He was always so gods-damned clever.

My heart thundered in my ears, drowning out the footsteps and the cries of my name behind me. Selfishly, I needed them here, but I couldn't allow them to join me on this last step of my journey.

"Skylar!" Daxton screamed, begging me to answer his call. I could hear the horror in his voice, his fear morphing into my own through the threads of our bond.

I withdrew the dagger from my back as a shimmering barrier appeared at the end of the tunnel.

The tunnel opened into a clearing at the volcano's epicenter, with the Heart of Valdor locked inside on a pedestal encased inside a magical barrier. The pools of magma below this raised platform blanketed the opening in a thick layer of heat that felt like pushing through a dense barricade. Still, I pressed ahead, sprinting toward the magical barrier encasing the Heart.

In one swift movement, I sliced through the veil of magic, allowing only me to enter as it sealed shut behind me.

My hands trembled as I froze, my voice catching in my throat. I dropped to my knees, the sharp rocks biting into them as the alpha's dagger clattered to the ground beside me. A surge of primal energy tore through me, my animal awakening as my eyes locked on the Heart, gleaming atop a pedestal, my ancestor's bones laid to rest beside it.

The ruby-red stone shimmered with a magical glow. It was beautiful, utterly breathtaking. Pulses of my magic intensified in my presence, as if the stone recognized my blood and whoever dared to enter in an attempt to wield its power.

"Skylar!" my mate roared, pounding his fist against the barrier at my back. His magic assaulted the divide between us.

"Daxton, *stop*," I whimpered, feeling the depth of his wrath. His rage masked the dreaded and all-consuming sorrow that threatened to shatter his soul.

I am doing this to save him, I reminded myself, *to save all of them.*

Rising from the earth, I braced myself to turn and face them.

"Skylar!" Daxton bared his teeth, pure outrage filling his stare. Yet, behind his veil of anger, I could sense his devastating heartbreak.

The guilt of hiding this secret from my mate darkened a piece of my soul. The look of painful understanding mirrored in his expression expanded the cracks in my heart, threatening to alter me from my destined fate.

"*Sky—*" Shaw skidded to a stop beside Daxton, his eyes widening in a desperate plea.

Castor was the last to join. His footsteps echoed off the stone walls of the darkened tunnel as he turned the corner to meet my gaze. He knew what I intended to do.

What I needed to do.

"Skylar," Castor whispered, pursing his lips. His eyes widened as color faded from his cheeks.

Daxton's head spun to his brother before rapidly returning to me. "Fuck this! No!" Daxton screamed as his fists pounded against the magical barrier. The tunnel threatened to collapse around them in his attempt to reach me.

"I'm sorry," I rasped. "Daxton, I'm—"

"No!" he roared again.

"*Dax—*"

"Don't you dare speak like that! Don't you dare *look* at me like that, Spitfire!"

My limbs hung lifeless at my sides. Summoning my courage, I forced myself to raise my gaze and find my mate's. He would never forgive me for this, but I prayed to the Gods above that he would someday understand.

"*Stop,*" I commanded inside each of their minds.

Daxton and Castor's expressions dropped as they heard my voice, and Shaw—Shaw's eyes widened in a pained understanding of what I was about to do.

"You will not pass through the barrier until my magic releases you." The power of my words settled as an unbreakable command none of them could resist.

"Shaw," I pleaded, biting my lip to keep it from quivering. "Bring the dagger back to our people. Guide Gilen in his role as alpha and help protect our pack. They'll need you now more than ever, my friend."

"No!" Shaw sobbed, followed by a bellowing roar as he shifted into his panther, trying but failing to resist my command.

"That's why you didn't kill him during the challenge," Shaw growled. *"You've known since then?"*

"Someone had to lead in my place," I answered. *"Gilen will become a strong leader and protect our people, but only if you are there to help guide him. I'm asking you to do this as a final request from your alpha, and as your friend."*

"Skylar, please, there must be another way."

"There isn't, Shaw. It must be an alpha, the same as it was before."

The roar from Shaw's panther shook the walls as he fought against my command. His forelimbs shuddered as his tail twitched, his head finally bowing in defeat as his eyes clenched shut.

"Castor," I said, turning my back toward them and stepping to the pedestal holding the Heart of Valdor, careful not to disturb the bones of my ancestor near the base.

"Bull-fucking-shit reason for having me here, Skylar!" Castor sneered, his anger a mask for the agony he tried to hide.

"I'm still holding the promise I made to you when first arriving in Silver Meadows," I said, meeting his hardened stare as I turned around the pedestal. *"But you, Castor. You must bring him back from this."*

"He won't... Daxton won't—"

"He must!" I screamed with angst. *"You must bring him back. Daxton is the key to this victory and the freedom of your people."*

I understood what I asked of Castor was steep, but that was why I needed him here. If anyone could help Daxton, it would be him.

Castor remained silent. His brows furrowed as he cursed under his breath, turning away and fisting his hair in frustration. "I don't... *Skylar*—"

"I know," I answered softly, feeling the emotion behind his words.

And for once, he couldn't seem to speak.

My hands trembled as I raised them to the Heart, the magic calling to me and my animal. The star markings on my arm began to glow as my fingers lightly brushed against the ruby-red stone.

"Skylar," Daxton cried out with pained emotion in his voice. "You can't—"

My body trembled as I gazed toward the barrier, feeling my mate's wrath daring to tear through the magic separating us.

"There's no other way," I sobbed, fighting to hold back my tears.

"We're in this *together*, Spitfire. This... This can't be it. I can't lose you when I've only just found you."

"You will *never* lose me, Daxton," I said, my heart shattering as I gazed into his eyes, knowing how much this decision was hurting him. "I'll wait for you," I whispered, my voice cracking. "At the crossing, when it's time for you to join me... I'll be there waiting for you."

"I can't," Daxton screamed, his fists clenched so tightly they turned white. "You can't ask this of me!"

"Daxton, you must!" I yelled, utilizing every facet of strength from my animal to keep my feet rooted in place. "You're the prince who was promised to unite your people, and... you promised to look after mine." My chest heaved as Daxton forced himself to meet my gaze. "You must keep your promise. You have to save them. Only you can."

"Not without *you* by my side, Skylar!" Daxton roared as his magic assaulted the barrier, blasting the three of them backward toward the passageway.

I gasped, my breath stilling in my chest at the force exerted against the veil of magic. The ricochet sent the three of them soaring across the opening.

Shaw and Castor collided while Daxton was thrown against the rocks on the far side. The volcano began to rumble. The pit of magma pooling in the vent beneath churned with the threat of an eruption.

We were out of time.

"Daxton," I yelled in a panic as he struggled to rise. "Immortality would never grant us enough time together—" The walls of the magma chamber rumbled as rocks began tumbling into the rising pool beneath the ledge. The heat became unbearably thick. "I will always find you."

I locked onto his stare, begging him to grant me this final gift of strength to do the impossible... To say goodbye.

"*Daxton,*" I cried as I gripped the stone.

Tears flowed down my cheeks as the magic swelled around me in a devastating vortex. My animal stirred inside my chest. Her soul and magic barreled into the stone with my own and unleashed the well of our power into the weapon that would require the ultimate price—*our lives willingly given.*

My pulse stuttered in an unnatural rhythm as the Heart of Valdor consumed every nerve, every fiber of my being. Snaring it inside the stone, stealing the breath from my lungs, and confining me to an inescapable fate.

"*Daxton,*" I whimpered as my life force began to fade.

Daxton's eyes glistened as a stream of tears cascaded down his face. He dipped his head as his body convulsed with a combination of rage and sorrow that would obliterate the world if it were set free.

Lifting his gaze, Daxton said, "We will always find each other, every day, until none are left."

My love for him transcended worlds and ignored the rules of time or distance that would tragically force us to part but never forget.

I would watch over him from afar until we reunited in the next life, where we would regain the time stolen from us.

My gaze drifted upward as a vortex of spiraling winds of flames and magic engulfed my world. Opening the floodgates of my power, I unleashed every droplet of strength and fragment of energy I held. My bones vibrated beneath my skin as a trickle of blood seeped from my nose and ears.

My animal rose from within, her soul's song igniting a melody that carried the pains of my death. Spiriting them away and shouldering the burden of my final act in this living world.

"*I love you,*" *I* called out to Daxton.

I felt my mate's scream, a raw and endless wail of sorrow. His grief wrapped around him like a suffocating ache, one that would never release its hold.

"*I love you, Skylar,*" he answered in a wounded roar.

Tears flowed down my cheeks as his final words echoed in my heart. Eternity would never be long enough with him.

I squeezed my eyes shut, a raw scream tearing from my throat like a burning inferno as the Heart consumed every fragment of me. This was the ultimate sacrifice, what was required to unlock the magic to save our world.

My body grew cold despite the blistering heat from the volcano, until there was nothing. I could endure the physical agonies of my death. I'd faced it before, and once again, a strange sense of calm washed over me. It started at my feet a subtle tingling that crawled up my legs and arms, until it settled deep within my heart.

"Are you willing?" an unknown voice called out.

I dared to open my eyes against the sting of the blistering winds.

"Are you willing?" It asked again, the voice sounding ancient and strong.

I bent my head forward as my fingernails cracked against the force of my fingers digging into the stone. I clenched my jaw, grinding my teeth as the taste of blood coated my tongue. My animal's presence surged inside me, flooding me with an unwavering courage that I desperately clung to.

Tilting my head back, I screamed into the chasm, "Yes!"

An explosion of light erupted from the stone. My hands were immovable as the power from the Heart of Valdor exploded from the confines of its cage, finally unlocked after my ancestor sealed it away.

"I'm sorry," I whispered, loud enough for only my animal to hear. "I'm sorry we were never able to shift."

With those final words, my eyes closed, the strength in my limbs gave way, and my final breath dissipated into ash. My life willingly given to the Heart of Valdor to heal our dying world.

Chapter Sixty-Eight

Castor Aegaeon

"*No!*" was all I could think to say, all I could fathom, as my premonition unraveled in a devastating tragedy.

Witnessing this nightmare felt like a dagger spearing my chest, the tip piercing my immortal heart and forcing it to cease beating. Scorching burns from smoldering embers of the magma chamber would be a welcome pain compared to witnessing this scene unfold.

"Not without *you* by my side, Skylar!" Daxton roared.

The panic in his voice teetered on sheer madness. I tensed as Daxton summoned every drop of strength his body could muster and hurled it at the veil of magic separating him from his mate on the inside.

Fuck, here we go.

I attempted to brace myself, but I'd seen the inevitable. Daxton's magic ricocheted against the barrier and exploded inside the volcano's chamber, blasting us with the full force of his powers.

I closed my eyes and braced for the impact as my body was thrown backward, colliding with Shaw in his panther form. Thankfully, I was not underneath him, or else I would have died from the impact of his body weight against the rocks.

"Fucking gods-dammit!" I cursed as I rolled onto the ground next to Shaw. "Fuck!" I was so angry I couldn't think of anything else to say.

How could she do this? How delusional was she? I thought I'd taught her better than this. I thought she'd understood…

But how could I be so furious with a sacrifice such as this? Willingly giving her life so others could carry on. Was there a more noble or brave cause?

Skylar was going to die.

And… And, somehow, I was responsible for keeping my brother from following her.

"I will always find you," Skylar cried out.

I trembled, my heart racing, knowing this was all the time they had left together.

My brother remained silent as Skylar's life force began drifting into the cursed stone destined to save us. I moved onto my hands and knees, shielding myself from the blinding vortex of magic building around her.

"Daxton," Skylar whimpered, and I knew… Gods above, I knew this was it.

My brother needed to answer her. He would never forgive himself if he didn't. I willed myself to glance at Daxton, praying for him to find the strength to answer her. To do the unthinkable and say goodbye.

I didn't hear my brother's final words to her over the thundering waves of magic, but I watched his lips move as he said farewell to his mate.

The sorrow in Daxton's expression broke my heart.

What was the point of all this power if Daxton couldn't use it to save the one who mattered most? The one who completed his soul, his very essence. I knew my brother would give anything, everything, to keep her. But he knew he couldn't.

Shaw moved beside me, tucking his massive head next to my shoulder as we braced against the spiraling winds. No words could be said to comfort Daxton. All we could do was watch this unfold, helpless to do anything to break this thread of fate.

A blinding white light sprang from Skylar's chest, filling the cavern with a flood of magic that raised the fallen stones from the floor and churned the magma beneath our feet.

It was indescribable.

Magic flooded my center, and I felt alive. More alive than I had been in the last five hundred years. My magic surged through me like a river breaking free of its dam, its untamed power awakening a dormant piece of my soul—something I hadn't known was missing, let alone lost.

And then I heard him, no, correction, I *felt* him.

As the flash of light settled in the cavern, Shaw and I gazed toward the inevitable sacrifice that would threaten to shatter the fabric of our worlds.

"Gods above," I cursed as silver tears pooled in my gaze.

Daxton stood with Skylar cradled in his arms. His ironclad grip on her lifeless body held her upright, refusing to allow her to fall. I helplessly watched as my brother collapsed onto his knees, pulling Skylar into his chest. His stare locked onto the motionless body of his mate, refusing to believe the reality of what his eyes beheld.

Shaw forced himself to stand on shaking legs as a stray tear trickled along his whiskers. Lowering his head, Shaw's lips pulled back in angst, revealing ivory teeth contrasting against his black coat. His claws extended and scraped the stone. Arching his back, Shaw released a loud, mournful roar into the chasm. The cry rattled my bones, filled with so much grief and emotion that it was hard to breathe.

I strained against the pain in my own heart as I willed myself to crawl toward my brother. I couldn't imagine the grief tearing him apart, how it felt to hold...

Gods-fucking-dammit.

I felt a tug at my center, and somehow, I knew it was Nyssa. Something was happening back at camp. My throat cracked as terror began settling in my core.

The silence inside the volcano was otherworldly as I cautiously approached my brother's side. Standing at his shoulder, I cursed the Gods for bestowing this fate on Daxton and Skylar.

How cruel was it to allow them this happiness and then tear them apart so shortly after? My brother experienced so little joy in this world. Skylar had become his light, a ray of hope in the bleak existence he was forced to endure.

And now? Now...

I swallowed a heavy breath, my voice cracking as I dared to step closer. "Dax?"

My brother didn't flinch at my word. Gods, he didn't even blink. His stare was isolated solely on the face of his lifeless mate cradled in his arms.

I stilled, watching Daxton's body tremble, and I swear even I stopped breathing. His hand quivered as he pulled back to gently cup Skylar's cheek. The reality of his mate's fate raged through his soul like a hurricane on the open seas.

Gently, Daxton brushed a strand of hair from Skylar's brow, tucking it behind her ear as he gently kissed her cheek. Almost as if she were sleeping, and he was patiently waiting for her to wake from a dream.

"Dax?" I questioned once more, yet he still didn't turn to look at me. Seconds passed in complete silence, five, ten, thirty... "Daxton!" I yelled.

Haunting silver eyes, not the gray ones I'd known all these centuries, snapped open to meet my gaze. I blinked and shifted backward, my eyes widening in shock at the vast well of power I felt emanating from my brother.

Daxton returned his focus to Skylar, lifting her closer and burying his face in her cascading golden-brown hair. His body shook as his grip on her tightened.

"No," Daxton whimpered in disbelief. "No... no... no. Spitfire, y-you can't—"

"Shaw, get back!" On instinct, I released my magic and created a barrier of ice to shield us. I didn't have time to question how I managed to create the blockade. My brother's magic was unstable, on the brink of exploding in a violent outburst.

"No!" Daxton roared into the chasm.

His scream was powerful enough to feel in the depths of your soul, followed by the most powerful blast of magic I'd ever experienced. I stumble back a step, holding onto anything I could to try and steady myself.

The pain of losing Skylar shattered him.

"No!" Daxton yelled once more. The depths of his loss echoed across the seas, atop every mountain peak and valley below—loud enough for all of Valdor to hear.

The magnitude of his grief caused the earth to tremble, threatening to tear the world apart as my brother's soul bond to his mate lay broken.

"Castor, the volcano is going to erupt!" Shaw rasped in his human form as the pool of magma bubbled with boulders crumbling from the walls. "Castor! We need Daxton to teleport us out of here. The tunnel's collapsed!"

"You think he's coherent enough to do that?" I hissed as I lowered my ice barrier.

"It's either that or we all die here with Sky!" Shaw inhaled a sharp breath as his expression hardened.

The admittance of his alpha's passing tortured him almost as much as the reality of her sacrifice. Shaw's eyes darkened as he scanned the rumbling ground near the entrance.

"I need to bring the dagger back to our people, and you need to settle Daxton enough to get us the fuck out of here."

Without hesitating, Shaw sprinted across the way, dodging fallen boulders and leaping over fissures that would lead to a molten death to retrieve the alpha's dagger.

Daxton's wordless roar rang out once more, causing the volcano to shake, throwing me against the wall as his power lashed out in response to his grief.

The depths of his sorrow struck a blade through the center of my soul. Gods above, his pain was manifesting in his magic, on the brink of tearing the fabric of Valdor to pieces.

Then I realized... The stone. The fucking Heart of Valdor was amplifying his magic just like it had done with Skylar's.

I will not lose my brother. I cursed the Gods. *You can't fucking have them both. Not this time.*

Determination set in as I pushed myself from the wall and raced to my brother's side. "Dax!" I roared, praying he could hear me through his grief. "Brother!" I screamed, reaching out to latch onto him.

I dug my fingers into his shoulders, which felt like hardened slabs of stone, trying to draw his attention away from Skylar and return to the current dangers threatening our lives.

My brother, my protector. The one who'd always been so strong.

"Daxton, please!" I cried out as he lifted his gaze to meet mine.

Tears streaked my brother's face, and the canyon in my heart widened into a never-ending chasm, feeling his pain radiate from every facet of his being.

In our centuries together, I'd never witnessed tears fall from my brother's face. Not when our mother's body was burned at her funeral. Not when Daxton told me about our father's death on the battlefield, nor when he finally returned home after a century in Minaeve's court.

But now, *this*.

For the first time in over five centuries, I witnessed my brother's true grief surfacing. Skylar's death would forever leave a constant bleeding wound on his heart and soul.

"We need to escape, Dax," I pleaded. "You need to get us out of here."

My brother didn't move. Gods, he didn't even appear to be breathing.

"Dax!" I roared as I reached to take the stone from Skylar's lap.

The movement toward her snapped him out of a trance. He bared his teeth with a feral growl, his eyes hardening as he abruptly got to his feet. Despite the stone no longer being in his possession, his eyes remained silver, his wild power pulsing in uncontrollable waves.

What in the Gods' names was happening to him?

"Castor! Daxton!" Shaw's voice broke the tension as he reached us, the alpha's dagger clutched in his hand. "The volcano is collapsing! Please... Please, Daxton, get us out of here!"

The volcano rumbled as the heat in this death pit rocketed to an unbearable degree. I could see a survival instinct click in my brother's mind, but I knew he was still lost in a haze of grief.

"Dax!" I yelled as I reached out to grasp his arm, motioning for Shaw to grab my shoulder. "Now!"

I don't know how, but thankfully, my words reached my brother. And in a silver flash, he teleported us away.

Chapter Sixty-Nine

Castor Aegaeon

A battlefield was a deadly dance of violence intertwined with chaos. Complete and utter *madness*. Which was exactly what Daxton unknowingly teleported us into the thick of.

The clang of steel and roars of battle filled my ears as we reappeared at the edge of our encampment. Floods of crimson stained the field. The cries of the wounded reverberated into the final hours of the darkened night.

The battle had begun. And clutched to my brother's chest was the first sacrifice of our hopeful future.

"Watch out!" Shaw yelled as he drew the alpha's dagger and lunged forward to block a sword wielded by a High Fae dressed in dark green armor.

With centuries of combat training ingrained into muscle memory, I instinctively reached for the blade strapped to my back. In one swift movement, I removed the head of our enemy from his shoulders.

"Don't hesitate," I told Shaw. "You do, and that pretty outfit Idris gave you won't be enough to stop a blade aimed at your neck." I reached for my other sword.

"You're welcome," Shaw huffed.

Blood marked the ground beneath my feet as Shaw and I formed a protective barrier around my brother and Skylar. Examining our surroundings, I inspected our position amongst the mass of warriors engaged in a bloody battle on all sides.

A familiar tug pulled at my center, drawing my attention toward an array of boulders near an overlook—*Nyssa*. I met her darkened stare from across the way as she motioned for us to climb to her.

"Shaw, Dax, this way," I commanded, drawing my second sword and preparing to fight through bloodied carnage to reach her.

Seeing Nyssa gave me an idea, and I prayed to the Gods that it would be enough. We needed Daxton to regain his senses—needed him in this fight. However, I was terrified that the loss of Skylar would prove too steep a mountain for even him to climb. To lead this fight, Daxton would need to don his mask of indifference yet again and embody the terrifying Silver Shadow of legend.

Ducking under an enemy's blade, I countered, slicing through their armor and rendering them lifeless at my feet. A flash of a premonition flickered across my subconscious, and I turned just in time to deflect a knife thrown at my back. I glared at the Aelius warrior across the way with venom spewing in my gaze.

He did *not* want to fuck with me right now. His mistake.

I envisioned the knife he'd thrown buried in his chest, and suddenly, it was no longer an idea. The warrior clutched his chest as blood spewed from a gaping wound, a blade not made of steel but ice—a weapon conjured with ice magic.

I stilled, dumbfounded by this new ability. Daxton was the only one able to conjure ice like this. I was only able to manipulate it. *What was happening?*

"Castor!" Shaw screamed as he charged ahead, barreling through two warriors at our front. The shifter proved his skill in battle, disarming the High Fae warriors in two quick movements before running his dagger through them. He was relentless in his endeavor to reach the safety of the outcrop, with Daxton close at his back.

My brother glanced over his shoulder with Skylar cradled in his arms, following my line of sight to the ice dagger embedded in the dead Aelius warrior's heart. His eyes widened with surprise as his grip around Skylar's lifeless body remained firm.

"Let's go," I said, motioning us forward.

Off to the side, magical flames skittered across the way, signaling the heir of Crimson City joining us. As we bounded up the slope, Gunnar's war cry echoed across the battlefield, and my heart leaped, knowing he was still alive and leading this fight.

They didn't need to know the tragedy of our long-sought salvation just yet, believing Skylar was only unconscious in Daxton's arms.

As I crested the final boulder, Nyssa leaped into my chest, her grip around my neck tightening as she settled into my embrace. Without hesitating, I dropped my blades and clutched onto her.

It was then that I sensed it.

The bond between us weaved together and settled into place, flooding me with a sense of clarity and euphoric bliss that I never thought possible.

Pulling back, I cupped Nyssa's delicate face between my hands, desperately seeking the understanding and recognition I had been dreaming of seeing for months. Amongst the utter madness encompassing us and the grief that my brother was suffering, I selfishly needed this. Needed her.

Nyssa clutched onto my arms and smiled at me, nodding her head as a stray tear stained her cheek. I bent and kissed it away, pressing my brow to hers.

"I swear to the Mother and Father above," I whispered against her ear, "everything I am or ever will be belongs to you. I am yours, Nyssa."

Nyssa released her hold on my arm and moved to tap my chest, once, twice, and then a third time.

I am yours. She didn't need to speak the words for me to understand.

Desperately, I pulled her lips to mine, sealing my promise with a kiss. Nyssa was my mate, my soul bond in this life and the next.

The familiar brush of shadows pulled our attention as Zola appeared in our outcrop. Our blissful moment turned to ash.

"Why are you not fighting with Crimson City and Silver Meadows warriors? Why the fuck is—" Zola's words fell silent as her eyes locked on Skylar's lifeless body clutched against Daxton's chest.

Nyssa went still at my side, with her hand springing to cover her mouth as she, too, realized the state of Skylar's condition.

"No... No, no." Zola gasped, turning toward Shaw, searching for the truth she didn't wish to see.

Shaw bent his head and pivoted away, every muscle in his massive frame flexing as he tried to control the grief inside an iron cage. "She... She sacrificed herself to the Heart. To eradicate the wilt."

"Well," Zola said in a hushed tone, trembling with the emotions we were all feeling, "she succeeded. Look."

I hadn't had time to notice, but even through the final hours of the night, I could see it.

The wilt was gone.

"The fallen are also—"

Daxton's head spun, his voice cold and distant as he addressed our spymaster. "What about the fallen? What is your report?"

"*Some* have transitioned into their previous forms."

"What?" Nyssa signed, stepping in front of Zola.

"High Fae, mostly. Some water nymphs, a handful of dryads... But not all chose to be saved. Some remain in their damned state."

The coloring on Nyssa's face dropped as she clutched her chest, shaking her head in disbelief. I felt a whirlwind of confusion spiraling through her as I reached out to try to lend her my support.

"When did Minaeve arrive?" Daxton asked, his eyes darkening as a wild flush of his magic caused my stomach to flip. "When?" he repeated.

"Moments after the wilt disappeared," Zola answered, tilting her head. "Daxton, your eyes..."

The High Prince of Silver Meadows, not my brother, stared her down.

Zola stepped back. "How did they turn silver?"

How did I suddenly develop the ability to wield ice magic? Just a few unknowns to scatter into this wonderful setting.

Daxton ignored Zola's question and turned his attention to my mate tucked at my side. "Nyssa." Daxton's ominous voice was laced with the promise of violence and death. "Watch over Skylar's body."

A body—that was all she was now. A lifeless shell of the bright and beaming essence she once was.

I swallowed heavily as Nyssa stepped forward, cradling Skylar's head in her lap as she knelt to hold her. Daxton stilled, his hand caressing Skylar's cheek one final time before he stood and turned his attention to the battlefield.

Silver Shadow's menacing gaze locked into the heart of the clearing, his wrath and rage fueling his battle-hardened stare. He summoned Valencia, the silver blade shimmering with a life of its own, fueled by Daxton's fury.

"I have a promise to keep," Daxton said on an exhale of breath as he vanished.

I was stunned at the effortless speed of Daxton's departure. Like me, his magic and abilities were amplified.

"Arm yourself with this," Shaw said, handing Zola the shifter's dagger. "I can't fight or carry it while I'm in my panther form."

"I'll fight beside you," Zola answered. "That way, it won't leave your sight." A silent understanding passed between them.

"I'll find Daxton and make sure he doesn't try anything foolish," I said, ready to charge into battle, refusing to voice my deepest fears about his self-preservation.

"Go," Nyssa signed with a firm nod. "Fight for tomorrow. Fight for the coming dawn and all those still to come."

Shaw and Zola jumped away with her shadow magic, leaving Nyssa and me alone in the outcrop. I paused at Nyssa's final words, thankful I held something precious to fight for and a reason to come out of this alive.

Chapter Seventy

Castor Aegaeon

Turning to descend from the outcrop, I reached into my pocket and withdrew the Heart of Valdor, tucking it safely away within the crevasse between the rocks.

It will be safer here.

Reclaiming my blades, I was ready and determined to fight for the days ahead—a future gifted to me by my friend.

Her death would not be in vain. I would keep my promise and bring my brother back from this. I would help carry the weight of his grief and ensure that he did not turn back from his promise to his mate. To fight for Valdor. To free our people and provide aid to safeguard the shifters across the sea.

Steel clashed against steel before it cleaved flesh and bone. The familiar feel of my swords slicing through my foes called to a darkness within me that was only satisfied with blood and death.

It was time for my darkness to be unleashed.

I felt powerful. My blood sang with a new song of strength, my magic flowing effortlessly through my limbs as I charged headfirst into the fight. My blades were extensions of my will, cutting down my adversaries without hesitation as they tried but ultimately failed to take me down.

My gift of foresight answered my call, no longer a hindrance but an ally in battle. Death bowed to my command as glimpses of my foes' attacks flashed through my mind's eye, mere breaths before they struck. I felt unstoppable, predicting their movements before they even made them. My twin blades dripped crimson; countless bodies left in their wake as I pressed forward to join my brother.

"Dax!" I called, guarding my high prince from any foolish enough to try and land a killing blow.

Daxton said nothing as he impaled a line of warriors with an ice spear. He teleported to my other side to cut down another charging in for an attack. "Leave her for me."

I glanced ahead at the edge of the lake where Minaeve stood in wait.

"Where is—"

"Seems I've arrived just in time," Seamus sneered as he attacked Daxton.

The two mighty foes clashed as their powers met with a thundering boom. Aelius was gifted with powers of the mind, but Seamus was a formidable warrior as a high prince of his realm.

Blades collided in a flurry of silver, and the two warriors appeared to be in a standoff. With Seamus catching Daxton off guard and seizing the upper hand, my brother had to summon every ounce of his skill and strength to overthrow the High Prince of Aelius.

"Gods-dammit, Anjani," I cursed, knowing she wasn't far.

Aelius's second could not be underestimated. My head swiveled, searching through the crowds of battle to find the magic wielder lurking amongst the disorder. Minaeve approached the two high princes, her magic casting shadows and mists in her wake as her intentions focused on my brother.

"No!" I roared as I hurled a spear of ice in Minaeve's direction.

The high queen easily deflected my attack, her shadows creating a shield. But killing her was not my endgame. My assault caused Minaeve to pause, and I grinned as her turquoise stare narrowed on me.

That's it.

"You always did have an aptitude for stepping out of line and thinking you matter enough to make a difference," Minaeve sneered.

"Can't disagree. I'm never one to shy away," I taunted, drawing her undivided attention.

Her shadows expanded, her mysterious magic granting her the power to command and wield them as lethal weapons. "How do you believe this ends, Prince Castor? You're no match for my power, let alone my guards. What do you hope to achieve?"

I grinned as I planted my feet on the ground, preparing myself for an onslaught. "What makes you think this," I said, gesturing between us, "is my goal?"

Minaeve looked me over, magic caressing my skin like a snake slithering amongst the rocks. It felt wrong, unnatural.

"I see," she said. "No matter. This will all be over soon."

An uneasy tremor crept up my spine.

"Enough! Stop!" Daxton's commanding voice boomed across the battlefield, bringing us to a halt.

I turned, seeing Seamus on his knees with Valencia pressing against his throat. Blood trickled down the high king's neck as his emerald-glowing eyes burned with a menacing vengeance. Seamus tried but failed to free himself. He was trapped, unable to regain control.

I couldn't help but grin.

"Release me," Seamus commanded inside my mind, causing me to jump back in surprise. *"You're not the only one who regained their true powers."* Seamus's grin widened as he took in my state of shock.

Seamus attempted to latch onto my mind, but I managed to construct a barrier around my thoughts to protect myself from his magic and push him out.

What kind of powers were unleashed from the Heart of Valdor?

Unfortunately, others nearby did not deflect his magic in time and began approaching Daxton with their weapons drawn. Daxton remained calm, creating an ice wall around them. Gods above, my brother didn't even blink at the effort it took him to construct his barricade.

"Ahh, I see," Seamus grunted as the blade at his throat pressed into his neck. "Your gifts advanced as well."

"Daxton." Minaeve spoke my brother's name with a familiarity she didn't deserve. "What is all this? Why are you fighting to—"

"I'll kill him," Daxton replied with a stone-cold edge. "And trust me, I'll enjoy it."

"Go ahead," Minaeve said as she clicked her tongue in annoyance at my brother's hesitation.

"What?" Seamus fought to gaze at his queen, to whom he dedicated the past five centuries of servitude and obedience.

Serves you right.

Minaeve dared to step closer, her guards materializing on all sides, unveiled by Anjani's magic. "Despite everything I've granted you, Seamus, I find that you're still insufficient to my cause."

I almost, *almost*, felt sorry for the unfortunate soul.

"*Kill him,* Daxton," Minaeve said.

The only reason my brother hesitated was because *she* was giving the command.

"Kill him!" Minaeve roared again, her shadows blasting outward into the night and latching onto Daxton's blade, willing Valencia to make the final strike and end Seamus's existence in this life.

"No!" I heard Rhett's exclamation without ever seeing him.

From behind an illusion, Rhett lunged for Minaeve and tackled her to the ground. The tendrils of shadow dropped as Minaeve's guards turned on Rhett in a flash. Anjani appeared behind them, her brows raised and eyes wide with panic.

Rhett was restrained and hauled to his feet. One of the guards gripped the back of Rhett's hair, revealing a unique patch of freckles in the shape of a crescent moon at the nape of his neck I hadn't noticed before.

Minaeve struggled to compose herself with Anjani's aid. "Get off me!" Minaeve spat, swatting Anjani's hand. "Go and find it!"

Anjani nodded before backing away and disappearing.

The queen's hands glided across the skirt of her overly extravagant gown before racing up to tame her raven hair, when her fingers stopped at the crown of her head.

"My, my—" Minaeve's eyes widened with terror as she spun toward Rhett. "No... You—"

Rhett only smiled as he freed his arm from a guard's grasp, lifting Minaeve's golden crown of three gems overhead before violently smashing it to pieces at his feet.

"No!" Minaeve roared as a blast of magic exploded across the Inner Kingdom.

A bright flash of white light illuminated the final moments of the darkened skies as my skull, my gods-damned skull, felt like it was splitting in two. I cried out and buckled to my knees. My hands pressed against my temples to try and prevent my mind from tearing. My vision became a blur as every living soul surrounding me also collapsed, the same tormenting headache assaulting their minds. I fell to my side, groaning with a foreign pain.

Was this some kind of attack?

Prying my eyes open, I saw Dax and Seamus grasping their heads. Their screams joined the choruses of others ringing through the fragments of dawn, daring to peek over the eastern horizon.

"Gah!" I roared as my vision blurred once more. It felt like a premonition was absorbing me, but no, not a premonition of the future. These were visions of my past.

My... My memories.

They cascaded like an open waterfall, smashing onto the awaiting rocks below in a violent collision. The current of them whipped and overflowed in every facet of my mind. Reforging all that had been stolen, painting them into a new tapestry of a vibrant array of colors before my eyes.

"My Gods." I could hardly breathe.

I trembled beneath the weight of the truth returned through my memories—our *stolen memories*. I braced myself to push onto my hands and knees. My eyes met my brother's with a newfound breath of life.

"Minaeve," I growled as every High Fae in the field turned their attention toward the false queen.

Minaeve stood her ground with her shoulders pulled back and the air of arrogance shining through her false sense of royalty. I beheld her with a new sense of loathing, finally witnessing the depths of her wicked nature.

Minaeve's skin, which always held a golden magical hue, was dull and ordinary. Her raven hair contrasted against the glow of the approaching dawn as her haunting turquoise eyes remained hard as stone.

But her ears... Her *curved* ears, now bore the reality of her true heritage.

The world itself fell silent as we stared at the *human* female who, for five hundred years, had held our people captive.

Chapter Seventy-One

Castor Aegaeon

It only took seconds, yet the flashes felt like years.

One by one, all our memories returned.

Five centuries ago, Minaeve stole our *mother's* memory stones and utilized them with the amplifying magic of the Heart of Valdor to conceal her identity and plant false memories.

The bitch would die for this.

All my forgotten thoughts clicked into place, connecting the missing pieces of the puzzle, with my mind becoming whole once more. Minaeve was *human*. A mage sent to infiltrate and exterminate our kind.

And all for what, power? Control?

"Fuck!" I cursed. I remembered everything.

During the initial bouts of the Great War, humans learned of the Heart of Valdor's existence and stole it from the shifter guardians residing in the Inner Kingdom. The shifters informed the High Fae of the travesty, desperate to stop the humans from leaving with the stone in their possession. Utilizing the magic of the three High Fae rulers and the shifter's alpha, they created the veil to keep the Heart safe and prevent humans from bringing it back to their territory and abusing its magic.

However, the origin of the wilt and Minaeve's rise to power were still unknown to me.

I shook my head to try and regain my senses. Pushing up and rising to my feet, my limbs convulsed as I fought to contain my wrath at the truth finally rising to the surface.

"You... Y-you," Seamus stuttered, unable to find the foul language worthy enough to spew at the false queen.

Gods above, Seamus.

His face paled as he clenched his fists, oblivious to the steady stream of blood staining his armor from the wound inflicted by my brother's sword.

Minaeve smiled, tilting her head back and releasing a piercing laugh. "You were such an entertaining toy to play with, Seamus," Minaeve said, examining her nails, appearing indifferent to his outrage. "Long before you welcomed us into your lands, we plotted the demise of your kind. We were simply biding our time, waiting for the perfect opportunity to strike at the heart of your world and conquer it for ourselves."

It was before I was born, but I recalled learning about Seamus's ascension to the throne. His father passed from an unknown illness during a visit to the human kingdom, granting Seamus reign over the largest population of High Fae at far too young an age.

"You bitch!" Seamus roared as he pounded his fist against the earth in disgust.

Memories of my youth sprang forth. I fondly remembered Daxton and Seamus sparring together in the training fields when he would visit our mother, who cared for and helped train Seamus as a child. On my tenth birthday, just before the humans attacked, Seamus gifted me the very weapons I used to this day.

I looked down at my twin blades, the intricate carvings along the hilt mimicking the tattoos I had inked onto my skin.

"You twisted my mind!" Seamus screamed, his voice raw, eyes wide in a vacant horror. "Planted false, spiteful memories and manipulated me." A wave of nausea overtook Seamus, leaving him convulsing as he vomited onto the grass. Gasping for breath, he struggled to steady himself, battling the suffocating guilt of the tormenting acts Minaeve had forced him to commit.

Before his corruption, Seamus had used his mind-reading ability to foresee his people's needs and seek the truth. He was young and firm in his rule, but in his heart, he was fair.

Seamus was our ally, our friend.

"Your magic was entertaining to twist and bend to my will, Seamus. Just like your father's." Minaeve straightened, pure enjoyment rolling over her features. "Admittedly, I siphoned too much too quickly during his visit to the human kingdom across the sea. A mistake that ultimately led to his demise. But I learned how to gain access to your desires through his gifts and, in return, planted a false memory that kept you faithful, kept you ever so *loyal*."

"You soulless witch!" Seamus snarled. "How dare you manipulate me like that!"

I had no idea what memory Minaeve was referring to, and I wasn't sure I wanted to.

"You personally invited me into your court," Minaeve said with a wicked laugh. "You allowed me to enter your world, High Prince Seamus. Don't you remember sending the invitation?"

Seamus swallowed, unable to form a rebuttal, screaming in disgust and frustration at his actions.

Minaeve's lips parted, her wicked smile growing. "And from then on, control over the Inner Kingdom was finally within *our* grasp."

Our? What did she mean by this?

I stared in horror at the human mage who infiltrated our world and began destroying it from the inside out.

"The initial attack on Valdor was well underway before you granted me access to the Inner Kingdom, Seamus. It began before the first human inhabitants set foot onto Valdor's shores," Minaeve continued. "Don't give yourself more credit than you deserve, High Prince of Aelius."

"The wilt," Daxton snarled, rising to his feet, Valencia once more clutched in his hand. "You're responsible for the wilt? How?"

"Dark magic," Minaeve answered, her shadows beginning to pool at her feet. "True power comes with a sacrifice sealed in blood, the magically gifted blood of my mother and father."

"You murdered your parents to obtain dark blood-magic?" I asked, barely able to fathom the act.

"Yes," Minaeve said. "Our mother, Serena, killed by my brother, was a human blessed with elemental magic, like many from our homeland. But our father, William, whose death came by my hand, bound not just one but two souls to our cause. You see, our father wasn't only gifted with elemental magic. He was also bonded to a guardian of earth and sky—a dragon."

Gods, no.

Dragons were virtuous, magical creatures of legend that once thrived in our lands. However, centuries ago, they vanished, migrating east over the vast open seas, never to be seen again. Sacrificing the life of a dragon was unfathomable, and the magic obtained from such a sacrifice was...

"Why?" I asked, unable to keep the question locked inside.

"Silver Prince," Minaeve purred, her crimson painted lips parting in a wicked smile. "I'm disappointed I never got to experience that silver tongue for myself. Your brother's, however, was ever so delightful."

I snarled, baring my teeth as I raised my swords.

"You managed to steal the Heart, but our people locked you inside our lands with the veil," Daxton said, his voice laced with icy fury. "Even with most of the shifters fighting on the mainland, here, you were outnumbered without your allies across the sea and your other magic wielders to aid you in battle."

I took in a sharp breath, remembering what happened. It was Daxton who rallied and united the three High Fae realms of the Inner Kingdom in one final effort against the humans. They were united under the leadership of the prince who was promised.

Daxton was, no, he is our *High King*.

"Yes, a tragic turn of events, but fortune smiled upon our cause. The knowledge about Arabella's treasured memory stones was a well-guarded secret that a royal from the Aelius court willingly shared," Minaeve said with a sickening grin. "After I obtained the stones, it was easy to amplify their magic with the Heart of Valdor and steal the memories of who and what I was."

"It's... It's all my fault." Seamus fell forward, the weight of his actions threatening to tear him apart. "She invaded my mind after she deceived me and siphoned my magic. I-I can't believe I doomed us all." Seamus paused, disgust and guilt consuming him. He swallowed a heavy breath and forced himself to turn and gaze at my brother. "I'm... I'm so sorry, *my* king."

"Not quite, cousin," Anjani sneered, appearing from her illusion as she walked to Minaeve's side.

"Anjani!" Seamus rasped, the betrayal of his kin cutting him deeper than any blade across his skin. "You... You knew about this? Why?"

"Their power is irrefutable, cousin. Unmatched," Anjani declared, her arrogance radiating like a badge of honor. "I've stood by Minaeve's side since she siphoned from your father, when she promised me dominion over the Inner Kingdom in exchange for my loyalty. At last, I'll claim what is rightfully mine," she added, her smirk twisting my insides with its cold certainty.

"You started this war and created the wilt as a by-product of your dark magic that devoured our world!" Daxton roared, stepping to Seamus's side. "For what? Power? Selfish greed?"

The other High Fae surrounding us began to right themselves. Shaw and Zola raced toward our position through the growing crowd, skidding to a halt on the outskirts of our standoff.

Minaeve's glare darted to Shaw. "*You*... filthy shifters."

Shaw refused to flinch as he met Minaeve's daggered stare.

"Their alpha," Daxton whispered, piecing the events together.

"Yes, their *alpha*," Minaeve growled. "Everything was working flawlessly, but their alpha somehow surpassed the magic of the memory stone."

"And stole back the Heart," I muttered. "The alpha surrendered his life to protect the stone, and thus, the magic of his sacrifice bore life to the trials." With perhaps a dash of divine intervention from the Mother and Father above.

"With only a shifter worthy enough to unlock its power," Shaw said. "Our alpha."

"What was given before must be willingly given again," Minaeve said.

"You knew she would die!" Daxton snarled. His brows pinched as his body shuddered, fighting to control his rage.

"The fact that she was your mate made this entire endeavor all the sweeter, *High King*." Minaeve laughed as she extended her hand to Anjani. "Thank you for retrieving the Heart."

My eyes widened as I shot up in a panic.

No, no, no. Fuck! How did Anjani find it?

My heart stilled as I frantically pivoted toward the outcrop where I'd hidden the Heart of Valdor.

Nyssa.

I reached through our bond to try and sense her, but nothing answered my call. There was no panic or pain, only silence—like she was hiding.

Nyssa, where are you?

"Return to me, Seamus," Minaeve commanded, drawing my attention. "We have work to do."

"What makes you think—" Daxton paused as he watched Seamus rise, his eyes widening in disbelief. "Seamus?"

"I-I have no choice," he said through gritted teeth. Every muscle in his body convulsed in response as he tried but failed to resist Minaeve's command.

The blood bond.

"Our marriage ceremony was so special, especially when it was sealed with High Prince Seamus's magical vow of servitude."

The veins in Seamus's neck popped as he forced his feet to stop.

"Seamus," Minaeve said in a warning tone. "Return to me."

Seamus clenched his jaw so tight I thought his teeth would crack. His emerald-glowing eyes turned toward my brother. He grunted as he fought the pull of the blood oath. His footsteps halted through the sheer force of his will.

"I will not..." Seamus's voice fell as his breath stilled, the power of the oath stealing the air from his lungs, demanding his obedience.

Suddenly, Seamus sprang forward and retrieved a dagger discarded from battle, angling the blade in a downward strike across his already bleeding throat.

"Stop!" Minaeve commanded, strengthened by the Heart of Valdor clutched in her grasp. "You will not kill yourself."

Seamus groaned against the power of Minaeve's command.

"Nor will you allow or command another to end your life for you. I forbid it."

Seamus remained motionless, locked between Daxton and the false queen.

"Drop the blade."

And Seamus was forced to obey.

"Call your warriors," Minaeve said.

"Why do you think any of Aelius would willingly side with you?" Daxton yelled, his gaze darting between Seamus and Minaeve.

"Who said anything about willingly?" Minaeve's wicked grin grew.

"Daxton, Castor." Seamus's voice echoed inside my mind. *"Do what you must."*

I swallowed a heavy gulp of dread, understanding Seamus's intentions for us to fulfill if he couldn't perform the task himself. *"I deserve far less than the kindness of a quick death. I'm sorry for everything."*

"Fall in line." Seamus's voice boomed over the clearing, and every High Fae warrior sworn to Aelius followed his command.

"Every citizen sworn to Aelius and High Prince Seamus's army is bound to him," Anjani said with a conniving look of glee. "The blood oath is an ancient tradition in the Aelius realm, of course, to ensure loyalty."

Minaeve wielded her siphoned magic, with the Heart of Valdor amplifying her power, as a massive glowing portal of light appeared. Through it stepped a tall figure wearing a dark blue cloak with painted stars and a trail of hooded figures following his lead.

"Istar," Minaeve said with a grin as the cloaked figure approached and openly embraced her. "Bless the dark."

"Banish the light," he replied as his hood fell back, revealing a mesh of black raven hair and hauntingly familiar turquoise eyes. "Finally, we have won."

Their likeness was uncanny.

"Arm yourselves!" Daxton roared as he hoisted Valencia above his head.

Finn sprinted to his side with flames illuminating his hands and traveling down his sword. "Crimson City is with you, Daxton," the young prince declared.

"Let's have some fun." Gunnar appeared at Daxton's other shoulder, blood staining his silver-lined leathers as he gripped a battle axe in one hand and his shield in the other.

The early rays of dawn trickled across the horizon, the Mother awakening from her slumber to find death at her doorstep. I clutched my swords in my hands, readying myself to charge into the fight, willing to defy the odds and overturn the human mage responsible for the destruction of our world.

"Charge!" Daxton yelled as the fighting began.

Chapter Seventy-Two

Skylar Cathal

Tap, tap... Tap, tap.

"What... What's happening?" I groaned, unfolding my arm from my face.

I gasped, mesmerized by the breathtaking beauty that surrounded me. Vibrant, colorful flowers dotted a canvas of soft green grass, while willows swayed gracefully in the warm, gentle breeze. Beyond this clearing, the forest seemed to stretch on for eternity, a never-ending array of pines and birch with vivacious greenery interwoven between the trees. My fingers gripped strands of grass, digging into the soil beneath me as a serene sense of peace encased me in a cloud of comfort.

The magical sound of elegant music filled my soul. The harmonious melody of string instruments flowed like the rushing waters of the nearby translucent turquoise river.

This forest was alive, unlike anything I could have ever dreamed.

"Get up," a voice commanded.

I turned to see a male no older than myself sitting back in the soft grass.

"You don't have time to waste lying around, Alpha."

I blinked rapidly at the shifter beside me, sensing a connection to him that spanned through space and time. A saccharine grin stretched across his clean-shaven face as he tilted his head and looked me over.

"Who are you?" I asked.

He remained silent, much to my dismay.

"Who are you?" I asked once more, using a dash of power through my alpha command.

He shook his blond, almost white, mesh of hair, feeling the magic in my words. "It's easier if I show you."

Reaching down, he rolled up the sleeve of his left arm to reveal the outline of three eight-pointed stars. The mark of the shifter champion.

"Stark?"

His grin returned as he moved backward, his magic rising to the surface. In a green flash, an owl with feathers matching a fresh snowfall stared at me with striking golden eyes.

"Where are we?" I asked, although I was pretty sure I knew the answer.

The owl tilted its head once more before spinning around and calling out into the forest. It turned its large eyes back toward me, flapping its wings as it hopped closer.

"Do you want me to follow you?"

A hoot and nod of its head was a clear sign.

"All right," I said, rising to my feet. "Lead the way."

The owl flew into the endless darkening sky above. The setting sun cast an array of pink and gold that made it difficult to turn away. Stark swooped over my head and circled me from above before diving past my shoulder and flying toward the river.

I didn't feel like I was walking; it was more like I was gliding, drifting across the land toward the soothing sound of the flowing river. The air had a sweetness to it, my steps felt weightless, and there was no trace of the nightmares, fears, or pain that once haunted me.

I felt at peace.

As we continued forward, the former champion as my guide, we approached a small cluster of boulders resting on the edge of the riverbed. The white fog around the bank began to clear, and I could see the outline of someone sitting along the water's edge.

"Hello, Skylar."

I skidded to a halt and gasped. My eyes widened as tears of joy flowed wildly down my cheeks. "J-Julia?" I clutched my chest, desperate to hear her voice again.

The fog parted as the darkened curls and tawny freckled face of my aunt came into view. "Julia!" I screamed, running as fast as my feet could carry me to her open arms.

I scooped Julia up off her feet, spinning her around and clutching her tight to my chest. The smell of warm spices from our kitchen in Solace filled my senses as she clutched onto my waist, laughing as I twirled. When I stopped, Julia cupped my face, kissing my cheeks and brow as I openly cried in her arms.

"There, there, love," Julia said softly. "Everything is going to be all right."

"No, no, it's not, Julia," I cried as memories of my last moments flashed inside my mind. The memory of Daxton's mournful cry and the looks of dread on Shaw and Castor's faces. Gods, I'd hurt them. Lied and deceived them. But I didn't have any other choice. They would have tried to stop me.

"Come here," Julia said as she grasped my wrist. "I want to show you something." Her gentle touch guided me toward the river. "Place your hand in the water and take a drink. There are things you need to know."

"What is this?"

"It's the waters of the great crossing, Sky."

I looked across the divide, realizing that this was the crossing to the afterlife. "Is it true that... that those who cross and are burdened by their sinful actions in their life sink to the bottom of the endless river and never reach peace?"

"Yes," Julia said somberly. "You've met one of these beings. I believe you made a bargain with it."

I stilled, swallowing heavily.

"But that's not what I wish to talk about," my aunt said as she knelt. "This water also holds memories, and you must see all that has happened to lead you here before you continue."

I hesitated.

"Don't worry." Julia chuckled as she cupped her hands and drank from the churning water. "You're already dead. What else could go wrong?"

Her playful wink relaxed me as I huffed a laugh.

"That's true," I replied, following her lead.

I cupped the cold water and gently brought it to my lips. As the liquid trickled past my tongue, I saw it all—the truth about the memories stolen, Minaeve's scheme to infiltrate and destroy the inner Kingdom. *Their* plan.

I coughed as I leaned forward. My mind raced with everything I had learned, "Minaeve... Minaeve and Istar, the human king's lead mage, are—"

"Twins," Julia said with a furrowed brow, "their unique bond links them together despite time or distance. Minaeve can siphon magic and lifespans, and, in return, Istar holds the ability to boost the magic of those around him, similar to the Heart. They've been working in unison since the humans first arrived in Valdor. Plotting and planning the demise of our world to take it for themselves."

That was how they survived all this time.

"But... But why?" I asked.

"Power," Julia answered plainly. "They were born with only a fraction of what they believed they deserved and sought more."

"They killed their parents," I heaved, sitting backward along the riverbank. "And, and a dragon—"

"I know." Julia softly patted my arm, tracing over my champion mark with the three stars now shaded crimson. "Not all of us have the strength in our hearts to do what must be done, Skylar."

"Gods, the High Fae," I stammered with a wave of sorrow crashing into me. "Even our ancestors..."

"Yes." Julia nodded, her lips pressed into a thin line and a narrowed brow. Her *serious* face, Neera and I named it from our childhood. "Our ancestors did not flee the Inner Kingdom. Our alpha sent us away to lead the fight against the corrupt human forces on the mainland. We were divided when the Heart was stolen. The veil was created by shifter and fae magic, but the memories of our elders were not spared in Minaeve's scheme."

"I can't even imagine how lost they were, how confused and defenseless—"

"Skylar," Julia interrupted. "*Shifters* are never defenseless. We are the guardians of the Heart of Valdor. Strong, dependable, and above all, brave. Our alpha, your direct ancestor, overcame Minaeve's magic with the help of his animal and then bravely sacrificed his own life to ensure it was locked away."

"Until a shifter—"

"Until a shifter clever enough, strong enough, and brave enough was able to find it."

I sat in silence, allowing the trickling sounds of the river to help me sift through my winding thoughts.

"Thankfully," Julia added, "not all humans are cursed with such evil in their hearts." My aunt beamed and stretched to cup my cheek. "Your mother Dawn, is one example of the truth in this."

"My, my—" I frantically spun around, searching. I'd never known her name.

"She's across the river," Julia said, motioning toward the opposing side. "Once your mother passed, Emery was here waiting for her, and then, they crossed over together."

Knowing that my father waited for my mother confirmed my suspicion that they were a mated pair, bringing warmth to my heart.

"All right, so this side of the river is some type of staging area? We aren't in the afterlife yet?"

"More or less," Julia answered. "It's a place for those not yet ready to cross over. A place where we can wait."

I swallowed heavily as my eyes threatened to release another stream of tears. I knew why Julia was here. She was waiting for Magnus. "How long?"

"As long as it takes," Julia said with a kind smile. "It's beautiful here, and we can watch over all those we love. It's not absolute peace, but..." Julia paused as she adjusted her knees beneath her. "Without your uncle, I'll never truly be at peace. A part of me will always be searching for him."

I cast my gaze away, tears stinging the backs of my eyes at the depth of love my aunt and uncle shared.

"Then I'll be waiting with you."

"Oh really?" Julia chuckled, covering her mouth. "You don't say?" she teased, lightly grasping my shoulder. "Daxton."

I nodded, my entire body trembling at the thought of my mate and how desperately I wanted to see him, hear his laugh, or feel the touch of his hand on my cheek—just one more time.

"That doesn't surprise me, Skylar," Julia said with an all-too-knowing grin. "He may be immortal, but I could see it. I told Magnus as such the day he brought you back to Solace. Daxton fell for you long before you even thought a pairing between you could be a reality."

"Was it that obvious?"

"Yes." Julia laughed.

The cracks that formed in my heart since hearing about her death began stitching back together.

"What?"

"I missed you," I replied, hugging her tightly. "That's all."

"Magnus isn't the only reason I'm here, Sky," Julia said, taking me aback. "One sip from the river doesn't give you all the answers." She chuckled lightly, rising to her feet.

The snow-feathered owl swooped past our heads and landed atop a nearby branch, fluttering its wings and giving us its undivided attention.

"Hello, Stark," Julia said.

"A friend of yours?"

"He's becoming one," Julia replied.

"I'm happy but also saddened to see you here, Champion," Stark said. *"I know what you had to sacrifice in order to fulfill this trial of fate."*

"Why are you still on this side of the crossing?" I asked.

"I'm waiting," Stark answered with a ruffle of his feathers. *"For him, but also you. We are all waiting for you."*

The fog along the river lifted, revealing the brilliant turquoise waters with vibrant-colored pebbles scattered along the bend. Red, blue, and even green stones lined a shallow pathway meandering across the distance to the opposing shoreline. My gaze followed the path, almost as if a higher power was guiding me to what lay on the other side.

The world stilled as a tall, commanding figure appeared along the edge. My throat went dry as my eyes locked with the male across the way. The green Cathal eyes that I'd passed by countless times in the hall of the alphas, which I saw in Magnus and Neera, were staring back at me.

"Father?" I stammered as I sprang to my feet.

A smile turned at the corner of his mouth as his expression softened, giving me a firm nod. He turned his head as a human female came to his side. My father wrapped his arm around her waist as he pulled her in close. The mating mark of a shifter visible along her neck. The sun-kissed skin, beautiful brown eyes, and vibrant, wavy golden hair were identical to my vision of her in the Labyrinth.

"Mother?"

She looked at me with tears glistening in her gaze, a deep sense of pride and love beaming in her expression. Emery bent and tenderly kissed her brow as she leaned into his chest. My heart fluttered joyfully at the sight of them together.

"They're proud of you, Skylar," Julia said, touching my shoulder. "So very proud."

I couldn't speak to them from the other side of the crossing, but I didn't need to.

Then, on Emery's other side, a familiar-looking male with the same Cathal eyes stepped forward. His shoulder-length blond hair lightly turned in the breeze, and I knew in my soul that this was the alpha who sealed the Heart of Valdor away.

He met my gaze, and, in a flash, he shifted into his animal, a proud, powerful lion with a mane the color of spun gold. He tilted his head back and released a thundering roar that reached us on the other side of the crossing. My mother stepped from my father's side as he shifted into his massive grizzly bear, adding to the chorus of my ancestors booming behind them.

"What does this all mean?" I asked.

"Your time among the living is not done yet, Skylar," Julia said, coming to my side and brushing my hair over my shoulder. "You must go back."

"What?" I shook my head in disbelief. "I'm dead. How am I supposed to go back?"

Julia grinned as a breeze played with the curls along her headband. Her dark eyes softened as she looked at me with the love only a mother could give. "You know how," she said as she touched my heart.

In the distance, I heard a faint melody drifting along the gentle breeze. "*Daxton*." I closed my eyes, feeling the pull of our mate bond trying to guide me home. "He's... He's still holding on."

"Stubborn males." Julia chuckled.

"But how? How am I supposed to—" I paused as the spark of fire from my animal kindled in my center. My soul ignited like the blazing sun, vibrant and overflowing with untapped power, finally ready to be unleashed.

I turned my gaze away from the river, hearing the song of my animal spirit.

"Go," Julia whispered, releasing her hold as my feet guided me from the crossing. "This was always meant to be."

I paused, glancing back one final time at my loving aunt, saying farewell. "I love you," I said to her before my eyes traveled across the river to my ancestors, who built the mountain for me to rise and touch the sky. "I love you all. Thank you—"

My father shifted into his human form and knelt, placing a fist over his heart with a bowed head, honoring me with his recognition of me as an alpha. My heart burst with gratitude at the pride in his expression. My mother gently pressed her fingers to her lips, releasing them toward me as she joined my father.

"Go!" Julia yelled, giving me the final push I needed.

I pivoted and raced across the clearing, toward the song calling me home.

"*Fly, Sky.*"

Chapter Seventy-Three

Castor Aegaeon

Fuck my life. Nothing about this battle was right.

Seamus faced off against Daxton, while Aelius and the human mages summoned through Minaeve's portal engaged with Crimson City and Silver Meadows warriors. Allies were forced to combat against each other, and the free will to defy Minaeve's wicked scheme was stripped from them all.

Having us destroy ourselves was far too easy. Minaeve's blood oath linked Seamus to her command, which extended to his people, granting her the ultimate plan for our kind to eradicate ourselves from this world.

The shifters on the mainland were outnumbered, their population depleted but never eliminated. No, they needed one of them to unlock the Heart of Valdor.

That was the only reason their kind was still alive.

Pivoting on my toes, I unleashed a fury of attacks aimed at disarming. Alas, some inevitably landed a killing blow, ending the life of a brother or sister. All while acting on a will that was not their own, sickening me to my core. I ducked and rolled under a strike to my backside.

Coming to my feet, I thrust my blades into the torso of a High Fae dressed in green armor.

"Thank you," the male rasped as the life faded from his eyes.

"Fuck!" I cursed as I withdrew my tainted blades. The crimson blood of my kin trickled down the metallic silver to stain my hands. "Is this what you wanted?" I screamed, turning toward the dawning sky. "This! This bloodshed... This death?" I cried to the Mother and Father above, my wrath and hatred for this damned fate of Valdor overtaking any remaining rationale.

Flames flared along the perimeter, and I knew Finn was in trouble. Turning in place, I searched for Adohan's heir, finding him along the base of the outcrop where I last saw Nyssa.

"Hold on, Finn!" I roared as I charged across the battlefield.

Gunnar was fighting at Daxton's side, but I still felt a pang of guilt for leaving my brother. Daxton would kill Seamus if he had to, but—

"Gahh!" I roared, my frustration boiling over as a premonition forced me to pause.

I sidestepped from my route and managed to duck under a blast of magic from a battling mage. Turning my darkened eyes toward the woman off to the right, dressed in a dark blue robe with stars etched into the seams, I bared my teeth and snarled. She looked at me and smiled, revving her magic for another blast of energy that would explode like the force of the sun.

The female fired her magic at me again, but my gifts allowed me to see where she was aiming her killing blasts. I dodged them easily, making my way toward her location. With the rising sun cresting over my backside, the female held up her arm to block the blinding rays. I smiled, confident that I had her.

"Try again," she said, aiming a blast of her magic at the outcrop.

"No!" My eyes widened in panic as I threw my blade at the mage, the steel slicing through her torso, but not before her magic collided with the side of the hill, sending boulders tumbling down the rock face.

"Fuck! Nyssa," I roared, desperately diving down our bond to find her.

Boulders scattered, and I felt my stomach drop, remembering that Finn was fighting at the base. Gods above, no.

I sprinted toward him. "Finn! Finn!" I yelled.

Shaw, in his panther form, joined me in my frantic search. His strength proved vital as he pushed aside massive boulders like they were mere pebbles.

"Finn!" I screamed, desperate to locate him.

A faint groan drew my attention, and Shaw sniffed the air with a nod, confirming my assumption. With one last effort, we shoved the final boulders to find Finn, with two of his guards surrounding him, protecting him from the falling rocks.

"*Cas?*"

"Thank the Gods!" I rasped, leaping into the pit.

"Don't move him," Zola said, appearing out of the shadows. "Castor, if you do, then—"

Shit, she was right. A stray blade protruded from his back, blood pooling beneath him. I looked at Finn's body entangled with his guards, who were already at the crossing to the afterlife. I spared a moment and silently thanked them for their sacrifice in protecting Crimson City's heir.

"Castor?" Finn coughed, his chest heaving.

"Hold on, Finn," I said, grasping his hand in desperation. "You have a sister to meet, I hear. You need to hold on. You need to meet her."

"A sister." Finn smiled as his eyes fluttered closed.

"Stay with me, Finn!" I roared. "Someone, fetch the healers. If we can get him out of here safely, he has a chance!"

"Castor, he can't—"

"Zola!" I yelled in fear.

"If you let me in, I can jump him to the healer's tent," Zola said.

I nodded, giving Finn one final squeeze before moving aside. The shadows cast by the surrounding rocks would allow her to transport them out of the debris.

Once out of the pit, I glanced at the continuing battle, searching for my brother and my mate amongst the chaos. Looking toward the east, I found her. Nyssa was dragging Skylar's body up the grassy knoll, her attention isolated on cresting the top.

"Nyssa!" I shouted, trying to get her attention.

What in the Gods' names was she doing?

As dawn broke along the horizon, Nyssa crested the hill with Skylar's body in tow. Nyssa fell backward, leaving Skylar on the mound's peak as the sunlight danced across her lifeless frame. In the next breath, an explosion of flames brighter than the Mother herself erupted atop the grassy knoll.

"Nyssa!" I roared as I shielded my eyes, running toward my mate in panic.

The flames continued to grow, drawing everyone's attention as the spiraling cascade of fire seemed to stretch up into the rising sun. I skidded to my mate's side, pulling her backward with me as we escaped the maelstrom of fire threatening to consume us.

"What is this?" I asked. "What's going on?"

Nyssa smiled, signing, "Skylar."

The flames spiraled into a swirling vortex as a familiar song echoed throughout the lands. It was a beautiful melody I remembered from my childhood. The same song my mother sang to Daxton and me. The same song I knew he sang to her—Skylar.

The heat of the flames skyrocketed, fluttering blue and then white, every pair of eyes entranced by the sight unfolding before us. The faint outlines of feathers began to dance amongst the wisps of crimson flames, followed by magnificent wings and tail feathers that draped behind a mammoth body cloaked in fire.

The flames swirled as a figure finally took shape, revealing a magical bird of legend, one I never thought I would see in my immortal life—*a phoenix*.

The flames dissipated, revealing the legendary bird of fire, hovering over the battlefield and looking down on us with a familiar amber stare.

"Skylar," I whispered as Nyssa grasped my hands.

Shaw's roar filled the silence as the phoenix's song answered his call, turning its sight to the mages rallying near Minaeve and Istar near the lake's edge. Blistering flames engulfed the phoenix's body as it swooped toward Minaeve. Skylar's power and rage erupted across the land below, creating an impenetrable wall of scorching wildfire aimed directly at the heart of our enemies.

Minaeve called upon a barrier, the Heart of Valdor clutched to her chest, as Skylar dove toward the shield. Flames and talons collided with the blackened wall, as dozens of smaller portals appeared around us. Aelius warriors were pushed through at the command of human mages.

Still, Skylar did not relent in her attack, determined to break through the magic that kept her from seeking vengeance and blood for the deeds cast by the false queen.

"Retreat!" Seamus commanded, standing along the opening of a portal. "*Do what you must,*" he said into my mind before stepping through the blinding light of magic.

I turned my attention back toward the mythical firebird, whose flames managed to crack through Minaeve's shield, causing her to panic.

"Through the portal!" Minaeve shouted at Istar and Anjani.

They both escaped without hesitation as Minaeve slowly backed up, struggling to keep her shield against Skylar's wrath.

"Until we meet again, shifter," Minaeve sneered as she stepped through the portal and disappeared with the rest of her troops.

Skylar violently flapped her wings as flames danced along feathers painted in red, yellow, and gold, blazing like the Mother herself. Traces of vibrant purple, white, and blue decorated the plumage at the tips of her wings and tail feathers, where the flames burned the brightest.

Skylar landed on the ground with her head tilted back. Her wings were gracefully tucked into her sides. She stood proud, her eyes shining with determination as she scanned the clearing, the flames cast by her magic burning brightly with the rising dawn.

She was mesmerizing.

Amid the smoke and chaos of the battlefield, I saw a lone figure marching toward Skylar. The flames surrounding her twisted and parted, clearing a path just for *him*.

Chapter Seventy-Four

Skylar Cathal

Daxton.

Exhaling a shuddering breath, I surveyed him, finding the face of the being I cherished most in this world, the soul I would always find in this life and the next.

Shifting into my human form, flames continued to dance around my naked flesh as my gaze locked onto a silver storm. Every nerve in my body and breath in my lungs ignited like the fire at my command as Daxton approached me in the clearing. He didn't spare anyone else a glance. He didn't look at his fallen comrades or slain enemies. He only saw me.

The world outside Daxton faded as I felt the mate bond click into place.

The threads that bound us glowed brighter than any flame, burning star, or sun in the sky. It was beautiful, illuminating any tinge of lingering darkness that dared separate us.

The overwhelming sensations soaring through our bond caused my heart to ache. Daxton's emotions ranged from hatred to sorrow, love to loss. But at the center of it was a profound feeling of hope that never dimmed or faltered. The unrelenting belief that our bond would lead me home—to him.

That we would *always* find each other.

My chest heaved as I stared at my mate, unable to move from where I stood as tears rolled down my cheeks. There was so much I wanted to say to him, needed to tell him, but I couldn't summon the courage to speak.

Any verbal declaration of love would fall short of what we felt, of what we shared together.

"Skylar?" Daxton murmured with heavy emotion.

"Daxton," I sobbed, overcome by the depth of devotion I held for this male.

Daxton's chest shuddered as he allowed himself to finally breathe. Tears formed in his eyes as he swallowed a heavy breath, bending to take a knee before me. Silently, he held out Valencia, bowing his head as he laid his majestic weapon at my feet.

"I bow before you, my queen," Daxton said. "I pledge my blade, my magic, and my life to you—and only you."

"I accept, on one condition," I answered, my phoenix's magic igniting our surroundings in a blaze of flames in agreement. "Only if *you* are my king."

Daxton lifted his gaze and stood to meet me in a rush. I fisted his hair and dragged his mouth to mine. The taste of him swallowed me in ecstasy, his tongue parting the way for us to consume each other, stealing this moment for ourselves. Our kiss deepened as his hands parted the flames covering my body, bending to his touch and his touch only.

"Take me away," I moaned against his lips. "Take us somewhere we can escape, where I can finally claim you."

"As you command, my queen," Daxton replied, bending to sweep me into his arms and teleport us away in a flash of silver.

Chapter Seventy-Five

Skylar Cathal

We reappeared in the hanging valley, the final petals of the moondance flower closing as the cresting sun along the eastern mountain peaks painted the meadow in a golden hue.

"Dax, I need to tell you—"

"No," he said sharply, carrying me toward a bed of soft grass near the trickling creek. "Don't. Not yet, I need—"

Heavy emotion rang through the bond as a whirlwind of intense feelings hammered into my heart, melting me against him. Daxton's grip on me tightened as he came to a stop, falling to the grass and tucking me between his legs. I reached out a hand to cup his bearded chin, longing to meet his gaze.

"Dax," I whispered, kissing his cheek as my tears trickled onto his face.

Daxton turned to kiss my brow, his hold on me refusing to give way as I looped my arms around his neck. I opened myself to our bond, vanquishing any remaining walls that dared to separate us, creating a safe place for us to retreat together.

"I-I'm so sorry." I sobbed as Daxton's grief drowned me in an endless sea of sorrow. His pain from watching me die was unfathomable, and I couldn't breathe. I couldn't think.

He was so gods-damned strong.

"I heard you," I rasped. "When I was at the crossing, I felt you calling me home." I pulled back to meet his gaze, the gray eyes I remembered now a brilliant silver rivaling the stars. "You saved me."

"You saved us all," Daxton answered, pressing his brow to mine as a wave of emotion crashed over us.

With my shift, our bond was uncaged, bringing us closer than I ever thought possible.

"I never lost hope that I'd find you, Spitfire. *Never—*"

"We will always find each other," I answered, sealing my promise with a kiss that broke the fabric of time itself.

I moved to straddle Daxton's hips, pushing him onto his back as I continued to kiss him. My mate's hands migrated over my curves, with his fingers digging into my skin, leaving marks where only his hands were allowed to hold me.

A deep-seated hunger—no, a need—began forming.

An instinct to claim him.

Our kiss deepened as sensual desire ignited through the bond. I moaned into Daxton's mouth as he ravaged my body with his rough hands, his growing length pulsating against the apex between my thighs.

"I need to claim you," I said, rising up. "Remove your armor."

A dark chuckle of approval shone within his menacing gleam. "Yes, Alpha." Daxton quickly stripped himself bare.

I moved to straddle him once more, drinking in the rippled muscles and scars of my battle-hardened warrior king.

I firmly grasped the base of his shaft as I traced the tip of his cock against my clit, teasing us both, savoring the build-up of heat.

"Yes," he groaned, his eyes mimicking liquid silver. "Use me. I'm yours."

Daxton sat up, gripping my ass with one hand to hold me in place as he worshiped my breasts, sucking on one pebbled peak before migrating to the other. I reached out and roughly tugged on the back of his hair, bending to devour his delicious lips.

I moaned as I broke our kiss, tasting the fevered flesh along his neck before nibbling on the base of his ear as I whispered, "I love you."

"Oh, Spitfire," Daxton rasped, his voice heavy with desire. "Love doesn't come close to describing the depth of my devotion to you." He grasped my chin between his thumb and forefinger, commanding my stare. "I could live a thousand lifetimes, conquer a million different worlds, and be granted the might of the Gods themselves. But none... *none* of these compare to one day, one night, not even one second, that I'm gifted with your presence."

I inhaled a sharp breath as a flood of emotions burst through the bond, the word "love" falling short of what we truly felt.

"You're my salvation, Daxton," I said. "You're my *everything*."

I leaned in and kissed him. The depth of our love screamed down the bond, so loudly that even those at the crossing to the afterlife could hear us.

I needed him inside me. Needed him to stretch and fill me like no other male could. I needed him to—

Fuck. I needed him to finally claim me as his mate.

Daxton sucked in a breath as I re-took control, pressing him flat onto his back as I moved to sheathe his length in one swift movement. Gripping his shoulders, I rolled my hips, watching my mate's eyes shine a brilliant silver.

And still, I wanted more.

Daxton released a deep moan as I increased our pace. His hips bucked to meet my fevered hunger. Our thriving bodies worked in perfect sync as waves of pleasure rolled through the bond. Still, we fought to be closer, to meet each other in a place of openness and pure bliss that we could only achieve together.

My release was building as Daxton's grip held me in place. His hips thrust in a euphoric rhythm with my own, taking my breath away as my core began to simmer into a raging inferno.

"Dax," I moaned, moving against him, my pleasure escalating higher and higher. "Daxton." My release tore through me as Daxton continued to ram his cock to the hilt. "Don't... Don't stop," I pleaded, waves of pleasure building once more.

"Not planning on it," Daxton growled in a dark, heavy voice.

"Good," I rasped, gripping his hands and pinning them over his head, moving atop his lap as I resumed our pace.

I raked my teeth over the base of Daxton's neck, my phoenix sending wave after wave of power through my body, causing my limbs to tingle until they trembled with the combined height of power and blissful pleasure.

"Are you ready?" I whispered into Daxton's ear. The power between us was rising and dancing to the melody of our bond.

"Claim me, Spitfire," Daxton said.

My grip on his wrists tightened as I held him in place. Clenching my thighs, I sat down, seating his cock deep inside me, raking my teeth along the side of Daxton's neck.

"You're mine," I growled as I bit into his flesh.

The heated iron liquid of Daxton's blood rushed across my tongue in sweet satisfaction. My mate groaned beneath me as he came.

My magic sank into the mark on his neck, sealing our bond and my everlasting claim of Daxton Aegaeon as mine.

Dax's groans of pleasure continued as I released my hold on his wrists, allowing him to clutch onto my hips and pump his release farther into me, feeling our connection transcend what we held before my claiming mark.

I released my bite, leaning back to admire the mark that I would make sure to re-stake whenever the opportunity presented itself. I slid from Daxton's lap, and he rose up and grasped the base of my neck, kissing me like a maddened male in search of a cure.

"Don't for one second think we're done yet, Spitfire." He huffed a dark laugh as he lay me on my back, drinking in the sight of me. "It's my turn."

The prospect of him laying a claiming mark sent a crazed thrill through me that floated through our bond.

Daxton stilled as he hovered over me, bringing my wrist to his lips. "My mark from before is no longer here. I won't stand for any other imagining they have a chance with you."

I didn't realize it until now, but his scar, likely all my scars, had disappeared. The only mark remaining was the three eight-pointed star design, now filled with crimson.

"Please, Daxton," I said in a breathy whisper. "Claim me."

A devilish smile crept across his lips. "As you command, my alpha queen."

I lay back as Daxton's massive frame towered over me. Gods be damned, we'd fought to get here. We'd earned the right to finally claim each other.

Daxton positioned himself between my open thighs, lowering himself to run his tongue along my clit before his fingers slipped inside.

"Daxton," I rasped as he devoured me, his fingers curling in just the right way to make me see stars.

"That's right, my queen," Daxton purred against me. "Say my name again. Scream it loud enough so the whole fucking world knows who you belong to."

"Daxton!" I cried out as the build-up spiraled through me, teetering on the edge.

My mate pulled back, licking his fingers as his eyes traced over my naked body spread out before him. "Fuck, you're perfection, Skylar."

"When you claim me," I said between rapid breaths, "the heat will likely settle in, and—"

"I'm aware," Daxton said with a grin, moving over me. "The need to take you will be all-consuming." Daxton's voice dropped, sending trickles of anticipation up my spine as he slowly kissed my lower stomach. "The need to satisfy my instinct to take you will be so intense that we won't have much sanity once under its sway."

"Do fae experience this?" I asked.

"We call it a frenzy," he said, a low possessive growl sounding in his throat as he looked me over. "I'm already feeling the effects of the bond, and I'm ready to take you again, my spitfire."

My eyes darted between us, heat pooling in my core, biting my lip at the sight of his length hardening.

"I'm warning you," he growled, grasping my chin and forcing my gaze back to him. "I'll be unhinged when it comes to you, Skylar. More than I already am."

My heart skipped as my phoenix sang in delight, approving of this male.

"I'm ready," I said.

Wetness dribbled along my inner thighs at the anticipation of him claiming me. Daxton's eyes darkened as he kissed me, adjusting his hips as he slowly, ever so fucking slowly, slid his cock into me—my body quivering with pleasure beneath him.

"You're mine," Daxton said as he thrust his hips forward, slamming to the hilt.

Arching my back, I moaned, clutching onto his shoulders as his teeth grazed over the base of my neck. His hot breath sent a trickle of pleasure radiating through my core, the anticipation of his mark driving me wild.

"Dax—" I pleaded as he opened his mouth, biting down onto my neck.

A wild rush of magic flowed through Daxton's bite as pleasure, not pain, soared through me. His hips bucked hard against me, each thrust sending me higher. I moved with him, his teeth still buried in my flesh as the magic continued to build between us, heightening everything. I fisted his hair, closing my eyes as I gave into the pull, allowing our magic to blend together, accepting his mark, and submitting, only to him.

My orgasm tore through me as my inner walls clenched around his pulsing cock. Daxton raised up; lips stained a beautiful crimson with wild silver flashing in his eyes. He grabbed my hips and pounded into me, roaring as he came, his chest heaving as I quivered beneath him.

Ice coated the ground beneath us as fire blazed along my fingers, bending when I reached out to touch him.

Daxton opened his eyes to meet mine as a wave of power vibrated between us.

Our bond was unbreakable.

Daxton was mine, and I was his.

Chapter Seventy-Six

Shaw Black

"Where the fuck did they go?" I roared.

"Do you really want to be a spectator to what they're likely doing?" Castor taunted in his annoying sing-song voice. I was beginning to tolerate his flamboyant facade, but it was still far from my liking. "How scandalous of you, Shaw. I didn't know you liked to watch."

"She's my alpha—"

"And he is my *king*," Castor shot back, emphasizing the final word as he released his hold on his mate.

My eyes widened with shock. "Excuse me, king?"

"The memories Minaeve stole," Castor began. "Daxton united the three realms against the onslaught of humans and mages. He's not *just* our high prince. He is High King of the Inner Kingdom."

"Their pairing unites Valdor."

"And the plot of the Gods becomes clear," Castor said with a huff of a laugh. "Can you believe it?"

I could. I did.

"Gods be damned," I cursed to myself, ignoring the questions following my abrupt departure from Castor and Nyssa.

Unable to do anything, I turned and marched across the clearing toward the healers' tents. To where the ever-present pull and feel of a thundering drum beat echoed in my chest, growing the closer I got to her.

My panther knew immediately.

The second I saw her and detected her scent, she consumed my world. I was as anchored to her as the moon was to the sun.

The High Fae were occupied with regrouping, and I was a lone shifter in these lands with my alpha currently occupied with her mate. I was angry at first that they vanished, but then again, if the roles were reversed, I would've done the same.

Skylar is a phoenix.

I still couldn't believe she returned from the dead, let alone shifted into the mythical firebird of legend. She was also larger than Gilen's roc, a fact that I knew Rhea would never tire of pointing out to anyone who asked.

"Shifter," a High Fae warrior in red whispered as I passed, giving me a nod of respect, which I returned.

Well, at least Skylar isn't the only one gaining ground with the fae.

My wounds from the battle were already healing thanks to my magic. The gashes along my back and shoulder added to the array of battle wounds I carried with a unique sense of pride. I had to. Otherwise, my scars would have led to my demise years ago.

I glanced at my hands, flexing them as the scars on my forearms gleamed in the morning sun against my skin. I steadied my breathing as I continued forward, forcing the familiar rising feelings of dread and hopelessness back down into the pit from which they came.

"Hurry up!" a female voice commanded.

I froze along the canvas tents aligned across the outskirts of the camp, a handful of paces in front of me.

"Move it. He's not dying. I refuse to inform Idris that she's lost a son today."

"Easy, Z," a male replied in a comforting tone. "He'll live. Let the healers work on him. I'll sit with you until he comes around."

Zola. I swallowed, hesitating at the level of concern in her voice for the fallen High Fae. *Did she already love another?* I huffed a laugh as I kicked at the grass beneath my feet.

Of course she did.

"*I never asked for this,*" Zola told me the night after our bond first appeared.

She didn't outright refuse me, which gave me hope—but perhaps I was wrong.

Crossing my arms, I leaned against a wooden post near another branch of tents. My eyes scanned the commotion of fae healers tirelessly working to tend to those in need. I should be helping, but I selfishly needed a moment to clear my head. My panther's roaring demands toward Zola weren't making things easy.

Off to the side, a healer with dark hair in a braid over her shoulder stumbled with a large bucket of water, losing her footing on a small rock along the path. I surged forward to grasp the handle, helping the High Fae keep the water from spilling over.

"Thanks," she said, looking me over, her dark eyes shimmering with flecks of gold. "Care to help me bring this inside?"

"Of course," I answered, easily lifting the load.

"Impressive." She sighed, wiping her brow with the sleeve of her dress. "Are all shifters this strong?"

"Most are, yes," I answered, thinking nothing of it.

"I see," she said, stepping to my side. "Are you injured?" She motioned to the bleeding wound on my shoulder.

"I'll survive." It was nothing I hadn't handled before.

"Perhaps, but not from the infection that will likely set in if you don't clean it properly," she scolded, reminding me of Latte back in Solace. "After you carry that in, you're my next patient. No arguing."

"Yes, ma'am," I answered.

She chuckled sweetly and flashed me a smile as she pushed open the canvas to the healer's tent.

Once inside, I set the cauldron down, and my eyes shot toward the corner. Zola sat next to Finn with

Gunnar, the fearsome general of Daxton's armies, splattered with the blood of those he had slain.

I watched as Gunnar tenderly cradled Zola's hands in his own, focusing her attention on him. "It's going to be all right, Z."

My magic flared in response to another male touching her. I knocked over a tray table and fisted the sheet of the bed. My panther roared so loudly inside my head that it made me stop and physically brace myself. I felt the overwhelming instinct to eradicate the male who held my mate's hands, calling for blood and the right to challenge anyone who dared even look her way.

Calm the fuck down.

Now I understood why Talon was a gods-damned lunatic for months before he was able to claim Rhea.

"You all right?" the healer asked, placing her hand on my chest.

All eyes, including Zola's and Gunnar's, darted toward me and the female healer.

Great, I've officially made a scene now.

"I'm fine," I said in a low growl, picking up the side table. "Where do you want me to sit?"

"Over here," she said, gliding her touch along my uninjured shoulder to lead me toward an open cot on the far side of the tent. And as luck would have it, it was the cot directly opposite Zola.

"Sit here, and I'll fetch the ointment for your wound."

"If others need it more than me, please give it to—"

"Did you fight in the battle?" the female cut in.

"Yes." I swallowed.

"Then you deserve care," she said plainly as she slipped toward the back to gather her supplies.

I didn't dare look Zola's way, although I could feel her stare burning into the side of my head.

"Remove your shirt so I can inspect your wounds closer."

I obliged the healer's request and reached down to remove the base layer gifted by Idris, which I was thoroughly impressed with during the battle. I would've had more wounds than just this gash on my shoulder if I hadn't been wearing it.

"Do you need help? If you'd like, we can attach a screen for privacy."

"No," I said with a shake of my head. "I'm used to it. I'll be fine." I tugged at the bottom of the shirt, wondering how much trouble it would be to fix the tear. It was impenetrable to most weapons, but not all strikes.

"By the way, I'm Kaia," the female said as she fronted me.

"Shaw," I replied. "Beta of the Solace pack."

"Beta?" Kaia repeated.

"Second in command," I answered, settling on the cot.

"Ah, right." Kaia's touch was gentle. Her hands delicate, just like the comely contours of her face.

Flecks of gold in her eyes shimmered as she focused on the gash along my shoulder, a strand of chestnut hair falling across her brow. I reached up to tuck it behind her pointed ear, which caused her to still.

I swallowed heavily. My hand slowly returned to my lap as I sat up straight, clearing my throat.

"Thanks," Kaia whispered, a flush of pink on her cheeks as her gaze wandered down my chest and toward my stomach. "Are there any other wounds you need tending or looked at?"

A pit of dread surged through my center as a large crashing sound caught my attention. I peered past Kaia to see Zola standing at attention, her darkened stare barreling into me like the wrath of the wilt itself.

"Outside, now," Zola commanded.

Gunnar crossed his arms and chuckled, raising his brows with a half-grin, mouthing, "Good luck."

I gritted my teeth. *Why does she believe she can command me like this?*

"Shaw?" Zola's voice echoed outside the tent.

I stilled, sensing the pleading tone in her voice, understanding the deeper emotion threaded beneath the hard bite of her command only seconds before. Instinct to run to her overtook me as I abruptly stood from the healer's cot, my eyes transfixed on the opening she stormed out of, the need to answer her call driving me forward.

And yet... Gods, I needed to be smart about this.

Without a word to Kaia, I marched outside the tent, fists clenched, as I prepared myself for only the Gods knew what.

I hadn't known my mate long, but I knew, like me, nothing was as it seemed. She was a spymaster with centuries of life experience, yet somehow, we were bonded. I admired the complex layers of her character. She intrigued me, and I would be lying if I denied my eagerness to learn everything and anything about her.

But did she feel the same?

The mate bond was not a guarantee.

I pushed past the canvas to see Zola waiting with crossed arms and a firm scowl. Her darkened eyes met mine, and I froze in place. But, instead of the cowardly fear she was accustomed to conjuring with her hardened stare, I met her with the same unwavering ferocity. My panther fueled me with a wave of power as my magic flowed around me, the green aura dancing in a faint light, highlighted by the morning sun.

Zola's expression remained stoic, but her eyes widened. She felt it. Uncrossing her arms, she inclined her head for me to follow her, a silent request this time, not a command.

I'd take it.

Chapter Seventy-Seven

Shaw Black

I followed Zola through the mass entanglement of High Fae scattered amongst the camp, yet my attention fixated on her.

Her long braid of ebony hair swung by her hip as she walked. I took the time to memorize her seductive curves as the heat rose in my core, my cock throbbing at the mere thought of running my hands along her dark-tawny skin. Her footsteps glided across the earth, barely making a sound as she led us toward the surrounding tree line.

My Gods, this female is as deadly as she is stunning.

Once inside the forest, I paused and closed my eyes to inhale a deep breath. My panther sprang to life inside me. I loved the smell of the trees and wild grass, allowing it to calm and center my damaged, restless soul.

"Do all shifters have this type of response to a forest?" Zola asked, breaking me from my trance.

"Not all," I answered with my eyes closed. "But nature calls to us in a unique way that's difficult to articulate. It settles our animals and helps ground us." I opened my eyes to find Zola staring at me. "This forest is brand new in a sense. It's come alive again. Reborn, and that is something to take note of."

"I can feel it," Zola said.

She was only a few steps away, close enough for me to reach out and touch her.

"You can feel it?" I asked.

"Through your emotions," she said, stealing my complete attention.

"The bond," I said, not needing her to answer, sensing a hint of jealousy that made my panther purr with delight.

We remained silent for what seemed like hours, even though it was only seconds. Neither of us knew what to say or do next, which was not a position I was used to navigating.

"This," I began, gesturing between us. "I don't know what to do, Zola."

She was unreadable. Her face gave no hint of what she felt or thought, likely a defense mechanism developed from centuries of building a protective wall around herself. Even though I lived only a blink of time in this world compared to her, I understood why she was like this. I understood the need to protect yourself against the darkness lurking behind shadows cast by the light.

Zola remained silent, and I chuckled to myself, admiring her cunning mind.

She raised her brow at me. "What?"

I couldn't hide my grin if I tried, running my fingers through my mesh of hair as I dared to take a half step closer. "Sorry, I can't help it."

She tilted her head and narrowed her brows. "Help what?"

"I like you," I said.

"You like me?"

"Yes."

"You don't know me," she replied, remaining in place.

Adjusting my weight, I dared to move closer, pleasantly surprised to see her position remain unchanged. "You're correct," I answered, noticing the slight twinge of her lips as she sucked in a breath. "But I'd like to."

"Why?" Zola asked with a fire in her tone that sent chills of excitement along my spine.

My female was fierce, and I loved it.

"Because of this bond that the Gods sought fit to bind between us?" she asked with false sincerity.

"I won't lie to you," I said. "I promise I never will."

Zola's expression softened at this, and for the first time, I could see a crack in her armor lift.

I inhaled a caged breath as waves of emotion echoed through the bond. "I'm prepared to let you in, Zola. To let you see the good, the bad, and even the ugly. To lay myself bare and give this a real chance."

My heart was racing as I hung in limbo, waiting for her reply. I had never been so bold with anyone, so open and willing to allow my walls to crumble. But somehow, it was different with her.

"I'm not sure you can handle *my* darkness," she whispered. "No one can."

"Try me," I said, closing the distance between us.

Through the bond, I felt a vortex of conflicting emotions ranging from fear to hope, longing, and isolation, and finally, a deep sense of yearning that teetered on the side of desire. I ran my fingers along the delicate curve of her chin, half expecting her to bite me in retaliation for touching her without permission.

Zola stilled against my touch. Those gorgeous eyes filled with shadows clenched shut as she reached to grasp my arm.

"You seem like an honorable male... I don't want to break you, Shaw," Zola whispered. "I can stand the world seeing me as a monster created by the wilt, but the idea of you, of my mate—"

I silenced her fears as my lips crashed into hers, lifting her off her feet and pressing her backside against a nearby tree. I didn't know what came over me, but somehow, I knew she needed this. I needed this.

My cock throbbed, begging to be released and fill my mate until the worries of her world vanished. Gods above, I longed to claim this female and make her forget everyone that came before me because there would be none after.

Zola wrapped her legs around my waist, interlocking her ankles as she kissed me with a ferocity I was all too eager to match. The taste of her on my tongue drove me wild. Her soft lips parted, and I dove in without hesitation.

I moaned into her mouth, gripping her perfect ass in my hands as I settled between her thighs, her nails raking against my back. Zola's moans of pleasure drove me into a high I never wanted to leave.

"Shaw," Zola whimpered as I ground between her thighs. "Shaw, wait."

I forced myself to pull back, allowing Zola to find her footing as I pressed my brow against hers. Our breaths were ragged as I fought to regain control over my panther's influence to take her against the bark of this gods-damned tree. A deep growl resonated in my chest. The drive to bite Zola's neck and claim her as my mate was fogging my mind.

"When you're ready to trust me," I rasped, stroking the wisps of black markings on her delicious neck, "you will share the story of these scars with me, and I'll tell you mine."

Zola reached for my right hand, bringing it to the light as she traced her fingers over the scars that damaged more than just my skin.

"I'm not asking you to accept the bond." I sucked in a breath, holding it captive before releasing it. "I'm asking you to give us a chance."

My female gazed at me like she was seeing the true depths of my soul, those dark eyes finding and accepting the truth I was laying at her feet.

"Very well," she breathed, sending my heart soaring.

I ravaged her mouth once more, needing to taste her like I needed air.

"They're back!"

"Hurry!"

"Come see them!"

Lost in our kiss, I almost missed the familiar surge of power and the knock against my subconscious. Reluctantly, I pushed away from Zola.

Skylar and Daxton had returned.

I gazed at the female in my arms with a renewed sense of life. I didn't want to leave our secluded hideaway, but duty demanded we both return.

I bent one final time to kiss the nape of her neck. "I will lay my mark on your flesh, my little shadow. But before I do, I want you begging me to do it." I pulled back, my voice becoming more animal than the male standing before her. "Because once I do, there's no turning back. You'll be mine, forever."

Zola smirked, causing my gods-damned balls to ache. "Confident for someone so young."

"Oh, I may be young, little shadow, but trust me, I'm far from inexperienced."

"We'll see," she answered with a smirk as she faded into the shadows cast by the overhanging canopy.

"Try to keep up," Zola mocked from behind, reaching into the pocket along her thigh and holding the alpha's dagger out to me. "You'll need to give this back to Skylar. It's a pity I have to return it, though." She sighed, clicking her teeth as her eyes darted along the steel of the weapon.

I strode toward her, holding out my hand to accept the dagger. "Thanks for keeping it safe."

"My pleasure."

I closed the distance between us. "Oh, my little shadow," I purred. "You have no idea what I have in store for you." I gripped her chin, bringing her lips to mine for one final kiss. "You'll forget every male or female in the centuries that came before me." I nibbled her bottom lip before pulling away, leaving her wanting more.

Zola went as still as death, her eyes closed as she sucked in a shuddering breath. "Well, we shall see, *shifter*."

I couldn't help smiling as Zola and I parted ways. She returned to their fallen friend while I ventured to find Daxton and Skylar.

Back at camp, I felt Sky's presence in the clearing, surrounded by citizens awestruck by their very existence. Daxton, the High King, commanded respect with his every breath, while Skylar, the shifter champion and alpha of the Solace pack, radiated raw, untamed power. Individually, they were forces to be reckoned with—Daxton's authority unyielding and Skylar's strength unmatched. But together, they were something more: a united front, a symbol of power and unity that inspired both fear and unwavering belief.

They stood as one. Even without the Heart of Valdor in our possession, I pitied anyone who dared stand in their way.

Wading through the crowd, I called to my alpha, *"Skylar!"*

Immediately, she turned to find me, keeping her hold on the male standing proudly at her side. Sky wore a simple black slip draped over one shoulder. Her golden-brown hair was pulled to the side, proudly exposing a bite mark along her neck. I smiled. Seeing the blissful joy on my friend's face brought happiness to my heart.

"Shaw," Skylar called out as she released her hold on Daxton and ran through the parting crowd.

When Skylar died, when I watched her die, our connection as alpha and beta snapped, damn near breaking me. I shuddered at the memory, with my mind still second-guessing what my eyes were seeing, still doubting this reality until she jumped into my arms.

She's here... She's alive. My alpha is alive.

Tears of joy threatened to fall, but I fought to keep them at bay. My friend was here, and this wasn't a dream. Pulling back, I cupped her face, finding those familiar amber eyes flaring to life with the fire I always knew burning within.

"What now, Sky?" I asked.

"Our actions of defiance may seem like nothing more than a pebble cast into the vast pool of injustice crafted by Minaeve's hand—" Sky paused, her voice steady but charged with a newfound resolve.

I watched, captivated, as she embraced the fire she had kept locked away for far too long.

"And yet," she continued, her gaze blazing with determination, "that pebble is enough to send ripples through the once stagnant waters. It is enough to disrupt, to challenge, and to spark a change no one thought possible."

Daxton stepped behind Sky, and I dared a glance at the High King of the Inner Kingdom, the look of pride beaming from every facet of his being as he held my alpha in his gaze.

"So, a phoenix, huh? Well," I chuckled, "we always knew you wouldn't be a stealthy animal."

Sky laughed. "What do you mean by that?"

"You are a firebird, Sky, a blazing beacon you can see for miles."

My alpha smiled, giving me one final hug as her mate joined us.

"Daxton," I said with a nod.

Daxton returned my gesture as Skylar returned to his side. Her arm wrapped around his waist as he pulled her close. I watched as he turned his head to kiss her brow, the mating mark on his neck visible along the collar of his shirt.

"Can you hear me?" I sent out a telepathic thought to my alpha's mate. *"Daxton?"*

The High King of the Inner Kingdom tilted his head in my direction. His once gray eyes, now glowing with an alluring silver hue, narrowed as he stared me down. Instinctively, I lowered my posture, waiting to see what would happen next.

"Beta." Daxton's voice boomed inside my head, confirming my suspicion.

Skylar glanced between us, only taking a second to realize what was happening. "I always knew power should be shared with a ruling pair," she said, smiling.

"And not just among the shifters," Daxton said, taking Sky's hand and turning to face the crowd. "Skylar Cathal is my mate." Daxton's voice boomed over the clearing, his magic amplifying his voice. "If you wish for me to remain your high king, then—" Daxton turned his head, locking his gaze on Sky's.

She gave him a firm nod, pulling her shoulders back and holding her head high.

"Then she is your high queen."

Silence crept across the meadow. No one spoke a word or dared to move. I silently knelt on the grass, allowing the High Fae to come to their senses and acknowledge Daxton's proposal.

Castor stepped forward from the crowd with Nyssa at his side. "Seems I'm a high prince after all." He chuckled with a sly grin that only he could master. "And you didn't have to die for it to happen. I'll take that victory," he said, kneeling before them while placing a fist over his heart and lowering his head.

Nyssa followed his lead, signing something with her hands before kneeling on the grass, while another dark-haired male joined the duo. Rhett, the High Fae who destroyed Minaeve's crown, also knelt before Dax and Sky with a small gathering of warriors dressed in green armor behind him.

I stilled, realizing that some citizens of Aelius were somehow spared from Seamus's oath and Minaeve's control.

"Hail, High King Daxton," a voice rang out.

Gunnar strode forward with Finn's arm around his neck, limping at his side with Zola on the other. Sky sucked in a breath at the sight of the injured fae, but Daxton held onto her hand, silently bidding her to wait.

"Hail, High King Daxton," Finn, the heir of Crimson City, declared. "Hail... High Queen Skylar."

"Hail, High King Daxton. Hail, High Queen Skylar!"

"Hail, High King Daxton. Hail, High Queen Skylar!"

The crowd chanted again and again until the deafening roar of Daxton and Skylar's names was all you could hear—all you could think.

Identical crowns appeared across their brows. One colored gold like the Mother's rays lay on Sky's, while the other, painted silver like the Father's moonbeam, rested on Daxton's.

I gazed at my alpha and admired how far she had come on this journey. However, a dark stain pulled at my heart, knowing we had so much further to go.

We might have won this battle, but a war was coming. And this *war* would be the toughest trial yet.

End of Book Three

Book Four
(Conclusion of the Valdor Series)
TBA: "A Trial of—"

Acknowledgments

Holy moly! Can you believe this is book three?!? I can't sometimes. Thank you so, so much for following Skylar's journey and embarking on this adventure into Valdor with me. You, as my reader, make this dream a reality, and I thank you to the crossing and beyond for your support.

Firstly, thank you to my husband and our girls for allowing Mama to daydream. Thank you to my family and friends, who let me ramble on about ideas and many different drafts. Thank you to my alpha readers, Megan, Kaiti, Andrea, and my mom, of course. Then my beta readers, Lina, Jade, and Shelby <3. You all have my immense gratitude for giving me your valuable time to help me on this journey. Inkpages… Thank you, Kris my book bestie across the sea, for the special edition opportunity and support. To Kat and Sharon for all your support and cheers on my side.

Secondly, thank you to Beauty and the Book, Fireside Books, and AK Enchanted Events in Alaska for hosting, selling my books, and helping me find my audience. The local support is unmatched <3.

Thirdly, I have an amazingly strong team of ladies with me that helped make this story sparkle and shine. Jen, my copy editor, gave me endless feedback and went above and beyond with her guidance and support. Cherie, my cover artist, brought tears to my eyes by bringing my cover and characters to life. And my proofreader, Eleanor, thank you for helping finish this project and making sure it was ready for the next step.

And finally, ***MY FATED FEW!*** I love you. Thank you for always being so supportive and staying with me on this journey. Three books down and one more to go in this series.

ABOUT THE AUTHOR

J.E. Larson is an "Alaskan-Grown" author, with a passion for being active and outdoors while daydreaming in her own worlds. Wife to an ever-patient husband and mother to a princess and a unicorn, J.E. has been writing and creating stories since she was young. And now, she finds the time to write in the quiet five a.m. mornings and secluded nights, hours after bedtimes.

Social Media

TikTok: j.e.larson

Instagram: j.e.larson_author

Made in the USA
Monee, IL
02 February 2026

43097217R00319